"Here in the for[...]
her to do what s[...]

"No, someone n[...]

"These woods are deserted. It will be fine."

She glanced around. They were so isolated. They could . . .

No! What was she contemplating? They couldn't!

He let go of her, guiding her so that she slid down his front, every titillated inch taking a leisurely trip across his anatomy. He unfastened her cloak and spread it on the grass. Pensively, she watched, not assisting or hindering him, not running off as she knew she should. He knelt and brushed the cloak flat, a smooth, inviting bed where they could romp and rollick. Then, he sat and held out his hand to her. She was so apprehensive, yet so excited, that she was paralyzed. If she joined him, she wouldn't be able to contain her baser impulses.

"Come to me, Emma." His ravishing eyes were beseeching, his smile beguiling her, luring her to her doom. He clasped her hand in his, his thumb tracing captivating circles in the center of her palm. "I won't hurt you."

Gently, he tugged on her wrist, and her knees buckling, she collapsed down. He reached out and petted her hair, her shoulder, his hand descending to her breast. He seized her nipple, squeezing the raised peak.

"What do you want from me, Em?"

There were dozens of potential answers she could give, from simple to difficult, from cheap to expensive. But what she said was, "I want you to touch me. All over. With your hands and your mouth . . ."

More . . .

COMPLETE ABANDON

Cheryl Holt

St. Martin's Paperbacks

COMPLETE ABANDON

Copyright © 2003 by Cheryl Holt.

Library of Congress Catalog Card Number: 2003009124

ISBN: 0-312-98460-X
EAN: 80312-98460-1

Printed in the United States of America

St. Martin's Paperbacks edition / September 2003

St. Martin's Paperbacks are published by St. Martin's Press, 175 Fifth Avenue, New York, NY 10010.

15 14 13 12 11 10 9 8 7 6 5

CHAPTER ONE

Wakefield, England, 1813

EMMA Fitzgerald left the groomed path that skirted Wakefield Manor. She rose on tiptoe and peeked through an open window into one of the lavish parlors. And what an eyeful she received! At ten o'clock in the morning!

Inside, a woman was reclined in the middle of the room, her body artfully draped across a fainting couch. She was buxom, striking, her lustrous auburn hair piled up on her head. Attired solely in a flimsy white robe that was loosely cinched at her waist, one of her breasts was completely exposed, the nipple large and attenuated. She sipped on a glass of wine—so early in the day!—clutching the stem of the ornate goblet, and swirling the contents round and round.

As she rolled to her side, her robe widened further to reveal her curved stomach, her shapely thighs, her long legs, her . . . her privates. Astoundingly, she had no hair down below, her nether lips smooth as a baby's bottom.

"Oh, my goodness," Emma murmured as she evaluated the lewd scene.

How—and why—would a woman do such a thing to herself?

Considering the stories circulating about John Clayton, Viscount Wakefield, and his dubious associates who'd ensconced themselves on the property, the extravagant woman's behavior was hardly surprising. But to have such an offensive, risqué episode so conspicuously displayed was reprehensible. Anyone might stroll by.

The degeneracy seemed beyond the pale, even for the notorious aristocrat.

The ravishing woman laughed, the sultry, feminine chortle billowing out, and Emma liked the sound. She paused, curious as to what was happening that had put the lady in such a playful mood. From the gossiping in the village, she'd anticipated that the mansion was inhabited by bossy, cantankerous snobs, so the spontaneous burst of merriment seemed peculiar.

She studied both directions, realizing that she was sheltered by the meander of the walkway and the shrubbery. If she dawdled, no one could see. Risk of discovery was slim, and a mischievous imp must have been egging her on, because she continued to observe, exhaustively examining every aspect of the indecent exhibition.

A man strutted into view. Partially clothed, he wore no shirt, but his lower torso was covered by tan pants and black riding boots. His back was to her, and entranced, she surreptitiously assessed his anatomy.

He was tall—at least six feet—and broad shouldered, but thin at the waist and hips. His arms were muscled and defined, and he had the countenance of a gentleman who utilized fencing or pugilism as a technique for keeping himself in commendable condition.

Whatever his mode of training, it worked. He had an amazing, manly physique that gave him an air of elegance.

He sauntered to the sideboard, converging on the spot where she was hidden, and she shrank into the foliage. With the angle of sun and shadow, she couldn't be detected. Not that he was looking. He was too intent on a beverage, and he reached for a crystal decanter and poured himself a glass of amber liquid, swilling it down in a quick gulp, then he poured another and drank it down, too.

Turning toward the window, he gazed across the lawn. His stance and nearness afforded her the ideal excuse to furtively spy, and spy she did. She was transfixed.

He was gorgeous. Nay, beyond gorgeous. Into the realm of godlike.

As though some deity had taken a special interest in his formation, his features were perfectly constructed, each bone and stretch of skin flawlessly situated for maximum effect. His hair was lush, blond, the color of ripened wheat, the type that made a woman eager to run her fingers through it. A few of the untamed locks dangled rakishly over his noble forehead and, as if he'd been too busy to have his valet render a necessary trimming, the back was too long and deliciously curled.

His eyes were blue and penetrating as the waters of the Mediterranean Sea were said to be. Not that she'd been to the Mediterranean, or would ever go, but she imagined that the shade was an exact match.

A tempting layer of hair coated his immense chest. It was a tad darker than the golden hair on his head, and it was matted in a thick pile across the top, then it narrowed to disappear into his trousers and masculine points below.

He tucked both hands behind his neck and stretched, and she was presented with a mesmerizing glimpse of the tufts of bristly hair under his arms, the bones of his rib cage.

As he arched out, the tightness of his pants was more noticeable, his powerful thighs splendidly delineated, his vital regions explicitly outlined. She could make out ridge and contour, and there was certainly a great deal to investigate.

He shifted to the side, furnishing her with a profile of his John Thomas. It was larger now, having increased in length, probably from his contemplation of the nude beauty loitering behind him. In visible discomfort, he pushed the heel of his hand at the erect rod, striving to ease the constriction.

Hung like a racing horse.

The crude phrase echoed past, and she blushed to the tips of her toes.

What was she doing, skulking and prying, while cogitating as to the genital size of the robust rogue? No doubt, he was about to participate in a tryst with the woman on the sofa, and Emma refused to watch.

In a temper, she reminded herself of why she'd come, of the righteousness of her mission. It had naught to do with the virile scoundrel, and she wouldn't be dissuaded by him or the sordid spectacle that was about to unfold.

Annoyed with herself, she stepped away, and above her, she could make out the white shutters and trim, the gray bricks of the majestic mansion. It was perched on a hill so that its wealthy occupants could loftily stare down on the land and the poor inhabitants living below. In the July sunlight, the panes in the dozens of polished windows sparkled like diamonds.

She peered across the expanse of rear yard. Despite the current dour state of the local economy, the estate grounds didn't look any the worse for wear. The bright green lawns were meticulously swathed, the gardens carefully pruned, the bushes and hedges painstakingly sheared, the flower beds weeded and arranged in eye-catching designs.

When people in the surrounding villages were struggling so terribly, the flaunting of such blatant affluence made her furious.

In her fist, she clutched the eviction notices that had been sent to various acquaintances the previous day by the viscount. The ruthless missives had targeted widows and the elderly, those least inclined to self-sufficiency, those who were most in need and, in some perilous cases, who were owed lifetime compensation from the Clayton family.

Most of the recipients couldn't read the horrid tidings. Seriously agitated, they'd rushed to the tiny, ramshackle cottage where she'd moved—with her disabled mother and younger sister—after her father had died and his housing and income allowances had been terminated.

Imploring her for information and encouragement, they'd come to her as they always had in the past, pleading for a reassurance she couldn't give.

Why, she, herself, had received one of the spurious orders for displacement. After her father's nearly half a century of dedication to the Wakefield district.

Had the viscount no shame? No sense of obligation or fealty?

Well, she wouldn't submissively tolerate such abhorrent nonsense, particularly when it was being dished out by a pampered, rich, self-indulgent ne'er-do-well such as John Clayton. She'd once relinquished the roof over her head without a whimper of protest, and she wasn't about to do so again. If the viscount was resolved to proceed, his edicts would not be implemented easily or peacefully.

Not if Emma Fitzgerald had anything to say about it.

With a fresh wave of ire and conviction shooting through her, she tried to picture him.

What would such a despicable lout be like?

"Majestic as an angel painted on a church ceiling," the housekeeper's sister had maintained.

"A silver-tongued devil, who could outcharm the snake in Eden," had been the opinion of the gardener's wife.

"Usually tippling hard liquor by noon," was the conclusion of the gardener, himself.

To her knowledge, the unrepentant villain hadn't formerly put in an appearance at the estate. At age thirty, he'd assumed the title the prior autumn after his father, Douglas Clayton, had passed away. He'd been the viscount for almost a year, and his total abdication of responsibility had left him with a steady, significant income, coupled with extensive leisure opportunity in which to squander it at his disreputable pursuits.

According to rumor—and there were many—his hobbies were reckless gambling, wild women, and intemperance. He was a man of town, a handsome, dissolute libertine who thrived on degraded activity. His history was a long line of debauchery, immorality, and vice, with nary an intervening interlude of exemplary behavior or ethical conduct.

There was no escapade in which he wouldn't wallow, no antic too outrageous, no indiscretion too scandalous, no abomination too disgraceful.

How dare he show up now, demanding more than his faithful crofters could provide? Just so he could hie himself back to London and waste their hard-earned money at the faro tables.

He'd traveled to the estate with a London retinue in tow. It contained a bevy of beautiful, unchaperoned women, and a collection of bawdy, impertinent men—the pair upon which she was gawking a consummate example of the scurrilous group. The interlopers had fully established themselves, running roughshod over the servants with their requirements and directives.

They reveled and caroused, staying up till dawn. An endless card game was in progress, with wagering for high stakes. Inebriation was rampant, as were flaunted forms of undress, and there was ample indication that Wakefield's companions were prone to lecherous fornications, systematically enjoying sexual congress with miscellaneous partners.

The viscount had been in residence for a week and had swiftly succeeded in twisting the placid mansion into a veritable den of sin and iniquity.

Her poor father, the beloved Vicar Fitzgerald, had to be rolling over in his grave.

She was determined to depart, when the woman spoke from the fainting couch.

"Is it a pleasant day outside?" Her voice was husky, tantalizing, and Emma wondered if it was natural or if it was a practiced affectation.

The man was distracted, but responded, "It's quite nice."

"Will we be able to go riding?"

"Perhaps," he said noncommittally.

"While you're up, darling, would you refill my glass?"

For some reason, the simple request had the man glaring at her over his shoulder. He was testy, irritated. "I'm not your *darling*, and I'm not your damned slave, either. Get it yourself."

A lovers' spat. How indiscreet. How uncivilized to listen to it. Yet, Emma wasn't about to desist.

The woman achieved a credible pout. "Don't tell me you're still angry over the incident with that insipid serving girl. She deserved to be slapped."

Emma's brows flew up in astonishment as she conjectured as to which girl had been the object of the shrew's temper. She couldn't wait for one of the neighbors to drop by and chat so that she could be apprised of all the details.

The man glowered, the irate force of his gaze making the woman fidget. He almost made a cutting remark then, in the next instant, his wrath vanished, as if he'd considered whether the matter was worth a quarrel and had decided that it didn't merit an expenditure of energy.

"These people are country bumpkins," he contended.

He was so flip that Emma was sincerely offended, and she questioned how she could have found him attractive. Clearly, he was handsome only until he opened his mouth and talked.

"They don't understand the concept of adequate service," he went on, "and they aren't discerning enough to comprehend their mistakes. I warned you before we came that you'd have to make do."

"You failed to mention that the domestic staff was comprised of untrained barbarians."

"You'll survive."

"Yes, well," she huffed condescendingly, "with the sloppiness that's allowed here, we might as well be camping in a cave."

"You can be such a bitch." He peered outside, rolling his eyes in repugnance—or maybe it was exasperation—and Emma was left with the distinct impression that the woman was goading him beyond his limits, but she was too self-centered to realize it.

"I thrive on it," she retorted puckishly, making a pretty moué with her lips. "But that's what you love about me."

"Not bloody likely." The man's rejoinder was so quiet that only Emma had heard him.

He lifted an arm, steadying it against the sill, the

posture extending his lank frame. Emma froze. She was so close that she could distinguish the individual hairs under his arm, the bumps on the brown ring of his nipple, could swear she perceived the earthy scent of his skin.

"Georgina"—he referred to the woman by her name—"I permitted you to accompany me for the sole purpose of entertainment. If you're not up to the task, I'd be more than happy to send you back to town."

Evidently, his comment was a threat, one that had a fascinating result. Georgina frowned at him with concern and panic, which were abruptly masked and replaced by what was an attempt at an earnest smile.

"Don't let's fight so early in the morning." Cooing, she was fairly dripping with sexual promise. "I didn't mean to upset you, darl—" She cut off just before expressing the loathed endearment. "Would it make you feel better if I apologized to the silly chit?"

He chuckled. "You wouldn't have the faintest idea how."

"I could do it. For you."

He chuckled again, and Georgina's relief was palpable—a catastrophe avoided—although Emma couldn't deduce what calamity she'd almost beheld.

Georgina slithered off the couch, gliding toward him and untying the belt on her robe as she neared.

They were going to engage in the marital act. Disgustingly, Emma couldn't compel herself away.

She was riveted, agog to finally have the opportunity to learn secrets about which she'd incessantly ruminated. The intriguing mysteries of libidinous conduct were about to be unraveled.

Her pulse rate elevated, her breathing escalated, her palms tingled.

She was a wanton at heart. Who could guess that

under the prim, proper exterior of a vicar's daughter, she harbored such base tendencies and corrupt character? Deep down, she was possessed of a weak moral constitution. How mortifying.

Georgina was directly behind him, and she spread the lapels of her robe so that both breasts were bared, and she rubbed herself across his back, her hands rounding his waist to stroke his stomach and chest.

"You're a bundle of nerves," she cajoled. "I'm going to relax you."

"That is what you get paid to do. It's about time you remembered."

His mistress! How decadent. Emma had never before encountered anyone so disreputable.

Georgina halted in mid-caress. "Don't be cruel. I said I was sorry."

They stood, paralyzed, on the brink of a more heated argument, but the man relented, taking one of her hands and guiding it lower. Whether he was giving permission, or commanding compliance, Emma wasn't sure, but Georgina avidly acquiesced.

With skilled dexterity, she fondled him, pressing and squeezing his cock, manipulating the fabric over the prominent crest. Scant effort had his hips flexing, and she teased and toyed while she slowly unfastened the buttons on his pants. She tugged at the placard, exposing him so that he was clutched in her hand, her fist making a tight circle into which he could languidly thrust.

Emma stared, then stared some more. She couldn't look away.

He was so beautiful. So manly.

Through her extensive nursing duties, she was no stranger to nakedness, and she had seen more than her share of male privy parts, but never like this. The appendage—usually small and withered—had regularly been viewed on dying old men or sick little boys.

His phallus was hard, onerous, proudly jutting out. It appeared so virile, so potent. So . . . so . . . gigantic.

Go. Go. Get out of here, a soft voice scolded, but she was immovable, no more capable of departing than she was of blocking the sun in its trek across the sky. Ashamed of herself, but utterly titillated, she scrutinized every second of the ribald display.

Plainly, Georgina had made love with him frequently, for she knew specifically what he wanted and when he wanted it. She prowled around his torso, until she was in front of him, then she yanked at her robe so that it slipped off and fell to the floor.

Emma analyzed the woman as though she were a curious laboratory specimen. She had voluptuous, swinging breasts, graceful, wide hips. In comparison, Emma felt downright skinny. Though she'd always deemed herself shapely, with a pleasing figure, next to the statuesque, generously proportioned femme fatale, she felt deficient, gaunt, and ordinary.

Amazingly, not only was the hair on Georgina's genitalia absent, but the hair under her arms and on her legs had been removed, as well. She was glossy, sleek, her skin smooth as silk all over. Her slick torso inflamed the man to an incredible plateau, his bodily tension heightening dramatically.

Gripping her hips, he twirled her and shoved her against the wall so that she had to brace her hands for balance. He kneed her thighs, raised her, then, with no restraint or regard for her comfort, he entered her with a fierce penetration, and he thrust in a deliberate rhythm, providing Emma with a thoroughly enlightening and educational demonstration.

At the incursion, Georgina inhaled sharply but, as if she were used to such rough handling, she made no verbal complaint. Bored, she held on to the wall, staring straight ahead. Obviously, she couldn't wait to be finished with the tiresome chore, and Emma was confounded.

How could a woman be mounted by such a dashing rascal and remain so detached?

It didn't take long for the man to reach orgasm. As he spilled himself, his legs quaked at the moment of impact, but other than that temporary trembling, he evinced no reaction. He was so apathetic that he might have been sipping his breakfast tea.

Then, without so much as a word being exchanged, he retreated from her, tucked himself into his trousers, and buttoned them.

Feeling cheated, Emma scowled. While she was definitely no expert on carnal affairs, she was no simpering miss, either. A confirmed, virginal spinster, she'd never had sex herself, but she'd delivered hundreds of babies in her twenty-eight years, and she'd heard just as many or more stories as to how each of them had been conceived.

Lovemaking was meant to be indulged with vehement passion, with a profound commitment toward enjoyment, yet this joining had been so devoid of emotion that she was almost disappointed at having stayed for the grand finale.

She was most surprised by the gentleman's impassive comportment. He was a lusty Lothario, vibrant and robust in all the ways that counted. She'd expected that he'd be so much more adept. Surely, he knew the pertinent methods for pleasuring a woman.

Didn't he hope for more? Seek more? Aspire to more?

If she was ever offered an opening to unleash his baser instincts, she wouldn't lightly pass up the chance.

What she wouldn't give to get her hands on that impressive anatomy. She'd show him a thing or two about desire.

With a start, she noted where her preposterous ruminations had strayed. As time went on, her musings were becoming more exorbitant and outlandish. Spinsterhood was gradually driving her mad.

Shaking her head, at her absurdity, at her foolishness, she crept away as Georgina spun toward the man. The paid harlot was struggling to pull herself together, to seem satisfied and thrilled, not wanting him to detect how unmoved she'd been.

Saucily, she patted the front of his pants, elated over the bulge that endured, confirmation of her hold over him. "Feeling better?"

Indifferent, he shrugged. "No."

"You are such a beast, Wakefield. I don't know why I put up with you."

Wakefield! The odious aristocrat, himself. She might have known it was he. How could she have not?

To think that she'd been dawdling in the bushes, mooning and drooling over him. How embarrassing.

Appalled, furious, she stalked off, not looking back, not wanting to see or hear anything further from the contemptible couple.

"Wakefield and his mistress."

She felt soiled by their debauchery. What a detestable pair. How could she have been enthralled?

So this was how the viscount spent his mornings. In between signing eviction orders for widows and cripples, he loafed, drank liquor, and fornicated with compensated whores.

Oh, wasn't he in for it.

Grumbling aloud, she traipsed around the side of the mansion, detouring past the verandah, and she was relieved that there were no guests lurking on the elaborate porch, but then, the slackers were probably still abed.

Out of habit, she started toward the servants' door, then she halted. She was on official business, and she wouldn't demean herself by slinking in the back door like a groveling supplicant.

She'd go to the front door. If the viscount didn't approve, too bad.

Righteous indignation spurring her on, she marched up the bricked drive and climbed the stairs, banging the knocker with three marked raps.

A thin, scrawny butler in an expensive black suit answered. He was no one local whom she knew, so he was likely a Wakefield employee from London.

"I'm here to speak with the Viscount Wakefield," she announced before the servant could take a breath.

Patronizingly, he stared down at her. "And you are . . . ?"

"Emma Fitzgerald. From the village." She wouldn't be cowed by the pompous lackey. "With a petition. I demand an immediate audience."

"I'm quite sure he's too busy to confer with you."

"When will he be available?"

"He won't be," and he commenced shutting the door in her face.

Ignoring him, she pushed with all her might, then swaggered across the threshold and pranced into the foyer. Apparently, people were more polite in the city, or perhaps he carried more authority there, because he was egregiously flummoxed by such a breach of polite etiquette. As he pondered what to do with her, his mouth flapped open and shut, like a fish tossed on a riverbank.

She planted herself in a chair. "I'll wait."

"You most certainly will not. I'll have the footmen escort you out."

She shot him such an evil grimace that he flinched. "Do you really suppose they could?"

He sputtered, then blustered, "It might be hours before the viscount is free."

Standing, she pointed an angry finger at his chest. "You tell that bounder for me that if he hasn't sent for me in fifteen minutes, I'm coming in to find him." She sneered malevolently. "And heaven help the man who tries to stop me."

The retainer harumphed and scampered off, destined for his master with the dreadful news that she'd arrived.

CHAPTER TWO

JOHN Clayton, Viscount Wakefield, sat up in his chair
and frowned at Rutherford, the butler he'd brought with
him from London since he'd been positive that none of
the provincial staff would be able to tolerate his proclivities. Rutherford wasn't shocked by John's bad habits.
Or if he was, he hid it well.

"Did you say there's a woman from the village?
With a petition?"

"Yes, milord."

"Are you sure you heard her correctly?"

"Definitely." Rutherford sniffed, offended at having
his competency maligned. "She demands an interview
without delay."

"Bloody hell."

Balancing his elbows on the desktop, he buried his
face in his hands. After a solid week of excessive revelry, he was tired, hungover, and grouchy. His head
pounded unmercifully, a painful throbbing behind his
eyes, and his stomach roiled, protesting his aborted attempt at eating some food. He'd be damned lucky if he
didn't pass out from exhaustion and immoderation.

Now this. As if he'd agree to being confronted by
some . . . some . . . woman. He'd already gone a few
rounds with Georgina, and it wasn't even noon. He
wasn't about to compound his annoyance by engaging
in verbal fisticuffs with a pushy, determined commoner.

"Tell her no, Rutherford. Send her packing."

"I tried, sir. She won't go."

"What do you mean, she won't 'go'?"

"Well, I informed her that you were too busy, but she just barged in."

How bizarre. "Have her forcibly removed."

Two spots of color marred the servant's cheeks. "I wouldn't recommend it, sir."

"Why not?" John chuckled. "Is she too large to carry? Is she brandishing a weapon?"

"No," Rutherford answered hesitantly, "but she seems quite aggrieved. And a bit mad. I do believe she'd be capable of bodily harm if provoked."

From one corner of the room, his half brother, Ian MacDonald Clayton, laughed uproariously. "This is a woman I'm dying to meet."

"Shut up, Ian," John grouched. A renewed hammering shot through his head, so potent that he began to worry that the top might fly off.

"Oh, chat with her, Wakefield," Georgina chimed in from the other corner. "It might be amusing. We could use some entertainment in this dreary domicile."

John glared back and forth, at his only sibling and his mistress, wondering if there was some way he could magically vanish. Would either of them notice if he simply disappeared? Wouldn't it be fun to find out where he'd end up?

Anywhere but here would be a vast improvement.

"What do you suppose she wants?" he asked Ian. His brother had a unique insight into the lower classes, being a member himself, a fact he took great relish in flinging at John on a regular basis. As if commonality were a noteworthy boon.

"Your assistance. What do you think?"

"I knew that," he grumbled. "But on what topic?"

"Obviously, there's some injustice afoot that she

feels only you—as the lord—can put to rights."

At Ian's mocking emphasis of the word *lord,* John glowered. Ian loved to sarcastically remind John of his exalted position, one that would have been Ian's in a fairer world, and one that John, himself, had never desired. The issue was an implicit wedge between them, and Ian could be so caustically derisive.

John could hardly alter the British laws of inheritance and entailment.

During numerous quarrels, he'd told Ian and their ass of a father that, if it was possible, he'd have dropped it all in Ian's lap, would have gladly let him assume the whole, damned nuisance.

If Ian had been in charge, John could have been in London where, at this very moment, he could be playing cards and wooing gorgeous women. Instead, he was stuck in the country, cleaning up the estate books after years of neglect by dear old da, and about to be challenged by an excitable, hysterical female.

"It doesn't sound as if she'll leave without making a fuss," Ian injected rationally. Always rational. Always reasonable. That was Ian. "You might as well see her."

The accursed scapegrace was grinning, anxious for the pending fracas, ecstatic to witness John squirming and on edge, and John seriously considered strangling him, just leaping over the desk, grabbing him by the throat, and . . .

"Oh, do, Wakefield," Georgina added, her sultry tone grating on his shredded nerves.

He scowled from one to the other, sighed heavily, then said to Rutherford, "Show her in. But caution her that if she creates a disturbance, I will personally pick her up and toss her out on the lawn."

"Very good, sir," Rutherford droned as he deferentially backed out.

"And you!" John spun on Georgina. "Keep quiet. I don't want to hear a peep out of you."

"But that will take all the fun out of—"

"Not a peep," he sternly repeated.

Shortly, footsteps reverberated in the hall, and Rutherford halted at the library door, announcing, "Milord, might I present Miss Emma Fitzgerald, daughter of the recently deceased Vicar Edward Fitzgerald, the longtime pastor of the Wakefield parish."

A vicar's daughter? John could barely stifle his groan of displeasure. Could the morning get any worse? Would afternoon never arrive?

A tiny woman, who couldn't have stood more than five four in her shoes, tromped across the threshold, and he choked down a guffaw at Rutherford's fear of the petite virago. From the retainer's description, he'd been prepared for an armed Amazon, who was ready to do battle on behalf of her minions.

In reality, she looked as if a stiff breeze could blow her over.

She was too skinny, as if she never had enough to eat. He despised thin women, preferring them to be voluptuous and buxom, although he had to admit that her breasts were shapely, plump and appealing, and just the size to fill a chap's hands. The slenderness of her waist emphasized her bosom, making her appear more busty than she actually was.

A pretty thing, she had the air of a fresh country maid: pink cheeks, ruby lips, bright brown eyes, unblemished skin, white teeth. Her hair was probably spectacular, but it was difficult to discern. Riotously curled, it seemed to be brunette, with streaks of auburn shooting through it, but she'd pulled it back in a tight chignon and capped off the wild strands in a confining snood.

Her gown did nothing to accentuate her innate comeliness. Drab and black—mourning clothes?—it dulled the sparkle in her eyes, and it was buttoned to her chin, with the sleeves clenched at the wrists, as if she daren't expose a hint of naked flesh.

A vicar's daughter, all right. She dressed the part. She looked the part. Would she be a devout shrew? A whiner? A complainer?

How he loathed contrary females. They were the bane of his existence, Georgina and his purported fiancée, Caroline, being the two most striking examples.

He examined her more rudely than was necessary, and as he did, he realized that his butler had had adequate cause to be wary. Though she was small, there was an arrogance about her that was disconcerting. Her poise and confidence made her seem bigger than she truly was, an ethical, honest woman with equity and justice as her banner, and he detested her on sight.

"Miss Fitzgerald." He nodded and rose, flashing her his most captivating smile, which was guaranteed to melt feminine restraint, and that had never failed to coax a reticent lover out of her undergarments.

To his colossal amazement, it had absolutely no effect.

"Viscount Wakefield."

She had a seductive, lusty voice that was at odds with her diminutive figure. It was the sort of voice that made a fellow fantasize about silk sheets and soft mattresses, candlelit bedchambers, and steamy sexual intercourse, but the arousing result was spoiled by how she was staring down her pert little nose at him—as if he were a putrid type of insect.

Stumbling to regroup, he inanely commenced with, "How nice of you to visit. What can I do for you?"

With a massive amount of evident disdain, she studied him, and the perceptiveness of her gaze was unsettling. Probing and astute, she seemed to rummage through a secluded area near the center of his heart where his wicked character and corrupt disposition rested just out of view.

She saw more than she should, as though she'd been apprised of every flaw and defect in his constitution, and there was nothing he could say or do that would surprise her.

Suddenly nervous, and needing to occupy his hands, he circled his desk and went to the sideboard, pouring himself three fingers of the Scottish whisky that Ian's relatives were kind enough to supply. He tipped the glass to his lips when she spoke sharply.

"I won't do business with a man who's prone to strong drink in the middle of the day. I insist that you be clearheaded."

"Well, I . . . I . . ."

He was at a total loss. In his entire thirty years of living, he hadn't had another soul tell him not to imbibe—no one except his father, but he didn't count.

Flabbergasted, he held on to the glass, not sure of what to do with it. Abruptly, it felt as if it weighed ten stone. He wasn't about to abandon the welcome libation merely because she'd ordered him to, but she was scrutinizing him in a derogatory fashion that made him incapable of swallowing any down.

Affecting nonchalance, he strolled behind his desk, once more, setting the liquor off to the side as though that's what he'd intended all along. Ian, wretch that he was, was chortling with mirth over her autocratic condemnation, a hand pressed to his mouth to prevent his jocularity from slipping out.

"Miss Fitzgerald," Georgina snapped. "How dare you condescend to the viscount. Remember your place."

Miss Fitzgerald didn't bother to glance at Georgina, keeping her keen assessment linked with John's, as she said, "Nor will I consort with any of your loose London strumpets."

Georgina gasped with affront, and Ian laughed aloud. John, himself, was stunned and impressed. Only a person who was very brave—or very stupid—would tangle with a tigress like Georgina. Miss Fitzgerald wasn't stupid, so she had to be made of steel.

"She's got you pegged hasn't she, Georgie?" Ian poked. Their animosity was legendary, and he deliberately goaded her by using the nickname she abhorred.

"Shut up," Georgina hissed. "Wakefield, you're not going to allow her to insult me so terribly, are you? I want her whipped—then thrown out."

As though neither Georgina, nor Ian, had made any comment, Miss Fitzgerald humbly proclaimed, "I'm a respected gentlewoman in this community. I shouldn't be compelled to fraternize with any of your doxies."

"Of all the nerve." Georgina leapt to her feet. "Listen here you pious, sanctimonious harridan . . ."

He appraised the two combatants—Miss Fitzgerald calm and composed, Georgina fit to detonate—and Ian who was snickering, and he longed to be in a salon of sane men, enjoying a cheroot and an amiable game of dice.

How he hated scenes. Yet, Georgina was so upset that she might render a slap, which he couldn't permit.

"Enough!" he roared. His shout was like a bolt of lightning blasting through his aching head, so powerful that it temporarily blinded him. Frantically, he gripped his scalp, as though he could keep his skull from exploding.

When his vision cleared, he was relieved to note that Georgina had heeded his command. Ian too was speechless. John never raised his voice, because ordinarily, he didn't care enough about events to be perturbed, and he'd startled them both.

"Georgina," he decreed, his attention fixed on his adversary, "you're excused."

She bristled, dying to remark, then she thought better of it and swept out in a dramatic huff.

"Ian, you, too." When the man didn't move, John scowled at him. "Begone."

"You need me," Ian infuriatingly pointed out, "so I can remind you of what was discussed."

With that veiled reference to John's tendency to overindulge, he tried to recollect why he and Ian had ever become friends. The cocky lummox could be overly vexatious, particularly in cases when John's reckless deportment bumped up against Ian's irritating sobriety and equanimity.

Ian came across as a virtual saint, while John was perpetually perceived as a sinner.

John had initially sought him out at the tender age of eighteen, and he'd been delighted at locating an unknown brother because he'd presumed that a cordial relationship would thoroughly exasperate their father.

Two years older, Ian was the scandalous love child, the dirty secret, of the illustrious Douglas Clayton. Consequently, Ian had been a temptation John couldn't resist. As soon as he'd been out on his own as an independent adult—an immutable terror raging through London—he'd befriended the man who had the same sire and who carried his same name, though a slightly foreign version of it.

He'd established the connection solely to incense their father but, as both the wife and the mistress involved in birthing the pair of sons had been deceased,

Douglas hadn't minded, and John had gained the only genuine friend he'd ever had.

So much for petty revenge.

"Fine," he barked at Ian. "Stay if you're so bloody interested."

"Don't curse in front of me," Miss Priss dictated.

"Miss Fitzgerald"—he struggled for patience— "you've invaded my home, slandered my companions, and made a general nuisance of yourself, and you haven't been on the premises for ten minutes. I'll curse in my own damned house if I feel like it."

There! He'd let her have it. But the nag didn't possess the discretion to hold her tongue.

"You, sir, are a barbarian."

"So I've been told. On copious occasions."

He tried to match her glare for glare, but couldn't. She had an aggravating ability to focus in that had him fidgeting like a miscreant. Under her austere evaluation, he felt like a lad about to be paddled by his tutor—a happenstance with which he'd been intimately familiar as a boy.

"I shan't tolerate it," she said snippily. "Straighten up. This instant."

Gad, but if she'd been wielding a cane, she might have rapped his knuckles with it.

"Don't tell me how to behave."

"Someone should. How old are you? Seven? Eight? You act like a child." She whipped around to Ian. "Who are you?"

"I'm the black sheep of the family," Ian fliply replied.

"I can see that you are," she concurred wholeheartedly. "Didn't your mother teach you to stand when a lady enters the room? Where are your manners?"

The unflappable Ian was caught off guard by her

blunt criticism, and astonishingly, her chastisement was successful. Chagrined, he rose.

"I seem to have misplaced them, Miss Fitzgerald. I apologize for my lapse." He walked over to her and made a courtly bow, the type that invariably had women swooning over the black-haired, blue-eyed devil. "Ian Clayton, at your service."

"You're the Scotsman, aren't you?" she inquired. "Some sort of elder . . . brother?"

"Well . . . yes," he ultimately confirmed, not choosing to delve into their convoluted patrimonial affiliation, when it wouldn't have been suitable for her ears, anyway.

"How can you expect this scoundrel"—she gestured at John—"to comport himself appropriately if you don't set an example?"

"You're correct, again. I'll try harder."

"I'd appreciate it if you would."

The woman gave Ian a radiant smile, and John stared, dumbstruck, at how winsome she looked, how enchanting. If she'd had a stylish outfit, and a flattering coif, she'd be downright beautiful.

Pity for such loveliness to be wasted, although with that caustic tongue, all the clothes in the world couldn't make her more appealing.

Ian was returning the woman's smile, and John was cognizant of how Ian's devious mind worked. Since any dawdling by Miss Fitzgerald would annoy John, Ian was considering striking up a conversation so he could delay her departure,

Lest Ian have the chance to activate his nauseating spigot of charm, John interrupted.

"Miss Fitzgerald, I'm extremely busy," he lied. In all actuality, he didn't have any pressing plans for the day, other than to further plod through the estate ledgers.

"Could you please be about your business? Why are you here?"

"I've come about the evictions."

"What evictions?"

"The ones you imposed yesterday." Distinctly rankled by his inability to recollect, she waved some papers.

"Oh, those evictions."

The economic condition at the estate was tenuous, and the removal of those malingerers who hadn't paid rent in ages seemed an elemental place to start in regaining financial ground. He'd signed the notices with barely a thought. Besides, it was only a dozen or so crofters. Why was she protesting?

"What about them?" he testily snarled.

"How could you?" Her devotion to her cause was so profound that tears welled in her eyes.

"Well, I . . . I . . ." he stammered again. The woman was turning him into a blathering fool. Frowning over at Ian, he visually pleaded for help, but of course didn't receive any.

He couldn't abide female histrionics, and he wasn't about to suffer through a bout of weeping.

Pulling himself up to his full six feet, he peered down at her in his most imperious fashion. "I won't be interrogated—or vilified—as to any decisions I make regarding the property. And I certainly don't intend to answer to the likes of you."

"Aren't you the high-and-mighty lord." She pronounced his title with the same contemptuousness Ian constantly used, infusing it with an ample amount of scorn so that John ended up feeling as though he were committing some horrid crime simply by existing.

"That is what I am, Miss Fitzgerald. Lord. And master, I might remind you." He wasn't about to subject himself to badgering by the termagant. The expulsion resolution had been the first he'd made concerning the property in years—a property to which he'd never wanted to be tied—and he wasn't about to be challenged over it by the village tyrant.

"Well, you may be the lord here, but you're making a brilliant mess of it. And you've scarcely arrived. I can only guess what idiotic steps you'll take if you're in residence a whole month."

How dare she? The little despot.

"I'll take your opinion under advisement." Oozing sarcasm, he motioned toward the door, specifying that her appointment was over, but she didn't leave.

How much more explicit could he be?

"But some of these people have loyally served your family for generations. Why, Mr. Gladstone, himself, toiled in the stables for seventy-nine years. It's not his fault that his rheumatism has gotten so painful that he can't continue. And Mrs. Wilson is a widow. With twelve children. Where will they go? What will they do?"

A widow? With children? A crippled, elderly man? Could he have . . . ?

No. He wouldn't wander down that disturbing road.

"Their problems are not mine," he loftily declared, sounding arrogant and pretentious even to his own ears.

"Isn't that a fine Christian attitude?"

He abandoned the safety of his desk and stomped toward her, but not too close, lest she was prone to bite. "Miss Fitzgerald, we're finished."

"We are not."

"I won't listen to any further drivel."

"Drivel!" she fumed. "Well, I've just begun, so you'd better sit down and get comfortable. We're in for a lengthy discussion."

"We're not discussing this," he wailed in a near shout.

Ignoring him, she rummaged through her documents, as though hunting for a list of grievances, and he looked to Ian for guidance, but his brother grinned and shrugged, immensely enjoying the squabble.

John was totally mystified as to what to do. Though he'd threatened to Rutherford that he'd bodily throw her out, he couldn't picture himself lifting her up and hauling her off like a sack of potatoes. Nor could he imagine calling for the servants to dislodge her. In light of her state of pique, it might take more than one footman and, despite how irksome she was, he couldn't bear to watch several burly fellows wrestling with her.

She was talking, having launched into an impassioned speech about the village, the estate, and the needs of the community. As she spewed an endless stream, her remarks were sprinkled with snubs and insinuations as to his intelligence, his reasoning capacity, and his aptitude for administration.

A zealous dynamo, she went on and on, haranguing about this family and that, naming names, providing ages, duration of service, depth of penury, and he was impressed with her presentation. In his social milieu, his associates gave new meaning to the term *detachment,* so it was refreshing and exhilarating to run across someone who felt so deeply, who cared so completely.

When was the last time he'd cared intensely about anything?

He couldn't recall.

Fascinated, mesmerized, he shifted back, resting his hips on the edge of the desk, and he was forced to admit that he'd never encountered anyone like her. She showed no respect for his position over her, paid no deference or heed to his edicts or commands.

Ian was the only other person of his acquaintance who wasn't exhaustively willing to ingratiate himself, to fawn or wheedle. People ceaselessly wanted dispensations from him: money, favor, patronage. They were in awe of his rank, his status, his wealth. They were frightened of him, envious, dazzled, cowed.

But not Emma Fitzgerald. Yes, she wanted things from him—her demands were coming through loudly and clearly—but she wasn't requesting any boons for herself. Each solicitation was made for the benefit of another. He'd never stumbled upon anyone who was quite so selfless, so altruistic.

Her benevolent nature was perplexing. Perhaps she was a genuinely nice individual, which, taking into account the buffoons and hangers-on who made up his circle of companions, was a pleasant notion.

Or, perhaps, she was a fool, not astute enough to comprehend how dangerous it was to risk offending him. With a snap of his fingers, a stroke of his pen, he could ruin her. Either she didn't understand that fact or wasn't worried about it.

How vexing. How marvelous. How insulting.

Had she no concept of his power, his authority, his omnipotence?

Apparently not.

He scrutinized her, thinking that he could put that pretty mouth to many tasks that were more advantageous than talking, but even as the risqué idea flitted past, he blushed, embarrassed to have grown so corrupt that he could muse lasciviously about a vicar's daughter.

His moral constitution had plummeted to a despicable low.

Gad, but he wanted her gone. His headache was worsening by the second, and he craved a dark room, where he could drink, play cards, and snuggle with a few cheery, spirited—silent—women.

The words flowed out of her mouth in a perpetual stream. How to make her stop?

He'd already decided against physical removal, and he wasn't about to engage in a verbal sparring match, because he wasn't positive he could win it.

Briefly, he pondered agreeing with her, revoking the evictions and letting the crofters remain, but as rapidly as the sentiment manifested, he shoved it away. He wasn't about to change his mind solely because she was a pain in the arse.

"So you see, milord Wakefield"—she rudely intruded into his reverie—"you can't proceed with your dastardly scheme."

He was taken aback. Not even his own father, when Douglas had ranted and raved, had ever labeled John's actions dastardly. It was an additional, disgraceful slur, and he wasn't sure if he should laugh, yell, or incarcerate the sassy wench.

She was too bold by half.

Cocking her head to the side, she folded her arms across her chest, waiting for his reply. The placement of her arms pushed her breasts up and out, and he impolitely perused them, taking a slow gander. Her outburst had elevated her pulse, and heightened her respiration, the result being that her nipples were enlarged. He could make out the tempting morsels through the fabric of her dress.

How had he judged her to be too skinny? She was rounded on top, and he would bet she'd be rounded on the bottom, too. Her hips would curve out from that tiny waist and extend down into long, lean legs, legs that could wrap around a man's waist and squeeze tight when he was . . .

Vicar's daughter! Vicar's daughter! The refrain screamed out like a fire bell, admonishing him as to her modest condition, and he lurched straighter, as if slouching before her was improper.

"Well?" she asked haughtily.

The answer to his dilemma, when it dawned on him, was so naughty—but so ingenious—that he didn't know why he hadn't thought of it sooner. He must be more fatigued than he'd suspected.

Though Ian was the bastard by birth, John was the one who'd deserved the designation. His comportment was regularly deplorable; his father had maintained that he went out of his way to be exasperating, which he did. Ninety-nine percent of the time, he was an unrepentant, unremitting blackguard.

He had the very mode by which to scare her off, and her egress wouldn't be difficult to achieve. Obviously, she'd heard stories about his reputation and repute. If he acted heinously, she wouldn't be surprised. Monstrous behavior was exactly what she would expect from him. A flagrant proposal, which she would be honor bound to refuse and would never accept in a thousand years, would goad her into a maidenly swoon, and he would promptly have her fleeing in terror.

If he was sufficiently vulgar, she'd be too mortified to ever return, so he'd never again have to be confronted by her righteous opinions or condescending disposition.

This was going to be so simple. And so amusing.

Poor Miss Fitzgerald. She was about to be shocked senseless.

"Well . . ." he echoed, pensively tapping a finger to his lip, and assessing her as a cat might study a canary trapped in a cage. A calculated grin creased his cheeks. Instantly, she noticed the transformation in his demeanor and took a reflexive step back, but he wasn't about to let her escape. Not when he'd courteously weathered her diatribe. He vacated his perch on the desk, and approached until he was so indecently close that the toes of his boots slipped under the hem of her skirt.

Amazingly, she retreated no further, bravely standing her ground.

"I might be persuaded to alter my course," he said.

"How?" Hesitantly, she smiled, eager to hope that her arguments had been effective.

He gazed into her brown eyes, momentarily distracted by how limpid they were, how penetrating. Her skin was smooth as silk, her cheeks rosy and delicate, and . . .

Vicar's daughter! The alarm rang again, and he visibly snapped himself back to the successful culmination of his machination.

He was a master at effrontery—he'd had his entire life to practice—so the unsophisticated, wholesome Miss Fitzgerald hadn't a chance against his rehearsed insolence.

"My decision was fiscal, not personal. So if I'm to change it, you'd have to provide me with a special remuneration."

"What do you mean?"

She was so guileless, so innocent and sincere. He almost hated to deceive her, but he was an indisputable cad and always had been. "If I let your friends stay," he cajoled, luring her in for the kill, "you'd have to reimburse me for my troubles."

"What troubles do they cause you?" she huffed. "They're old, sick, and overburdened."

"I would sustain a financial loss if they remain"— he fought to appear contemplative, then earnest—"but I'd be amenable to forgoing the income if you could do something to make it worth my while—so to speak."

"Me? I don't have any money."

"Well, I wasn't referring to money."

"What then?" She was still without a clue as to where he was deliberately and crassly leading her.

"A reparation that would be more likely to"—he paused, winked—"tickle my fancy."

Over in the corner, he could see Ian stir, uneasy with the sudden tenor of the conversation, but he knew his brother. If Ian had any qualms about what John was doing, he'd voice his misgivings when they were alone.

Unfortunately for Miss Fitzgerald, she wasn't familiar with John's penchant for mischief, nor did she realize how adept he was at impudence. Her face was an open book, and he could effortlessly read what was written there: It was gradually occurring to her that he was making an inappropriate advance.

Impertinent as any princess, she inquired, "What—precisely—are you suggesting?"

"You have only one asset that might be of any value to a man such as myself."

Shamefully, he let his prurient regard travel over her torso, lingering on every delightful spot, then he meandered back up till their stormy gazes locked.

"Lord Wakefield, you're making a . . . a . . . lewd proposition to me."

"Naturally. What else do you have to offer?"

As he'd anticipated, she gasped. "You would steal my virtue, in order to . . . to . . . erase the debts of my neighbors?"

"You're quite fetching," he said bluntly, as if he seduced chaste women as a hobby, "and it's been a long while since I've had a country lass. I imagine I'll be enormously entertained."

Horridly affronted, she scowled. "I do believe that's the most offensive comment anyone has ever uttered in my presence."

"I'm sure it is." He shrugged, laughed facilely. "I'm

renowned for my reprehensible conduct. I have a base character, I'm afraid."

"You are an unmitigated lecher."

"Without a doubt."

He'd presumed that she'd be unnerved, outraged, or aghast, but she wasn't eliciting anywhere near the indignation he might have predicted. His Miss Fitzgerald was made of stern stuff. Time to raise the stakes. To have her running from the room in a cloud of repugnance and loathing.

"I don't know how well versed you are at dalliance, but I'm infamous for my abilities as a lover. I can guarantee that you'll be satisfied."

He imbued the word *satisfied* with as much inflection as he could, drawing it out so that even the most sheltered virgin couldn't help but get the general drift of his intent.

"Are you planning for us to lie down together as man and wife?"

"Yes. But not just once. I'd have to require numerous assignations before I'd be fully compensated." Furrowing his brow, he pretended to mull a commensurate recompense. "How about one tryst for each person on your list? That ought to make us come out about even."

"You're actually saying . . . you deem me to be the sort of woman who would . . . you assume that I might acquiesce in . . ."

He smiled. She was so unschooled that she had no vocabulary to describe his sordid overture. This was going much better than he'd conjectured. A few more deftly delivered insults, and he'd be shed of her forever.

"And don't forget, if you please me, there'll be a little extra in it for you. Any of my mistresses can tell you that I'm generous when contented. I especially like to give gifts of jewelry."

The last statement was a bit much, but he wanted to send her into a frenzy of moral wrath. He braced for a furious slap, or a shriek of disgust, or a sob of despair, but to his out-and-out consternation, she did nothing of what he'd foreseen.

Instead, she initiated an intimate survey of her own, and it was much more torrid, and much more thorough than the visual tour he'd just taken of her anatomy. She journeyed down to his chest, to his stomach. Lower, to his groin, where his unruly phallus had the audacity to swell under her examination, enough so to bulge and make his trousers unaccountably tight.

Boldly, she tarried there, evaluating length and girth, then her ardent appraisal rolled back up, fixating on his mouth, giving it such an avid inspection that he flushed.

Roaming those final few inches, her eyes linked with his, once again, and she smiled, too, a sly, shrewd feminine smile that had him frantically questioning what he'd set in motion.

"Why not?" she consented, out of the blue. "How vile could it be? And if you're half as good as you claim, it might even be fun."

CHAPTER THREE

EMMA maintained a straight face, delighted that she could exude calm under such blazing scrutiny. As her acquiescence was not what he'd expected, Wakefield was confounded and flabbergasted, and nervously fidgeting—as though wondering if she was about to ravish him.

Warily, he kept peeking over at his brother, wishing the other Clayton in the room would rescue him from his folly, but the man judiciously chose to stay out of the debacle.

She wasn't sure when she'd deduced that Wakefield wasn't serious about his solicitation, but no one could be that despicable! Somewhere in the middle of his asinine performance, she'd realized that he was trying to ferment a surge of maidenly umbrage that would chase her away. Unfortunately for him, she was no shrinking violet and refused to go peacefully.

For some reason, she understood much more about him than she ought, and her excess of insight had nothing to do with the fact that she'd already seen him mostly naked and participating in a sexual rendezvous.

He was magnificent, extraordinary, unlike any person she'd ever met before. His charisma and elegance were sweeping over her like a tidal wave, making her eager to linger in his presence as long as he would allow.

Surprisingly, he wasn't the devil that she and others had painted him to be, but an outrageously handsome, sophisticated, and fascinating man. Deplorably, the animosity she'd intended to harbor toward him had vanished, only to be replaced by curiosity. She was intrigued and enthralled, their pithy discussion the sole bright repartee in which she'd engaged in ages.

There was an odd connection between them. She'd sensed it the moment she'd stepped into the room, and he'd focused his amazing blue eyes upon her. When she'd been spying on him from outside the house, she'd noticed those eyes, but she hadn't been prepared for how mesmerizing they were up close. She felt as if she could stare into their azure depths and see all the way to his soul.

Regrettably, what she'd discovered wasn't very encouraging.

He thrived on acting the part of a knave. He liked people to think he was a cad, an amoral villain, which he clearly could be, but he'd flaunted his dissolution until he'd displayed it so frequently that others assumed he really was a perpetual scapegrace.

Though he rigorously strove to hide any stellar attributes, deep down, he was a principled gentleman. His ethics—if one could call them that—had a bizarre twist that might take some acclimation. She had to comprehend what drove him so that she could ascertain how to finesse him. By appealing to his more honorable nature, she could get him to do what needed to be done.

All sorts of cordial relationships developed between the most diverse types of people, and she was optimistic enough to suppose that there was some purpose to her meeting the wanton scoundrel. Both for him and for her. Her peculiar cognizance as to his character quirks would be a boon, and being that he was a typical male, he'd never suspect that she was using him to accomplish her own objectives.

Though he'd tried to hide his response, he'd been shocked and dismayed when she'd mentioned Mr. Gladstone's plight, a glaring indication that he had a conscience. He could provide tremendous support to the community, if he was cleverly lured in the right direction—but she couldn't pressure him if she didn't spend any time with him.

He was short-tempered and intelligent, but easily distracted by vice and debauchery, and he didn't tolerate insubordination. No one talked back to him, contradicted him, or repudiated his absurd opinions. He was extremely impressed with himself and his exalted position, and he was smarting from her astute remarks and observations, so he wouldn't condescend to suffer her company again, unless she took exceptional measures to protract their acquaintance.

She'd quickly assessed her situation: If she wanted extended opportunities to fraternize, he had to be persuaded that she could occupy his hours as enticingly as any doxy. Unless he could be convinced that their association would be amusing, he'd bar her from the manor, and thus, she wouldn't be able to work her wiles.

She was an expert at getting men to do what they should, at prevailing upon them to embrace their responsibilities. Why, just the previous week, she'd induced a village boy to marry a girl who'd needed a husband. She was adept at the utilization of manipulation and ruse in order to effect her ends for the greater good. She'd learned her tricks from her father, who'd been proficient at subtle coercion.

Wakefield was no different from any other man. He could be led, he could be pushed, he could be downright shoved, and she was more than willing to be the one doing the shoving. So long as, at the conclusion, she got him to revoke the evictions, and it hadn't occurred to her that she wouldn't prevail.

She couldn't have been a vicar's daughter for nearly three decades without absorbing some of her father's teachings: On every occasion, *right* was destined to triumph over *wrong*.

If she had to consent to an affair, she would, but that didn't mean she had to follow through. Her goals were lofty and just, and she would promise him anything—even wild, deviant sex acts—if it would garner her the appointments she would need to dissuade him. She would tease and flirt, and constantly lead him to believe that he was about to seduce her, but he would never succeed, though he didn't need to know that.

While normally, she was an honest, candid individual, who wouldn't dream of lying or enmiring herself in falsehoods, she was looking him in the eye and prevaricating with nary a ripple in her rectitude. As he shouldn't have raised the repugnant proposal in the first place, she didn't have any reservations about deceiving him.

If she later recanted, so what? No one would cry foul. He didn't dare tell anyone what he'd done, and assuredly, she would never confess. If by some stroke of bad luck, their accord became public knowledge, there wasn't a person alive who would reprimand her for declining to yield to the craven aristocrat, although she had to admit that she wouldn't complain too loudly should a small amount of *yielding* actually happen.

She wouldn't consider their arrangement a total failure if she managed to steal a few kisses before their transaction ended. What female would lament being kissed by such an insolent rogue?

Not herself, certainly.

She'd been kissed before—passionately and many

times—and she'd liked it. Too much. So much so that she'd frightened herself and had not attempted such frivolity again.

The autumn of lusting, she'd invariably referred to it.

She'd been seventeen when a crew of traveling thrashers had journeyed through to help bring in the harvest, and she'd been smitten by one of the field laborers. Charlie had been a totally inappropriate sort, a burly, strapping lad, who'd oozed charm and virility, and she hadn't had the strength to resist his allure.

For an entire week, she'd sneaked out in the night to be with him. He'd been a randy boy, and his enthusiastic kisses had stirred such unremitting corporeal torment that she still wasn't sure she'd recovered from them.

After that brief capriciousness, she'd shunned male company, devoting herself to aiding her father in his ministry. In the process, she'd deprived herself of the likelihood of further bodily transgression. Her self-imposed, eternal chastity was a penance for the sins she'd committed.

But in the night, when she lay in her lonely bed, she'd recall that superb episode, and how it had felt to be a woman. Even after all these years, she could graphically recollect the splendor that ardor engendered and, as she'd once proven herself to have such a weak moral constitution, she'd always suspected that she might impetuously seize the opportunity again should any dapper-looking fellow be bold enough to indicate any interest.

A fellow such as Wakefield, for instance. She'd never encountered anyone like him before, and probably never would again, so she couldn't regret an ardent kiss or two.

And if he tried to turn them into something more,

she wasn't worried about her ability to handle him. She wasn't an adolescent girl who was out of control with physical yearning. She knew how to adamantly say no, and though he struggled mightily to pretend otherwise, she perceived the integrity lurking under his bitter outer shell. He would heed any restraints she imposed on his behavior.

He was standing so near, trying to intimidate her, that she could smell the starch in his shirt, the soap with which he'd bathed. There was an earthy odor about him, a mixture of fresh air, leather, and other manly aromas like tobacco and horses.

It called to the lusty, bawdy side of her secret self, the side she religiously strove to stifle and had only revealed to a potent itinerant field hand.

The sensations made her feel unencumbered and wicked, naughty and mischievous, a female who was disposed to revel in any debauchery.

In other words, a woman completely opposite from herself.

Shifting forward an inch or two, she narrowed the distance between them. Wakefield's perplexity spiraled. He was so easy to read! He couldn't figure her out, what she intended, or where his indecent approach was conveying him.

This was going to be so gratifying! And profitable for so many indigent folks.

"Now then," she said, all business, "I'm sure you won't blame me if I insist we put our pact into writing."

She couldn't say where the brilliant impulse had come from, but if she had his signature on an agreement, she was positive she could use the written record to coerce all manner of compliance from him.

"Into writing," he stupidly repeated.

"No offense, milord, but you can see my point. I'd

be a fool to surrender my virtue on no more than a private conversation. If I succumbed to your copious charms, but you defaulted on your end of our bargain, what recourse would I have to compel your performance?"

"You won't accept a verbal commitment from me?"

"I hardly know you, and what I do know is quite horrid. Why should I credit what you have to say?" She glanced over at his brother. "Would you take his word for anything, Mr. Clayton?"

"No. Absolutely not."

At his answer, Wakefield grew so furious that she was even more satisfied as to the wisdom of her scheme.

Wakefield was sputtering and stammering for a valid retort, so she aimed her comments to his brother. "Mr. Clayton, would you be so kind as to transcribe the terms for us?" She smiled up at Wakefield. "It will be beneficial to have a witness, don't you agree?"

"By all means," he ground out.

Wakefield glowered at Mr. Clayton, and a silent communication passed between them, which she tucked away for later dissection and analysis. Obviously, they were very close, and she would have to factor Ian Clayton into her plans. If the two brothers were as attached as they appeared to be, she might be able to utilize him in her handling of the viscount.

"Glad to be of assistance, Miss Fitzgerald," Ian Clayton finally said, and he moved to the desk, but only after Wakefield had given him some type of taciturn permission.

Another fascinating detail to mull!

He made a great show of seating himself and dipping pen to ink, and she was overcome by the notion that he was acutely enjoying the interlude. Evidently, she had bested Wakefield in a way that didn't often transpire, and Ian Clayton was humored that she had.

"Where would you like to begin?" He seemed innocent and obliging, and he conspicuously kept his attention from settling on Wakefield.

As for the viscount, he had stepped away from her, creating space, or perhaps staking out his territory. His arms were crossed over his chest and, visibly angry, a ponderous frown marred his brow.

"Let's start out with a title," she suggested. " 'Agreement Between the Parties' or some such. Then list our names and identities."

The pen scratched across the page as he filled in an introductory paragraph.

"How about this?" Mr. Clayton queried, and Emma scooted behind the desk to read over his shoulder.

"That's excellent." She looked up at Wakefield whose scowl hadn't lessened a bit. "Would you like to see what he's composed so far?"

"No."

"Fine, then. Let's continue." She recited, " 'Viscount Wakefield stipulates that he will rescind the eviction notices for the following fourteen tenants.' " She laid her list on the desktop and smoothed it out, indicating each of the names as Mr. Clayton affixed them to the document. " 'In exchange, Miss Fitzgerald will perform fourteen episodes of sexual intercourse.' "

At her blunt phrasing, the tips of Mr. Clayton's ears turned bright crimson, but he persisted with his writing as though she'd uttered nothing untoward. As to the viscount, he gulped down a strangled sound.

Hoisted on his own petard! Wonderful! Before they were through, she hoped he'd suffocate from embarrassment.

Feigning naïveté, she asked him, "Is that language amenable to you?"

He paused, his steamy regard sweeping over her in a blatantly carnal way, and he said to Mr. Clayton, "I want the sentence to end like this: ' . . . sexual intercourse in any fashion Wakefield requests.' "

Smirking, his rabid gaze locked with hers, and he seemed to crow, *Top that!*

He didn't grasp that he could preen and strut forever but his arrogance wouldn't have any effect.

Mr. Clayton peered up at her. "Will that addition suffice?"

"Yes. Now this: 'The viscount will not initiate any other evictions for a period of one year. At that time, should he feel the situation still warrants such drastic action, he will not proceed without consulting Miss Fitzgerald and giving her a chance to change his mind in whatever style he demands.' "

Wakefield stiffened. "Just a damned minute. I'm not about to enter into an arrangement where I'm eternally beholden to your whims and—"

"Don't curse in front of me."

He bit down on his lip so hard that he might have drawn blood. "My apologies," he muttered, "but you talk as if I'll be taking advantage of you in perpetuity."

"I guess you will be, but I'd like to think you'll come to your senses long before then." She nodded to Mr. Clayton. "Jot that last down. About our cohabiting a year from now—if it's required."

He was grinning. "It that all right with you, John?"

"Splendid!" the viscount barked. "Dandy!"

"Is there anything we've omitted, Miss Fitzgerald?" Mr. Clayton inquired.

"There are two other items," she said, "but I don't know if they belong in the contract or not, so I'll let you advise me."

"What are they?"

"Well, I can't abide a drunkard—"

"A drunkard!" Wakefield snapped.

"—so he must refrain from imbibing. Should that be included? Or can I trust him to stay sober?"

"Miss Fitzgerald," the viscount griped, "you will not direct me in my drinking habits!"

"Sir, *you* are bartering for the privilege of regularly violating my person, so I'll be surrendering much more than you. You ought to give up *something* as a concession."

"She's got you there, John," Mr. Clayton chided. Conspiratorially, he murmured, "We'd better include it. He can be stubborn about his vices." He scribbled away. "And the other?"

"His loose women and sluggardly companions will have to go back to London."

"What!" both men complained together.

They were jointly appalled by her ultimatum, stunned that she had the gall to raise the scandalous topic. No doubt about it, she needed to keep the upper hand with the pair of bounders. "I'm afraid I'm going to have to insist."

She saw a propitious opportunity to rid the property of the wastrels and scalawags who had traveled with the viscount, and who had been driving the staff crazy with their despicable antics.

The peace and quiet generated by their departure would be welcomed, plus she wanted Wakefield all to herself, without the distraction of his rough crowd. With the two of them in seclusion, she'd have better odds for altering his conduct.

"You are a marvel, Miss Fitzgerald!" the viscount exclaimed. "You've insulted me for nearly all of my perverse tendencies. Is there anything you've neglected to enumerate?"

"I don't believe so."

"I pity the chap you marry. You're already a proficient nag. You'll have him thoroughly unmanned before your wedding night!"

"I'm sure you're correct." She laughed gaily. As if any man would marry her! The only one who'd ever evinced a heightened interest was the new vicar, Harold Martin, and Emma shuddered at contemplating what a miserable existence that would be.

The viscount and his brother were glaring at each other, Wakefield enraged, Mr. Clayton mystified by her effrontery. They were speculating as to how they'd gotten into this fix, and how they were going to get themselves out of it. They'd commenced the spurious discussion as a lark, a joke that would provide a slew of hilarious stories to bandy about.

They hadn't counted on the prospect that she'd outwit them.

Another imperceptible communication occurred between them, and they seemed to shrug in unison. In tacit accord, they'd decided to placate her, while ruminating over how to subsequently weasel out of the bargain.

Weren't they in for a surprise!

Mr. Clayton dipped the pen and adjoined her resolution that Wakefield's visitors return to town. Finished, he held the document so that she could peruse it. "How's this?"

"Perfect," she affably concurred. "Let's sign it and make it official."

"Let's do," Wakefield grumpily mimicked.

Mr. Clayton drew three lines at the bottom. One for herself, one for Wakefield, and one for Mr. Clayton, who would serve as their witness. Emma took the pen, and wrote her name in her usual tidy script, then she extended it to the viscount, who stared at it as though it were a venomous snake.

"You're next," Mr. Clayton goaded him.

Seeing no way out of the conundrum, Wakefield stomped around the desk and yanked the pen out of her hand. To reach the contract, he had to jam himself into the confined gap between herself and Mr. Clayton and, as he did, he was wedged up against her.

Convinced as to her wantonness, she didn't move away, but allowed the improper contact, inhaling his luscious scent, scrutinizing the intriguing golden color of his hair then, at the last second, she jerked her eyes away so he'd have no clue as to where she'd lingered.

He inscribed his name with a grand flourish, then he offered the pen to his brother, and as Mr. Clayton scrawled his name, Wakefield whispered to him, "Cheeky little baggage."

She grinned, champing down on a giggle, barely able to conceal her elation.

Mr. Clayton sanded the ink, and Wakefield snatched up the paper. Most likely, he was bent on hiding it, and she plucked it away, folded it, and tucked it into the bodice of her gown before either of them could react.

Wakefield was horrified. "You're not going to keep it!"

Oh, how she relished being close to him! She couldn't remember when she'd previously stumbled upon a man who was so handsome, so dashing and distinct.

He towered over her, his masculine heat and essence overwhelming her, making her skin tingle, her pulse escalate, her senses come alive. But while she treasured his proximity, she was too shrewd to be deluded by his magnificence.

"I'm not about to let you have it," she caustically

pointed out. "I'm quite sure it would disappear."

From the invisible daggers the two men traded, it was disgracefully apparent that they'd had every intention of destroying it once she'd left, but their prank wasn't progressing at all as they'd foreseen. They'd assumed they could send her off, foolishly surmising that she had a deal, when she'd have had no method of proving it, or holding Wakefield to his promise.

Much to their communal chagrin, she hadn't submissively done as they'd calculated.

"When should we start?" she asked Wakefield.

Plainly, he longed to answer, *Never!* but he was too egotistical to say so aloud. Instead, he stomped around the desk, while he pretended to be magnanimous. "When would be convenient for you?"

"How about now?"

Luckily, he wasn't swallowing a bite of food, because he would have choked on it.

"Now?" he echoed faintly. Maneuvered into an ambush, he rapidly regrouped. "An immediate commencement wouldn't be possible for me. I'm extremely busy today." He frowned at his brother. "Isn't that right, Ian?"

"You don't have anything on your schedule."

If looks could have killed, Mr. Clayton would have been dead on the floor.

"I'm sure you've forgotten"—Wakefield tersely clarified—"that I'd planned to go riding with some of our guests."

"Had you?" Mr. Clayton smiled, all ingenuousness. "This is the first you've mentioned it." Wakefield took a menacing step toward him, and Mr. Clayton held up his hands in surrender. "But then, I'm never fully apprised of your calendar."

"Tomorrow, then?" she interjected. She'd had enough of the obnoxious duo and whatever game they were playing. "I'd really like to get on with it, so I can give some early assurance to those who've received your eviction letters. Many people are packing their belongings—and in grave despair—even as we speak."

Wakefield yearned to object, but she'd neatly boxed him into a corner. She had the endorsed agreement crumpled between her breasts, and short of wrestling her to the ground and snagging it from her, he couldn't get it back. As long as she kept it in her possession, she would have a chance to reverse his decision; he couldn't renege.

"Tomorrow will be fine."

"At one?"

"Yes," he irritably acceded.

"You'll be sober, and your friends gone?"

"Yes, Miss Fitzgerald! Yes!" Exasperated, he gestured toward the door. "Will that be all?"

He was so piqued that she was amazed he wasn't down on his knees and begging her to desist and depart, and she couldn't resist tweaking his temper a tad more.

She knew she should leave while she was ahead, but she was having such an extraordinary time in his company that she couldn't make herself walk out.

These few minutes had been so invigorating and vital, a pitiful indicator of the state of her life, and she couldn't force herself to end their initial encounter. She liked having his attention focused on her, wanted to dawdle in his presence.

"Actually, there is one more thing."

"What?" he snarled.

"I thought you might give me a good-bye kiss. So I'd have some idea of what to expect."

"What to *expect*? You've just negotiated a sexual contract, and you don't know how to kiss a man?"

"Well, of course I know how to *kiss* a man. I'm

more worried about . . . well . . . if the experience will be repugnant or not." Which was a bald-faced lie. She anticipated that it would be remarkable, but it was so entertaining to have him fuming.

"Did you hear that, John?" Mr. Clayton chimed in, chortling merrily. "She's concerned that kissing you might be repulsive!"

Wakefield had suffered through her other slurs without becoming overly upset, but this slander of his masculine abilities was too much. Especially that she would question his aptitude in front of his brother. He was obviously conceited as to his reputation with the ladies, but from the apathetic copulation she'd seen, she didn't understand why any lover would rave.

"Come here, Miss Fitzgerald."

She'd egregiously poked at his ego, and she'd reap the consequences, but she was anxious to have this inaugural foray terminate on a bold note. Oozing bravado, she sauntered around the desk and approached him until they were toe-to-toe. His body was taut as a bowstring, and she supposed that he would roughly grab her, that he would maul her with a punishing kiss.

Astonishingly, he placed his hands on her shoulders so lightly that she could scarcely feel them, then he bent down and tenderly melded his lips to her own. It was the most chaste, most precious, moment of her life. His breath brushed across her cheek, it was warm, he tasted like . . .

Abruptly, it ended. He pulled away, concluding the embrace before she'd had occasion to shut her eyes.

Their gazes linked, and the strangest sensation of connection and affinity leapt between them. He'd noted the sweetness, too, and he was bewildered and confused.

Hastily masking his perplexity, he cleared his throat. "I trust that wasn't too . . . *repugnant*?"

"No," she tartly replied, "just disappointing."

"Disappointing!"

"You seem like such a virile fellow." She let her assessing regard meander down his torso, then back up. "I'd imagined you might imbue it with a little more . . . *passion* . . . I guess."

Why did she persist with baiting him? Wasn't it enough that she'd triumphed in every instance? She'd already garnered most of what she'd hoped to gain and they hadn't even begun their struggle toward a resolution.

The knave made her willing to do or say any crazed thing, merely to see the rise she could get out of him. Absurdly, she felt a burning desire to provoke a response, as if the Good Lord had specifically sent her to shake him awake after a lengthy slumber. Yet, her prodding was very much like nudging at a sleeping giant.

He was glaring at her with such cool, controlled fury that she grew apprehensive. Behind her, Mr. Clayton was guffawing jovially, making veiled, sarcastic observations about Wakefield's sexual prowess, but Emma couldn't decipher them. The intimidating strength of Wakefield's concentration was deluging her, and it was like being sucked into a whirlpool.

"Ian," he said quietly, not bothering to turn about, his tone brooking no argument. "Leave us be."

"I really can't bear to." Mr. Clayton was still chuckling. "This is more fun than I've had in an eternity."

"Go!" Wakefield commanded softly, but the vehemence with which he'd pronounced the word was so fierce that it reverberated off the walls like a shout.

The room grew silent, and Mr. Clayton pushed back his chair and stood. Emma could hear nothing but the tick of the clock over the mantel, and the thudding of her pulse in her ears. Mr. Clayton passed by them and he paused, bothered by the level to which she'd elevated Wakefield's ire.

"If you need me, Miss Fitzgerald—" Mr. Clayton gallantly proclaimed, fretting about her being alone with the angry nobleman.

"I won't," she confidently retorted. "I'm not afraid of Viscount Wakefield. He'd never hurt me."

He might grumble and roar, but he'd lash out with no more than his caustic tongue, and she'd beheld how verbally vicious he could be: not very.

Mr. Clayton looked from one to the other, then strolled out.

They were caught in a mind-boggling staring match, until the door latch clicked after him, and the second it did, Wakefield swaggered in, his body impacting with hers all the way down. Chests, stomachs, thighs, feet, they were tangled together, and the surge of stimulation that erupted from their anatomical attachment was so powerful that she flinched, only to find her rear planted on the edge of the desk.

Wakefield pressed his advantage, hovering over her and tilting in, so that he had her off balance and plunging backward. Before she could sink onto the desktop, he arrested her descent with the palm of his hand between her shoulder blades. He held her just there, examining her features, and totally unsure of what to make of her.

"Never let it be said"—he moved even nearer, with a subtle shift of his hips, insinuating himself between her legs—"that John Clayton left a lady *disappointed*."

Nervously, she licked her bottom lip, instantly capturing his undivided attention. "Perhaps *disappointed* was a tad strong."

"Shut up, woman! You plague me with your ceaseless chatter!"

Deliberately, tantalizingly, he lowered her down, until her back reached the expanse of polished oak. He came with her, stretching out, his immense chest flattened to her breasts, his private parts positioned against her own.

He was hard! His erection was heavy and huge, and she inhaled sharply at detecting the massive bulge.

With his arms braced on either side of her, she was efficiently trapped, but she wasn't fearful. She was ablaze, titillated, fascinated. She didn't know what he intended, and she didn't care. It felt incredible to have him situated so familiarly, and she hooked her feet behind his thighs, urging him on.

He was excited by the small encouragement, his eyes widening, his nostrils flaring. "Whatever I might decide to do to you now, you'd deserve it. You realize that, don't you, you silly strumpet?"

"You don't scare me, so stop trying. And I'm not a *strumpet*!"

But then he proceeded to show her that she probably was.

He mumbled something she couldn't interpret, then he kissed her, his lips settling on hers. The action was impulsive, swift. With no warning, his tongue entered her, and she stiffened, then relaxed, her hands cradling his neck, to tug him closer.

His mouth molded perfectly with her own, as if it had been sculpted for kissing her and no other purpose at all. Her eyelids fluttered down, and she let herself be swept away.

As she'd suspected, he was an ardent man when he chose to be. There was a fire and intensity simmering beneath the surface that was carefully banked. The aloofness and detachment she'd perceived when he'd made love to his paramour were absent.

Teeming with suppressed ardor, his arousal was blatant and evident against her loins. Unashamed of his condition, he brazenly let her feel his splendid cockstand, so ready, and she smiled, celebrating their naughty indiscretion.

He tasted so fine, like brandy and mint, and she moaned with delight. The sound rumbled into his being, seeming to rush down to his phallus, and he began to flex and thrust at her, through her skirts, the rhythm corresponding with that of his tongue.

Her body was ripe, she was wet at her womanly core, stirred with longing and craving his touch, but maddeningly, he wouldn't advance, not allowing his hands to stray, and keeping them firmly anchored on the desktop.

Past any sensible limit, he continued on, until his cock was unrelenting in its need for completion, until her torso was rigid, and she was insanely wishing that he'd do something much more abandoned than this turbulent kissing, which neither of them seemed disposed to halt. It was too delicious, too decadent, taking her into an entirely new realm that was far beyond any possibilities she'd ever imagined.

Finally—finally!—he broke away. Their respirations were laborious, their bodies primed for mating, and it occurred to her that, if he but asked, she might commit any reckless act. Nothing prior had prepared her for this urgent, unremitting combustion that had her zealously wild to ruin herself.

He peered down at her, mere inches separating their mouths, his breath coursing over her face, his eyes penetrating, and she was ecstatic.

The lust that had engulfed her had been as potent for him.

Arrogantly, he inquired, "Have you—on this occasion—found my kiss to be more than sufficient?"

"I'd say it was . . ."—she delayed for maximum effect—"*adequate.*"

He barked out a laugh. "Sassy wench."

Transferring his weight to his feet, he stood, but not before resting his palms on her shoulders and stroking them down in a lazy, languid path, tracing over her collarbone, her breasts, her ribs, her crotch and thighs. Then he straightened, adjusting his clothes and composing himself.

"Go home, Miss Fitzgerald, and don't come back," he cautioned. "Because if you are idiotic enough to provoke a subsequent confrontation, I can't guarantee that I will stop."

With that, he spun around and marched out, closing the door behind. Left by herself, she loitered, obscenely draped across the desk, and gazing up at the ceiling. Her skirt was rucked up, her legs bared and dangling over the edge, her bodice askew, her hair falling down. She was a sight, and she needed to stand and right herself before anyone else could wander in, but disgustingly, her knees were weak, and she slid to the floor, huddled on the rug in a pile of skirt and petticoat.

The man was a sorcerer! With no more than a kiss, he crushed her defenses, fractured her restraint, wreaked havoc on her common sense, making her eager to acquiesce in any depravity.

For the first time since meeting him, she was frightened. Not of him. But of herself, and of what she might be capable at his instigation and direction.

What had she set in motion?

She stumbled to her feet and, without encountering another soul, she sneaked out of the manor and headed for home, her signed pact discreetly tucked away in her chemise.

CHAPTER FOUR

"YOU'RE not planning to go through with it?"

John glared at Ian over the rim of his whisky glass. "What do you think?"

"Considering how you act, anymore, who could say?"

"What the hell's that supposed to mean?"

"It *means* that you might do any reckless thing. What possessed you to initiate such a foolish stunt?"

Ah, a question he'd asked himself a few dozen times since their auspicious rendezvous with the indomitable Miss Fitzgerald the day before.

What had possessed him?

During the appointment, he'd had a valid motive for the ruse, though now he couldn't remember what it had been. He'd wanted to rid himself of the bothersome female in a fashion that would ensure she wouldn't return, but the subterfuge hadn't proceeded as he'd intended.

How had the diminutive shrew so deftly turned the tables on him? He was bloody glad she didn't gamble! The hellcat was so shrewd! So sly! Had they been betting against one another, he'd likely have lost everything he owned. She kept a man off balance, prevented him from choosing the wiser course, from staying on the proper path.

Why . . . he wouldn't be surprised to learn that she'd had training as a witch!

His eyes stung from his blasted insomnia, from cigar

smoke and too much liquor, his head throbbed, his body ached, and he wished he'd been discerning enough—as had been his guests—to fall into bed before dawn.

The house was quiet, himself and Ian the only ones roaming about the cavernous, hollow rooms that he hated.

"Don't worry," he said. "I took care of Miss Fitzgerald. She won't be back."

"Hah!" Ian snorted. "If that's what you believe, you've become an absolute dunce."

"I scared the living daylights out of her."

"How?"

"I kissed her to the point of ravishment."

Even to his own ears, his actions sounded stupid. How was it exactly that his lips had come to be joined with hers? How had he gotten provoked to where he'd had her flat on the desk, her legs wrapped around him, his cockstand urgent and pulsating against her loins?

This unpalatable sojourn to the country was driving him mad! It was the only explanation.

"Oh, I'm sure that struck the fear of God into her." Incredulous, Ian rolled his eyes. "For a man who purportedly knows all there is to know about women, you can really be an idiot."

"Trust me. She won't show her face here again."

"No, *trust* me. She'll arrive in about fifteen minutes."

"Why fifteen?"

"Because it will be one o'clock."

"So?"

"You agreed to meet with her at one."

"I wasn't serious."

"Well, unfortunately, Miss Fitzgerald was."

Ian strolled over to the window and gazed out at the rolling lawns behind the manor.

With each passing year, his brother's disposition changed so that, frequently, he appeared downright sanctimonious in his renunciation of vice and revelry. The more John indulged, the less Ian seemed to, although he usually kept his opinions to himself over John's penchant for excess. Apparently, with Miss Fitzgerald front and center, Ian felt it was his duty to ingratiate himself, convinced that the tiny termagant needed a champion.

As if Miss Fitzgerald required any help at handling herself!

The woman was a harridan, a viper, with claws like a big cat that sank in and latched on. Refusing to give in or relent, she was like a starving dog at a bone, her teeth clamped around what she wanted. He shuddered just from recollecting how voraciously the little harper had dug in and wouldn't let go.

She scarcely needed Ian's intrepid aid!

John stared at Ian's stiff shoulders. Lately, he'd been so morose, so discontented and out of sorts. John was curious as to why and was about to inquire, when Ian emitted an eerie laugh that made the hair rise up on John's neck.

"What is it?" John queried.

"Not only is our formidable Miss Fitzgerald tenacious"—he whipped around and leveled a virulent look that spoke volumes—"but she's early."

"You're joking."

"No, I'm not. She's traipsing across the yard even as we speak."

"Bloody hell." John leapt to his feet and stumbled over to the window.

There she was! Bold as brass! Didn't the female have any sense?

In a taut silence, they watched her draw nigh, and John experienced the oddest sensation that his destiny was approaching—much like Death knocking on his door. Once she entered the house, he would never be the same, and he fleetingly pondered whether he should hide so that she couldn't find him.

"Told you so," Ian aggravatingly remarked.

"What is it with her?" John didn't expect a reply. Ian didn't comprehend the fairer sex any better than did John.

"All of this matters to her, you dolt. These people, this place." Ian made a wide gesture, indicating everything in sight. "But I doubt you could understand."

"Go intercept her. Don't let her in."

John pronounced the order in his customary authoritative manner, temporarily forgetting that Ian never heeded his commands, nor did John issue them to his brother. Though their birth statuses were completely divergent, Ian was one of the few people John respected as an equal, and the instant the dictate left his mouth, he regretted uttering it.

A flash of ire simmered across Ian's face but was quickly masked.

"No. You got yourself into this mess. You can get yourself out of it. For once." He started toward the door, but stopped at the threshold. "Don't you hurt her."

"Oh, for pity's sake!" As if he'd *hurt* the accursed nuisance. How could Ian conceive he would?

"She isn't some jaded doxy from town. She's a chaste, honorable gentlewoman."

"Chaste!" he scoffed. "She is no virgin."

A virgin couldn't have had the skill to kiss like she did. With full engagement of hands, tongue, and body. His balls wrenched on recalling how lusty and bawdy the interlude had been.

Kissing Emma Fitzgerald had been thrilling, intriguing. She put her heart and soul into the embrace, relishing the episode in a way his other lovers never had.

He regularly wallowed in carnal activity, but it had grown so tepid and routine. When had the newness and excitement worn away? When had he last kissed someone—and really meant it?

Since he generally paid for his pleasure, the foreplay leading up to the ultimate act was a waste of energy. Why delay gratification with frivolous, feigned ardor? His paramours weren't consenting to gain physical satisfaction. They were in it solely for the cash they could earn, so why pretend it was more than an uncomplicated business transaction?

"Don't you dare pursue that asinine contract you signed with her."

"After her shenanigans, she'd deserve it if I did."

"She's desperate. You're ousting poor people!"

"They're malingerers and—"

"You can be such a prick!"

He and Ian rarely quarreled, and the testy comment set a spark to John's temper.

Though his anger was immature and unreasonable, he bristled at having his competence maligned. His whole life, he'd had to listen to his father's harsh criticism that he'd never amount to anything, that he had none of the necessary characteristics to be a viscount.

His sainted, deceased older brother, James, was to have inherited the title, but he'd drowned in a boating accident when John was a child, and John had had to repeatedly hear how he couldn't fill his dead brother's shoes.

After having constantly been told that he was a failure and an imbecile, he'd spent two decades bolstering everyone's low expectations until his conduct was ingrained. With his father's death the previous year, the responsibilities were his own, even though he hadn't wanted them.

For as long as he'd been able, he'd avoided assuming his obligations, but he couldn't keep dodging them. The fiscal situation was dire at all the properties, and he grasped what had to be done to correct their father's mismanagement, was prepared to make the difficult choices.

Who was Ian to oppugn his abilities?

As Ian had resided in John's home for the prior twelve years, and reaped quite an affluent standard of living due to the largess yielded by the Wakefield estate, who was he to complain about how John chose to salvage it?

"What would you suggest? That I cancel the evictions simply because she batted her pretty brown eyes at me?"

"I don't give a shit what you do with your holdings," Ian acerbically claimed. "It's entirely your affair. All I'm saying is: Don't maltreat her." There was a dangerous pause, then he added, "Or I guess you'll finally have to answer to me."

What the hell was he ranting about?

Ian stalked off before John could ask him.

Irritated, hungry, hungover, he walked to the sofa and slouched down, sipping on his libation and contemplating his pathetic state: no genuine friends, no money in the family coffers, a brother who loathed him, a mistress he couldn't abide, a purported fiancée who lied to herself and professed to be in love with him merely because her overbearing father demanded she be.

How had he ended up at such a pitiful juncture?

Voices floated down the hall, and he strained to make out who it might be, though he was positive that Ian was being his charming, gracious self and personally welcoming Miss Fitzgerald into the house. Shortly, a solitary set of footsteps was briskly winging toward him, and he heaved a sigh of resignation.

Ian had extracted a petty revenge, giving Miss Fitzgerald specific directions as to John's location, and in a few seconds, she marched into the library.

She was garbed precisely as she had been the morning before, same severe hairstyle, same drab dress, and he fleetingly wondered if she only had one. How sad for someone so fetching to have such scant opportunity for individual embellishment. If she'd belonged to him, he'd accouter her in red to accentuate the color in her cheeks, and he'd decree that, whenever they were alone, she have her hair brushed out and flowing down, and he'd—

"Wakefield, you're drinking!"

"Yes, I am, Miss Fitzgerald." Rudely, he tipped his whisky at her, then imbibed in a deep swig.

"Your companions are still on the premises, too! Your mistress is here! I saw her coming down the stairs."

"Is she up and about already?" he flippantly inquired.

"You've violated every term of our agreement—and we haven't even commenced!"

"There is no agreement."

"Oh, yes there is!" She stomped over to him and snatched his glass, tossing the contents into the hearth. He was so astonished that he didn't even object. Furious, she hovered over him, hands on hips, ferocious as any put-upon governess he'd annoyed as a lad. "I'm not about to let you worm your way out of it!"

"Miss Fitzgerald, I know I have a miserable reputation, but you can't realistically presume that I would permit you to disgrace yourself into being seduced by me! Despite how noble your cause!" He strove to look conciliatory. "I was jesting."

"I wasn't! Your promises may not hold any value to you, but mine are sincere and earnestly made!" Flabbergasting him, she went to the door and turned the key in the lock. "We're proceeding! Whether you want to or not!"

What on earth did she propose?

He actually suffered a frenetic moment when he worried that she was going to force herself on him. The notion was so absurd that he laughed aloud, a robust, hearty belly laugh such as he hadn't enjoyed in ages, but his mirth faded when she sauntered to the windows and closed the drapes, tightening them so that no one outside on the path could see in.

With a smile as old as Eve's, she advanced on the couch, and before he could register a protest, she climbed on top of him and straddled his lap. Her knees were balanced on the cushions, her thighs cradling his own. She rucked up her skirt and lowered herself so that her privates were in contact with his phallus, and his cock jumped to attention, swelling his trousers, as she temptingly shifted across it, then she leaned forward, breasts to chest, her lips inches from his own.

"I can stay for two hours, Wakefield, and we have so much to do." She threaded her fingers through his hair, sifting through the curly locks at the back, then she bent down and initiated a kiss, her delectable mouth uniting with his, the impact electrifying and magnificent.

The woman was an absolute mystery, and he was stumped as to how he should carry on. He'd tried to humor her, he'd tried to warn her, he'd tried to frighten her, but nothing had succeeded, and he couldn't fathom how to make her desist and depart.

As it was, her fabulous anatomy was pressed to his, setting off sparks in numerous erotic spots. His erection was so hard it was painful. Those marvelously enticing lips of hers were molded to his own, yet he was sitting like a nitwit, inert as a marble statue, hands at his sides, and declining to participate as was imperative.

For once in his despicable life, he'd resolved to act the gentleman that birth and breeding said he was. He had no intention of encouraging her, or of progressing down the road she seemed determined to travel.

He would save her from her folly!

She licked across his bottom lip. "Kiss me back, Wakefield."

"I can't."

"Yes you can."

"This is wrong." Had those words come from him? What was happening? In her presence, he was becoming a certifiable prude!

"You're right, but we're going to do it anyway." She caressed his shoulders, his chest, massaging in languid circles.

"Don't do that," he ordered, but without any punch behind the command.

He took hold of her hands, halting the circular motions, but she linked their fingers together, in a dear manner, much as if they were adolescent sweethearts. Like a contented cat, she arched, thrusting out her breasts and rubbing them up and down, her aroused nipples poking at him in a way that incited his manly instincts.

"Imagine how grand it would feel to have my hands on you," she said, breathless and eager. "To have my mouth on you. You'd like that, wouldn't you?"

Shocked that she would raise the possibility, he could only stumble around for a reply.

Was she insane? What man wouldn't plead to have those ruby lips envelop him? What a lush haven she would be!

The image she painted, of her kneeling before him,

undoing his pants, slipping those slender fingers inside to manipulate and tease, was more than he could tolerate. He was a mortal human being, not in the habit of denying himself.

Restraint was stupid! Hadn't he cautioned her as to the consequences if she persisted? Yet she was foolish enough to throw herself at him, to offer the most succulent of delights. He wasn't about to resist.

Reaching for her, he took over the kiss, intensifying it, and she groaned her acquiescence. His hands roamed downward, to her buttocks, clasping the two globes and using his grip as leverage to stroke her across his raging phallus.

He was so ready! So fast! What was it about her that attracted him so? A brief kiss, and he was set to spill himself in his trousers like a callow boy!

Her adept fingers drifted down to his cock. She played with it, squeezing, pressuring it through the fabric, until he was vigorously flexing, rabid for the next, in a frenzy to be bared for her ardent assessment.

She unbuttoned his shirt, then blazed a steamy trail down his neck, to burrow her nose in his chest hair. Snuffling and rooting about, her tongue flicked out in blistering bursts as she scooted across and found his nipple, nibbling with her teeth, then sucking at it until he was squirming and writhing beneath her.

Why wasn't he cooperating?

With a sudden urgency, he needed to have her stretched out and spread wide. He was frantic to impale himself, to pleasure himself at her expense, and he grabbed her hips to rotate her, to ease her off his lap so that he could assuage his masculine drives, but as he made the move, she pulled away, her lovely brown eyes scrutinizing his own. Dismay and consternation furrowed her brow.

"You've recently lain with another. I can smell her perfume on you."

Amazingly, he was embarrassed and baffled, and he couldn't recall ever being so at a loss as to what he should say. He blushed to the tips of his toes, feeling as though he'd been caught in an unaccountable, compromising peccadillo.

She was so appalled—so hurt!—that he'd had a lover. With the troubled way she was studying him, he was overcome by the ridiculous impression that he'd been cheating on her, that he'd been detected and needed to beg her pardon or justify his behavior.

He didn't explain himself! To anyone! He was the Viscount Wakefield. His conduct and comportment were not topics to be bandied about, and others knew better than to reprimand him. Yet Miss Fitzgerald deemed it totally appropriate to voice an opinion on the amatory subject, just as he sat there, thinking he ought to be profusely atoning.

It was one of the most ludicrous, farcical moments of his life.

"Miss Fitzgerald, you can't expect me to have—" He was too mortified to finish the sentence!

"But you knew I'd be here"—she appraised him, hoping to find a reason for the incomprehensible—"yet you didn't have the decency to wash first. Have you no respect for me? As a woman? As a person?"

Her grievance was real, her insult authentic, and he felt like the cad he was repeatedly accused of being. Oddly, at witnessing her upset, he was ashamed. He was so accustomed to dissipation and intemperance that it hadn't occurred to him to bathe—not that he'd believed she was about to arrive!

But still, he was used to lechery, and had indulged so flagrantly, and for so long, that he'd forgotten how those with a more normal life might view his proclivities. As Ian faithfully reminded him, he could be a disgusting fellow. Sometimes, he acted so outrageously that he even offended himself!

"I'm sorry." The apology slithered out before he realized he was going to utter it. "I truly didn't anticipate that you'd deign to visit. I've been up all night, and I—"

"You never made it to your bed?"

"No."

"Wakefield!" she gently chided, and her tender intonation did something to his insides, causing his heart to twist and expand as though it didn't fit between his ribs. "I suppose you haven't eaten, either."

"Well—"

"All you've done is carouse and tipple? Since yesterday?"

"Yes," he admitted. His demeanor, when considered through her eyes, left him contrite and sheepish.

"Honestly! You must take better care of yourself!" With a sassy smile, she inquired, "How will you keep up with me if you don't?"

How, indeed?

With a kind of envy, he observed as she deftly arranged and rebuttoned his shirt, then sprang to her feet, nimble and energetic, equipped to take on the world and reform it to her version of how things should be.

There must have been a time when he carried on with such enthusiasm, but he couldn't remember when. Many activities that he'd previously treasured had lost their appeal. Sporadically, he managed to practice at fencing, but other than that recreation, not much interested him beyond his vices.

She walked to the windows and yanked on the drapes, jerking them open as far as they would go. Sunshine flooded the room, making his eyes burn and his head pound. "Miss Fitzgerald! Do you mind?"

"Not a whit," she impertinently responded. "What's your butler's name? Rutherford?"

"Yes. Why?"

He was reclined on the couch, an arm flung over his eyes to shield them from the onslaught of daylight, when abruptly, she was hollering into the corridor.

"Rutherford, come at once. I need you."

"Good God, Miss Fitzgerald. Are you trying to raise the dead?"

"With the condition of that indolent servant, I might be."

Eventually, the retainer showed himself. He was in a snit, obviously mistaking Miss Fitzgerald for one of John's London colleagues. Though Rutherford tried to hide his feelings, he abhorred most of John's acquaintances.

Little did he know that the individual doing the shouting was his newest nemesis!

"You!" He was aghast to discover that she'd sneaked in without his knowledge or permission. "What are *you* doing here?"

"Didn't Lord Wakefield tell you? I'll be here every afternoon. For at least two weeks. Perhaps longer if it suits me." She rotated so that Rutherford couldn't see, then she winked at John. "I'm helping him to evaluate the financial situation of the estate."

"Holy cripes," John grumbled. He'd speculated as to how she'd rationalize her repetitive appointments to those who might question her goings-on. So she was *working* for him, was she?

He bent over and rested his chin in his hands. The lady had more audacity than anyone he'd ever met.

"He's paying me an exorbitant amount for my *as-*

sistance," she breezily prevaricated. "I couldn't pass up the opportunity."

For a vicar's daughter, the lies certainly rolled off her tongue! In his dealings with her, he couldn't overlook that fact. She was capable of all sorts of duplicity, and he had to be on his guard, lest he be ensnared in one of her schemes—of which he was now convinced she had many.

"She hasn't done much—yet—to prove that she's worth it, Rutherford," he pointed out.

"But I will," she baldly rejoined. "I'll be worth every penny."

Did she ever let a man have the final word?

"Now then," she continued, "Lord Wakefield advises me that he's been involved in debauchery all night—"

"Miss Fitzgerald!" John sputtered, flustered by her public dissection of his profane tendencies, but she didn't miss a beat.

"—so he's having difficulty settling down to business. He needs a pot of tea. Strong as Cook can make it."

"Coffee," John countermanded.

"And breakfast," she added. "Whatever Cook can scrounge this late in the day, but a full plate."

"His Lordship doesn't eat breakfast," Rutherford imperiously droned.

"He does now. You're to feed him each morning before I arrive."

John noted in a huff, "You talk as if I'm an infant!"

"Well, you act like one," she said with great equanimity. She peered at Rutherford. "And he needs a bath. Right away. Have it delivered abovestairs immediately. If I'm to spend time in his company, his sloppy personal habits must end."

Rutherford almost choked, and he stared at John, his puzzlement clear, but as John had already learned, who could fail to comply with one of Emma Fitzgerald's edicts? It was like trying to stop the wind from blowing.

He tipped his head. "See to it."

"Very good, milord."

He departed, and Miss Fitzgerald called after him. "By the way, Rutherford, *all* of Lord Wakefield's friends are leaving for London in the morning."

"Whoa!" John shot up in his seat. "What did you say?"

"Even now," she persisted, "his brother is spreading the news to the guests, so you might inform the staff that they'll be busy with packing."

"Wait just a damned minute!"

"Don't curse at me," she admonished as his butler scurried off, and John was positive the bastard had been smiling. Rutherford had been in John's employ for years, and he was well aware that no one told John what to do, and no one was about to on this occasion, either!

He had no appetite for languishing in the country, with no companions or nocturnal revelry to relieve the tedium, and no mistress to tend to his carnal requirements.

But then, he mused wickedly, *there is the delightful Miss Fitzgerald to take Georgina's place.*

A fascinating conundrum.

He stood. "I've humored you quite extensively, Miss Fitzgerald, but you've finally gone too far."

"You agreed, Wakefield. I won't permit you to renege." She jerked at the door and gestured for him to proceed to his room, and he blindly obeyed without arguing.

How did she do that? Why did he let her?

Usually, he was completely intractable, but when

interacting with Miss Fitzgerald, she was so adamant, and he was so indifferent, that it seemed easier to simply go along. Plus, he liked listening to and watching her. He couldn't recollect when he'd been with someone who was so passionate about every little thing. Her attitude was so bloody refreshing.

"My friends are staying," he contended as he stomped by her.

He had to locate Ian and rescind her decree! How could his blasted brother follow the termagant's instructions without first garnering John's consent?

"They are not."

As though she were lord of the manor, she promenaded to the staircase and climbed, and he was behind her, focused on how her skirt swished across her charming bottom with each step.

"Your reputation will be irrevocably soiled if you accompany me to my bedchamber."

"I don't intend to loiter."

"Then why are you coming with me?"

"Because I'm not letting you out of my sight until I'm assured that you've been restored to an acceptable state. I can't abide your sloth."

She bustled on, not sure of the route, and he steered her around. As they progressed, he grew eager. Very soon, they'd be sequestered in his bedchamber. She might assume that she was merely ushering him upstairs, but she didn't understand the male animal.

As if he'd allow her to go once he had her alone!

Checking out the sway of her hips, the curve of her delicious ass, he trailed after her. He wanted to take her hair down, to ascertain if it felt as silky as it looked. He wanted to remove her clothes, to have her naked.

His desire for her spiraled to such a dangerous height that, as they entered his room and he shut the door, his cock was so enlarged that he was afraid he might burst the placard on his trousers.

Offering her no chance to demur, he fell on her like a wild beast, pushing her against the door and gripping her thighs to wrap her legs around his waist. Trapping her, balancing her with his hips, he took her mouth in a searing kiss, while his hands dipped to her breasts, kneading and pressing the flawless mounds.

"Wakefield, we have to stop," she protested, wrenching away, so that he had to nip and bite her cheek, her ear. "Rutherford will be along with your bath and your breakfast. He'll see us."

"He's used to my promiscuity. He won't bat an eye."

"Wakefield!" she scolded, her sharp retort like a bucket of cold water on his raging lust. "Shame on you."

"What? What did I say?"

"How often must I remind you that I am not—and never will be—one of your London harlots?"

With a shove, she forced him away, then opened the door, as burly footsteps sounded in the hall. Several men brought in jugs to fill the tub in the dressing room. Miss Fitzgerald knew all their names, and supervised the preparations as if she were his housekeeper or—perish the thought!—his wife.

The servants snapped to when she spoke—in a fashion they'd never exhibited for him!—and they did her bidding without dispute or vacillation. It was evident that she was highly respected, so beyond reproach that no one seemed to find anything indecent about her presence in the viscount's private suite.

"Ah, here's your breakfast," she said as two maids carried in trays.

She made distracting, innocuous chatter with the girls, supplying caustic remarks as to her reason for being in his bedchamber that had to do with her discussing the estate and some of the Viscount's recent decisions. The way she pronounced *decisions* left no doubt that everyone was cognizant of—and furious about—the evictions.

All ears were perked in her direction, and whenever she referred to him, the employees stole furtive, angry glances at him that made him shift uncomfortably.

She arranged the dishes and accouterments on a side table, then she shooed the servants out. As they went, she asked one about a new baby, and another about an ailing grandmother, waving and prattling until they'd withdrawn down the hall and around the corner.

When it was apparent that no one would notice, she closed the door, and his hopes soared that they might tryst again, but she displayed no signs of the ardor that had had him nearly doubled over in the library. She'd been so hot and bothered, extremely proficient in her exploration of his erection, and he wanted to lure her back to the erotic crest where they'd left off.

What would it take to rekindle her flame? He was bound and determined to reap some satisfaction.

She kept maintaining that they had a deal and needed to stick by it. So be it. She'd insisted that he comply with the terms, and he was beginning to reflect upon the advantages. If she could demand his adherence, he was definitely within his rights to demand hers.

She rendered the perfect solution to his dilemma when she queried, "Would you like to have your bath? Or your breakfast?"

"I'll start with the bath." He held out his arms. "Undress me."

How could she refuse?

CHAPTER FIVE

EMMA gaped at him, trying to think of a way to balk, but lamentably, nothing beneficial surfaced, and it occurred to her that she couldn't devise an excuse because, deep down, she was a slattern. She'd love to shed him of his apparel. Slowly. Piece by piece. Until he was naked and at her mercy.

He wasn't aware of her spying indiscretion, so he didn't know that she'd had a glimpse of what was shielded behind those fashionable trousers. A bit earlier, she'd briefly gotten her hands on it, and what a glorious adventure that had been!

She'd made him so aroused! Herself! Emma Fitzgerald!

The virile rogue had been excessively provoked, but she kept her pride in check over the role she'd played in inciting him. He was an unmitigated libertine, and he'd probably have gotten an erection if a female dog had walked by! He was that loose with his favors—evidence the odor of perfume hanging about his person.

Thank heaven she'd detected it, or there was no telling into what predicament she'd have landed. The bitter aroma had rudely jolted her. She was here to prevail upon him to cancel the evictions. Not to fornicate with him, despite how loudly her poor, untended flesh was begging for the opportunity.

Having scarcely slept a wink, she was running on adrenaline. The kiss they'd shared the previous day had left her testy, uncomfortable, and aching in places she hadn't noted in years.

In the wee hours, she'd paced and scolded, trying to rein in her careening emotions, endeavoring to put what they'd done into perspective, to lessen its impact and importance, but to no avail. With an almost insane gladness, her body had cried out for more, while her heart . . .

Oh, her stupid heart!

She'd always been by herself. Had peered down the road of her life and seen naught but struggle and loneliness. Isolation and despair. No joy. No happiness. No contentment.

Like a foolish, lovestruck girl, she'd found herself asking, *Why not?* Why not jump in farther than she'd meant to go? Why not seize the moment? Why not use him as badly as he intended to use her?

Certainly, he could be objectionable, dictatorial, and overbearing. But he could also be engaging, witty, clever. He was smart, educated, and interesting, in a manner that only a prosperous gentleman could be. Plus, he was too handsome for his own good, and she shamelessly pined for the chance to know him in the biblical sense. And not once. But over and over.

She recognized all the reasons to stay away from him, was conscious of his faults and flaws. He'd end up wreaking havoc on her staid existence if she allowed it, but while she comprehended the perils, he was arrogantly posed across the room and commanding that she divest him of his clothing. Madly, heedlessly, her feet were traipsing across the floor, her entire being disposed to assent.

As she'd been up all night, her usual acuity was absent, her self-discipline shot to Portsmouth and back, so it was risky to proceed. There was no guarantee that she could keep her wits about her, that she could keep her skirt down, her knees together, and her chastity intact.

What he was offering was so immoral and so appetizing that she couldn't deny herself. His potent rod was pushing at the placard of his pants, summoning her to release him from his confines.

Just this once, she bargained with herself, *and then never again.*

Disgusted, she shook her head, realizing that this was how every sinner started down the road to perdition. And she'd been raised knowing with what the road to Hell was paved. None of it mattered. Before the hour of three arrived and she was due at home, she would see John Clayton in the altogether, would pet, and stroke, and fondle. And taste, too, if it came to that.

She neared, insolently took his hand.

"In here," she said, ushering him to the dressing room, and he followed, a definite strut in his gait. He was preening over her acquiescence, having not doubted that she'd comply with his wishes.

A fire was burning in a brazier, even though it was July, and the air was toasty and muggy. The tub was opulent, spacious and broad, designed for Wakefield's larger proportions. It was situated behind a painted screen, and a small table was next to it, stacked with washing cloths, towels, and soaps.

They stopped, turned toward one another, and the encounter grew incredibly intimate. It was just the two of them, no one to intrude or interrupt, and a marvelous expectation hovered around them. Any extraordinary event might ensue, any licentious behavior would be permitted.

Wakefield slipped his hands around her waist and pulled her close. His cockstand prodded her belly, igniting tingles of agitation that rushed outward through her extremities, to her nipples, her womb. There was no awkwardness in their informality. They were so compatible that, bizarrely, she felt as if she'd been in his bedchamber a thousand times before, that she'd regularly assisted him with his bath.

The perception scared her to death!

"You make me so hard," he asserted, and he bent down and bestowed a kiss that was so sweet, she sighed with pleasure.

"Rascal."

"Help me with my shirt."

She knew she shouldn't, but she set to the task anyway, unhooking his cuff links and laying them on the vanity. Then, she unfastened the buttons until his chest was bared, his beguiling matting of hair luring her to caress him. He yanked the lapels aside, wresting the hem and jerking at the sleeves, so that he was nude from the waist up.

"Touch me again," he implored. "I like the feel of your hands on me."

Tempted beyond her limits, she forced an image of him and his paramour into her mind, recalling them in the throes of their bored, restrained passion, vividly recollecting the tang of an exotic cologne, and what the couple had likely been doing that had resulted in the fragrance being smeared all over him.

"Not till you've washed. I can't."

"Of course," he gallantly responded. "You're so fetching; you make me forget myself."

Ooh, he was an unrepentant flatterer, who adeptly appreciated how to overwhelm a woman's saner impulses and inclinations. In her forlorn circumstance, it was a hazardous combination. He smiled, a devilish grin that creased two dimples in his cheeks, and she could picture how he must have looked as a naughty boy when he was causing his nanny all sorts of trouble.

Caution was so imperative!

"Why don't you get in the tub? I'll be right outside."

"Promise me you won't leave."

He was sincere! He truly wanted her to be there when he finished! The insight made her heart pound.

"I won't."

She went to the outer room, anxious to distract herself, but his presence was too blatant. One of his coats was tossed over the bedframe, a pair of riding boots was balanced in the corner, his shaving equipment and extra cuff links were scattered across the dresser. Proximity to his belongings was exhilarating, and she quivered with anticipation, eager to peek into the wardrobe, to riffle through it so that she could examine and handle his garments.

Instead, she went to the table where the maids had deposited the breakfast trays. In a thrice, Cook had prepared a scrumptious repast, enough for an army, and she furtively nibbled at the eggs, at a morsel of scone. The flavors made her stomach growl, and her oral glands salivate.

While it was inappropriate to partake of Wakefield's feast, she was hungry. Anymore, her diet was so meager that, sporadically, she wondered from where their next meal would come. With the loss of security her father's job had rendered, the preceding six months had been a nightmare as she'd fretted and stewed over the fate of her meager, poverty-stricken family.

The new vicar, Harold Martin, had moved into the rectory where Emma had been born and raised. She could scarcely argue over his legitimate usurpation of the property, so she'd packed and gone quietly, meekly abandoning her home without a fight. Since that dreadful day, she'd been forced to endure the eternal humiliation of surviving in a hovel, of having little to eat, and no means of supporting her mother and sister who depended on her.

People were aware of the Fitzgeralds' dire straits, but no one could intercede. Economic conditions were too extreme for all.

When her father had been alive, parishioners had rewarded their good deeds by donating supplies to the vicarage, so she'd kept on with her nursing, considering it as employment whereby she could procure sparse rations of provisions. She delivered babies, attended the sick, prayed with the dying, but in light of the area's acute financial austerity, few had anything with which they could afford to part, so hunger was an incessant problem.

Plucking a berry from the scone, she held it on the tip of her tongue in order to savor its tartness. The astringency was like a poke with a sharp stick, graphically reminding her of her dire plight.

She whirled away, only to discover that she could peek into the dressing room through the crack in the door. Wakefield was disrobing, having removed his shoes, and he was in the process of drawing down his pants. Dry-mouthed, she scrutinized him as he revealed his backside, and she couldn't prevent herself from staring, at the bumps of his spine, the rounded globes of his bottom. His thighs were covered with a wiry dusting of the same blond hair that was on his chest, and she was deluged by a maniacal desire to strip herself, to hurry in and press her torso to his.

In dismay, she shut her eyes, and she could hear him stepping into the tub, the water lapping, his hiss of breath as he sank down into the steamy cauldron.

Absurdly, she was jealous of his luxury. She hadn't bathed in a tub since they'd moved out of the rectory and lost the stove that had so easily heated the water. Her ablutions had been reduced to quick swipes with a cloth, and her envy of such a minor amenity only underscored—more so than her deplorable diet—the pitiful level to which her fortunes had descended.

"Miss Fitzgerald," he beckoned, "come here. I need you."

"For what?"

"To wash my back." There was a pause, and a significant chuckle. "And my front."

Oh, Lord, give me strength!

She bit the inside of her cheek, worried her fingers on her skirt. The prospect made her weak, but in spite of her misgivings, she went. It was a method by which she could experience some of what she coveted without going overboard.

After all, what could happen when the man was immersed in a vat of water?

To be safe, she dished up a plate of breakfast and took it with her. In case she ran out of innocuous chores to accomplish with her hands, she could feed him. Head high, courage at the fore, she entered the room, marched to the screen, and peered behind it.

Submerged in the water, he was reclined, his elbows and knees relaxed against the edges. Warm, drenched, slippery all over, he'd dunked himself, and his hair was dripping and slicked off his forehead.

Feigning bravado, she approached and knelt beside him, bringing over a stool and resting the plate upon it.

"Let's get some food in you. You'll feel better."

"I already feel pretty damned good."

"Don't cu—"

"I know, I know." He snickered and waved away her protest. "Don't curse."

"You're learning."

She grabbed the spoon and scooped up some eggs, extending them to him as if he were a babe. He assessed her, a smile quirking his exquisite mouth then, without complaint, he took the bite she'd rendered, then another and another, until he'd gobbled up most of it.

When she dispensed the final spoonful, he steadied her wrist, grasping the utensil and setting it and the plate away, then he linked their fingers. "You're constantly taking care of people, aren't you?"

For some reason, she blushed. "I try to be helpful."

"It's more than that. You're a natural. It's in your blood."

"Perhaps."

He leaned forward and kissed her in that tender way she was coming to expect. It was always dear; it was always a surprise.

"Thank you for taking care of *me*."

"You're welcome."

He clasped her neck and tugged at her till their cheeks were joined, his face in her hair, and . . . and he was sniffing her!

"I like how you smell," he contended after a protracted sampling. She couldn't devise a suitable reply and was striving to develop one when he added, "I want to call you Emma."

"No."

He laughed, a seductive, bewitching sound that rattled her innards. "Woman! You're alone with me. In my dressing room. I'm naked. I'm calling you Emma."

"It's too familiar." If they discarded all semblance of propriety, where would that leave her? Such liberty was the very worst thing that could transpire. How would she maintain any emotional distance if he was repeatedly murmuring her name? "I don't want anyone to know that we've established a casual relationship."

Momentarily, he was stunned, then he laughed again. "You'd be embarrassed if people knew we were friends?"

"Well . . . yes."

"God, but you're deadly to my ego. I'm not sure why I put up with you."

"Because you like me?" she tentatively ventured.

"Yes, I believe I do." Scrupulously, he evaluated her, then he sat back, slouching down into the water. "We'll compromise. I'll call you Emma when there's no one else about. And you'll call me John." He winked wickedly. "That way, when I'm inside you and you're crying out in ecstasy, I won't have to listen to you saying *Milord Wakefield*. I don't think my pride could stand it."

The knave was so convinced of his prowess! She'd seen him having sex, and she hadn't been impressed, so she couldn't deduce how he'd drive her to cry out—in ecstasy or for any other purpose. Besides, she didn't plan to ever spread her legs for him, but she didn't suppose this was the best time to admit it.

"You'll never persuade me to call you by your given name."

"We'll see." He urged her nearer and whispered in her ear. "Take off your clothes. Get in the tub with me."

Her breath hitched in her lungs. Did men and women really conduct themselves so decadently?

How spectacular it would be, both of them nude and rubbing against one another! Her avid imagination soared with the possibilities of what she wouldn't dare attempt. She couldn't conceive of parading before him, undressing while he watched, then climbing in to frolic.

"I can't"—he kissed her cheek, her mouth—"I can't."

"I want you in here with me."

He pulled her to him, so that she was precariously

positioned over the tub, her breasts flattened to his damp chest, but she had no fear that she might fall in. His arms were strong as a vise, and he held her as if she were cherished and special.

"It's too soon. You're asking too much."

"I keep forgetting," he mused.

"About what?"

"That you're not like the other females of my acquaintance."

"No, I'm not, and I wish you'd stop mentioning them. The comparison makes me feel cheap and common."

"My darling Emma," he said, "there's nothing *common* about you."

He regarded her, not sure what to make of her or the peculiar association they'd formed.

She pondered the same. Where would it lead? Where would it end?

He reached behind her and retrieved a cloth, swished it in the water, wrung it out, then he offered it to her, encouraging her to misbehave with complete abandon.

It seemed such a venial sin, to merely brush it across him. How could she resist?

Recklessly clutching it, she snatched the soap, too, and worked up a lather. Commencing at his neck, she laved his shoulders, his arms, his back, his chest. In alluring circles, she stroked lower and lower, until she was dipping into the water with each swipe, coming closer to the provocation that awaited, but not courageous enough to slide all the way down.

She settled for rinsing off the soapy residue, until his upper half was clean, and he smelled so fine that she could hardly keep from sniffing at him as he'd done to her.

All finished, the cloth dangled from her fingertips,

and she was ready to drop it, when he directed her hand under the water and guided her to his erection. He swathed her fingers around it, tightening their combined grip, and he flexed, the velvety skin going taut then easing as he retreated. He was enormous, her fist barely able to round the circumference, and a flutter charged through her secret, feminine regions.

He moved his hand away, to let her proceed on her own, and once he did, she withdrew, too, so he enveloped her again and held on.

"Fuck me with your hand, Emma," he gently commanded.

The vulgar word electrified her, inducing a swirl of chaos, and she was overcome by such a confused mix of physical craving and imposed restraint that she was paralyzed. She turned to him, burrowing into his chest.

She was so conflicted!

"You can do it, Em," he coaxed. "Just for me."

Brazenly, he rose up on his knees, his flanks and loins exposed, and she glanced down, rejoicing in the chance to observe him. His cock was tempestuous, angrily pulsating, demanding her immediate attention. She flicked her thumb across the incited crown, causing him to shudder and tense his stomach muscles.

"You're so beautiful—" she managed, before her mouth united with his in a torrid kiss, and of their own accord, her unruly hands drifted down, meticulously massaging the cloth over his privates, his cockstand, his balls, the cleft of his ass.

The rough nap titillated and excited him to a thrilling, outrageous peak, but ultimately, he was the one to halt. He seized her wrist, slapping at her hand seconds before he lost control and spewed himself into the water.

She wasn't sure why he'd hesitated at the critical apex. She couldn't credit it to shyness or modesty, and definitely not to any sudden decision to remediate the pace.

Slumping into the water, he reposed against the tub as he rapidly reasserted his aplomb, and he analyzed her, trying to deduce how they'd so swiftly arrived at this erotic juncture. The room was quiet, and he was staring at her so intently that she couldn't match his gaze. She looked down at the water, humiliation sizzling her cheeks.

"I thought I could go through with this," she explained. "I want to. I really do, but . . ."

But what? a voice in her head screamed.

Now that she knew how glorious she felt when he was near, she yearned to stretch out with him on his bed. It would be so splendid to have him pushing her down into the plush mattress, to have his body heavy and insistent against her own. She'd want to dabble and trifle over and over until she ignited in the flames of a sin from which there could be no salvation.

"I want your hair down, and your clothes off." As he spurred her to commit one trespass after the next, he was kind, understanding. "I want you to lie down beside me."

"Oh, Lord . . ." She buried her face in her hands, feeling as though she could burst into tears.

It would be so simple. The bed was a few feet away. He was thoroughly aroused, her own self in no better condition. She could say yes, but she would be giving the most precious part of herself to this bounder, this stranger, and the fact that she was considering it, that she was so pathetically eager, was frightening.

What was happening to her? Perhaps his penchant for dissolution and debauchery was catching—like a bad cold!

Initially, she'd meant to toy with him, to flirt with

him as a ruse to get what she wanted for her neighbors, but her plan was folly. Her life was a solitary vacuum, and he filled it with his amazing vitality. She wished she could capture some of his charisma and charm in a bottle, so that the contents could linger and cheer her when she was back at her dismal, dreary cottage.

He was like a healthy tonic, a bracing restorative, a shining star in her dull universe.

Sensing her distress, he rose up and hugged her, nestling her in the crook of his neck, while he nuzzled and kissed her hair. It had been a long while since anyone had held her or crooned endearments. The solace was welcome, like an unexpected gift on a rainy day, and she wrapped her arms around him and embraced him in return, wallowing in the sweetness.

Astonishingly, he appeared to treasure the moment every bit as much as she did, and it occurred to her that maybe his lofty world of wealth and affluence was a forlorn place, as well. Maybe he had no one to render sympathy, a pat on the back, a needed hug, either.

They were a sorry pair!

A clock chimed the hour of three. She sighed, hating that it was time to go, but relieved that the lateness would preclude her from making unwise choices. At home, with distance between them, she could regroup, could regain her equilibrium, while she came up with a way she could be in his company without demeaning or surrendering herself.

When she was with him, the man reduced her to a baser sort of individual, whose corporeal drives were unchecked, and she had to find a procedure whereby she could circumscribe her behavior.

You can do it! she scolded.

"I must go."

She removed herself from the security of his arms.

Her bodice was moist from being pressed to his wet skin. The humid air had curled her hair more than usual. Tendrils had escaped from her combs to tickle her cheeks and neck, and he twirled a lengthy strand around his finger.

"It's only three o'clock."

He was genuinely displeased that she would leave, and the realization was dangerous and magnificent.

"I have other appointments."

Her most crucial one was locating some food for her family's supper. There wasn't a single scrap left in the house.

"Cancel them," he authoritatively decreed, and she smiled, thinking how grand it must be to be rich and idle.

"I can't."

"But I'm not ready for you to depart."

He was astounded that she would go after he'd told her no. He was so selfish, had perpetually been coddled, and people jumped to obey whenever he snapped his fingers. The total subservience of those around him was most likely the reason he was so impossible.

"Well, Wakefield, you can't have everything you want."

"Yes I can." He smiled, too, his eyes twinkling with merriment. "I'm a viscount, remember?"

Oh, yes, she remembered, all right. He was of the nobility, a peer of the realm, who dined with kings and queens, and he was so far above her that it was ludicrous for her to be mooning over him, and fantasizing over what could never be.

"Yes, you are, and you're horridly spoiled."

"I'll be crushed if you don't let me have my way."

"You'll get over it."

"No I won't." He pouted, making her chuckle, then

he sobered, kissing her, endeavoring to cajole away her inhibitions. "I want you to stay, so I can make love to you. All afternoon. All night."

"Not even you could have that much stamina."

"Would you care to bet?"

Oh, he was incorrigible! His invitation was so enticing, and a hairsbreadth from acquiescence, she was appalled by her foolishness. "You make me crazy to do things I oughtn't."

"You agreed that you would. In writing!"

The scoundrel had the audacity to toss their bargain back at her! "Yes, I did, and you're a cad to remind me of it."

"Being a cad is only one of my abominable habits." He grinned, unrepentant. "Isn't your word your bond, Emma Fitzgerald?"

"It is," she grumbled.

The light banter ceased, and he grew serious, turning so that his elbows rested on the rim of the tub, their forearms folded together. "I want us to be lovers."

"I know you do."

"In the beginning, you were disposed, but now you're scared. Why?"

Because you're all I've ever wanted! All I've ever dreamed about! She swallowed and said, "It's so much more intense than I'd imagined it would be."

"This connection between us"—he gestured back and forth, incapable of explicating what they both sensed—"it's powerful."

"Yes. I've never felt anything like it."

"Nor have I," he claimed, and she speculated as to whether his disclosure was true, or if it was merely a flattery he successfully utilized to wheedle recalcitrant women into lifting their skirts.

He traced his thumb across her bottom lip. "I pushed you too fast. Next time, we'll go slower."

"It's not the *speed* we need to worry about. It's—" She cut off, unable to verbalize why she was afraid.

"How far we might go?" he completed for her. She nodded, and he kissed her, a quick, dear peck on the lips. "It will be wonderful. I promise."

Which was what she feared.

In the outer bedchamber, the door opened—stupidly, neither of them had thought to lock it!—and a sultry, unmistakable female voice inquired, "Wakefield, are you in here?"

As his mistress boldly entered, reality crashed into Emma with the force of a runaway carriage. What was she doing in this room? With this man?

Frantically, she lurched away, but he was squeezing her hand, refusing to release it. His eyes searched hers, probing for something she couldn't define, and his cheeks flushed, as if he were embarrassed by the intrusion, but he made no comment. Perhaps he couldn't.

After all, what could possibly be apropos?

"Let me go," she begged in a whisper, but he only tightened his grip, so she yanked her hand away, and leapt out of reach.

There was only one exit, so she couldn't avoid his paramour, but she didn't want the beautiful doxy to stumble upon her as she was huddled over the tub, with Wakefield naked as a jaybird.

She patted her hair and jerked at her damp clothes, uselessly trying to straighten herself. She was a sight, but there was nothing to be done about it, and desperate to appear calm, she strolled out.

"Tomorrow at one, Emma," Wakefield said softly to her retreating back. "I'll be waiting."

Her insides clenched. Dare she come on the morrow?

No! She absolutely would not!

She stepped into the bedchamber, and the imposing courtesan—had Wakefield referred to her as Georgina?—was so stunned that her painstakingly plucked brows rose to her hairline. Her shock instantly metamorphosed to a scowl, then full-on hostility.

The encounter might have been comical if Emma hadn't been so utterly mortified. She and the demimondaine stared one another down, and they didn't require pistols for it to be described as a duel. Though Emma hid her trepidation well, she felt the loser. Too short, too thin, too poor, and obviously too free with her favors. Her drab, dowdy dress was sodden in several spots where it shouldn't have been, and Georgina took careful note of every incriminating mark.

When she'd seen Georgina on the stairs two hours earlier, she'd been immaculately attired in an exquisite gown, but in the intervening period, she'd changed her apparel, slipping into a robe that was all but transparent. Her hair was down, her feet bare, and she was clearly intent on an assignation with the viscount.

The belt at the waist of the robe was loose, the lapels widened so that the center of her torso was visible. Emma could see her large nipples, her tonsured privates.

"What are *you* doing here?" Georgina barked.

Her haughty tone was terrifying and would have made a normal woman cringe and tremble. As it was, Emma's legs were wobbly.

She despised the other woman, for all that she was, for all that she represented, but mostly, Emma loathed her because she was entitled to waltz into the other room and finish what Emma had started. Wakefield would spend the evening having sexual relations as he'd proposed to Emma, but he'd have a different partner.

Dismayed and confounded, Emma recognized that she was jealous. A red-hot rage surged through her at the idea of Georgina reveling with Wakefield as Emma, herself, could not.

"Wakefield asked me to attend him." Emma was deliberately vague and suggestive, wanting Georgina to stew and fume over what exactly they'd been doing. "We've been . . . *busy*."

"Be off, you little harlot." Georgina was seething, disdainful as any princess, and she floated by Emma as if she were invisible.

Emma was rooted to the floor, and she flinched when, behind her, Georgina gushed, "John, where have you been? I've been looking everywhere."

"Shut the door," he said, his voice husky and altered now that Georgina had sauntered in with no clothes on.

"Certainly," Georgina cooed.

The door was firmly latched, and Emma cocked her head, attempting to eavesdrop, but she couldn't hear a peep, which was the worst torture of all. She whirled away to flee, impatient to be off lest amorous sounds begin to emanate. Wakefield was aroused, so it wouldn't take much to spur him into carnal play, and she couldn't abide contemplating the myriad ways he might garner satisfaction.

Could he—would he—substitute one lover for another in the blink of an eye?

Just as she would have moved into the corridor, she noticed the table of food that had been laid out for Wakefield. There were baskets of breads, pastries, cheeses, fruits, more than one person could eat in a week. She'd fed him till he was stuffed, so what would be done with the leftovers?

Her stomach protested loudly, and she was tempted

by how delicious everything smelled, how fabulous it would taste, what a treat it would be for her younger sister, Jane. Without pausing, so that she wouldn't have the opportunity to talk herself out of it, she walked over, pulled the cloth from the table, made a sort of bag, and stuffed the food into it. Then, she flung it over her shoulder and pranced out, flouncing down hall, then the stairs, as if she owned the accursed mansion.

If she was observed, she doubted that she would pique anyone's curiosity. Wakefield's acquaintances would ignore her, and she knew most of the servants. They wouldn't question her as to why she was marching off with the viscount's belongings.

So, Emma, you've always been a wanton. Shall we add thievery, avarice, and gluttony to your list of sins, as well?

The stern chastisement reverberated through her, as if God, Himself, were directly admonishing her, but she vociferously shoved away the censure, declining to heed the reproach.

I'll bring the tablecloth back tomorrow, she vowed. *I swear it.*

Even as she did so, she perceived that it was a pretext whereby she could contrive to visit Wakefield again.

CHAPTER SIX

EMMA approached what was her home, a minuscule, decrepit shack the estate agent had located for them after her father's death. Though it had enabled her to keep a roof over their heads, it was a sorry excuse for familial lodging. Especially taking into account the comfortable house in which she'd spent the prior twenty-eight years of her life. But she wasn't about to complain; devoid of options, her finances totally depleted, she'd been ready to accept anything.

The cottage was a thirty-minute walk from the manor, another thirty from the village, so it was secluded and quiet, and their existence was very different from being next to the parish church, where they'd constantly been overrun by visitors.

Now, unless they ventured out, they rarely saw anyone, which Emma didn't particularly mind. Their fortunes had fallen so low that she was glad they were out of sight from the general community where she would have had to deal with the pity of others on a daily basis.

As she stepped out of the woods, she was dismayed anew by the dismal appearance of the building. She never became accustomed to how dreary it was. Scant more than a shed, it had two small rooms and a loft. The roof sloped, and whenever it rained, water poured in, and they had to set out pans to collect it. The two windows had been broken and were boarded up. Except for the meager flower bed she'd managed to plant by the door, the yard was covered with tall weeds.

There was a stove, and it currently worked well enough to heat the dank interior, but in a few months, winter would be upon them, and she was greatly worried by the prospect.

Reality slapped her like a cold cloth, monotony and invariability pressing down on her with crushing intensity. She was tired of having to be valiant, of having to carry on in the face of adversity.

Hadn't she contributed enough to those around her? Hadn't she ceaselessly accepted more than her share of ordeal and tribulation?

Recently, she'd spread herself so thin that she'd begun to feel invisible, that there was no Emma Fitzgerald, but merely an empty shell of a woman who perpetually immersed herself in others' woes, who was cursed with having to cure everyone else's ailments.

Surprisingly, she pondered the female visitors sequestered up at the manor, and she found herself wondering what it would be like to be one of the ravishing, opulent—unprincipled!—courtesans who'd joined Wakefield for his sojourn in the country.

Wickedly, she thought that it would be so marvelous to subsist in such an unrestrained environment. If only she could trade places with one of them. For a week—or even a day. She'd have no duties, would suffer no guilt over her failures, would have no one to look after or tie her down. She'd lounge and loaf, flirt and philander, dally and trifle.

For a frivolous moment, she let the impetuous fantasy take wing and flourish, and she decided that a life of repose and recreation would suit her. She'd excel at it. She'd rapidly adapt.

She'd wear only the most expensive gowns, would hire a personal maid to wait on her hand and foot. A

French coiffeuse would style her hair. She'd accouter herself in the finest jewels, would feast on the most scrumptious diet, imbibe the rarest wines, while being courted and wooed by dozens of cultured swains.

What an extraordinary adventure it would be! A restorative holiday! A grand lark!

From the time she was a babe, she'd longed to be someone different. Throughout her childhood, she'd chafed over what couldn't be changed, even going so far as to speculate whether a huge, celestial error had been made, if the stork had deposited her in the wrong house. She was so distinct from her humble, modest parents. They were decent folks, who hadn't hungered for more than they'd been given, while she'd constantly envisioned herself in a bigger world, filled with gaiety and excitement.

As a result, she'd never fit in, had never belonged, and clearly, she hadn't learned any lessons from her contrariety, either. Her father had regularly counseled her about the dangers of craving too much, yet she persisted in clinging to fruitless illusions.

The flamboyant life relished by the likes of Wakefield and his friends wasn't for her. Her sedate, ho-hum existence was meant to be, and there'd be no variation. Not on this day or any other, and immature daydreaming wouldn't accomplish anything, except to exacerbate her discontentment.

Happiness came from within, as her father was wont to say. She appreciated the wisdom of the statement, but still, every once in a while . . .

Jane was lingering by the stoop. She jumped up and, with a lovely smile on her face, rushed out. Almost eleven, she was pretty, with Emma's same brown eyes and slim figure, but her hair wasn't quite so curly or uncontrollable, and it was a lighter shade of brunette, an auburn with blond highlights. She was happy, sweet-natured, gangly and lanky as a colt, and perched on the verge of blossoming into a charming woman.

Emma adored her and had from the moment she'd been born, having assisted the local midwife in the miraculous delivery. Although she'd helped at hundreds of births since then, her first encounter with childbirth had been seeing Jane slip from their mother's body. It had made the two sisters inordinately close. Emma had been sixteen, and with their mother's precarious health, Jane's upbringing had been fully placed into Emma's hands, so she usually felt more like the girl's mum than her sibling.

"Did you meet with Viscount Wakefield?" Jane was bubbly with excitement. With Emma's revelation the night before—that she would have several appointments with Wakefield—Jane had been delighted and fascinated.

"Yes, I did."

Flinching at the reminiscence, she couldn't stop ruminating over how phenomenal it had been to be with him, but also about how dreadful it had been when his mistress had ambled into his dressing room and shut the door.

On the solitary trek from the mansion, she'd been besieged as to what had likely transpired. Hundreds of grotesque visions rampaged, and she couldn't keep them at bay.

She'd pictured Georgina embracing him, or maybe letting him mount her from behind as he had when Emma had spied upon them.

Miserable and forlorn, in a dither, she'd stomped through the forest, struggling to come to grips with her envy and jealousy. She felt as if Wakefield were cheating on her by having sex with his mistress! An absurd notion all the way around! But there it was, and she couldn't put it aside.

Such vice and dissolution were destructive for him—damaging to his person and his soul—and Emma was inexplicably troubled about both, though why she should fret over the bounder was a mystery.

"Tell me everything," Jane begged. "Was he very grand?"

She'd developed a fanciful, adolescent-style crush on John Clayton that had Emma realizing how fast she was growing up.

"Aye." Emma grinned, not having to prevaricate about that fact, at least.

"Would you say he's handsome as a prince?"

"Definitely."

"What was he wearing?"

There at the end, nothing at all!

Emma's cheeks blushed scarlet at the recollection. Lord, but wasn't he a dangerous, enticing rogue? "A flowing white shirt and tan pants, made from very expensive fabric. And jaunty black boots that came up below the knee."

"He was very dashing, wasn't he?"

"You're right about that."

"And is he kind?" Romantically, she professed, "I couldn't bear it if he wasn't."

"He's extremely kind," Emma answered. "Look what he gave us." She opened the tablecloth so that Jane could peek inside at the feast Emma had stolen.

"Scones!" Jane breathed the word as if she were beholding a precious gift of gold or jewels. She clasped her hands and pressed them to her chest. "Did you tell him I love scones?"

"I did"—fornication, stealing, and now lying! She was transforming into a criminal with scarcely any effort!—"and he went straight out and advised Cook to pack a big bag so you could have all you want."

"He sent them for me?"

"Yes."

Jane skipped along with Emma, thrilled to suppose that Wakefield would have taken an interest in her. In her short life, few people had. Their father had been too preoccupied with his duties, and their mother too sickly to be attentive. Jane was a darling lass, but lonely, being too solitary and isolated due to their mother's declining condition.

To earn them coins or food, Emma often had to leave for hours or days. When she was summoned by their neighbors, Jane had to stay by herself to watch over their mother, Margaret.

Margaret's physical constitution had perpetually been unstable, but recently, her mental acuity had started to go, too. Disoriented, careless, she was prone to wandering off, so someone had to be with her every second.

Too much of the burden was teetering on Jane's slender shoulders, and Emma ceaselessly fretted about the hardship, but it couldn't be rectified, and the onus was one more item about which Emma had to feel guilty.

"How is Mother?" It was painful to inquire. Long ago, she'd conceded that Margaret would never improve. She was steadily fading away—even her body was shrinking—and it seemed as though she might soon disappear altogether.

"She had a fine afternoon," Jane said, but then, Jane invariably claimed their mother was doing well; it was an essential deceit she utilized to cope with the irreparable situation. "She's been rocking in her chair."

The rocking motion soothed their mother, and whenever she was distressed, they would lead her to it and give the chair a gentle shove. Emma was relieved that the time had passed so uneventfully for both of them.

"Let's go in and unpack these goodies."

Jane raced ahead, Emma following more slowly. As they reached the door, the sound of wheels crunching down their narrow lane had them stopping and turning to see the new vicar, Harold Martin, drawing nigh. He was exceedingly proud that he could afford a carriage, and he always pretentiously arrived in it.

In his peculiar manner, he presumed himself to be courting Emma and, on one stunning occasion, he'd proposed marriage. As he'd been strutting through the rectory and taking possession of her home when the offer was tendered, she hadn't been inclined to say yes. He'd been too gleeful over his usurpation of the property, while having virtually no regard for the incapacitated widow and her two children from whom the house was being confiscated.

He had garnered his post through an attenuated connection to the Claytons, and he periodically and aggravatingly alluded to his distant association. Since he'd acquired a sufficient income through his job as vicar, he'd decided to marry, an act he'd had to delay as a bachelor with no means of support.

Emma was the sole female in the vicinity whom he deemed worthy of his elevated status, but she hadn't been able to imagine herself as his wife, though disgustingly, she hadn't entirely abandoned the possibility. Unduly wary, she felt that, as yet, she hadn't descended to rock bottom, and she needed to keep the alternative available should her quandary worsen.

His chipper conveyance rattled to a halt, and as he fiddled with the reins, Jane fidgeted, reminding Emma of another reason she had no genuine fondness for him. His dislike of children was palpable, and Jane sensed it.

"Why don't you take our treats inside, while I cha
with Vicar Martin?"

Jane stood on tiptoe, and whispered, "Would you be
upset if I hid them so we don't have to share?" Emma
was shocked by the comment, and Jane quickly added
"Or would that be too un-Christian?"

Emma pondered her request, taking in Harold's
smart vehicle, his sporty clothes, his shined shoes, and
she winked at Jane. "Put it all away."

Jane bounced in, elated to be out of the vicar's pres
ence. His relief was reciprocal.

"Emma"—he neared, smiling a smile that was a tad
chilly—"it's such a pleasant afternoon. I thought you'd
like to join me for a ride."

While she wasn't overly enthused about his com
pany—he could be an exceptional boor—she frequently
went with him, enjoying the excuse to gad about, to do
something fun and frivolous. A fair fellow, of medium
height and stature, he had blue eyes and thinning blond
hair. In a few years, he'd be bald, but for now, he was
well dressed and dapper.

He was precisely the type of gentleman a woman
should have been flattered to entertain. Was she mad to
reject him? In view of her dire plight, what did she hope
to gain?

She sighed. This was not the day she could tolerate
his insincere prattle. Not after she'd been fondling and
caressing the very naked, very virile Viscount Wakefield
an hour earlier.

"I can't, Harold. I've just returned, myself. I haven'
even said hello to Mother yet."

Her mother was another barrier between their having
a future. He detested Margaret's increasing senility and
avoided her as if the affliction were catching.

On hearing that she'd been out, his brows rose. He

was regularly amazed to learn that she had a life beyond the cottage, and he was determined to guide her in her private affairs. As she'd consistently been an independent female, his pomposity rankled.

"What have you been doing?"

"I dropped in on Viscount Wakefield."

"He received *you*?"

"Yes."

"Why would he?"

"Because I asked him to."

"But I've been trying to obtain an audience for the past week!"

"Really?" She feigned innocence. "I can't fathom why you couldn't. He didn't seem to be busy."

His mouth firmed into a tight line, and he pretended no affront, that he hadn't been deliberately snubbed by the nobleman. "I wasn't eager to meet with the man. I merely felt I should pay my respects, but with all the gossip . . ." He let the implication trail off.

"About what?"

"About the viscount and his . . . his *colleagues*. From what I gather, there is a lot of mischief occurring at the manor." He paused for dramatic effect, fiddled with his watch, tugged on his vest. "If you get my drift."

"No, I don't," she lied. "What's happening?"

"Let's just say it wouldn't be fitting for a man of the cloth to visit, and I must order you not to go again, either."

She wondered if Harold would suffer an apoplexy should she confess some of what she'd seen and done—by her own choosing! "Sorry, but I can't accommodate you."

"Emma, you must acquiesce to my guidance in this matter. It won't do for my fiancée to be discovered on the premises."

"We're not engaged, Harold."

He ignored her contradiction. "The viscount is not a proper individual for you to know."

"Well, Wakefield can be a bit of a—"

"You call him *Wakefield*?" he petulantly remarked. "Aren't you a virtual pair of chums!"

"I'm hoping he'll ultimately consider us to be friends. It will enhance my chances of success."

He groaned and rolled his eyes. "Don't tell me you accosted him with your foolish petition!"

"Of course I did."

"But you're aware of why I objected."

"Yes, I am, Harold." He'd been excessively vocal in his command that she not meddle.

"Emma, you must desist with these impractical quests. You're tilting at windmills."

"You can't convince me not to try, Harold." His pessimism was the biggest obstacle between them. She saw incessant opportunities where he was certain none would ever exist. "Besides, I'm gradually swaying him. He'll change his mind like that." She snapped her fingers, her show of bravado so impressive that she almost believed it herself.

"Such a worldly, sophisticated chap doesn't wish to be inconvenienced with petty complaints." He assessed her, making it obvious she had nothing of value with which to persuade the infamous aristocrat. "You forget that I'm well acquainted with the Claytons. Lord Wakefield won't oblige you."

"We'll see." Thankfully, she was rescued by her sister beckoning to her from the cottage. "Jane must need my assistance with Mother."

"What about our drive?"

"Invite me next week."

She spun away and bustled inside, resolutely shut-

ting the door and peeking at him through a crack in the
boards. As his carriage vanished down the rutted lane,
she shuddered with distaste.

What if desperate circumstances forced her hand,
and she ended up married to the lummox?

She'd rather take up harlotry. Full time.

Ian Clayton lounged on his bed, a pile of pillows
propped behind him, peering at the flame of a candle as
it flickered and extinguished. A warm summer breeze
rustled the curtains, and a refreshing gust of wind blew
in, smelling of moist earth and impending rain. Far off
in the distance, thunder rumbled and lightning flashed.

Across the room, movement caught his eye. Surprisingly, his door was opening, and someone sneaking
in, when he couldn't conceive of who it might be. Before
they'd left London, he'd made a decision to steer clear
of the females who'd tagged along, and he'd been cat-
egorical in his disdain so that none of them would mis-
construe. While John relished their licentious tendencies,
and felt they were worth the bother, Ian couldn't abide
any of them. They were loose with their favors, and foul
of character.

Perchance he was odd, but when he had sex with a
woman, he liked to assume he'd been her only lover in
the previous twenty-four hours or so. John wasn't nearly
as discriminating, so his feminine associates weren't
usually the sort Ian would solicit when he wanted carnal
companionship.

As the intruder stealthily prowled across the floor,
he evaluated her, searching for her identity, but it was
her beguiling perfume that gave her away.

"Shit," he muttered, upon recognizing that his
brother's mistress was slinking toward him on silent feet.

What the bloody hell could she want? He loathed her, his aversion plainly apparent and repeatedly displayed.

She approached the bed, and he could see that she was wearing a transparent robe and naught else. It was slack and flowing behind her, the belt untied to reveal the middle of her torso.

Evidently, she was bent on seduction, though he couldn't figure out why. He hadn't given her the slightest indication that he might be interested. She was a shrew, a classic manipulator who wangled people and events so that she always got what she wanted, a dragon-lady who ate men alive.

Even had she been unattached, he wouldn't have been attracted to her and, as it was, she had been his brother's paramour for over two years.

Ian had few scruples where John was concerned, and had committed many unforgivable sins against him, but he drew the line at cuckolding. In his own distorted fashion, John had been a trusted friend, and a fine sibling, so cohabiting with his mistress seemed beyond the pale.

Besides, though John denied any fondness, it was possible that he harbored some affection for the sly vixen. He'd kept on with her much longer than he should have, despite Ian's urging for caution, so he must feel some affinity—though with John, one never knew for sure what he was thinking.

Perhaps he'd continued to provide for her solely because few ladies could match her in beauty or poise. Or perhaps it was her purported skill in the bedchamber, where she was reputed to be amenable to performing any obscene act. There was something to be said for a woman who had no qualms about what she did with her body. Gazing upon her brought on dozens of libidinous notions and, although he couldn't stand her, his cock stirred.

"Ian," she crooned enticingly, sounding exactly like the expensive whore she was, "are you awake?"

"Yes, Georgina, I'm awake."

She advanced on the bed and had the audacity to perch her shapely hip on the mattress. "I must speak with you."

Well, well, wasn't this intriguing? What could the curvaceous wench be up to? Her hand crept out to rest on his thigh, and involuntarily, his randy anatomy responded. He raised his knee, not wanting her to detect how his phallus had swelled and tented the bedclothes.

"About what?"

"I need your help with John."

She hadn't asked for it before—she wouldn't have dared—and he masked a smile. She was the most mercenary witch he'd ever encountered, and if John was plaguing her, it had to do with money. Or her sudden fear that he might quit giving it to her. It was the only incentive that would cause her to debase herself by seeking him out.

What had happened? Had she finally pushed John too far? Demanded too much? Bitched too loudly?

"How could I *help* you with John?" He didn't give a hoot as to how John might have vexed her, but he was curious as to where her supplication would lead.

"He's told me that . . . that I must return to London." She leaned in, her bounteous breasts swinging out so that her nipples were bared and, as she'd unmistakably intended for him to do, he looked his fill.

Ooh, what a delight it would be to suckle one of those elongated tips!

"Everyone's going."

"But he can't mean to include me."

"His instructions were very explicit."

Actually, John had been royally pissed that Ian had told the entire, sordid crew to withdraw in the morning, but Ian had discounted his diatribe. Ian liked how Emma Fitzgerald had John running around in circles and jumping to attention, and it humored him to see the two of them sparring. Plus, the frisky Miss Fitzgerald suited Ian's purposes.

When she'd insisted the slackers be expelled, he'd agreed without hesitating, knowing John would be irked, but not giving a rat's ass.

From the day they'd begun making travel plans, Ian had adjudged it a bad idea for John to bring his cadre of hangers-on, but he hadn't been able to dissuade John. The rowdy crowd was a distraction that kept John from getting down to business so that they could finish and leave with all due haste. Ian detested the estate, having to witness firsthand and up close what could have been his had his parents wed, and he had no predilection to remain a minute longer than necessary.

If he had other—more dubious—reasons for wanting a speedy exit, he tried not to reflect on his personal motives.

Though John valiantly struggled to hide his abilities, he had a shrewd head for financial dealings, and it simply wouldn't do to have him delving into the ledgers too deeply. There was no telling what he might determine if he sobered up and accomplished more than a cursory mathematical analysis.

A rapid departure was best for all parties.

"But I had thought"—her hand slid up, loitering over the spot where he'd love to have it arrive, and mesmerized, he watched it slither on—"you could talk to him for me."

"Why would I want to?"

"Because you care for him, and so do I." In a practiced move, she wet her bottom lip. "I'm willing to stay."

How ludicrous for her to claim that she *cared* for John! For his fortune, maybe. And his position and the status it gave her in the demimonde. "You hate it here."

"I'll make the sacrifice. For him."

She didn't have a benevolent bone in her body, so what was really going on? "John doesn't need you."

"But what of his manly . . . *drives*? He requires regular entertainment."

"He'll fuck anybody, Georgie," he crudely pointed out. "If that's why you want me to believe you should tarry, you're not making a very good case of it."

"But who could satisfy him as I can?" To demonstrate how consequential she could be, she brushed his erection then moved on, up his stomach, to his chest, where she brazenly toyed with his nipple.

"He'll snare himself a country lass. There are plenty about who'll tumble a viscount." His comments were deliberately goading, and she could hardly refrain from reverting to form with a caustic reply, but she reined in her temper, keeping herself in check until she could coerce him into an alliance.

"He's already found one! As if he should lower himself to copulating with some vicar's *daughter*."

Ian grinned. She was jealous! Of Emma Fitzgerald! How absolutely hilarious!

When he'd viewed John in the library with Miss Fitzgerald, he'd perceived a strong connection between them, and obviously Georgina had, too. John was infatuated, but then, he was enchanted by anything with breasts and legs. John had many faults, but in spite of his notorious reputation and behavior, he wasn't so idiotic that he would compromise the perspicacious female. He knew better; he understood his place and hers.

Still, to ascertain that Georgie felt threatened by the rural virago was a marvelous discovery. How could he use the information to her detriment?

"She is exceptionally pretty," he needled. "I noticed that John seemed smitten."

"We can't let her work her wiles on him. We'll both lose out if he falls victim to her charms."

Ian chafed at the insinuation. Georgina was laboring under the common misconception about his relationship with John: that Ian maintained his elevated circumstance through John's beneficence.

No one stopped to ponder whether Ian might have his own funds, and that he resided with John because he chose to. The arrangement was extremely lucrative, but he wouldn't explain himself to the likes of Georgina Howard.

Clearly, she assumed he was an ally. "What would you have me do?"

"Prevail on him to let me stay. I know you can. He respects you; he'll do what you say."

"What's in it for me?"

"You'd be surprised." A suggestive brow rose in invitation.

How desperate was she? How far would she progress in her attempts to secure herself with John? "I suppose you could try to convince me."

Arrogantly, she smirked, confident she could subordinate him with her sexual prowess, but she didn't realize he could see her facial expressions in the shadows.

What a witch!

She bent over, licked and sucked his nipple, then she kissed a hot trail down his abdomen, dallying at his navel, sequentially prodding the blankets away until his cockstand surged up to greet her waiting lips. With a salient detachment, he observed as one might a sporting contest between two unfamiliar players, and he had to concede that she was fantastic at her trade, utilizing her tongue and teeth in myriad ways that incited him to recklessness.

No wonder John kept her around. She was exhaustingly adept.

As she opened wide and took him far inside, her silky auburn hair swished across his stomach and thighs, her fingers deftly massaged his balls, his ass, and he luxuriated in the sensations that shot through his loins. His hips began to flex, and he thrust into her with great relish.

Cuckoldry wasn't so bad after all! Surely, John would absolve him if he learned of the indiscretion. It had been a while since he'd philandered, so the release would be welcome, and it would take scant effort to spew himself in her throat.

For a few minutes, he exercised his excessive control while he seriously debated the pros and cons of letting go, then he came to his senses. He abhorred Georgina, and he could definitely find better locations to deposit his seed than in her lying, crafty, treacherous mouth.

Immediately, he calmed, shielding his emotions—an artificiality at which he was notably proficient—then he pulled her away as though she'd had no effect on him.

Baffled by his disinclination, she sat up, frowning.

"What is it, darling?" she cooed.

"I'm not in the mood."

Her lovers never spurned her, and she wasn't certain how to react. Glowering, she reached for his cock again, ready to commence anew. "Let me try to—"

"Georgie"—he chuckled meanly—"you could go

down on me for the rest of my life, and you'd never persuade me to betray John." On his own, he was perfectly capable of duplicitous conduct toward his brother. He didn't need her assistance.

She studied his cool demeanor, his apathetic mien, and it dawned on her that she'd been duped. "You hadn't contemplated helping me."

"No."

"You were using me!"

"You're such a whore."

"You bastard!"

"Now, now," he flippantly admonished, "be careful what you imply about my mother."

She lashed out and tried to slap him, but he grabbed her wrist to forestall the blow. His own temper raging, he yanked her close so she could get an undiminished glimpse of how much he despised her.

"I'm not John," he warned. "If you hit me, I'll hit you back." He shoved her so that she skidded off the bed and stumbled to her feet. "Get out of my room, and don't bother me again with your shenanigans."

Furious, she sputtered and stammered, finally blustering, "I'll tell John what we did. I'll say you instigated it."

"Have at it," he countered casually. "He'll be thrilled to know how disposed you are to sleep around—while he's paying through the nose for your exclusive company."

She paled, her magnificent bosom heaving, not having considered that Ian might have no qualms about confessing the incident to John.

"I hate you." Seething, she stormed out, her ire so vicious that he could only speculate as to how and when she'd retaliate.

With the door shut, he snuggled under the covers,

and his unsated cockstand demanded alleviation. He took himself in hand, positive that he'd achieve more pleasure on his own than he could with any of the women of his acquaintance.

John dawdled by the window, gazing across the rear lawn to the break in the trees where Emma, bearing down on him much like the wrath of God, had come marching out of the woods the previous day. After her arrival, he wasn't exactly sure what had happened between them. He couldn't describe or characterize events, or the lingering sense of expectation he'd enjoyed in planning for their next rendezvous.

When she'd charged into his library, he'd been hungover and miserable, and she'd scraped raw his flaws by scolding and chastising him in a fashion that no one ever had. She'd made him feel terrible, like the rogue he usually was, and he'd really and truly wanted to make it up to her.

There was something about her that urged him to decent comportment. Perhaps it was her refusal to accept his penchant for indolence and vice, or the temerity she possessed to inform him when he was behaving boorishly. It was fun to watch and listen to her, to witness so much passion bubbling out.

She was a veritable volcano of potent sentiment. On every topic.

And she was so damned sexy. Which was craziness. What man in his right mind would be titillated by such impudence and sass?

They'd almost made love in the library, but before they could, she'd dragged him upstairs for breakfast and a bath. Then, he'd nearly had her again, but she'd had an attack of panic that had prevented them from proceeding to the logical conclusion.

As a result, he was testy, cranky, irritable. He was stunningly popular with the ladies, and he couldn't remember when he'd had one rebuff his advances, yet Emma had. Twice!

He'd overwhelmed her and needed to slow down, to woo her so that she was comfortable with the notion of their becoming lovers. If he pressed, she would honor their signed agreement, but he didn't want her to acquiesce merely because she felt compelled by their asinine contract.

He'd had enough of paid paramours and disinterested partners.

For once, he wanted to join with a woman simply for the joy of it, for the jollity and delight it would render to his sorry condition. It had been a long while since he'd encountered someone who cared for him. Emma did. She was cognizant of his defects and failings, but she liked him anyway, and her esteem was like a breath of fresh air.

He had to have her. He'd been mired in decadence forever, and for some bizarre reason, he felt that her goodness might rub off on him if he could have some intimate appointments with her.

Peering over his shoulder at the clock on the mantel, he was annoyed to note that she was fifteen minutes late. What if she didn't come? At the realization that she might not, he suffered a twinge of alarm. Was she angry with him? Hurt? Insulted?

Before Georgina's inopportune entrance into his bedchamber, they'd been linked emotionally, had shared an incredible moment, and he could imagine what Emma must have thought as she'd stood on the other side of the dressing room door, with himself and Georgina sequestered inside. Very likely, she deemed him to be a rutting beast who could flit from one female to the next in the blink of an eye.

While he'd been known to redefine lechery with his shameful habits, he couldn't have fornicated with Georgina if he'd been offered all the gold in the Bank of England. Oddly, he'd have felt as if he were cheating on Emma!

No doubt, Emma suspected the worst, but he'd instructed Georgina to close the door solely because his mistress had a sharp tongue, and he hadn't wanted Emma to hear whatever snide comments Georgina might have made.

The situation had been hideously awkward, and he hadn't been able to rapidly devise a feasible solution, so he'd done what seemed best at the time, but in retrospect, he'd been horridly callous. He'd wounded Emma with his ostensible lack of regard, and he wished he knew what to do to mend his gaffe.

Well, if she didn't appear shortly, he'd have to hunt her down. One of the servants had to know where she lived. He'd give her till one-thirty, then seek her out.

The house was quiet, his clamorous associates having departed for London. They'd grumbled and complained but, confronted with Ian's staunch adamance, had ultimately gone.

Although John would never admit it, he was relieved by their egress, but he loathed the isolation and seclusion left in their wake. The large mansion was too serene, the vast salons echoing with old messages from his father. He yearned to jump on his horse and catch up with the entourage, but there was too much to be done, too many changes to be set in motion before he could leave.

Just then, Emma burst out of the trees and tramped toward the manor, her tenacity evident in her dogged stride. It had rained in the night, and the temperature had cooled. She was swathed in a dingy brown cloak and straw bonnet.

As she approached, he spied on her, a smile creeping across his face, and suddenly, his sojourn to the country didn't seem so oppressive. He was deluged with a special kind of happiness—as if he were smiling on the inside, too—and he gleefully anticipated being in her presence once more. She turned the corner of the house and was out of sight, and he loitered, impatient as she knocked, as she was let in, as Rutherford escorted her down the hall.

She waltzed into the room, and he was lurking by the door, scowling and pretending to be irked by her tardiness. "Miss Fitzgerald, you're late."

"I wasn't going to come at all." She was in a merry mood, declining to heed his feigned pique. "Are you sober, Wakefield?"

"As a judge, Miss Fitzgerald."

"We're making progress."

"According to whom?"

"Rutherford advises me that you've sent your friends to London." He glared at the retainer who was busy studying the ceiling, and the man scurried out, securing the door behind.

The instant it was latched, he covered the distance that separated them, wrapped his arms around her, and swept her into a torrid embrace that went on and on. When their lips parted, he was hard, aching for her and what was coming. On several occasions now, he had put off having her, and there would be no delay.

"Don't ever make me wait," he murmured. "I hate it."

"You're spoiled."

"Absolutely."

"Do you always get your way?"

"Yes."

He clasped her hand and attempted to lead her to the couch so they could begin their afternoon of love-play, but she dug in her heels and wouldn't budge.

"Not so fast." Before he grasped what she meant to do, she'd opened the door again, and there was Rutherford with John's outerwear.

"Grab your coat," she ordered. "We're going visiting."

"I don't want to go visiting."

"Too bad, because we are."

"Who?"

"One of the tenants you're evicting."

"Now just a damned minute!"

"Don't curse in front of me."

"I'm not about to meet with some poor sod who—"

Ignoring his protest, which exasperated him beyond measure, she walked into the corridor and started out, fixed on her destination, and if he wanted to spend any private time with her, he had to follow.

Rutherford extended his coat and hat and, gnashing his teeth, he snatched them up, then obediently trailed after her.

CHAPTER SEVEN

"How long did you say Mr. Gladstone had worked for my family?"

Emma smiled. Wakefield was behind her, so he couldn't see. "Seventy-nine years. He started in the stables when he was a lad of six."

"Hmm . . ."

He added nothing further, and she continued down the winding path through the woods that led to the mansion.

She hadn't planned to visit John Clayton again. After their disastrous, fantastic encounter during his bath, she'd fumed and ruminated until she'd ultimately concluded that the perils far outweighed the benefits.

They shared a hazardous physical attraction—a compelling emotional one, too—that made her heedless to commit any negligent act, and she'd convinced herself that she couldn't travel down such a risky road. But as day had dawned, as morning had slowly ticked by, as one o'clock had approached, her honorable intention had flown out the window.

The notion of not being with him was too depressing to ponder. She couldn't desist, yet she didn't dare let him sequester her in a private parlor. He was so adept at cajoling her to lustful behavior that he'd have had her on her back, her clothes off, in a matter of seconds. Where he was concerned, she had no willpower. She couldn't tell him no.

She wasn't sure how or when she'd devised the fabulous inspiration of going to Mr. Gladstone's, which allowed her to dawdle with Wakefield, but without any opportunity for illicit flirtation. It had been the perfect solution to her dilemma.

Wakefield had barked and complained, griping about her tyrannical manner with every step, but still, he'd acquiesced.

By her standards, the appointment had been an enormous success. Mr. Gladstone, in his eighties, almost blind, mostly crippled, had been named on Wakefield's despicable ejection list. Though he scarcely had the ability to care for himself, he refused to abandon the cottage that Wakefield's grandfather had provided for him three decades earlier as a reward for meritorious service.

Despite his infirmities, his mind was sharp as a tack. He was a spry fellow who hadn't been cowed by the aristocrat. He'd chatted amiably and, in a surprising revelation, he'd mentioned that he'd taught Wakefield's grandfather to ride, his father and older brother, too.

Emma had been shocked to learn of an *older* brother. She'd always thought Wakefield to be the eldest and hadn't known that he'd inherited as an adolescent.

What effect had his sibling's death had on molding him into the dissolute, ne'er-do-well he'd grown to be?

Intrigued and enthralled, she'd discreetly observed their conversation from the corner, while she'd thoroughly analyzed Wakefield who was suddenly her favorite topic in the entire world. She couldn't have predicted how he'd relate to the aged man's predicament, but he'd impressed her tremendously.

He was possessed of an interesting capacity to adapt, to mold himself to his environment, so he hadn't seemed awkward or out of place. He'd curbed his rampant imperiousness, had been diplomatic, courteous, and respectful. It was a fascinating glimpse that made him appear even more remarkable.

"Fine!" he grumbled, halting. "I agree!"

She spun around. "What?"

"He can stay."

"Mr. Gladstone?"

"Aye."

"I don't have to bed you first?"

"No."

He was so irritated by his decision that she grinned. "Do you mean it?"

"Of course I *mean* it. What do you think? That I'm talking simply to feel my lips flapping?" She giggled, and he snapped, "Why are you laughing at me?"

"Because you've done the right thing, and you're angry about it."

"I'm not angry." He stopped short. "Well . . . maybe a little."

Underneath the bluster, he was the sweetest man— as she'd sensed from the beginning. A serene joy swept through her, commencing at her heart and flowing outward to her extremities.

"Thank you," she said quietly.

"You're welcome." He tipped his head in acknowledgment, then straightened, folding his arms across his chest, his domineering demeanor reasserting itself. "But he's the only one. Do you hear me, Emma?"

"Yes. Now about the others—"

"Don't pester me!"

"I have an interview arranged every afternoon. Tomorrow, we're to call on Mrs. Wilson so that I can introduce you to her children."

"I'm not about to chitchat with some strange woman's children!"

"You'll like them, especially baby Rose. She is such

a darling." Chattering a mile a minute, she went off, jabbering about the Wilson family's poverty, about the father who'd been killed in a haying accident.

He frowned at her, then his glower softened, and he gazed at her in amazement.

"What?" she queried on noticing his curious expression.

"You have more audacity than any person I've ever met."

"Why do you say so? Because I'm trying to help my neighbors?"

"No-o-o." He dragged out the word as though he were about to instruct a moron. "It's because I give you the earth, and you demand the moon and stars, too!"

"If I never ask, I'll never receive, will I?"

"*You*—Miss Fitzgerald—are a mercenary! I'm lucky I'm not facing you over a negotiating table." He bent nearer. "Or across the barrel of a pistol!"

"You're not about to make me feel guilty. You shouldn't have issued any evictions. And you know it."

"I know nothing of the sort."

"What you really need to do is cancel the rents."

"The rents!"

"Yes."

"Miss Fitzgerald"—he was excessively exasperated— "I am the Viscount Wakefield. I take it you're aware of my position in the community?"

"Yes, I am."

"I'm here at the estate because it's in horrendous fiscal condition. I must salvage a calamitous situation but how, exactly, am I to accomplish this feat?" Annoyed, he threw his hands up in the air. "I'm not to oust any tenants! I'm not to collect any rents! Just what is it you would have me do?"

"I have many good ideas."

"I'm not foregoing any rental payments!" He shot her a fierce glare. "And that's final!"

"They'll be null and void for one year," she adjoined calmly as though he hadn't shouted at her. "Then, when you reinstate them, you'll lower them, so that people have a fair chance to get back on their feet. It's the drought, you understand, and a drop in the price of wheat, and then there was the—"

He grabbed her forearms, dipped under the rim of her hat, and kissed her, cutting off the rest. It only took an instant for the wonder to sink in, and she relaxed against him, pressing her torso to his so that they were connected from breasts to toes. He'd developed a marvelous cockstand, and it prodded her stomach, making her feminine regions tingle and throb.

When their lips separated, his eyes were sparkling with delight. The sun shone down on him, the leaves swished in the trees, a warm breeze rippled around them. It was tranquil, a brook rustling off in the distance, birds clamoring in whistles and squawks. The only other sounds were his steady breathing and the furious pounding of her pulse.

It was a magical moment, the two of them alone, surrounded by the dense forest, and he was showering her with such stunning affection that she longed to weep with how precious he made her feel.

"You talk too much," he declared.

"So I've been told all my life."

"You fill up my ears with your prattle."

"You should listen to me."

"I like you better when your mouth is busy."

"With what task?" she saucily inquired.

"With entertaining me." He molded his lips to hers and, when he ended it, she was sighing with pleasure.

"I love how you kiss me," he said. "As if you truly want to."

It was an odd comment, and she swore she wouldn't reflect upon it. Besides, he was kissing her again, commanding her full attention, and she wrapped her arms around him, and gave her whole self over to the embrace. Their tongues mated in a frantic rhythm that made her womb stir, and swarms of butterflies surge through her stomach.

Her hat was in his way, and he yanked at the bow that was tied under her chin and tossed it into the weeds, then he gripped her bottom, whirled her around, and braced her against a tree. He was settled between her legs, his phallus pushed into her, so that if he shifted, even the slightest amount, he rubbed himself over her animated parts.

In a thrice, she was wet with desire, her body on fire. She wanted to have his hands on her, to have him fondle and nuzzle and caress.

His need spiraled in direct proportion to her own, and he thrust ardently, then abruptly, he quit, his respiration ragged, his control frazzled.

Moderating the conflagration, he nibbled across her cheek, down her neck, taking small bites that made her squirm and writhe. Her nipples were so hard they ached, straining at her dress, flagrantly imploring that they be released. She was so aroused that, if he so much as looked at them, she would likely do anything he suggested.

"I want to make love to you." His voice was tempting, seductive, urging her to do what she oughtn't. "Here in the forest."

"No, someone might come by. Someone might see us."

"These woods are deserted. We haven't stumbled on

another soul all afternoon. It will be fine."

Fine? Was he mad? They couldn't frolic in the out-
doors like a pair of rutting animals? Or could they?

She glanced around. They were so isolated. They
could wander farther off the trail. They could ...

No! What was she contemplating? They couldn't!

He let go of her, guiding her so that she slid down
his front, every titillated inch taking a leisurely trip
across his anatomy. Linking their fingers, he led her off
the path and, like a ninny, she offered no resistance,
eagerly following wherever he went.

In a secluded meadow, he turned to her, unfastening
her cloak and spreading it on the grass. Pensively, she
watched, not assisting or hindering him, not running off
as she knew she should. He knelt and brushed the cloak
flat, a smooth, inviting bed where they could romp and
rollick.

Then, he sat and held out his hand to her. She was
so apprehensive, yet so excited, that she was paralyzed
and couldn't move to him or away. Physically, she was
inclined to whatever he proposed, and if she joined him,
she wouldn't be able to contain her baser impulses.

"Come to me, Emma." His ravishing blue eyes were
beseeching, his smile beguiling her, luring her to her
doom.

"I'm scared."

"I know you are." He clasped her hand in his, his
thumb tracing captivating circles in the center of her
palm. "I won't hurt you."

"I hadn't imagined you would."

Gently, he tugged on her wrist and, her knees buckling, she collapsed down. She huddled before him, out
of her league and unsure of what to do. If he touched
her, she might shatter into a thousand pieces. If he
didn't, she was worried over the same result.

"I want to take your hair down."

"If I remove the combs, I won't be able to fix it."

"I'll help you."

As if she were a puppet on a string, she permitted him to rotate her, and he snuggled her to him so that her rear was nestled into his loins. With a few deft flicks of his fingers, which vividly reminded her of his experience with other paramours, he had the combs extracted, the curly brown wave tumbling down to graze her hips.

Cuddling with her, he burrowed his nose in the wavy mass, sifting through it, arraying it across her back, then he lay down, bringing her with him so that they were side by side on the ground. Casually, he looped his thigh over her legs, his foot impelling her nearer so that their bodies were united, and he scrutinized her intently while she stroked lazy circles, round and round, on the middle of his chest.

It was phenomenal to have him evaluating her. He did so often, as if he didn't quite know what to make of her. No one had meticulously dissected her before, and she treasured how he roved and probed, searching for her very essence.

"Why are you staring at me like that?"

"You're a great mystery to me."

An enigma! How thrilling! "Why?"

"On the outside, you're so prim and proper, but on the inside, you're a teeming cauldron of sexuality. Your carnal nature bubbles to the surface, and then you rein it in. Every time." He was teasing, but serious, as well. "Are you always so forward with the men you meet?"

"Only with you. You overwhelm my better sense."

"I'm glad."

"Bounder." She chuckled, and he did, too, then their mirth faded, and the interlude grew intimate and dear, and she felt she could confess any secret to him. "I guess

I'm terrified of what might happen if I let go."

"So am I." He reached out and petted her hair, her shoulder, his hand descending to her breast and massaging the pliant mound through the fabric of her dress. "You do something to me. Being around you makes me feel . . ." He broke off, incapable of explaining.

"Splendid? Miserable? Ecstatic? Panicked?"

"All those. And more." He seized her nipple, squeezing the raised peak, causing her to chafe at the agitation. "What do you want from me, Em? I need you to say it."

There were dozens of potential answers she could give, from simple to difficult, from cheap to expensive. He'd taken a fancy to her, and could aid her in innumerable ways. She wished he would ease her burdens, carry her woes. Cancel the eviction from her cottage, save her family from ruin, supply her with money, food, security.

But what she said was, "I want you to touch me. All over. With your hands and your mouth."

Solemnly, he analyzed her again, then he nodded. "We'll go slowly."

"All right."

"If I frighten you, tell me, and I'll stop."

"I won't ask you to stop. That's why I'm afraid."

"Lean on me for a change, Em. I'll take care of you."

He kissed her, gradually rolling her onto her back, then coming over her so that his weight was partially on her. His hips melded into her pelvis, his phallus rigid and insistent at her leg.

With his tongue, he tormented her lips, and she opened for him, taking him inside, inhaling his taste, his smell, imprinting each superb detail.

He tarried, while his inquisitive hands roved and investigated, traveling over her torso, lingering, journeying on. Eventually, he undid the buttons on her dress. She did naught to impede him, keeping her hands anchored in his hair so that she wouldn't stupidly prevent him from going where she was desperate for him to be.

The bodice loosened, it fell away, and he drew the sleeves down her arms so that the top was pooled around her waist, her breasts covered only by her functional chemise. His fingers glided into the undergarment to her nipple, and the impact was so invigorating that she arched up, but he held her down, slithering the straps of her chemise so that her arms were pinned to her sides with her breasts revealed. The air rushed over her naked skin, her nipples constricting further, until they were painful buds.

"My, my, Emma." He studied her bosom, estimating size and abundance. "So pretty. And all mine."

He lay on her again, taking both nipples, twirling and pinching them until she was in agony, then he kissed down her nape, her bust, finally—blessedly!—arriving at her cleavage. Nipping under the swell of her breast, he licked and taunted.

"Do you want me, Emma?"

"You know I do, you cad!" she bit out through clenched teeth.

"Should I kiss you here?" His teeth skimmed an extended nub.

"Yes, yes," she wailed. "Wakefield, please—"

"I love it when you beg me," and he sucked the provoked tip into his mouth, abrading it relentlessly.

"Sweet Jesu . . ." she moaned.

He tortured her until she was sore and raw, then he went to the other, trifling with it, continuing on far past the point of pleasure, but she couldn't get enough of the potent stimulation.

Brazenly, she spurred him on, lifting her breasts so that she contributed more of herself for his total, decadent enjoyment. He took what she offered and more, inducing her to give him everything, to hold nothing back.

Her loins were damp and aflame, incited beyond bearing. Their impassioned wrestling had rucked up her dress and furnished him with an inviting cushion against which he could flex, propelling them deeper into the inescapable quagmire, and she was growing so hot she fretted that she might ignite.

His hand sneaked down to cup her, then slip under her skirt. She was unclothed beneath it, with no drawers to shield her privates from his questing fingers, and she braced as he converged on her most sensitive area.

He tangled through her womanly hair, delving inside to explore. Her inner muscles spasmed, holding him tight, but it wasn't enough.

She was no stranger to orgasm, having occasionally inflicted the wanton gratification on herself, but she hadn't known how much more intense and satisfying it was for it to occur at the instigation of another.

Deliberately, he manipulated her. "God, you're so ready for me."

Grinning up at her, his mesmerizing eyes glittered with mischief, and a lock of blond hair fell rakishly over his forehead. Hovering over her breasts as he was, he looked beautiful, exhilarated, wicked, resolute.

"Do it!" she pleaded irritably.

"Now?" He halted the erotic path of his thumb.

"I can't wait any longer. You're killing me."

"We can't have that, can we?"

She'd thought that he'd progress with his hand, but he surprised her by sliding down her torso, urging her skirt up and baring her core.

She knew what he intended, and in a perverse fashion, she was thrilled that he would attempt the depraved act, but the notion made her overly uncomfortable, left her feeling too exposed, and she didn't want to be so much at his mercy. She yearned to pull her legs together, to hide herself from his zealous appraisal, but he was wedged in, too heavy, and she couldn't dislodge him.

He widened her nether lips, so that he could examine the folds, the pink cleft, and she threw an arm over her eyes, striving to absent herself from the embarrassing predicament.

"Wakefield, don't. I don't like this."

"You will."

"It's too . . . too . . ." She couldn't describe her sentiments. Undone. Ashamed. Titillated beyond her limits. Out of control.

"Ssh . . ." he soothed, as if she were a skittish horse that required gentling. "It will be all right. Relax."

Relax! As if she could with the virile scapegrace poised between her legs!

He elevated her bottom, and he sampled her, parting her with his tongue, running it along the middle, then probing inside.

"Please—" she implored again, not certain if she was begging him to desist or to proceed with all due haste.

"You taste so fine. As if you were created just for me."

He toyed with her nipples, and his tongue perturbed her until she was set to explode. The sensations were ascending, her body stiffening with the approaching pinnacle and, with a crazed fervor, she chased after the elusive apex.

"John—" she keened, not meaning to use his given name, but she was beyond the juncture where she could keep it from creeping out. It was a capitulation and, arrogant rogue that he was, he chuckled.

"Come for me, Emma. Come now."

In her condition, she couldn't refuse him. He latched on and sucked vigorously, and she raced to the edge and hurtled over, spiraling higher, higher, until she was careening across the universe.

Vaguely, she perceived that she'd cried out—loudly—but she couldn't restrain herself. She plunged into the voluminous force of the orgasm, relishing every second of the zenith that had no boundary. Ultimately, the upheaval began to abate, and she floated down, only to find herself cradled in Wakefield's arms.

Without her being aware, he'd scooted up so that he could nestle with her through the tumult. He was kissing her hair, her eyes, her cheeks, whispering soft declarations that she didn't understand. They sounded French, or perhaps Italian, and she pretended that they were endearments, and from the magical foreign cadence, they very well could have been.

"What a joy you are." He murmured the comment against her lips, and the tang of her sex was on his mouth.

He thought she was a *joy*! What a precious remark! Like a foolish ninny, she burst into tears, and he balanced her chin in his hand and swiped them away.

"My adorable Emma," he sympathized, "what is it?"

"It was so . . . so wonderful."

"Aye," he concurred, "it was at that."

"I didn't know it could be like this."

"Neither did I."

"And . . . and . . ."—she hiccuped, scarcely able to speak—"I want to do it again. Already!"

He laughed heartily, and snuggled her into the crook of his neck so that she could have a good cry. It was a fabulous spot to linger, and she sobbed as she hadn't in ages. Shedding enough tears to fill an ocean, she wept for her father, her mother and sister, for herself and her plight, for all her dreams that would never come true.

He withstood it well, as though he consoled hysterical women every day, which she knew was hardly the case. Down below, his erection was evident, his disturbed anatomy not having attained any assuagement.

She fathomed that he needed tending, but she couldn't alleviate his situation—she wasn't sure how!—though he didn't appear to be unduly concerned.

Selfishly, she grasped for all the solace he was disposed to render, soaking it in, letting him calm her with his body, with his words. The hum of his voice reverberated through her bone and marrow, and it lulled her. The lamentation ceased, and her eyelids drooped.

She was so tired! She yawned, a most unladylike gesture, and before she realized it, she'd nodded off.

When she stirred later, she couldn't have guessed how long she'd lain there. She'd felt so content and safe that she'd slumbered heavily, and she stumbled to consciousness, stretching, reveling in how extraordinary it was to awaken in his arms.

He was on his back, clutching her to his chest and, as though he hadn't a care in the world, he was leisurely contemplating the forest above their heads.

As she fidgeted, he turned to his side and kissed the tip of her nose. "Hello, sleepyhead."

"Hello." She was so happy; every pore in her body seemed to be smiling.

"I didn't think you were ever going to wake up."

Glancing around, she noticed that the shadows were much more lengthy than when she'd dozed off. "What time is it?"

"Almost five."

"Five!" Aghast, she sat up. She was still naked to the waist, and possessively, he stroked one of her bared breasts.

"Stop that!" she commanded, slapping his hand away.

"You have the nicest tits," he said.

"Do be silent!"

Frantically, she leapt away and adjusted her clothes, yanking at them while he did his level best to impede her efforts.

He was reclined on her cloak, assessing her brisk actions, but providing no assistance, and showing no signs of being in a hurry, himself.

"Let's go to the manor," he suggested, "and have supper. Then we'll make love in my bed all night."

"Wakefield!"

"John," he insisted. "That's what you call me when you're crying out in passion."

"Well, I don't plan to make a habit of it." She searched for her combs, but found only two of the necessary six. She held them out. "Help me with my hair."

"No, I like it down."

Exasperated, she glared at him, but he was mellow, insouciant, and completely disinclined to aid her. She'd have to wear the hood on her cloak and sneak home, praying she encountered no one, hoping that inquisitive Jane wouldn't question her messy coiffure.

"Get up!" She jerked on her cloak, but he was securely moored upon it and wouldn't budge.

"Why are you in such a rush?"

"Because—as opposed to you—I have a life and I've got to get back to it."

"Cancel what is so imperative. I want you with me."

"I can't snap my fingers and make my responsibilities vanish"—she glowered at him—"like some people I know."

Jostling the cloak, she managed to wrench it out from under him. Arranging it over her shoulders, she fussed with the clasp, but she was too shaky to fasten it. She couldn't recall where they'd left her hat, so she'd have to hunt for it another day when she wasn't quite so discomposed.

"Can you find your way to the main house on your own?" she inquired.

"Of course." Apparently, he'd deduced that she was going, that despite his autocratic manner, he couldn't convince her to remain. Disconcerted, he stood, taking her hand, hugging her close. "Stay with me."

"I can't!"

"Tell me what you need done, and I'll have someone see to it for you."

Depressed and weary, she stared up at him. He could never comprehend the pressures she underwent, and she wouldn't even try to explain them to him. To a man of his affluence and station, her problems would seem so petty.

"No one can perform my chores for me."

"You'd be surprised by what I can accomplish if I set my mind to it."

"So you're not an idler and a sluggard as your detractors claim?"

"What do you suppose?"

"I *suppose* that you pretend you're an impossible lout, but I can't figure out why you go to so much trouble to garner everyone's adverse opinions."

He scrutinized her as if she'd expressed an extremely profound observation, then quietly he said, "I don't want to be alone up at the house."

It was an astounding admission. She wasn't sure

what to make of it, and could formulate no appropriate reply.

"Stay with me," he murmured again, and he kissed her, coaxing and cajoling.

"I can't," she repeated, and she eased away before he could tempt her into agreeing. With him, she was forever on the verge of doing what she oughtn't, and it would take so little for him to overwhelm her resolve. She had to get home!

Jane was probably frightened by her protracted absence, and Emma couldn't believe how greedy she'd been, how inconsiderate, just so she could engage in an illicit tryst.

Her moral compass was broken!

"I must go."

She whirled away and started toward the path.

"Emma!"

There was such yearning in his voice that she pulled up short.

"Don't ask it of me," she beseeched, alarmed by how she'd react to whatever enticement he might utter next.

After an attenuated pause, he said, "Tomorrow, then. At one."

"At one."

She scurried off without looking back. He didn't follow after her, and she was so relieved.

CHAPTER EIGHT

HAROLD Martin tugged at his hat and slumped his shoulders, slouching on his horse so that he looked nondescript—a commonly dressed, uninteresting traveler passing by. With night approaching, it wouldn't do for speculation to fly that the new vicar from Wakefield village had been seen rambling down the rustic lane.

People would talk. In this godforsaken rural area, they didn't have anything else to do but gossip about their betters, and though he'd deny till his dying breath that he'd made a clandestine journey across the countryside, rumor was difficult to quell. Should he ever be interrogated, which he doubted would happen since his reputation was impeccable, he would swear that he'd had supper at the vicarage, had read before the fire, and had retired early.

In a few minutes, he'd reach his destination, and the sense of anticipation was thrilling. He made the trip twice a month, and wished he could stop by more often, but circumstances and distance rendered it impractical to indulge more frequently. Besides, he refused to submit to his scurrilous urges too regularly, reluctant to acknowledge that he was ruled by his sordid propensities.

A vision of Emma flashed into his head, and he shook her likeness away, furious that his cerebral meandering allowed her to intrude as he was about to pervert himself.

It was offensive to contemplate her—his future

bride—when he was so near to committing such horrid sins. He couldn't abide that he might tarnish her image by what he was about to do. In his mind, she needed to be pure and untainted.

She was innocent, demure, all he desired in a wife. His own proclivities were so deviant that he had to wed a woman who was his opposite, someone like Emma who would convey chastity and modesty to their marriage bed. Her virtuousness would impel him to rein in his predilections so that he wouldn't disgust her with his raging passions.

Hopefully, some of her stalwart decency would rub off, and his constant need for degrading amusement would wane. It was simply a matter of character, of strong will. He was determined to prevail over his wanton nature!

He couldn't recollect when he'd become so enamored of decadency. When he'd gone to university, he'd been a virgin, an honorable chap with lofty ethical standards. His roommate, Adrian, had been the catalyst that had led him astray. Adrian had had a penchant for abhorrent pleasures, and thus, he'd had an uncanny aptitude for ferreting out those unsuspecting souls who were disposed to dissolution.

It had been a slow descent for Harold. He'd valiantly struggled to resist Adrian's attempts to lure him from the straight and narrow, but eventually, he'd succumbed, trying a meager taste of the carnal diet on which Adrian had thrived, savoring more and more of the degenerate feast until he'd acquired his own insatiable appetite for depravity.

He'd fallen so low that there'd even been those glorious occasions that he and Adrian had . . .

Well, he wouldn't mull on that. Rehashing that rough, heinous interlude was a waste of energy. Fleetingly, he'd immersed himself in Adrian's world, but he'd managed to escape, having not surrendered to any invidious manly fascination since that wretched relationship.

But still, he couldn't abstain completely. His repressed cravings were so unbearable that he'd begun to conclude they weren't healthy, that it wasn't prudent to keep such tumultuous impulses bottled up.

He'd been a bachelor much longer than was wise, and with Emma declining to set a wedding date, what was he to do? His lust for her was escalating so rapidly that he could scarcely risk spending time in her company, lest the beast rampaging inside leap out and he devour her with his rising ardor. She was so unschooled that she'd be alarmed and shocked, perhaps repulsed, if she had any idea of the blatant drives that churned inside a man, so he couldn't let her surmise how badly he wanted her.

Luckily, he'd learned of the Back Door, the information having been unwittingly furnished by another minister whom he'd met at a neighboring congregation. The pastor had regaled his listeners with the worst transgressions of his flock, and when he'd honed in on the sins of the flesh, Harold had paid particular note, gleaning enough detail to infer where the house of ill repute was located.

Upon making the discovery, he'd debated for weeks, pondering whether he dared visit, until finally, he'd gone on an intelligence-gathering mission, telling himself it would be a single sojourn and no more. Unfortunately— or fortunately, depending on one's point of view—the establishment had been everything the other vicar had railed about and much more, the proprietress inclined to orchestrate any nasty diversion if the price was sufficient.

What with the ample income endowed by his post, he had plenty of money, and he'd quickly ascertained that the madam was a veritable master at deducing what entertainment he might like to try.

He mused as to what perversion might await, and his reflections set his manly parts to swelling. His trousers were uncomfortable, and with each clop of the horse's hooves, his genitalia rubbed the saddle, making him anxious for the reckless abandon stretching ahead.

At his prior appointment, he'd had a girl, eleven or twelve he'd guessed, and such a juvenile that she'd had no breasts to speak of, no feminine hair covered her pussy. Her bottom had been smooth and bare, her cleft painfully tight. Pitiably, she hadn't been a virgin, but what had he expected in a brothel?

Previously, he'd never had a child, and copulating with her had been splendid. She'd fussed and cried over how big he was, and he'd had to hold her down, had had to force her to do the dirty deed, and oh, how wicked it had been! He kept at her most of the evening, his masculine rod repeatedly inflamed by the naughtiness.

He hadn't known that he harbored such a sinister obsession, and now that he'd had a sampling, he couldn't quit ruminating over the episode, and he hoped that the madam offered him the lass again—or another just like her. The prospect tempted him in a vile fashion that went beyond what he'd tried or dreamed about before.

It had him considering Jane Fitzgerald in a totally new light. Formerly, he'd believed he loathed her, but now he wasn't positive. Once he married Emma and moved her family into the vicarage, Jane would be under his control, would be wholly dependent on him. Surely, she would have to obey him, might be pressured to . . .

Aghast, he let the thought trail off, finding it so appalling that he couldn't pursue it. He absolutely would not fantasize about Jane Fitzgerald!

He was foul, despicable! A brute! A monster! How could he conceive of such iniquity? To where had his rectitude disappeared? His prurient voracity was growing ungovernable, was pushing him to limits he couldn't contain.

Kicking his horse, he spurred it to a trot, and momentarily, he arrived. A boy came out from the stables to tend the animal, and he provided Harold with a lamp so he could walk down the dark path, through the untrimmed hedges, to the porch and the red door that was shielded by the shrubbery.

Upon rapping the special knock, he was admitted and instantly whisked upstairs to a private chamber, which suited him very much. There wasn't a chance that he'd encounter other patrons. His anonymity was assured.

As he was a valued customer, the madam assisted him, herself. He didn't have to deal with her servants, another boon for which he was grateful, as every bit of furtiveness was appreciated.

"What'll it be, luv?" she asked, her huge bosom heaving under the fabric of her dress, her large nipples jutting out.

"I'll try a young girl. The youngest you have in the house."

He extended a pile of coins, which she briskly snatched up and stuffed into a purse that hung at her waist.

Georgina Howard reclined on her fainting couch in the receiving parlor of the lovely town house procured for her by John Clayton. Pensively, she assessed her elegant surroundings, remembering the numerous guests who had called upon her in the cozy, welcoming room. The ambiance was typical of her entire residence.

Wakefield was a generous man, and when she'd shrewdly allied herself with him, he'd spared no expense at accoutering her in a style that would proclaim her elevated station. Her home was a flawless example of color and design, as well as a visual testimonial to her cunning and greed.

It had taken almost three years to finagle Wakefield's support, and while others presumed that their joining had been a flip decision by John, their association hadn't been an accident. Meticulously, she'd plotted and schemed to bring it to fruition, and after all her hard work, she wasn't about to let it slip through her fingers.

Sipping her glass of wine, she insolently gazed out the window into the yard where her gardener trimmed her rosebushes. She had twelve employees—twelve!—which was an enormous amount for a single female of her humble antecedents. It was a confirmation of how far she'd come, of how strenuously she'd scrimped and saved, of how successful she'd been.

Due to Wakefield's largess, her servants were liberally compensated. They knew upon which side their bread was buttered, and they were excessively courteous and helpful, coddling and pampering her, deeming her to be a person of substance, so she carefully hid how their fate was riding on Wakefield and her enduring ability to hold his attention—which she knew from vast experience was prone to wander.

As a child, Georgina couldn't have predicted that she might rise so high. Her father had owned a taproom, and she'd assumed that she'd always live in the village where she'd been born. But her father had died when she was eleven, and her mother had remarried. Georgina had already been maturing with her voluptuous figure, and her stepfather had been titillated by the changes.

For months, she'd fended off his crude advances until he'd caught her alone in her room. He'd tied her to her bed, gagged her with a towel, then violated her.

The rape had been vicious, profane, and had left her torn and distraught, terrified and confused, and he'd ravished her on four subsequent occasions before she'd fled to the city.

A distant cousin, a jaded actress who'd been ten years older, had initially supplied Georgina with a place to stay and food to eat, had even escorted her to the barber's wife so she could rid herself of the babe her stepfather had planted, but Georgina had had to devise a method for making her own way.

With her cousin's guidance, she'd perfected her only marketable commodity—that being her looks and anatomy—so that by age fourteen, she'd secured her first protector. He'd been elderly, and extremely patient in their physical affairs, more excited about having an attractive, adolescent woman on his arm than anything else, so she'd been able to ignore her revulsion to corporeal interaction.

Gradually, she'd learned how to beguile and enchant, to charm and cosset, to fornicate in every manner a man could possibly seek to do it, and to accomplish it with her smile firmly affixed, despite how repugnant she found some of the behaviors to be.

At her benefactor's death, she'd made one calculated move after the next, grappling for position in the scandalous circle inhabited by herself and the other hapless women just like her.

Ceaselessly, her eye had been on the maximum prize—a nobleman with the resources to bestow a refined mode of living.

Wakefield had been her preference and, as he'd been the most handsome and virile of the idle, extravagant fellows with whom she'd socialized, she'd felt that the sexual fraternization wouldn't be quite so detestable.

Biding her time, she'd dawdled on the periphery of his world, ingratiating herself, courting his friends. She'd studied him, had taken flattery and coquetry to a nauseating level, until she'd contrived to entice him into their arrangement.

When he was happy, he was magnanimous, and her engaging abode was a virtual trophy to how commendably she did her job. She spent her allowance judiciously, wanting his peers to see how well he'd chosen, wanting *him* to be inordinately pleased whenever he came to relax and unwind.

Nostalgically, she glanced around, taking it all in, recalling the raucous fun she'd instigated, the nights of drink and frolic she'd accommodated, and she wondered how much longer she'd have the opportunity to host the guests who flocked to her soirees because of her connection to the notorious viscount.

She had no illusions about why she was currently such a powerhouse in the demimonde. Wakefield might be a scapegrace and a libertine, but he was rich and prominent. People were drawn to him, they curried his favor, and the simplest means of reaping it was to win over his mistress.

Though he was purported to be a scoundrel and a loafer, in all actuality, he was clever and astute. With his title and fortune finally inherited, he would succeed beyond anyone's wildest imaginings, and Georgina planned to be with him through each step of his ascent to eminence and acclaim.

Though he perpetually denied the inevitable, he would wed that ninny, Caroline Foster, a trembling, blathering fool whom Georgina couldn't abide. If it wasn't Lady Caroline, it would be some other simpering, vapid girl just like her, so he would need a strong woman in the background, who was smart and resourceful, who could read people and manipulate them to beneficial effect.

Georgina intended to be that woman.

She couldn't lose her influence over him. Her livelihood, her future—why, her very life!—rested on her capacity to persevere with him, and she wasn't about to relinquish what she'd toiled so exhaustingly to attain, which was why she was so gravely troubled by the vicar's daughter who was with John at Wakefield Manor.

His fiancée, Georgina could handle. Miss Fitzgerald was another story. John felt an affinity for her that was potent and unwavering, the likes of which frightened Georgina to her very core and was the reason she'd debased herself by approaching Ian Clayton.

She'd been so sure that Ian would have perceived the inherent dangers created by Miss Fitzgerald, though with him, it was difficult to discern his motivations. As to his loyalties, she'd erred hideously, and had embarrassed herself in the process, but she wouldn't rue her mistake. In the prevailing situation, it was advantageous to know who her allies were—and weren't. Besides, she had many bigger issues with which to cope.

During the period she'd been Wakefield's consort, he'd had many flings. An opera dancer here, a randy widow there. Georgina had spies everywhere and kept close tabs on him. None of his petty dalliances had lasted more than the time it took him to drop his trousers. He'd always come back to Georgina, satisfied with their alliance, yet when Georgina thought of how he'd looked at Miss Fitzgerald, a frisson of panic slithered down her spine.

Miss Fitzgerald was tough, tenacious, a fighter, a winner. She was the type who focused on a target and never vacillated until she'd achieved her goal, precisely as Georgina might, though they'd use different procedures.

What if she set her sights on Wakefield? The pious carper was poor as a church mouse. If she concluded she could improve her circumstances by allying herself with the wealthy viscount, where would that leave Georgina?

She'd witnessed them together that day in the library at Wakefield. There'd been a spark and energy flaring between them that she hadn't wanted to admit. Even more odd was the afternoon that she'd broken the rules and brazenly gone to John's bedchamber—uninvited—in the hopes of convincing him to let her remain.

The prim and proper Miss Fitzgerald had been in his dressing room, and obviously assisting him with his bath. Though she'd been fully clothed, Georgina had observed enough to be distressed. The little witch had generated a furious cockstand for him, and he'd refused to permit Georgina to tend it. Then, he'd insisted that she depart for London posthaste.

She didn't dare defy his direct order to stay in town, yet she was frantic over what might transpire in her absence. She couldn't sit idly by, unable to deduce how her destiny was unfolding, and thus incapable of altering the course of events.

"What to do?" she muttered to the empty salon.

Someone needed to intervene, someone who could subtly remind Miss Fitzgerald—in no uncertain terms—that she didn't belong with Wakefield. Ian would be of no help. So who else might suffice?

Desperate measures were called for, and consequently, a devious, underhanded idea popped into her head. For an eternity, she mulled the benefits and detriments before proceeding.

Rising from the couch, she went to her writing desk, retrieved a blank piece of paper and dipped her pen, weighing her words.

Dear Lady Caroline . . . she began, then halted. The formal salutation set the wrong tone. She crumpled up the page and started over.

Dearest Caro . . .

She wanted Wakefield's alleged fiancée to believe the letter—which would be succinct, explicit, and anonymous—had been sent by a concerned friend. She brooded and deliberated, then dipped her pen once more.

. . . *I endlessly debated as to whether I should write you, and ultimately, I couldn't keep quiet. You have such a great affection for John, and I decided you would want to know. I am incredibly worried about what is occurring during his extended visit to Wakefield Manor* . . .

She read the opening lines, read them again, then smiled malevolently.

"Perfect," she murmured and continued on.

Ian lounged on the sofa in the library, swirling the whisky in his glass, and glaring at his half brother's back, but the intense regard couldn't goad him into turning around. John was lingering by the window and staring across the rear lawn, unduly intrigued by whatever he beheld.

Recently, he'd changed. It was just after the noon hour, and he was sober. The boredom that habitually plagued him had vanished, his personal demons conspicuously trounced. Their cadre of acquaintances had retired to London on schedule, but John hadn't grumbled about the tranquil pall that had descended once they'd gone.

Ian couldn't figure it out, but he wasn't about to question the boon. Or complain. There were so few things that made his sibling content, and Ian welcomed any development that would elevate his mood.

"Georgina stopped by my bedchamber before she left." Absurdly, he was dying to confess, as well as to see what sort of response he'd garner with the news.

"What for?"

"To give me a French kiss."

Casually, John peered over his shoulder. "What did she want from you?"

"What makes you think she wasn't merely inflamed by my fabulous anatomy?"

"Hah! She loathes you." He laughed at the notion, which was hilarious considering the state of Ian's and Georgina's mutual dislike. "I know her too well. She never does anything unless she expects something in return."

Too true. That's why Ian hated her. She was a mercenary. "She wanted me to talk you into letting her stay here in the country."

"Did she say why?"

"She was afraid that if you were separated too long, you'd realize you didn't miss her, and you'd boot her ass out the door."

"I wouldn't, simply because it would be such a nuisance to replace her." He shrugged. "Besides, she's extremely talented with that mouth of hers. I wouldn't want to forego that bit of delight."

"She was definitely proficient."

"Did you enjoy it?"

"I didn't allow her to finish."

"Why not?"

"Because I had no desire to scheme against you."
Not with her anyway.

"You could have done the deed but not told me."

"It crossed my mind, but it didn't seem sporting."

"Who cares what's *sporting* when a woman has her
lips wrapped around you?"

"I'll remember that next time."

They both grinned, an identical quirking of their
cheeks.

Then, lost in thought, John spun around to scrutinize
the yard again, and Ian assessed him as he leaned against
the window frame. The silence was companionable,
making Ian glad he'd broached the topic of Georgina,
and relieved that John hadn't been royally pissed, but
how sad that John had no staunch feelings about her.

Gad, she'd been his paramour for over two years.
What a waste of cash and effort!

Just when it appeared that the conversation wouldn't
resume, John peculiarly queried, "What do you suppose
your mother saw in our father?"

"Besides that he was handsome, rich, and could
charm the bark off a tree?"

"Yes. Besides all that."

John chuckled, and Ian rolled his eyes at how thick
his brother could be.

Ian's mother had had a three-month revel with the
dashing, dynamic Douglas Clayton, when he'd traveled
to Scotland on a protracted hunting trip. According to
stories that clan members had shared, she'd been young
and foolish, and very much in love with the charismatic
foreigner, and Ian hadn't begrudged her her conduct,
though he'd never told her so. She'd died in childbirth.

"Money and status," he baldly pronounced. "What
do you suppose yours saw in him?"

"*Touché*," John retorted.

John's mother had wed Douglas because her family had commanded her to, the union having been contracted during her childhood, but the underlying reasons were the same. With affluent men, they always were.

Ridiculously, John inquired, "Was your mother happy with him?"

"It was a ninety-day lark."

John winced. "Sorry."

"You know what he was like."

"Aye. A bounder and an ass."

"And those were his best qualities." Ian sampled his whisky. "In fact, as you dig into the various estate books, I'm wondering if you'll find expenditures for more of his children."

"He might have sired others?" John was aghast at the prospect.

"Well, he went to Scotland every autumn. For decades. My uncles inform me that he was quite randy."

"Oh, Jesus." John rubbed a weary hand over his face. "So there might be dozens of little *Ians* running around the Highlands?"

"If you're not careful"—he smiled wickedly—"you might end up supplying shelter for an entire household of people just like me."

"I'd shoot myself first."

He flashed Ian a comical glower, feigning pique, but though he acted like a malingerer, and griped about his responsibilities, he didn't shirk the important ones.

"I'd never let you," Ian joked, "because I couldn't bear to learn who'd inherit after you. I'd likely have to start being polite to someone more offensive than you, and I couldn't bend over much more than I have. It's not in my nature."

"The heir is my second cousin Henry. Or so I've been notified."

"That dolt?" Ian gave a mock shudder. "Shouldn't you be setting up your nursery?"

John cringed. "God, but you sounded just like Father—risen up from the grave—when you said that."

"What a haunting that would be!" Ian agreed. "But you know he was correct."

"Who the hell would I marry?" John grimaced. "I take that back: Who the hell would marry *me*?"

"Anybody would. You can have your bloody pick, so stop being difficult."

"I'm not jesting," John contended. "I truly need your advice." With a last, yearning glance at the yard, he came over and sat across from Ian on the other sofa. "Of all the suitable women we know, who would you suggest?"

"Well, how about Caroline? She's crazy about you—when I can't begin to imagine why—and her father insists the engagement is binding."

Lady Caroline's father, the Earl of Derby, had negotiated the match with Douglas when she was a babe. Caroline's spouse was to have been John's older brother, James, and when he'd died, the two pompous men had sought to obligate John—without seeking his opinion—but John hadn't been inclined to honor James's betrothal. His repudiation had been the cause of interminable strife and discord between father and son.

"Will you listen to me? I'm *not* marrying Caroline, and that's final."

"Why not? She's beautiful, sweet, educated. What's not to like?"

"I've known her all my life, Ian," John grouched. "Fucking her would be like fucking my sister."

"Oh," he sagely pontificated, "so that's the problem."

"Precisely. Could you conceive of instructing her to

go down on you? She'd quake herself to death."

Actually, Ian could absolutely picture it. In his view, Caroline was a repressed, ripe spinster, who was prime for the plucking, but there was no convincing John. "She might surprise you."

"I doubt it. I mean, honestly"—he was up again, pacing, then marching over to gawk out the window—"could you see yourself hiking through the woods with her, maybe having her up against a tree, or tumbling her in the grass? Her hair would get mussed, and she'd have an apoplexy."

"I thought that your kind was constantly in pursuit of a chaste, biddable wife."

"My *kind*? Ian, how do you come up with such rubbish?"

"Seriously," he said. "Why would her lack of sexual spontaneity matter? You could bed her a few times a year, she'd dutifully give you the sons that you require, and you'd still have Georgina—or someone like her—to perform whatever nasty acts appeal to you."

"I should grit my teeth and forge ahead even though Caroline and I would both be miserable?"

"Certainly." Although it was a mystery how any man could anticipate that copulating with Caroline would be a chore. If she'd stoop low enough to look in his direction, he'd jump at the chance to have her, but it would never happen. She was such a snob that she pretended he was invisible. "Then you wouldn't have to fuss over your choice. Caroline's family would cease their pestering, you could go about your business free and unencumbered. You'd have it all. It's that have-your-cake-and-eat-it-too nonsense."

"That would be a hell of a way to commence, don't you think? Marrying somebody I never wanted, merely to get it over with?"

Ian discreetly evaluated him. Was John a romantic deep down? Was he searching for fondness and devotion in a bride? If so, he wouldn't find them in that river of vipers that occupied the marriage market in which their father's demise had forced him to swim.

"You hope to marry for love?" Ian prodded cautiously. "Is that your plan?"

"No," John scoffed. "I'd just hate to land myself in the type of relationship my parents had. Father had a paramour lurking behind every door, and my mother was heartbroken because of it."

"Really?" Ian had never heard John mention as much, wasn't aware that John harbored this observation about his parents.

"In many ways, your mother was lucky that Father didn't stick around."

"Perhaps." Ian hadn't contemplated the possibility. What would it have been like if Douglas had stayed on? It was a fascinating puzzle to ponder.

"I want to be happy." John was more testy than the discourse warranted. All that sobriety was wearing on him. "Is that too much to ask?"

"No. But your craving of contentment can't preclude your marrying and siring an heir."

"What time is it?" John impulsively posed, completely changing the subject.

"Ten minutes after one. Why?"

"I believe I'll take a walk outside."

"A walk?" Ian echoed, incredulous.

"Yes."

"Are you feeling all right?"

"Just grand." On observing Ian's skepticism, he added, "Can't a bloke take a bloody stroll in the fresh air without the whole world commenting?"

"So who's commenting? Go! I don't care what you do."

John stomped out, as Ian watched, curious as to whether they were fighting and why.

He strained to discern the footsteps that would ensure John had departed then, on stealthy feet, he sneaked to the door and locked it. He waited, holding his breath, then he went to the desk, and centered himself in the large chair.

Removing a small key from his pocket, he fiddled with the secured drawer, then eased it open. As he'd guessed, the estate ledgers were inside, and he lugged them out, and arranged them in a tidy pile. Eagerly, he located the book containing the most current entries, and he scanned the rows of numbers.

CHAPTER NINE

THE instant the library door shut behind them, John reached for Emma and braced her against it. He wasn't about to let her bat her pretty lashes and persuade him to traipse off on another expedition to interview his tenants. Though he couldn't figure out how it happened, he couldn't refuse her requests, and when she compelled him to accompany her, he couldn't say no.

Well, he'd had enough. They weren't going anywhere, except across the room to lie down on the couch.

He gripped her shapely thighs and lifted her, bunching up her skirts and widening her thighs so that he could lean in to steady himself at her center, so that she could wrap her legs around his waist.

She'd worn her straw bonnet, and he dipped under the brim, zealously taking her lips in a torrid kiss as he fumbled with the bow so he could untie it and yank it off. The blasted hat regularly irritated him, shielding her so that he only caught occasional glimpses of her smile whenever she peeked up at him, and he nearly ripped it to pieces in his haste to have it gone.

Her hair was down, the curly locks secured with a single ribbon, as if she'd resigned herself to the fact that the assignation would end with his running his fingers through it, and she hadn't wanted to place herself in the position of having to pin it up when she was in a rush. The ribbon was easily removed, and he tossed it away so that her fabulous tresses cascaded over her shoulders.

As he sifted through the soft strands, he cherished the gesture she'd made, recognizing it as a compromise, an admission that what sparked between them couldn't be ignored or avoided. It was too potent, too overwhelming, and trying to fight it was futile.

He knew because he'd rigorously endeavored to combat the burgeoning temptation, but when he wasn't with her, he couldn't concentrate on anything but how slowly the clock was ticking, on how soon the moment would arrive so that he could be with her.

On those afternoons when she didn't show up by the hour of one, he'd be frantic with worry, and as she'd finally come marching across his rear yard, he'd feel exuberant. Usually, he didn't even mind as she dragged him off to convene with his crofters. He'd enthusiastically escort her, entranced and stupidly anxious to bask in her company in any fashion she'd allow.

The innocuous visits around the estate were wretched. She was affable and courteous, doing naught to suggest that she might be amenable to seduction, or that she was thinking about any subject beyond their task, while he could focus upon nothing but how rapidly he could get her alone, and what he intended to do with her once he could locate a sequestered spot in the forest.

In front of others, he donned the role of aloof aristocrat, pretending that he and Emma had no connection other than for business purposes. She'd tease him unmercifully, gazing at him with a particular amount of naïveté and artifice, or brashly slipping her hand into his arm as they strolled side by side.

The subtle touching made him crazy, and he hadn't decided if she was doing it deliberately, or if she was merely prone to excessive corporeal contact, but whatever her motives, she'd impelled him past his limits.

After their latest appointment at a crofter's shack

had concluded——with his once again revoking his eviction decision, and Emma sweetly kissing him on the cheek and telling him she hadn't had any doubt that he would——he'd been so aroused that he'd pondered whether it was possible for a man to burst the seams on his trousers. He'd been that hard and ready. But as they'd sauntered into the woods, she'd declared she had important chores to complete, and she couldn't dally with him as he'd hoped.

With a brief exchange of a few dangerous kisses, she'd vanished like smoke, racing off to the responsibilities that hampered her from tending to his rising ardor.

He was irked that she declined to do his bidding, that she felt her personal concerns equaled or superseded his own. In his world, he asked people to jump, and they said, how high? They never argued or maintained that they were too busy.

At the same juncture, he was amazed that she was strong enough to rebuff his edicts. With the exception of Ian, no one disagreed with him. He was a dictator in a universe where others grasped that their province was to make him happy, to blithely and cheerfully carry out his commands.

She didn't comprehend this principle, or if she did, she chose not to abide by it. When he tried to point out his eminence, she'd laugh and inform him he couldn't always get his way——when he didn't see why not——and that he was horridly spoiled. Which was true, but it didn't mean she had to so vigorously flaunt her independence.

For some bizarre reason that he was still striving to unravel, he wanted her to rely on him, to be beholden, to be inextricably bound, but the more he attempted to constrain her, the more distance she imposed. Instead of

their advancing on to full sex—as any sane chap would
have anticipated after their indecent romp in the forest—
their encounters grew more and more chaste, until he
was convinced he'd explode if he didn't alter the direction in which they were traveling.

Each day, they would assemble in his library, but
before he had a chance to so much as hug her, she would
maneuver him outside so that she could introduce him
to another of her poverty-stricken neighbors. While he
had to admit that he was coming to enjoy their lengthy
walks, that he treasured the fresh air and the balmy summer temperatures, that he was enthralled to view the estate and the inhabitants' difficulties through her eyes, he
wasn't about to persist with their celibate friendship.

He was fed up with her evasion and subterfuge. She
had a knack for trifling with him, for making him believe
that an amorous event would transpire, but she constantly escaped before he could initiate any ardent activity. Reticence was not in his nature, but he'd played her
game, and he was weary of it. He wanted what she kept
promising with every one of her sly smiles, with every
tempting sway of her curvaceous hips.

Deceptively, he'd lulled her into presuming that she
could usher him where she wished, but she was about
to learn a tidbit that few people knew about him: He
could be nudged and prodded when the end result didn't
signify. Others deemed him to be a slacker or apathetic
as to what occurred around him, when in truth, he could
be relentless if the outcome was meaningful. His dilemma was that there weren't many issues about which
he was inclined to expend any energy.

Apparently—though he couldn't have explained
why—Emma Fitzgerald had become one of those topics
about which he cared deeply, so he would be ruthless in
getting what he wanted from her. His quiet acquiescence

was over, and their meetings would now progress according to his dictates. Not hers.

He wouldn't permit her to leave without his getting the opportunity to make love to her. He wouldn't put off for another second what he should have insisted upon days earlier.

How had she bewitched him so thoroughly? Why had he yielded to the infatuation? Where would it lead?

"Open for me." His tongue was toying with her lips, demanding entrance, and she obeyed, folding her arms around him and holding him close.

Down below, his cock was rock-solid, his balls clenched and aching and, unable to stand the suspense, he speculated as to how quickly he could be inside her, how marvelous it would feel, how tight she would be, and if—once he'd had her a time or two—some of his infernal longing might abate.

He was so bloody intrigued as to what it would be like to copulate with her. Why was he so desperate to find out how it would be?

He massaged her breasts, began to unbutton her dress but, as he'd suspected she might, she tried to stop him.

"Wakefield, no." She pulled away, tipping her head so that he kissed across her cheek, down her neck. "One of my neighbors is expecting us."

"We're not going out today."

Hefting her up, he had her off balance, and she yelped and slapped at his shoulders.

"Put me down, you beast."

"No."

She weighed no more than a feather, so it was a simple feat to cart her to the couch, to recline on his back, to bring her with him. Her knees were situated on either side of his lap, her skirt rucked up, her loins perched above his own. His phallus was pulsating, awaiting her to lower herself so that her privates impacted with his.

From prior experience, he knew she didn't wear drawers, so her pussy would be bare, would be hot and slippery against the placard of his pants, and he couldn't tolerate the space separating them. Yet she didn't make any move to exacerbate their conjunction, so he clasped her flanks and tilted her so that she was slanting forward and powerless to prevent the inevitable.

The shock of feeling her crotch to his ignited an eruption of stimulation that blasted through what little was left of his chivalrous tendencies. He yearned to rip away her clothes, to pin her down and take her in a rough, unbridled mating. She goaded his manly senses to outrageous, hazardous heights, that had him recklessly eager to have her, and damn the consequences.

The palm of her hand was propped on the arm of the sofa, and she glared at him with an exasperated look that should have annoyed him, but didn't. Her face was so expressive, and he never tired of studying the emotion that swept across it. He was amused by her aggravation, oddly tickled that she was about to enumerate all the ways he was a bounder and a scapegrace.

Throughout his life, he'd been told how despicable he was in his habits, how he couldn't fill his brother's shoes. The message had grown so tedious that he'd quit listening.

Surprisingly, he wasn't rankled by her complaints. She had an ability to communicate her castigations in a manner that made him want to heed her, that made him want—for a change—to better himself so that she would be gladdened by his rectified conduct. He reveled in pleasing her, in seeing her smile and knowing that she was elated because of something he'd accomplished just for her.

Her gratitude and delight over the most trivial deeds were so genuine that he conjectured that few people had ever done her a good turn. She was lauded for helping others, but it didn't appear that many of her generously lavished favors were returned.

He was thrilled that he had the resources to coddle her as she deserved, and he longed to aid her more extensively. She inspired him to all sorts of out-of-character benevolence.

"What are you doing?" she scolded as he manipulated her nipples.

"I want to make love to you."

"But I have plans for us, and I've—"

He settled a finger to her lips, silencing her.

"No."

She scrutinized him, and he could read every agonized thought skittering through her devious, charming head as she tried to deduce how she could coerce him outside so that physical interaction would be impossible. Previously, her ploy had succeeded, but she'd exhausted his patience. His level of titillation had exceeded his willingness to indolently tag along to wherever she went.

"I don't want to do this," she ultimately contended.

"I don't care."

She bristled with irritation. "You're a pompous bully, Wakefield. I don't know why I keep spending time with you."

"Because you're crazy about me."

"Don't flatter yourself."

He dropped her further, so that he was nestled in her cleavage, so that he could root and nuzzle between the two dangling mounds. He tormented her nipples, squeezing them firmly, and she hissed out a breath, though she struggled valiantly not to let him hear it.

A pattern had developed between them. She flirted and vamped, tantalizing him, while contriving to remain out of his reach. An elusive barrier was hindering her, and he couldn't conceive of why. She was an exceptionally passionate female, her libidinous vitality so blatant that—to him, at least—it seemed to shimmer around her. He'd never witnessed anything like it, and he was obsessed, smitten, fascinated, and he couldn't hold his nefarious proclivities in check.

"It will be wonderful, Em, you know it will."

"I've never said otherwise."

He took her nipple between his teeth, rolling it around, and the fabric of her dress and chemise rubbed enticingly. She arched her back and groaned.

"Why are you afraid?"

"I'm not."

"Liar." He meandered to her other breast, dabbling and provoking. "If I don't know what's wrong, I can't fix it."

"Nothing's *wrong*."

He sat her on her haunches. She was so sincere, and he was coming to understand her so well. If he could see her eyes, she couldn't fabricate. "I'm not without a bit of expertise at erotic diversion."

"Don't remind me; I detest it when you do."

"You can't hide how much you desire me."

"I don't," she claimed.

He ignored her denial. "So we're proceeding."

"You'd force yourself on me?"

"I don't think *force* will be necessary."

Proving himself correct, he slid a hand under her dress, and let it glide along her cleft, then he entered her with two fingers. She was shamelessly, exhilaratingly damp, and the discovery lurched his own state of arousal to a drastic peak. "You are so wet. So ready for me."

Blushing, her cheeks burned a furious crimson "You don't play fair."

"No, I don't."

"I don't want this," she mournfully alleged. "I don't want *you.*"

She was so miserable over the prospect that he snuggled her to his chest, her breasts flattened to his own, her stomach relaxed into him. He couldn't bear to have her so forlorn, as if the notion of engaging in sexual congress with him were painful, and he consoled her, soothing her as one might a distraught child.

Though restraint was torture, he moderated his pace, steadied himself, and stepped himself back from the brink. As he calmed, he was able to concentrate on what was happening, to recall how much he liked the cuddling, too.

Formerly, he hadn't lain with a woman solely for the joy of holding her. From the beginning, when he'd bedded his first tavern maid at age fourteen, his carnal trysts had been instigated for the exclusive purpose of fleshly alleviation. No greater design had ever motivated him. Why waste time on foreplay, on courting or wooing? His partners were welcomed to his bed so long as they satisfied him. And they did, without question.

With Emma, the rules were different. He relished embracing her, watching over her. That afternoon in the woods, after she'd had such a staggering orgasm, she'd fallen asleep in his arms, and he'd held her for two hours.

Over the years, he'd had an occasional paramour who'd doze off after the fireworks, but he wouldn't stay when they did. Without fail, he'd slipped out and departed, yet with Emma, he'd never considered going, and by tarrying, he'd learned a lesson about the simple pleasures: There was no need to race to the end. Most of the contentment could be found in the protracted, languid journey.

"Who do you rush off to be with when you leave me?" While typically, he was a selfish man who rarely pondered his lovers' circumstances, he was peculiarly, inordinately curious about her.

"My family. My mother and younger sister, Jane. Mother is ill, and one of us must always be with her. When I'm out, Jane is alone, and she's only eleven."

He remembered the estate agent's prattle about her father's passing, about their dire straits afterward, but as was his wont, he hadn't paid much attention. "There's just the three of you?"

"Yes."

"How do you manage?"

"I work, you silly oaf. How do you suppose?"

"Work at what?"

Sitting up, she gawked at him as if he were an imbecile. "Various tasks. I tend the sick, minister to the dying, I deliver babies—"

"You deliver babies?" She was so competent; he could absolutely picture it.

She wiggled her brows. "I have many talents."

"You certainly do." He ran his thumbs across her palms. They were callused, rough—a working woman's hands—and the complete opposite of the soft, creamy hands of the highborn ladies with whom he normally consorted. "I hate that you work so hard."

"Why? A bit of sweat and toil never killed anyone." She tweaked his chin. "You should try it sometime."

"Very funny."

"Besides, how would we eat if I didn't?"

She casually threw out the statement, as if scrounging for her supper were a common occurrence and of no import, but he was gravely disturbed by the remark.

Many perilous replies were suddenly poised on the tip of his tongue. Replies as to how he would like to help her, to protect her, to look after her.

An impulsive offer of financial assistance was so near to being voiced aloud that he had to gulp it down, lest he utter a commitment he wasn't prepared to make.

The abrupt urge was like a tangible object, and he was frightened and confused by its intensity. With one problematic mistress plaguing him, he didn't need another, so what exactly was he contemplating? While he wanted many things from her—amiable companionship, lively conversation, terrific sex—they were temporary. He wasn't about to acquire an inane emotional attachment, which definitely meant he wasn't equipped to make a pledge as to support.

They were at the commencement of a brief, amusing fling, and when it was over, he had a superlative life in town to which he was enthusiastic to return. Emma did not, and never would, have any place by his side in the city. For pity's sake, she was a rural do-gooder, who thrived on acting as a nursemaid for the infirm, as a champion for the downtrodden. He couldn't take her to London; his arrogant, vicious, unaccepting peers would devour her.

Shaking off his fleeting insanity, he clutched her hands in his and rested them on his chest.

"Touch me, Emma." He guided her in lazy circles. "Touch me all over."

For once, she didn't argue. With her seductive, slender fingers, she undid his shirt, starting at the top, then descending to the waistband of his trousers, until the lapels were loose, and she could reach inside to caress him. The sensation of skin to skin was so dramatic that he felt as if he'd been jolted with a bolt of lightning.

She riffled about, then bent down to burrow her nose across the furry pile of hair.

"I love your chest," she said.

"Feel free to indulge."

Wickedly, she chuckled as she rooted and sniffed, flicking her tongue in tiny strokes that led to his nipple. She laved the pebbled nub, making his stomach muscles clench, his cock throb, as she sucked and teased, nipping at it with her teeth.

He pulled her closer, spurring her on with murmured praise, and she increased the pressure until he could scarcely tolerate the stimulation. She was thoroughly attuned to him and perceived his need to compose himself, and she sat back, appearing sly and wise, as though she comprehended all the secrets men tried to hide from women but never could.

"Do you want me, Wakefield?"

What a coquette! She seemed so chaste, so innocent, but she had a ribald streak that drove him wild, whenever he was lucky enough to coax it to the surface.

"You know I do." She was twirling his nipples, making him writhe and squirm. "Take off your dress."

"No."

She'd refused, but he was unbuttoning the front anyway, and he pushed the bodice apart and eased it off her shoulders. He finessed her chemise in the same fashion so that the fabric was bunched around her waist, her breasts unconfined and exposed.

"My, my!" he complimented admiringly. "Look at you!"

Like a shy virgin, she crossed her arms over her bosom. On observing her modesty—wholly misplaced after all they'd accomplished so far!—he laughed and forced her hands away so that he had an unimpeded view.

"Don't stare at me like that."

"Emma, you're so pretty."

Blushing a deeper shade of red, she momentarily struggled, striving to elude him so that she could cover herself, but he wouldn't let her, and after a brief wrestling contest, she gave up.

Until now, he'd foolishly imagined that he favored voluptuous women, with large, heavy breasts that made for an intriguing pillow after a bout of raucous love-play, but he'd been mistaken.

He liked them smaller, just the right size to fill his hands. Hers were impeccable, pale and delicately rounded, the areolae a soft pink. The nipples were taut, peaked, and he rubbed his thumbs across them, the motion causing her to shift her loins, to rock herself across his phallus as he'd been longing to have her do.

He tugged her down, and her upper torso connected with his for the first time, their bared flesh pressed together, no clothing to inhibit perception. Clasping her hips, he moved her so that her breasts were merged to his, her nipples tickled by his chest hair. Dipping down, he took after one of the succulent tips, nursing at it until he could feel her tension mount.

There was a battle raging inside her. Mentally, she didn't want to be doing this with him, but physically, she couldn't resist. Her body was crying for what he was lavishing on her, and the physical was winning out. She couldn't prevent herself from succumbing.

His hand slid between them, to her core. She was so aroused that he didn't bother with any niceties. He proceeded directly to her clit and tossed her over the edge.

"John—" she moaned.

"I'm here," he assured her, holding her as she soared to the heavens and beyond.

Her orgasm was more extreme than the initial one he'd achieved in the woods—if that was possible. Her anatomy was rigid, as she strained and wrenched against

the potent agitation, and a wail of despair erupted. H
captured it, swallowing down her groan, lest a servan
hear her, and suspect what they were actually doing i
the locked room.

As she retreated from the pinnacle, her muscles re
laxed, growing weighty with satiation, and she wa
stretched out, molded to him, and they were a flawless
fit. She was the correct height, her head nestled unde
his chin, and she was curvaceous and pliant where h
was flat and compact, brawn to lean, bowed to straigh
It seemed as if she'd been created with him in mind. A
perfect match. An ideal mate . . .

Wrong choice of words! Fidgeting uncomfortably
he speculated why such absurd sentiments kept flittin
about whenever he was in her company.

If he was searching for a *mate,* it was in the im
mediate, carnal sense only. Despite how people wer
clamoring and laying bets, he wasn't in the market fo
a bride. If he had been, he could have married Carolin
in the time it took to have a special license drafted.

When he eventually broke down and made a deci
sion, the woman he selected would be distinctly divers
from Emma Fitzgerald. He'd pick a wife who wa
trained to her role, one who wouldn't begrudge him h
faults, who would politely pretend he had no bad habit
and who wasn't in some godawful hurry to shape hii
into a better man.

He wouldn't shackle himself to a female who wa
constantly chastising him, denoting his shortcoming
and railing at him over his blunders. A fellow coul
drive himself mad trying to live up to Emma's loft
expectations. .

As their ardent kiss ended, her cheeks were flushe
her heart pounding furiously at the base of her neck.

"How do you do that to me?" She was genuinel

erplexed as to how proficient he was at goading her
nto a climax. He was amazed, himself, at how readily
he surrendered.

"You're easy," he jested, and the instant he uttered
he quip, he regretted it. She froze, a combination of
orror and dismay marring her brow.

Often, she seemed immensely experienced at sexual
ffairs, but then her mien would alter and she'd appear
) be a disconcerted virgin. Erotic banter was beyond
er, but why would it be? With how adept she was, her
eticence was ludicrous.

She was an enigma, and he couldn't solve the riddle
hat made up her entire self. Who was the real Emma?

"I don't mean to be. Truly I don't." She was ap-
alled by her libidinous proclivities and apparently be-
eved he was denigrating her for exhibiting them. "I try
) control myself, and I—"

"Ssh," he soothed. "I was joking."

"You don't think I'm a wanton?"

Well, yes, but he could hardly say so. He didn't nec-
ssarily consider a modicum of wantonness to be an ad-
erse trait in a woman, and he liked every corrupt,
centious bone in her body. In fact, if he could figure
ut how to nudge her so that she journeyed beyond wan-
)n and into the realm of complete abandon, he'd be
cstatic.

"No, Em. Don't be ridiculous."

"If I'm not loose, then why does it happen so fast
nd so, so—" Evidently, the question frequently vexed
er, and he took it seriously. They were tiptoeing around
he gist of why she regularly reined herself in—just
hen things were getting interesting.

"We share an affinity, Em. But it's good that we do.
)on't worry about it."

Tentatively, she nodded. "What produces it?"

"I don't know. It's one of life's great mysteries.

We're compatible—in a physical way—but there's n
explanation for it."

"It's a curse."

"Or a blessing, depending on your point of view."

"A curse," she repeated. "Definitely a curse."

He grinned, in total disagreement, and he flexed h
hips, his untended, inflated phallus arching up to vivid
notify them that only she had been sated.

Remarkably, for once, she didn't stumble abou
grabbing for her clothes and frantically arranging h
hair, so that she could race out the door as she routine
had in the past.

She was studying him carefully, and it looked as
she'd crossed an emotional bridge. There was a glea
in her eye, and a wily smile creased her cheeks, as
she knew something he didn't.

"I want to take you in my hands." She gripped t
waistband of his trousers. "In my mouth, too."

"Oh, Jesus."

"Would you like it if I did?"

Evaluating her slim, skilled fingers, her pouting rul
lips, he recalled every naughty, sensual detail of th
afternoon in his dressing chamber, when he'd lured h
in as he'd soaked naked in his bathing tub. She'd m
ticulously washed him, running a cloth over his heate
skin, his private parts.

With a minimum of cajoling, she'd effortlessly in
pelled him into a jeopardous lather, had roused him
a critical zenith. That encounter had involved only h
hand. He didn't know how he'd survive if she pleasur
him with that sexy, sassy mouth of hers.

"You'll kill me if you put your mouth on me."

"Really?" Laughing, she licked her lips. "Let's s
if I do."

She opened the top button on his pants and scoote
down.

CHAPTER TEN

EMMA didn't pause, because she didn't want to nervously reflect on what she was about to do. When she'd begun this idiotic charade, she'd had such noble intentions, had been so certain that she could garner what she wanted from the worldly viscount by playing games and leading him on, but her strategy was a dismal failure, her scheme foiled. She could no more resist him and his advances than she could stop the sun from rising.

What a fool she was! She'd had one, fleeting romantic spree with a boy when she was seventeen, and because of it, she'd convinced herself that she had the maturity and sophistication to go head-to-head with a bounder like John Clayton.

The attraction she'd had for adolescent Charlie all those years ago was so tepid that she didn't dare refer to it as arousal. By contrast, her feelings for Wakefield were in another league entirely, so potent and overwhelming that she didn't understand how she could be expected to control them, and it occurred to her that this was the reason young ladies were chaperoned, guarded, and counseled as to their virtue.

Others knew, as she had not, that a person could experience magnetism so intense that there was no way to fight it, that desire could be all-consuming, indiscriminate, that it could sweep away wisdom, caution, and discretion.

Better than any virgin in England, she comprehended the results of sexual intercourse. She'd been present at the birth of many unwanted babies, and she had no illusions about how they were created. Yet despite her excess of knowledge, at this very moment, with Wakefield half-naked, and herself isolated with him where no one would ever find out what they were about to do, she was prepared to progress to any reckless conclusion without regard to the consequences.

No wonder women regularly got themselves into trouble!

Since the afternoon they'd dallied in the forest, she hadn't been able to concentrate on anything but him and how badly she yearned for them to rush to perdition, once again.

She couldn't eat, couldn't sleep, as she'd incessantly debated how she had to avoid him at all costs. But even as she reprimanded herself, she couldn't stay away. He was a shining star in her monotonous universe, a brilliant sun to her dull moon. His presence at Wakefield Manor had delivered excitement and joy, where there was nothing but misery and despair, so she couldn't prohibit herself from visiting him.

Mightily, she'd striven to keep him at bay, to hold her own licentious impulses in check. On this occasion too she'd planned to be strong—she really and truly had—but when he'd dragged her into the library, where he'd locked the door and sequestered them inside, her wicked nature had surged to the fore with such an urgency that she couldn't tamp it down.

He'd said that what they were doing wasn't wrong, that she wasn't depraved, and she was so relieved to have him discount her corrupt tendencies. Her lust for debauchery raged below the surface, luring her to immorality, coaxing her to vice, and she was ready to throw off the restraints that fettered her.

The orgasm he'd given her had been so stunning that she'd nearly wept from the force of it, and she wanted to supply him with some of the same dazzling gratification. So far, she'd managed to dodge his requests for carnal assuagement, and he'd been kind and patient about her dawdling, but she no longer wanted him calm and composed. She wanted him testy, chafing, at the edge and anxious to jump off.

Gliding down, she blazed a trail down his stomach, tarrying to nip at his navel, then she traveled on, to the front of his trousers, where his cockstand was so deliciously manifest. Nuzzling at him through the cloth, she rooted and bit, stroking and fondling him, then she reached for the top button and slipped it through the hole. The next one followed and the next, until the placard was undone, and all she needed to do was push it aside to have him bared, in her hands, in her mouth.

Could she do it?

She knew that women habitually performed the indecent procedure, just as she knew that men enjoyed it above all else, so Wakefield would be thrilled by her lack of inhibition. Where he was concerned, there were no confines to her conduct. She wanted to savor and touch and smell, and she was inanely enthusiastic to make him happy.

What did this portend? When had his contentment become so significant?

Until this instant, she'd viewed their relationship as a marvelous lark, a spot of exotic fun in her dreary existence, but of a sudden, his pleasure was vital, and her ability to bring him satisfaction and serenity was paramount.

Was this love?

The very idea was terrifying.

Not prone to doing anything halfway, if she fell for

the scoundrel, it would be a total, complete, wretched plunge. As was her wont, she would give all to a man with whom she had nothing in common, who was rich and titled, and who would return to London as soon as his business in the country was finished.

She'd never see him again, would never hear from him again, and she would be left behind, forlorn and bereft, and devastated at having to carry on without him.

If she lost her heart, how would she persevere?

The risk of succumbing was too dire. She needed to be clear on her established priorities, to focus on what she could accomplish, and to remember what she couldn't. Her arrangement with Wakefield had been entered into for the exclusive purpose of helping her neighbors. Whatever privately transpired was transitory and not connected to her loftier goals.

As she'd hoped to delight in some of his fantastic amorous attention, he'd provided her with the perfect opportunity to indulge, but she couldn't forget that it was only a naughty fling, a brief romp, and would never be more than that. No one would ever know what she was about—except herself—and what a luscious memory to have long after his departure!

Sliding her fingers under the placard of his pants, she shoved at the fabric, and his cock jutted up, extending out to her. Red and pulsating, his life's blood pounding through the ropy veins, it seemed angry, alive, with a will of its own, and it demanded recognition, handling, satiation.

She ran her fingers through the bristly hair that nested his erection. It was rougher, darker than the blond hair on his head, and she burrowed her nose in it, rubbing her cheek across his lower abdomen. Each subtle shift had him flinching, his stomach muscles clenching as he restlessly endured her exploration, but she didn't caress him where he needed it most.

Finally, she took pity, gripping him in her fist, massaging her thumb over the sensitive end, and he hissed out a breath. Clutching him tightly, she had him flexing and pressing, but she was too hampered in her movements and didn't have the space to tend him as she wanted.

She tugged his trousers off his hips, so she could behold the length of his phallus, the two sacs dangling below, and she cupped him in her palm, then bent down. Laving him with her tongue, she started at the bottom of his turgid rod and advanced toward the crown.

As she hadn't formerly attempted the feat, she wasn't exactly positive of how to go about it, but she vivaciously set herself to the task, letting Wakefield be her guide. By judging his reactions, she could deduce what he liked best, and with each passing minute, he grew more strained, his body tense, his cock rigid.

What power she had over him! He was at her mercy. How stupendous it was to dominate and subordinate the jaded knave.

Arriving at the tip, she licked at his sexual juice. He tasted so fine, his essence tempting her on a primal level, and he made her ache and hunger in an acute fashion. Her nipples were taut and in need of manipulation, between her legs she was wet and throbbing. She wanted to swallow him whole, to take him into herself, to meld with him forever.

She gazed up his lank torso, and he was staring at her with a fire in his eye that enchanted and provoked. There was only him, the quiet room, and the magnificent expectancy of what was about to happen.

"I want to know you like this," she declared.

"Are you sure, love?"

The endearment slithered by and, because it was so dangerous, she tried to pretend that he hadn't uttered it. The word ignited a swarm of butterflies deep in her belly. They cascaded out, flitting across her nerve endings, confusing her, rattling her.

A thousand frantic questions darted around in her mind: Why had he said it? What did he mean? Was it simply an appellation he impetuously expressed to any female imprudent enough to lie down with him? Or—a most sinister thought!—had he voiced it because he was developing profound feelings for her?

What if he was?

The notion was so preposterous, and so exceptional, that she couldn't credit it. Extreme affection on his part was impossible, inconceivable, yet she found the concept to be extraordinary, and she could picture herself collapsing into that word, ominously wishing for it to be true so fervently that she drove herself mad with the magnitude of her craving.

Ignoring its gravity, she declined to ascribe it any import. There was only one thing he wanted from her, only one thing of any interest she had to confer. That was her body, and she was ardent and burning to share it with him. Sexual congress was the sole motive behind their interaction, and she had to be careful, lest she allow her lonely heart to wander where it should not go.

"Aye, I'm sure," she told him.

"I'm so hard for you. I don't know if I can slow my pace or hold back."

"Don't hinder yourself on my account." She intended to luxuriate in every decadent, depraved aspect of the maneuver. "I want it to be spectacular for you."

"Trust me, lass, it will be." He settled himself on the cushions. "No matter how it goes."

The position centered his cock directly beneath her

mouth, and she grazed the end, then opened wide and took him inside. Immediately, he began to thrust, not permitting her to adjust or acclimate. Obviously, he was accustomed to the deed, the awkwardness, the crudeness, and he was unaware that she hadn't previously engaged in the lewd pursuit.

He didn't constrain his baser proclivities, and he paid no heed to her untried condition, but she couldn't blame him. From the moment they'd met, she'd acted like a whore and had done naught to furnish him with a higher opinion of her character.

Absurdly, she'd been anticipating something mundane and sedate, polite and civil. But as constantly ensued during her trysts with Wakefield, she was surprised at how the reality varied from her fantasies. The escapade was contrary to what she'd imagined, bawdier, turbulent and risqué.

Ashamed as she was to admit it, she had numerous disgraceful facets to her personality, and this impropriety called to each and every one of them. She reveled in the indiscretion, relishing how their situation was reduced to the barest elements: her mouth, his cock.

He rolled to his side, and she went with him, snuggling herself into the gap between his torso and the couch. Cradling her head, he draped a leg over her, keeping her close so that he could obtain maximum enjoyment. As he approached the apex, he was ready to let go, and she braced, pondering how the end would come, how it would feel, how his seed would taste.

How she would survive the ordeal!

She wasn't precisely certain what she was supposed to do, and it wasn't as if she could pause to ask. Since she had played the role of trollop exceedingly well, he'd envision that she would be schooled in the conclusion.

At the last second, he pulled away, grabbing for her,

trying to drag her up his chest, and she didn't know what he proposed, but she suspected it involved the absolute relinquishment of her virginity.

Balking, she used her weight and placement to prevent him from moving her to where he could finish in a manner she wasn't equipped to attempt.

"I need to come, Emma. Now."

"In my mouth, John."

"I'm afraid I'll hurt you."

"You won't."

They glared at each other, and a battle of wills resulted. She was desperate to satisfy him, to learn what the staggering event would be like, and she flicked out her tongue and stroked across him, making him groan.

"Em,"—he tried to dissuade her, but without much vehemence—"stop."

"Let me do this for you." Hesitantly, she smiled, her brown eyes pleading. "Please?"

"Oh, Jesus . . . The way you look at me . . ."

He flopped against the pillows, and she took his reclining as acquiescence, guiding him to her lips, as he mumbled a remark that sounded like, "I wanted the first time to be different," but he was beyond reason.

Rapidly, he was overcome by desire, and a handful of thrusts lured him to the precipice. Embedded, he shuddered, then came in a fiery rush. A haunting wail echoed from his chest and reverberated around the room. He spilled himself, salty and hot in the back of her throat, and she gladly took all that he rendered, cherishing that he'd granted her the chance, that he'd let her be the one.

A lush eternity passed before his climax waned. His body slackened, and he withdrew. A gush of air was released from his lungs as if he'd deflated with the strenuous effort.

For a long while, she lay motionless, rejoicing in the aftermath, speculating as to what would occur next, what they would say, how they would act. Eventually, he reached down and petted her hair.

"Come here," he softly commanded.

Without vacillating, she obeyed, clambering up so that she was stretched out on top of him. She stacked her fists and rested her chin on her hands, watching him as he pensively studied her.

He appeared terribly young and innocent, his cynicism and haughtiness had temporarily vanished, and he seemed distinctly perplexed by their budding attraction, at a loss as to how to explain the potency of their affinity. He was searching for answers from her, as if she were a great mystery he was trying to solve, or that he needed to determine whatever it was that made her tick. Or perhaps he was wanting to comment on what they'd just done, but he couldn't verbalize his impressions.

Neither could she. The episode had been amazing, incredible, more sublime than she could possibly have dreamed before they'd commenced, but such a divulgence would make her seem more like the harlot he believed her to be. Nor could she mention, without sounding thoroughly immoral, that she was eager for a repeat performance.

Both lost in thought, they stared, their lips inches apart, their bodies merged, their hearts beating as one.

"Are you all right?" he finally inquired.

"Yes. How about you?"

"I'm still alive," he teased, referring to the quip he'd made before they'd begun as to the drastic effect she might have on his mortality.

"I didn't kill you?" she joked.

"I survived it well."

"I'm relieved you're such a hale fellow. I couldn't

have rationalized your abrupt demise to Rutherford."

Her grin spread from ear to ear and, joyful and exhilarated, he smiled, too. Clasping her buttocks, he urged her upward, till he could initiate a gentle kiss. He deepened it, his tongue gliding inside, and he moaned his delectation.

"I love the taste of my sex in your mouth. It's as if you were made for me."

"I liked what we did," she shyly confessed.

"So did I." Suggestively, he wiggled his brows.

"Let's try it again," she said impulsively, before she could keep the prurient proposition from slipping out.

"Give me a minute, my little strumpet." Merrily, he swatted her on the bottom. "I need to catch my breath."

"I don't want to wait."

"Well, you're going to."

He rotated them so that he was lying along the rear of the sofa, and she was spooned with him. His front was nestled against her back, and his naughty fingers lingered on her waist, then slid up to cup her breast. Though she was bewildered by her response, she was aroused, merely through her participation in spurring him to orgasm.

Her nipples were firm and ready for stimulation, and she writhed and fidgeted, anxious for him to apply pressure, to take the steps that would send them traveling down the road of passion once more, but he was content to repose.

There was barely enough room for the two of them, and she burrowed nearer, relishing how they were wedged together, his skin warm against her own, his chest rising and falling.

"I want you to visit in the evening," he said, "so that you can stay the night with me. In my bed upstairs."

"I never could." But even as she dismissed his invitation, her mind was awhirl with miscellaneous scenarios as to how she could bring it to fruition, how she could hide her protracted presence in the manor, how she could keep from being missed at home.

"Do it for me."

She sighed. "You tempt me beyond my limits."

"Good."

A companionable silence descended, then he broke it. "I hate your dresses."

"You're such a flatterer, John." She nudged him in the ribs with her elbow. "I bet the ladies in London can't resist that silver tongue of yours."

"I like it when you call me John."

"I know. That's why I don't. You always get your way; you're entirely too spoiled."

"I want to buy you some new clothes."

"Absolutely not."

"I'd like to see you in red. Or maybe a bright blue." He caressed her hair, her arm. "Let me."

"Where would I wear a fancy gown? Besides"—she peered at him over her shoulder—"if you started purchasing my apparel, it would seem as if you were paying me for spending time with you. It would make our friendship so tawdry."

"Oh, Em. I didn't mean it like that."

"But that's how I'd perceive it."

Analyzing her, he struggled to comprehend her position. No doubt it was radically foreign to him. Most likely, he'd offered expensive gifts to many women in his life, and had been turned down by few. Ultimately, he wrapped his arms around her, kissing her hair.

"I suppose," he grumbled, "that if I bought you a dress, you'd make me feel guilty for being affluent enough to afford it."

"I probably would at that." She chuckled. "You're coming to know me extremely well."

He chuckled, too, then yawned. "You make me happy."

Her heart lurched. What a divine, perilous sentiment! There were dozens of sweet, endearing retorts she could have murmured in reply, but she forced them away, scared to let them out. He wouldn't want to hear any mawkish drivel that he couldn't return in kind.

Why, if she professed an inappropriate emotion, he might become concerned about her level of affection; he might refuse to meet with her again. She'd come to count on their assignations as the only thing that kept her going in the dark of night when despair threatened to overwhelm her. Their affair would end soon, and she didn't need to hasten their separation with a foolish, insipid declaration of undue regard.

She closed her eyes and tucked the statement away, memorizing his exact tone when he'd said it so that she would never forget, and she cuddled to him, treasuring his heat and size, how she felt secure and protected in his arms.

His respiration steadied and slowed, and before long, he was snoring lightly. She delayed a few minutes, then she sneaked off the sofa. Quietly, she buttoned her dress, tied her hair, and scooped up her bonnet. There was a knitted throw on a chair by the fire, and she draped it over him, but he didn't stir.

Scrutinizing every tiny detail, she observed him, and he looked so peaceful. She yearned to lean over and kiss him good-bye, but she worried that she'd wake him, and he wouldn't let her get away, though truth be told, she wouldn't exert much energy in attempting to leave if he coaxed her to remain. She'd love to dawdle by his side forever, to bask with him in his easy existence of wealth and prosperity.

Shaking her head at her absurdity, she tiptoed out.

Just as she would have exited out the front door, his brother appeared almost from out of nowhere. Other than that initial, horrid afternoon, when he'd been a witness as she and John had negotiated their contract, she'd rarely crossed paths with him. She hadn't quizzed John about Mr. Clayton or their relationship, and she wasn't sure what to make of him now.

He was appraising her as though he'd stumbled upon her doing something she oughtn't—which she definitely had been!—and she wished she could magically vanish into thin air.

"Hello, Miss Fitzgerald," he cordially welcomed. "I didn't know you'd arrived. What brings you up to the manor?"

"I've been working with Wakefield on the estate finances." She was a terrible liar, and her cheeks flushed crimson.

"Really?" From the tenor of his question, she could tell that he didn't believe her. "I hadn't been informed that he'd sought your assistance."

"It's true," she contended, much too ardently. "We've been discussing solutions that are less dramatic than eviction."

"You wouldn't—by chance—be forging on with that ridiculous bargain the two of you had me write down?"

"No," she scoffed. "No."

"Because I advised him that if he followed through with it, he'd have to answer to me."

She gulped. "You did?"

"Yes."

"Well"—she grappled for levity—"we had a good

laugh over it, then we got down to business."

He rested a reassuring hand on her arm and said "You could confide in me if you needed my help."

Numerous frantic thoughts swamped her. What did she actually *know* about John Clayton? If his own brother deemed him capable of nefarious conduct maybe her usually astute intuition had gone awry, and she didn't know him at all.

"I don't need any help," she asserted. "We're friends."

"Friends. Hmm . . ." He mulled the word, rolling it on his tongue as though it were a novel flavor he'd never sampled. "I wasn't aware that John had any female *friends*."

"Well, there's a first time for everything, isn' there?"

"Where is he?"

"He . . . ah . . . he fell asleep in the library."

"He fell asleep?"

Her admission of his sudden nap was stupid, and she kicked herself. If she and Wakefield had been having a fiscal meeting as she'd claimed, why would he have dozed off in the middle of it? He had many damning faults, but even *he* wasn't that rude.

Mr. Clayton was meticulously evaluating her, and she peeked at her dress, wondering if she'd left a button undone or if a garter was sticking out, but her outfit seemed to be in order.

"He was very tired," she volunteered lamely.

"He certainly must have been."

Her idiocy was only making matters worse, and she had to escape before she said something even more asinine. "I'm sorry, but I'm late for another appointment I've got to go."

"By all means," he graciously agreed, proceeding to

the door and opening it for her. "Don't let me detain you."

Marching out, she exhorted herself to take deliberate, measured strides but, sharp as any dagger blade, his assessing gaze cut into her back.

She reached the corner of the house and scurried around, out of his sight, hustling toward the woods and the safety of home.

CHAPTER ELEVEN

LADY Caroline Foster peeked out the window of her carriage as it meandered down the drive toward Wakefield Manor. Having never been to the estate before, she critically appraised the gardens, memorizing every aspect so that when she returned to London, she'd remember what she'd seen.

She knew all there was to know about the Wakefield holdings, having thoroughly studied the available information, but even though she'd read about the area on paper, it couldn't render the crucial sort of detail supplied by a visual inspection.

With relish, she could recite the acreage, the number of employees, the annual income from the crofters, the amount of wheat, barley, and other crops produced in the fields. When she married John and became his viscountess, the sprawling property would be one of many over which they'd have dominion, so she'd made it a point to be fully apprised of the specifications before that auspicious day arrived.

Her impending role was daunting, and she yearned for John to be proud of her. For so many years, she'd waited faithfully for him to decide he was ready to wed, and when he finally relented and they walked down the aisle, she wanted him to be glad that he'd yielded to the inevitable.

She would be the best viscountess ever!

Her future had always involved marriage to the

Wakefield heir. Her grandparents and parents had wanted the alliance, and so had the late viscount, Douglas Clayton. Their plans had been set in stone when Caroline was a babe in her cradle.

Originally, she'd been slated for John's older brother, James, but he'd died, so with his passing, she'd gained a different fiancé, and the modification hadn't really affected her. She'd been so young, and the concept of a husband so distant, that one boy had been the same as another.

It had happened ages ago, and she scarcely recalled James, so it seemed as though she'd been groomed to marry John, and John alone, that there'd never been any Wakefield heir but him.

He hadn't said as much, but she had a niggling suspicion he didn't like that she'd initially been his brother's intended. They hadn't discussed his opinion—she wouldn't be so crass as to raise the topic!—but she was haunted by the perception that he felt as though he hadn't been her first choice, that he'd won her by default.

Often, she wondered if that wasn't what kept him from declaring himself. John diligently labored to separate himself from James's image, and he took affront whenever there was the slightest intimation that he should carry on as James might have done. If anyone was idiotic enough to counsel him as to how he should act more as James might have, he did exactly the opposite of what was suggested.

He could be exceptionally contrary, so she pretended that his reticence to tying the knot was simply due to his obstinate nature and not—heaven forbid!—any feelings he might harbor about her personally.

With her father's estate adjacent to one of the Wakefield properties, she'd grown up around John, viewing him as a kind of detached, affectionate elder sibling.

Though he was six years older, they'd frequently socialized. Even as an adult, after he'd established himself
in London, they'd encountered each other at various
events.

Why, they were so close that they'd sat in the same
pew at the church during James's funeral!

She understood his strengths and weaknesses, his
proclivities and flaws, and she was convinced that her
placid demeanor would offset and complement his penchant for wild living and dissipation. They were friends
and, as her mother constantly indicated, the length of
their acquaintance would form the bedrock for a steady
partnership—if John could move beyond the reservations that hampered him from making a decision.

Others thought she was crazy to persevere—after
all, she'd just turned twenty-four!—but she acknowledged her duty, and she wasn't about to shirk her responsibilities, although she would privately admit that
she was irritated by his lack of initiative. She'd given
up much to be his bride. As one season after another
had come and gone with no grand celebration, she'd
sustained excessive derision and ridicule, and while she
courageously tried to ignore the barbs, the mockery hurt.

People laughed at her behind her back, calling her
a fool, a harlequin, claiming that she'd ruined her
chances by allying herself with John. If he ultimately
refused to marry her, she wasn't sure how she'd react.
She was a spinster merely because she'd cast her lot with
him, not doubting that—as her parents perpetually insisted—he'd settle down and do the right thing. Should
he demur in the end, she'd just die!

Despite her mother's admonitions, she was positive
that she could change him, that she could rein in his
exorbitant tendencies and make him a better man. He
could be an adequate husband, even if he might not be

the dashing, romantic swain she'd fantasized about as a girl.

Certainly, she liked him well enough, notwithstanding his numerous foibles and fondness for mischief. He was amiable and polite, familiar, like a comfortable pair of riding boots.

If she sporadically wished that he made her heart pound, that he'd gaze at her with the fire of manly desire in his eyes, that he would sweep her away into a life filled with passion and excitement, she pushed the notions aside. Theirs would be a sound union, based on entrenched principles of obligation to family and country, and it was imprudent to crave what was never meant to be.

The carriage rounded a corner and rumbled out of the woods, and she managed a glimpse of the residence. It was beautiful, situated on a hill, the windows gleaming in the afternoon sunshine. A thrill of anticipation and worry skittered down her spine.

She hadn't written to notify John she was coming, and he would be astonished. She never did anything unexpected, never broke a rule or behaved impetuously, so she couldn't explain what was motivating her.

Assuredly, there was the need to have John regard her as spontaneous—he often teased her for being too repressed—but the anonymous message she'd received had also played a part in her resolution to travel to Wakefield.

John had an affinity for loose women, a propensity her mother had expounded on at length, and she had no illusions as to the type of marriage she would have: With John as her husband, she would have to feign naïveté as he consorted with the Jezebels of the world.

Caroline didn't grasp the sordid particulars, but her mother had hinted that females of the lower classes would provide John with an entertainment that she—as the daughter of an earl—shouldn't have to furnish. Though this incomprehensible, implicit dictum was distasteful, she'd assumed she'd acceded to it, but upon learning of his current trollop, she'd reeled with frustration.

The harlot would afford him a further pretext to evade matrimony, and even as she valiantly struggled to hide her pique, she was out of patience.

When his father had died, her parents had promised her that—with the title weighing heavily on his shoulders—John would come up to scratch, but she'd been looking forward to a proposal for months! The unsigned letter had forced her hand, and she wasn't about to tarry in London as her destiny was, once again, delayed.

She'd send the coquette packing, then she'd have John all to herself for an entire week! Such confined fellowship would work miracles on their relationship!

Her parents were in Scotland, and their absence had given her the perfect opportunity to make the furtive trip, with no one being the wiser. She would use every second to remind John of why they'd be so good together. His procrastination was about to end!

The coach rattled to a stop at the front of the mansion, and she continued to peek out as the coachmen performed their tasks. Eventually, the door was open, the step down, and she exited. With her stomach churning in knots, she smoothed the anxious marks from her brow, and fixed a serene smile.

John would be delighted to see her! She wouldn't contemplate any other possibility!

Rutherford was present to attend her, and she started toward him, eager to be announced, when she caught her reflection in a windowpane. Other than a few wrinkles in her skirt, she was relieved to note that she looked immaculate.

Her blond hair was pulled into a neat chignon, her blue eyes and attractive mouth were accented with a dainty coating of facial paints. She'd worn an off-the-shoulder, cream-colored gown that underscored the delicate shading of her pale skin. Slender, shapely, wealthy, a privileged noblewoman about to greet her fiancé, she boldly waltzed into the house as though it already belonged to her.

Unduly pleased, she entered and spun around only to come face to face with Ian Clayton.

When she'd left town in a giddy rush, she hadn't calculated that Mr. Clayton would also be in the country, when she should have known he would be. He and John were two peas in a pod, and where one went, the other followed. It was a reality that irked and vexed her.

The brothers were inordinately devoted, and John would likely want Mr. Clayton at the wedding. Why, he might ask Mr. Clayton to be his best man! How would she tell him no?

After the nuptials, the pair would carry on with their male association, which would include Mr. Clayton's free run of her home. That he'd lived in the selfsame house for the prior decade was a factor she discounted. She'd be a bride who ought to be permitted to select who would be welcomed under her own roof, but how did a wife mention such a complaint to her spouse? How did she confess that his half brother frightened her out of her wits?

When she was around Mr. Clayton, she didn't know what to do or say. Seeming overly large in size, he intimidated her, which was silly. He was the identical height as John, but with how he strutted about, he appeared bigger. They were enough alike to be, well . . .

brothers . . . but while John's features were angelic and beautiful, his were rugged and untamed.

"My, my," he derided sarcastically, "if it isn't *Lady* Caroline."

He purposely stressed her title in a manner that was designed to enrage and, mute and furious, she glowered at him. Though she endeavored to avoid him, there were times—such as now—that a confrontation was inescapable. He made her feel inept, unimportant, as if she were conceited and vainglorious, and his acerbic attitude incensed her.

She was a very nice person—to those meriting her courtesy. Which Mr. Clayton clearly did not! Neither by his birth status nor his conduct did he warrant any attention at all.

"Did you inform John of your plans?" He leaned in, trying to alarm her with his proximity, and he was succeeding. Her pulse rate increased, her nostrils flared, her stomach muscles clenched.

For some reason, when he was near, her senses were especially acute. She could smell the soap with which he'd washed, the aroma of tobacco clinging to his jacket, could discern the heat emanating from his lanky torso. She couldn't figure out why he unnerved her, but she wasn't about to ponder her peculiar sensitivity.

Ignoring him, she turned to the butler, undoing her wrap and holding it out.

"So it's an impromptu visit, is it?" he chided when she didn't respond. "Well, John is definitely going to be *surprised*."

She wouldn't attempt to interpret his emphasis on the word *surprised*. It could have any meaning; she wouldn't try to decipher it.

He watched her with those shrewd blue eyes of his, and she tamped down a shiver, unwilling to let him ascertain how completely he disturbed her equilibrium. As he inappropriately assessed her, his rudeness was unbearable, and she glanced away, declining to pay him any heed.

"What will *Daddy* say when he finds out you've trotted off by yourself?"

"Rutherford"—she spoke to the retainer—"show me to the drawing room. I'll wait for John there. I don't care for the conversation here in the foyer."

"Ooh," Mr. Clayton jeered, "a direct hit, milady." Dramatically, he clutched a hand over his heart as though she'd wounded him, which she could never do. He was made of ice and steel. Then, he snapped to, oozing false civility. "I'll escort her, Rutherford. Order refreshments, then be about your duties."

The butler crisply bowed to Mr. Clayton's obvious authority—rather than her own—and sauntered off, leaving her alone with the domineering oaf and more angry than she'd ever been.

In the ensuing hush, they studied each other, combatants in an undeclared war. His sizzling concentration roved over her, boring into her, so that he seemed to peer into her very soul, and she shifted uneasily, suffering the insane sensation that he'd unearthed each of her petty secrets.

She shattered the tense silence. "I can locate the parlor myself, thank you very much."

He scowled. "Stop being such a snob."

"I?" She was aghast at the uncivil remark, and she haughtily enlightened him. "I'll have you know that I'm considered quite a friendly individual—when I'm in *friendly* company."

"No," he countered, "you're an out-and-out snob. And you go out of your way to be a bi—" He checked himself before he would have pronounced whatever else he judged her to be.

"A what?" she petulantly inquired.

"Never mind," he arrogantly replied, and she fumed again. She hated it when men treated her as less than an equal, as though she were dainty or frail or—worse yet!—stupid.

"I can't abide your churlish behavior. Now, if you'll excuse me—" He was consistently determined to instigate a verbal brawl, but she wouldn't oblige him. She tried to go, but somehow, he'd moved and efficiently blocked her retreat.

She bristled. Though she couldn't fathom why, he was bent on tormenting her. Yes, she'd insulted him on that one horrid occasion, but it had been years earlier, when she'd impulsively and immaturely made an indecorous slur about his lineage, as well as the conceivable, dishonest financial incentives that might have spurred him to share the town house with John.

As she'd voiced her innuendos too loudly, a servant had overheard and had apprised John, so she'd had to apologize, lest he suppose she had a temper.

The taste of that atonement was still bitter on her tongue, and though Mr. Clayton had accepted her expression of regret, she'd been left with the impression that he hadn't really forgiven her.

He slithered closer, the toes of his boots dipping under the hem of her skirt. "John won't be glad to see you."

How dare he comment! "I can't understand why you'd deem my arrival to be any of your affair."

"Everything that occurs in John's life is *my* business." He glared at her as if she were a fool. "You shouldn't have come. He'll be upset."

"I'll take my chances," she argued between gritted

teeth. She absolutely would not explain herself, not when she'd been so thrilled by having braved an adventure. She wouldn't let Mr. Clayton spoil it!

"Why do you persist?" he suddenly, vehemently asked.

"With what?"

"With chasing after my brother? He's not worth it, and he doesn't deserve you."

Several cutting retorts were perched on the tip of her tongue, and with every pore in her body, she longed to lash out so that he would feel the sharp edge of her ire. Just once, she'd like to toss her composure on the ground and stomp on it. She'd relish the prospect of reproving the impertinent bounder, of letting her carefully restrained, spirited constitution shine through.

But fortunately, John's opportune emergence down the hall prevented her from making a scene. Abruptly, she calmed, adopting the tranquil disposition for which she was renowned, and Mr. Clayton—knave that he was—recognized how quickly she brought herself under control so that John wouldn't notice her fury.

As she seethed, he chuckled, and she contemptuously snubbed him—a tactic at which she excelled—focusing instead on John, and immediately, she concluded that the troublesome letter had been accurate.

There was a thin, rather plain woman with him. She was outfitted in a drab, functional black dress, a straw bonnet, and a threadbare cloak. They were promenading arm in arm, chatting as if they were bosom buddies, and he was smiling down on her in a fashion that was never manifest when he was with Caroline. Though she'd convinced herself that love and affection were not to be achieved through her marriage, his displaying them to another stabbed like a knife at her self-esteem and prodded her latent competitive instincts to the fore.

They approached, not aware of her, and Caroline was able to analyze her nemesis, allowing that the woman could probably be pretty if she'd had the advantage of stylish attire or coiffure. She was so far John's opposite that it was laughable, except for one teeny detail: They exuded an energy, or a chemistry, so potent that Caroline could distinguish it with scant difficulty.

She stiffened, ready for battle, and to her dismay and horror, Mr. Clayton was inspecting her as she evaluated the couple. He raised a brow, as if to query, what do you think of that?

With ease, he'd deduced that she'd rushed to Wakefield to lock horns over this very situation. Why was he so adept at reading her? How embarrassing that he could!

John gaped down the corridor and saw her. His usually glib demeanor slipped, and he missed a step. For a brief instant, he looked terribly culpable, as if he were doing something wrong and she'd caught him in the act. Good! Let him stew! It was about time she garnered improved treatment for herself!

Then he smiled—the bland, affable smile he reserved just for her—and her heart sank. Why couldn't he gaze at her the way he was ogling at his new *friend*?

"Caro?" At least he used her pet name! "Is it really you?"

"Yes, John, dear." Unruffled, poised, she strode forward, both hands extended for him to grasp, and he didn't disappoint. He moved away from the other woman as if she'd been rendered invisible.

"What are you doing here?"

"I was so lonely in London without you"—she rose up on tiptoe to collect her ritual kiss on the cheek; he'd never kissed her on the lips, but oh, how she wished he would!—"that I decided to visit."

"I see." Frowning, he exhibited no evidence of the glowing adoration he'd been lavishing on his colleague. "Does your father know you've come?"

"No." Flirtatiously, she grinned, but inwardly she flinched. How had it happened that she was twenty-four years old, and no one believed she could take a breath without her father's permission? "He and mother are in Scotland." Leaning nearer, she hoped to have his companion stewing over their familiarity. "I ran off all by myself." With her maid, of course. She wouldn't be wild enough to abandon all semblance of propriety.

"What if someone finds out?" he lectured gently.

"No one will," she confidently insisted, though she wouldn't worry if the news circulated. Perhaps damage to her reputation would provoke a proposal.

"Caro, I must say that—"

She couldn't bear to hear his admonition. If he was displeased by her brazen conduct, as Mr. Clayton had vigorously contended, she'd expire from mortification!

"Let me tell you about my trip," she interrupted. "I had a marvelous journey."

Boldly, she took his arm and spun him toward what she trusted was a receiving parlor. Efficiently and briskly, she maneuvered him away from his most recent temptation. He sighed and dragged his feet, but she tugged him forward, and he accompanied her, too much of a gentleman to stop when she was so intent on her destination.

As they crossed the threshold, she regally peered over her shoulder at his consort. Caroline could perceive the dozens of emotions that were bombarding the guileless woman. She was appalled, thunderstruck, and hurt, and Caroline braced herself, refusing to feel any guilt over her actions. John belonged to her and always had!

She was tired of sharing him with every lightskirt who strolled by!

As though it were an afterthought, she decreed, "You there, girl! Have my bags taken upstairs and unpacked. Then inform the housekeeper that I'd like a bath delivered to my room. In about half an hour."

John stiffened, angry by what she'd done, but she shut the door so that her scolding would be leveled in private.

Ian shook his head, wondering why John had trailed after Lady Caroline with nary a complaint, and why he hadn't so much as cast a farewell glance in Miss Fitzgerald's direction.

Naturally, any chap confronted by his fiancée, while dallying with his paramour, had to be discomfited, so Ian could hardly rebuke him for a lapse. With John's lackadaisical attitudes regarding women and their feminine sentiments, he didn't possess the requisite courage to navigate such a disastrous bog.

No doubt, escape had been the better part of valor.

What a dreadful encounter! For all of them!

Lady Caroline's appearance hadn't been impromptu or ill considered. She'd come because of Miss Fitzgerald, for once evincing a bit of fortitude—misplaced though it might be.

How he hated that she'd exert so much effort on John's behalf!

As the thought materialized, he shoved it away, declining to ruminate over her. Why did he permit her to bother him? He couldn't care less if she disgraced herself, year after bloody year, mooning over a man who wasn't interested.

But didn't she have any pride? Any sense?

Yes, her accursed father had arranged her marriage when she was a child, but when would it dawn on her that the agreement had been a mistake, that John wouldn't honor it? Caroline was no longer an insipid girl, and she didn't have to blindly comply with her father's edicts. What would it take for her to realize that her opinion mattered? Where was her backbone? Would she never have the mettle to say *enough* and move on?

He had no illusions about why he obsessed over her so often and so thoroughly: He was desperately attracted to her, his fascination fueled by a complex combination of resentment and jealousy. She exemplified everything he'd ever coveted, everything that might have been his had the world been fairer. Yet she was so far beyond his station that it was ludicrous to ponder her at all, and the fact that she was so unattainable made her more desirable. Plus, she was John's, had perpetually been meant for him, which only added to her forbidden allure, making his fixation more absurd and illogical.

She could never be his, but he regularly fantasized about the possibility. What man wouldn't want her to grace his bed?

John presumed she was a cold fish, but Ian saw a fire and vitality that were vigilantly banked. There was passion bubbling just below the surface, which was why he goaded her so severely. He wanted to be present when all that pent-up calenture came tumbling out. What a sight it would be!

He focused his attention on Miss Fitzgerald, who seemed to have been turned to stone.

She was also glaring at the closed door, the force of her gaze steadfast, as if she were trying to burrow through the wood so as to discover what was occurring on the other side.

If he'd been disposed, Ian could have clarified: John

was being cordial and sociable, while explaining to Lady Caroline—as if she were a wee lass—that her trip had been overly rash. Then, with no concern for her feelings, he'd make plans to send her home with all due haste so that she'd be in London before others were aware of what she'd done.

Smooth talker that he was, John would persuade her that he was doing it for her benefit and, like the obedient child she'd ceaselessly been, Caroline would go without a fuss.

Unfortunately for Miss Fitzgerald, she wasn't cognizant of the odd dance in which John and Caro habitually engaged. She was stunned and heartbroken, and he detested having to distress her further, but it couldn't be helped. In all likelihood, she was living out some fantasy of her own: the vicar's daughter and the wealthy viscount commencing a clandestine, exhilarating romance.

It was pathetically touching. She and John were squirreled away in the country, so it was easy to forget their respective positions, and Caroline's arrival was a huge dose of painful reality.

He'd grown to like Emma Fitzgerald. Though he'd initially fretted about her motives and her ability to stand up for herself, he'd quashed his misgivings As she'd repeatedly proven, she was no incompetent ninny. She could hold her own against the likes of John Clayton, although Ian did occasionally chafe over what was transpiring between them during their peculiar appointments. Their affinity was powerful and so blatant that, after that mysterious afternoon when she'd left John *napping* in the library, he'd conjectured that it might have burgeoned into a dangerous realm.

As he tarried there with her in the quiet foyer, her anguish patently apparent, he grasped that his suspicions were correct: Miss Fitzgerald was precariously attached

to John, maybe even in love with him, which was foolhardy and disastrous.

Intervention was essential. She needed to be jolted
out of her idiocy, though he'd sound his alarm kindly.
Emma Fitzgerald didn't belong in John's life and never
would, and she had to be vividly advised of that pesky
detail.

"Don't mind her," Ian said, referring to Caroline.
"She doesn't mean to be rude; she's just never had to
act any differently."

Miss Fitzgerald blinked and blinked, as if she'd
stumbled out of a dark room into the bright light. "Who
is she?"

"Lady Caroline Foster. Her father is the Earl of
Derby. She's John's fiancée." It was a small lie but important and timely to utter.

"They're betrothed?"

"Since they were children," he fibbed again.

The tidings had her so aghast that he almost couldn't
continue with his ruse, but she had to be dissuaded from
her dubious course. "Previously, John felt no urgency to
wed"—an understatement if there ever was one!—"but
with his assumption of the title . . ." He let the implication trail off, let her conclude that the ceremony was
imminent.

"Have they set the date?"

"Soon." Pensively, he nodded but didn't elaborate
so that she'd infer the worst.

"My . . ."

For a lengthy interlude, she peered toward the room
where John was sequestered with Caroline. Anyone who
wasn't versed in the intricacies of their bizarre relationship might have imagined them ardently kissing. Tender
sweethearts reunited.

Her woe and longing were agonizing to witness, and

when she faced him, her eyes were glistening with tears.

"I had no idea," she insisted. "He hadn't told me."

"A wise woman," he delicately counseled, "might reflect upon the futility of persisting in a venture fraught with such peril."

"Yes," she softly agreed, "a wise woman might."

"John will return to London shortly."

"I've never supposed he'd do anything else."

"I've known him for many years, Miss Fitzgerald." Gad, but he felt as if he were kicking a puppy! "It wouldn't be prudent to hope that he'd follow through on a promise or that he might change his behavior."

Her eyes searched his. She was so genuine, so sincere, and her affection for John was obvious. What a depressing and dear notion! She'd been so swept up in the excitement that she'd failed to recollect their divergent antecedents, but she was smart, and she understood what needed to be done. For John. For herself.

Nervously, she licked her bottom lip. So fetching. So refreshing. So misguided in the affairs of the heart. "Would you give the viscount a message for me?"

"Certainly."

"Would you tell him that I . . . that I . . ." She had to swallow twice before she could finish. How she would rue the separation! "That I've been neglecting other duties so I could tour the estate with him, but I won't be available to assist him from here on out."

"I'll notify him."

"And would you"—she swallowed again, more tears threatening—"would you work to ensure that he heeds my decision? He might not be inclined to listen."

Too true. Miss Fitzgerald knew John well. If he didn't want to cry off, it would be extremely difficult to convince him to desist. "I'll see to it."

"Thank you."

"You're welcome."

Scrupulously, she observed him, as though she would say something else, and he was relieved when she decided against subsequent discourse. No sense prolonging the inevitable. Besides, he didn't want to be furnished with more reasons to like her.

She was remarkably astute, and if she expounded on John in any fashion, if she initiated a discussion about his faults or her fears for him, Ian would readily join in, would end up seeking ways for the two star-crossed lovers to be together, when there was no excuse for exacerbating their insanity.

"Good-bye," she said. "I wish—"

"Wish what?"

"That you and I had gotten to know each other. We're both worried about John"—so it was *John*, was it?—"and I think we might have been friends."

He nodded. "I believe we might have been."

"Take care of him for me."

How intriguing that here, at the last, she dropped any pretense that they'd been more than casual acquaintances. "I will."

She nodded, too, then she shuddered, her body trembling violently, as if shaking off a heavy burden. Without another word, she departed, choosing to use the rear door utilized by the servants rather than the front that she'd enjoyed when she'd called on John.

For many minutes, he lingered, staring at the spot where she'd been and feeling lower and more despicable than he had in a very long while.

CHAPTER TWELVE

JOHN trotted his horse to the break in the trees and reined in, stretching his legs in the stirrups as he surveyed the pitiful scene before him. The estate agent had been explicit in his directions, so there was no doubt that he had the correct location.

His fascinating, amazing Emma lived here? How could it be?

While he'd known that her home was within walking distance of the manor, in his usual detached fashion, he hadn't paid attention to her domestic arrangements. As he didn't spend much time with commoners, particularly poverty-stricken ones, it hadn't occurred to him that someone with whom he'd formed such an intimate bond could exist in such squalor.

Chagrin had delivered him to her door, though not the fiasco with Caroline. His abashment was due to the disconcerting fact that he'd finally noted she was on his original list of evictions.

Why hadn't she said anything? Why hadn't he noticed sooner?

He'd been sitting at his desk in the library, too distracted to accomplish any work. The ledgers had been strewn about, but he'd kept gazing at the fainting couch, daydreaming about how Emma had lain with him there.

In between his erotic ramblings, he'd pondered Caro, her resolution to come, her refusal to go. She was so habitually tractable that he couldn't comprehend what had happened to make her so adamant about remaining. She was so sweet-tempered that he'd never been able to put his foot down with her and mean it. If he knew how to be stern, she wouldn't still be tagging after him, confident they would wed.

In the midst of his scattered musings, he'd glanced down at the names of those scheduled for removal, and the surname Fitzgerald had leapt out at him. After a few quick questions to his agent, he'd ascertained the devastating truth: Emma, her mother, and her sister were some of the purported reprobates he'd intended to render homeless.

During the extensive, agreeable hours they'd passed, she hadn't said a word! Had never hinted at her plight or pleaded her case. How typical of her. Tending to everyone else's needs first, declining to fret over her own miserable condition.

If he wasn't so worried about her, he'd be furious. Didn't she realize that, with the stroke of his pen, her troubles could have been solved? From the moment they'd met, she'd been pressuring him to perform some of her accursed *good deeds*, but could she let him toss a bit of his largesse her way? No, she could not!

Who was more deserving? Emma made him smile, brought him joy, provided him with copious reasons to be a better person. She pushed him to find a viable purpose for the detested responsibilities his title and heritage had placed upon him.

Gad, but she furnished him with an incentive to stay sober! No small feat!

Most of all, she was his friend. Outside of Ian, who could claim the dubious distinction? She liked him, relishing the good and fussing over the bad. She was constantly optimistic, and when he shared her pleasant company, she made his adversities seem petty and negligible.

Would it have been so terrible to depend on him? Even a little? She was so damned tough. Hadn't she been informed that it was permissible to solicit aid from friends when one was in dire straits? Couldn't she let her guard down—just once!—so he could be strong for her? He had wide shoulders; she could lean on them, and he'd proudly assume her burdens.

People regularly petitioned him, but he was surrounded by villains and scoundrels, and few were worthy of his support, so he hardly ever granted it. Yet, on this occasion, when he was incredibly eager, he couldn't get the bloody recipient to so much as admit that she could use a tiny bit of help.

He hadn't seen her in two days. Two days!

The winsome vixen had thoroughly ingratiated herself, had given him something to look forward to, had left him so impatient for her arrival that every afternoon at one o'clock he tarried like an imbecile at the back of the house.

Then, *poof!* No Emma.

How was he supposed to cope with such an eventuality? Didn't the blasted female grasp that she'd grown important to his happiness? How dare she disappear!

Presumably, she was trying to teach him a lesson after the debacle with Caro. Wasn't that just like a woman! Blaming the man for every infinitesimal thing that transpired! It wasn't as if he'd invited Caro to Wakefield! In all the years he'd known her, she hadn't committed a single impulsive act, and he wouldn't speculate as to why she'd done so now. Whatever insane delusions were motivating her, he wouldn't bother to unravel.

Besides, what did Caro's presence have to do with

Emma? The two women, and the sections of his life they represented, were totally disconnected.

Caro's stunt had had him so perplexed that he'd mishandled the encounter, but to be confronted by his alleged fiancée and his current lover! In the same instant! It had been a no-win situation.

He'd rudely abandoned Emma in the foyer, being dealt with by Caro as though she were a servant. Then, he'd had Caro crying in the parlor, after supplying an out-of-character tongue-lashing, the type of which he hadn't previously dispensed, lest he wound her delicate sensibilities. By the time he'd been shed of her, and free to search for Emma, she'd departed.

Ian had shown her out, and the bastard had confessed that he'd lied and told her Caro was John's actual betrothed! He'd deliberately chased her off so as to keep John from making a huge mistake.

As if John required Ian to manage his romantic affairs! Ian was no more proficient at maneuvering the feminine quagmire than John was, himself. For Ian to willfully hurt Emma was unconscionable. No wonder she was piqued and hadn't stopped by again.

She had a moral disposition that was at variance with his own. In light of the kinds of knaves with whom he consorted, he'd never had to aspire to virtuous conduct or civilized behavior. He saw nothing inappropriate in having a mistress, various transitory paramours, and a fiancée.

But Emma wouldn't see it that way. While she might rationalize their dallying despite his having a disreputable mistress, her ethical constitution would draw the line at a fiancée, which was foolish. He would be at Wakefield briefly, so they had a limited opportunity in which to explore the boundaries of their odd, exciting association. What goal was served by denying herself?

He urged his horse out of the trees and into the clearing, and he was increasingly disgusted as he received a close-up view of the dwelling she inhabited. The cottage was a hovel, too pathetic to be referred to as a *house,* and he couldn't believe humans would reside in such a wretched lodging. Once he had her transferred to suitable shelter, he would have the sorry shack torn down so there wouldn't be a future pretext to offer it to another unlucky occupant.

No one observed his approach, but from the isolation of the area, he suspected they had infrequent visitors, so there was scant need to watch for guests. He tied his horse to a nearby bush and marched to the door, knocking briskly.

It was opened by a girl who had to be Emma's sister. She was pretty, young, with Emma's curly hair and beautiful brown eyes, an exact duplicate of how Emma must have been as a child. Lank and gangly—like a colt learning to stand on its feet—she was perched on the cusp of womanhood. She would develop into a beauty, like her older sibling. How tragic that she had such dismal prospects.

"I am John Clayton, Viscount Wakefield," he announced as she gawked, astonished.

"How do you do," she answered politely. "I'm Jane Fitzgerald."

"Hello, Miss Jane." He smiled disarmingly. "I'm here to call upon your sister, Emma. Is she at home?"

"Yes. Won't you come in?"

She held the door, and he started in when Emma popped up, blocking his entrance.

"What are you doing here?" she barked.

"I need to speak with you."

"Didn't your brother give you my message?"

"Of course he did, but I didn't listen." He smiled

again, just for her. "I *never* listen to others. It's a failing of mine; you know that."

He'd anticipated that his self-deprecation would coax a smile in return but, dispirited and resigned, she simply studied him as if he were an interesting curiosity. In the ramshackle setting, she seemed so altered, so dejected and beaten down, and she sighed painfully, the weight of her world crushing her, and he suddenly felt ashamed. For who he was. For what he was.

Incessantly, she'd chided him for not appreciating all that he had, for refusing to acknowledge the blessings his position had bestowed, and he'd laughed off her admonitions, but he couldn't any longer. He'd never conjectured as to what befell a woman when the man who'd been her sole support died, so he was disturbingly startled by the glaring evidence.

She was so remarkable, and to be apprised of her seedy environs was shocking and discouraging. How could he utilize his superior status and affluence to her advantage? If he couldn't exploit his wealth to improve her circumstances, what was the use of any of it?

"You should go," she churlishly declared as Jane interrupted.

"We were about to sit down to our daily meal. Won't you join us?"

Appalled by the invitation, Emma maintained, "The viscount is much too busy."

"No I'm not," he said, and he turned to Jane, whom he now regarded as a valuable ally. "I'd love to stay."

Emma was furious, and he brushed past her before she could slam the door. As he walked by, he stroked a comforting hand across her waist, hoping she'd perceive the gesture to mean that he'd take care of everything.

Adjusting to the gloom, he critically surveyed the incongruous sight. There was a main room, a bedroom

in the back, and a loft overhead. Crammed into the di
minutive space were several tasteful pieces of furniture
indication of a prior familial prosperity. An oak dinin
set, a matching hutch, a sofa, embroidered doilies an
knitted throws, were scattered about on an earthen floo

Emma misunderstood his scrutiny and felt con
strained to proclaim, "We didn't take any items from th
vicarage that didn't belong to us."

"I never considered that you might have."

"These things were part of my mother's dowry."

She glanced away, unable to face him, and with th
intensity of his gaze, he tried to compel her to look a
him, but she wouldn't, so he shifted his inspection be
yond her, to the corner. By a boarded window, the
mother—an aging, serene, gaunt woman—rocke
repetitively in a chair, blindly peering outside throug
the cracks, not seeing any of the bright summer su
shine.

Jane whispered, "That's Mother. She's been havin
a bad day."

Jane was abashed, as well, by their reduced re
sources, but she strove to cover it by chattering ne
vously and interminably, plainly trying to smooth ov
the tension between himself and Emma. She pulled a
extra chair up to the table, held it out, and he sat.

There were two servings of soup, dished up in fi
china bowls, with silver spoons laid out—remnants fro
a more plentiful period. Jane ladled a third bowl a
placed it before him, then seated herself.

Unmoving, Emma remained across the room, un
Jane said, "Emma, come. Your soup will get cold."

Emma hesitated, wanting to decline but not havi
the heart to disappoint Jane. She sidled over and sat, to
still without meeting his eye.

A dreadful hush descended, but Jane was determin

be cheerful and fill the void the two adults had cre-
ted. "Milord Wakefield, thank you for the treats you
nt me."

"What treats might that be, Miss Jane?"

"You remember: the scones and other pastries.
mma mentioned to you how much I like scones, and
ou insisted I have the whole batch."

She was so earnest in her belief that he'd recall the
oon, that he acted as if he knew precisely to what she
ferred. "Oh, yes. *Those* treats."

Tendering no comment, Emma blushed a blazing
d, as Jane obligingly quipped, "We washed the table-
loth, and Emma brought it back. Good as new. Isn't
at right, Em?"

Emma stirred her soup. "The viscount doesn't want
hear about it, Jane."

"Yes I do," he responded. "I'm absolutely en-
ralled." He wanted to get a reaction out of her, but
ort of poking her with a sharp stick, he couldn't figure
ut how. "Next time you're hungry for pastries, Jane,
ave Emma inform me, and I'll deliver them by the bas-
etful."

Jane stared at him solemnly, then gushed, "I knew
ou were kind. I told Emma I couldn't bear it if you
eren't."

What a sweet girl! How distressing to have her liv-
g like this. The quiet grew, once more, and he waited,
ttentive, while his female companions ate, then he
pped his own spoon only to discover that the paltry
oncoction was a flavorless broth. Not so much as an
nion was floating.

Were they starving in addition to their other trou-
les? Emma was very slender, but he'd assumed she had
slim build. He'd never supposed that her thinness
ight be caused by hunger. The likelihood outraged

him. Would she have kept such a ghastly exigency fr[om] him?

He'd thought they were friends!

Exasperated, he pointed out, "There's nothing here but carrots and water."

"Yes," Jane said optimistically, "but we pretend i[t's] a delicious stew, packed with yummy vegetables. Th[en] it doesn't seem so awful." She halted and beamed at [her] sister, not grasping how much she'd revealed. "W[hat] shall we imagine is in it today, Em?"

Emma was paralyzed with mortification, and s[he] muttered, "Would you excuse me, please?" Tears ca[s]caded down her cheeks, and she stumbled from her ch[air] and scurried outside.

John sighed heavily, unsure of how to procee[d.] Emma was proud, and she'd been humiliated at havi[ng] him behold her dilemma. He wanted to go after her b[ut] doubted she would welcome the solace.

The stream of sunlight through the opened door co[n]fused Mrs. Fitzgerald, and she rose and blankly gap[ed] around as if she might go, too. Jane went to her a[nd] efficiently settled her in the rocker, then she returned [to] the table as if naught were amiss.

"Do you ever have anyone in to watch over yo[ur] mother?"

"No. Who would?"

"One of you must always be with her?"

"She can't be alone. She wanders."

Adversely affected by the news, he nodded, rec[ol]lecting the occasions he'd trysted with Emma, when he[']d pressured her to delay her departure. She'd repeate[dly] alluded to her obligations, but he was an aristocrat w[ho] could snap his fingers and have others do his biddi[ng,] so her travails had seemed nebulous and insignificant[.]

"Do you have any other food in the house?" [He]

adn't needed to inquire. A visual scan clarified that the
helves were bare.

"No."

"Why not?"

"Well, Emma delivered a baby a few days ago,"
ane clarified, "and the father promised to drop off some
ictuals in payment, but he didn't, and Emma doesn't
ike to pester people over what they owe her. She says
hey give what they can, when they can, and we mustn't
e greedy."

"I see."

And he really, really did. She'd starve before she'd
sk others for help! The foolish woman! He was fuming,
ut he hid his temper from Jane. "Emma was upset; I
hould probably talk with her."

"Tell her not to be sad," Jane beseeched him. "I hate
t when she's sad."

"I'll tell her," he gently vowed.

From the stoop, he glimpsed her strolling aimlessly
lown the rutted lane that led away from the cottage. He
ushed to catch up with her, which wasn't difficult, and
nomentarily, he was behind her. She'd discerned his
resence, but she didn't slow down.

"Emma—"

"Go away."

"No."

"Why aren't you up at the manor," she bitterly que-
ied, "entertaining your fiancée?"

"I'm not engaged."

"Not *engaged*, indeed!" she scoffed.

"It's true. Caroline would like to be, but it won't
appen."

"Do be silent!" She glowered at him over her shoul-
ler. "Next you'll be contending that she doesn't under-
tand you."

"She doesn't."

She rolled her eyes and continued walking. "You'r
embarrassing yourself. And me. Stop it."

He stepped in and wrapped his arms around he
waist, arresting her forward progress, and she rewarde
him with a hard elbow to his ribs, but he didn't releas
her.

"Hold still, you vicious minx."

"Leave me be."

She struggled against his restraint but not vigor
ously, for the fight had gone out of her. As if her bone
had melted, she slumped into him.

He embraced her for a long while, kissing her cheek
her hair, as the sounds of the forest billowed aroun
them. She was crying, but she didn't try to mask he
tears or swipe them away, and he hugged her tighter.

"Why didn't you confide in me?"

"About what?"

"That you were on the eviction list?"

She balanced the back of her head on his shoulder
"What good would it have done?"

"Did you think I wouldn't change my mind?"

"No, I didn't," she truthfully admitted. "Besides,
don't want your assistance."

"Big, strong Emma Fitzgerald!" he scolded, bu
kindly. "She doesn't need anybody!"

"Especially not you." She gazed up at the sky, ex
haling a breath of anguish and despair. "Do you eve
wish you could be somebody else? That you'd wake u
one morning and everything about you would be differ
ent?"

"Yes, I wish it all the time."

"So do I," she choked out. Then abruptly, she con
fessed, "I stole those blasted scones. It was that after
noon when you had your bath, and your mistress wa

with you in your dressing room. I was angry, and there was so much food—more than you could ever eat!—and I was jealous. So I dumped it all in a tablecloth and stole it for Jane, and I lied and told her it was a gift from you. That's how pathetic my life is! I've taken to thieving leftovers from rich peoples' houses!"

The tears flooded again, and he felt like clamping his hand over her mouth so that he wouldn't have to hear more. Every word she uttered cut like a blade to the bone.

Gruffly, he declared, "I don't give a rat's behind about a basket of scones."

"Well, I do."

Though she resisted, he turned her, nestling her to his chest while she had a lengthy cry. He liked consoling her when she was distraught, and he suspected that she didn't let loose very often. She wouldn't permit others to witness her woe, and he felt privileged to be the one with whom she shared it.

Eventually, the torrent subsided, and she was limp, spent and exhausted, and he speculated as to how she kept on, day after day. "As soon as I can locate a suitable accommodation, I'm moving you out of here."

She stiffened. "You are not."

"I am," he ordered, but for once he wasn't certain of the authority he wielded. She was exceedingly stubborn, and if he insisted too strenuously, she'd refuse just on principle.

"I'll purchase something small, that's clean and safe, and I'll—"

Furious, she shoved him away. "You are such a pompous ass!"

"What? What did I do?"

"I said *no,* but you never listen."

"That's because you're so obstinate! And you're always wrong!" He crossed his arms over his chest. "In case you haven't noticed, Miss Fitzgerald, you've gotten yourself into a damned fine fix, and you need some assistance to get yourself out of it."

"Not when your solution is so ludicrous."

"What—may I ask—is so *ludicrous* about your having a proper home?"

"Do you have any idea how my neighbors would gossip if I let you proceed? What pretense could I use that wouldn't be hideous?"

"Who the hell cares what other people think?"

"I care! Me!" she shouted, clutching her fist over her heart. "This is where I live, where I'll remain long after you've hied off to London—to your mistresses, and your fiancées, and Lord knows who else. *I* have to stay here." She swallowed down a huge gulp of air. "My reputation is all I have left. I've lost everything else."

"But we're friends, Emma, aren't we? Surely, I could help you because we're friends."

"Don't you understand?" She slapped her arms at her sides. "We're *not* friends! We're not anything at all!"

"How can you say that?"

"You put your hands on me, and I put my mouth on you. I'm sure a hundred other women have done the same with you in the past."

Her bluntness startled him, and he detested that she had such a low opinion of his character. He wanted her to picture him as a better man—the man he *could* be, instead of the man he was.

Adamantly, he asserted, "It's much more than that, and you know it."

"I know nothing of the sort. I *know* that you're bored in the country, and you're searching for a way to pass the time. For some reason I can't begin to fathom, you've decided to pass it with me."

"And it's been grand." He smiled, escalating her wrath.

"No it hasn't. You make me forget myself, my duties, my place."

"What's wrong with that?"

"What's wrong with that?" Totally aggravated, she was nearly shrieking. "I'll tell you what's *wrong* with that: I have a life! That's important and fulfilling. And there's no room for you in it. You make me dream for things I can never have! You make me yearn to become a woman I can never be. I try to curb my immoral conduct by staying away from you, yet you come here anyway, ingratiating yourself with my sister, pretending you're concerned for our welfare—"

"I am concerned—"

"—and you have the gall to stand there, smiling at me, looking so damned magnificent. Like a bloody prince—"

"Emma"—he blinked, astounded—"you cursed at me."

"Yes! Yes, I did, John Clayton. Are you happy now? You drive me to perpetrate every wicked trespass known to mankind. Covetousness, sloth, avarice, envy, fornication, profanity. Pick your sin!"

Charmed, he laughed uproariously. "You're a virtual felon."

"I hate you!"

"You're crazy about me."

"I am not!"

Clasping her bottom, he lifted her up, twirling her in circles while she batted at his shoulders.

"You're in love with me."

"You are so full of yourself."

"Say it out loud. Say that you love me."

"Not in a thousand years, you arrogant bounder!"

He stopped spinning them and loosened his grip, sliding her down his torso till her feet touched the ground.

No one had ever loved him. Not his distant, aloof parents. Not Ian, who found him to be—as Emma did— spoiled and impossible. Not Caroline, who was so steeped in ritual and ceremony that she couldn't recognize a valid emotion. Not any of the promiscuous women, such as Georgina, who had various motives, none of which had to do with excessive ardor.

If Emma was in love with him, he'd be swamped, deluged, bowled over by the force of her affection.

How frightening! How extraordinary! How glorious!

He cradled her in his arms, relishing how natural it felt to have her there. "You can't keep living where you are, so I want to find you other lodgings. Let me."

"We've been through this before. Any gift would make it seem as if you were paying me."

"I wouldn't intend any disgrace."

"But still, that's how I would feel. I'd be naught but another mistress to you."

"Em—"

"I would! Don't deny it. Knowing you brings me joy, and I won't let you ruin my happiness by transforming our relationship into something shoddy."

She was so forlorn, so tragic, that he was ashamed of every base tendency to which he'd ever succumbed. "I could never think badly of you."

"Then, how do you *think* of me? Are you ready to speak vows? To commit yourself to me and your responsibilities here at Wakefield? Or are you simply eager to copulate at your leisure, compensate me for it, and be on your way?"

He couldn't reply. The notion of proposing was so distressing that it made him weak in the knees, and he had to physically brace himself lest he fall over in a panicked swoon.

She couldn't expect that they would wed!

But the instant the supposition materialized, he realized that of course she would! That's what all women craved—except the dubious types with whom he was well acquainted. Yet marriage to her was out of the question. As was dishonoring her by setting her up as his mistress.

So what—precisely—did he want from her? Uncomplicated fornication? For which he paid? Which he received for free?

Neither concept was palatable, nor did they adequately address what he was growing so frantic to obtain.

He wanted to delight in her company, to bask in her glow, to wallow in the magic that erupted when they were together, but other than those obscure abstractions, he couldn't explicate what he desired. A fleeting sexual fling seemed the only viable outcome. It was an incredible conclusion for himself, but how could it be fair to her?

"I'm sorry, but I'm not very good at this," he admitted candidly. "I have to return to London soon, so I'm not positive where you fit. All I know is that I need to spend time with you while I'm here. I can't formulate an answer beyond that."

The perceptive look she flashed said that she hadn't anticipated anything better from him, and he felt petty and shallow.

"Come visit me tomorrow at the manor," he cajoled.

"Not while your fiancée is there."

"Get this through your head!" He grasped her shoulders and gave her a firm shake. "Caroline is *not* my fiancée."

"*She* believes she is."

"She's not."

"Why would your brother allege differently?"

"He likes you, and he doesn't want you hurt through your association with me. So he lied." Skeptical, she studied him, and he insisted, "Em, I'm not engaged."

"Swear it to me."

He placed one hand over his heart and raised the other as though pledging on the Bible. "I swear it."

She scoffed. "As if I'd take your word for anything."

He bent down and kissed her, a lush meeting of their mouths, and he was relieved when she didn't pull away. It had been an eternity since he'd last kissed her, and he tarried, cherishing every detail.

When they separated, he gripped her neck, and rested his forehead against hers. "I missed you."

"Don't say that."

"Why?"

"Because I want it to be true."

"It is, you silly wench. I missed you every second."

He kissed her again, and the embrace developed into something more, something stunning and bewildering. He couldn't fathom the moment in the future when he'd travel to London without her. How would he persist with his normal routine when she had so subtly altered his reality? What was there about his habitual method of carrying on that still appealed?

"Come to me tomorrow," he repeated.

"No."

"Caroline's leaving in the morning." At least, he hoped she was. For once, he would be abnormally blunt with her. The woman had to go! She couldn't be allowed to prevent him from fulfilling his abbreviated destiny with Emma.

"John—"

"At one. As always."

Shrugging, she nodded in defeat. She couldn't resist the mutual temptation any more than he could. Triumphant, elated that he'd worn her down, he took her arm and led her to the cottage.

Jane hid behind a bush and peeked down the lane. She could see the viscount and Emma. They were kissing!

She was so thrilled that she could barely restrain herself from whirling around in merry circles.

As she'd imagined, he looked like the picture of a prince in an old storybook Emma used to read to her as a child. He was so tall and handsome, so dashing and gallant. And he loved Emma! She just knew it!

Would he rescue them, like in the storybook?

Making a wish, she crossed her fingers. Then, doubling her chances for success, she removed a pretty rock from her pocket and buried it under a leaf for the fairies, reciting the same wish for them to hear.

Seizing every option, she murmured a prayer to God, imploring Him to bless them by giving Emma the viscount to love and treasure.

She peered down the lane again, and they were strolling toward her, so she scampered off and rushed into the house. A huge smile lighting her face, she sat at the table, toying with her soup as though she hadn't moved from her chair.

Harold Martin perched in his jaunty carriage, staring through the thick woods.

He couldn't believe it! He simply couldn't believe it! His Emma! Kissing another man!

It wasn't their first kiss, either. They were extremely familiar with one another.

When he'd rounded the corner and gazed down the road, he'd noted the pair and stopped. It had taken a minute to deduce the identity of whom he was watching, and his original reaction had been that some brigand was forcing himself on her. He couldn't conceive of the virtuous woman behaving immorally of her own accord, but as he'd spied upon her, he'd surmised that she was willingly participating.

She responded to the man as a harlot might, with hands, body, and tongue involved.

How could this be? Emma had defiled herself, had let a man—who wasn't her husband—touch her. Had she gifted him with her virginity? Her chastity belonged to Harold! How dare she cuckold him!

He'd strained to ascertain with whom she'd perverted herself, and after a thorough assessment, he'd been shocked to determine that it was Viscount Wakefield.

The scandal! The shame!

Wakefield was a libertine, a rake, a roué of the worst sort! He was disposed to any heinous conduct, and he regularly humiliated himself in London. Now, apparently, he'd decided to perform some of his depraved deeds in the country.

How had he gotten his dastardly clutches on Emma? What did it portend for Emma and himself? He couldn't marry her after this abomination!

Furtively, he continued to evaluate them as they ceased their torrid display and sauntered back to the loathsome cottage. As though they were old friends, they paraded arm in arm, disgustingly comfortable with one another.

Seething, he waited until they were inside, then he

found a clearing and turned around, proceeding to the
vicarage, with no one in the cottage aware that he'd been
on the Fitzgeralds' deserted road.

With each clop of the horse's hooves, he pondered
what he should do with the information he'd gleaned.
He was fond of his position, so he couldn't rile the viscount in case the eminent nobleman became irked and
had Harold's career terminated before it had really begun.

So how could he utilize his discovery to best advantage?

Emma was no more than a whore. Considering what
he'd learned about her proclivities, he didn't want her
as a bride, but could he garner other boons? On what
conditions might he coerce her into acquiescing?

Outraged, aghast, overtly offended—yet titillated by
the carnal prospects of her sordid nature—he hastened
on, his mind awhirl.

CHAPTER THIRTEEN

EMMA wasn't sure why she'd made the journey to Wakefield Manor. The disaster in John's foyer, with the beautiful Lady Caroline, had persuaded her that she must stay away. It had been one thing to philander with him when she'd believed that he dallied solely with scandalous mistresses. It was quite another to continue on after being apprised that he was engaged.

Since that dramatic encounter, she'd let the exalted lady's image constantly fill her mind, so that she'd be deluged by the reasons she had no place in John's life. The excuses she'd used to justify her wanton behavior were ludicrous.

As his brother had pointed out, Lady Caroline had always been slated to marry John, their parents having decided ages ago that their two exceptional, dynamic children would forge an alliance of power and influence about which Emma could only fantasize. If he didn't wed Lady Caroline—as he insisted he wouldn't—then some other gorgeous, poised woman of the aristocracy would ultimately be his bride.

It would never be Emma, which she knew absolutely and hadn't considered even a remote possibility, so her absurd attraction to him was insane, and she'd assumed she'd talked herself out of calling on him ever again. Her doldrums, her thriving discontentment, were inadequate pretenses for licentious comportment.

Yet, here she was, furtively climbing the rear stairs

of the mansion, hand in hand with John, creeping in like a pair of love-starved adolescents. They were bound for the safety of his bedchamber and the privacy they would enjoy once they were sequestered inside.

He was especially good at stealth, and she guessed it was a knack he'd developed as a child when, she was positive, he'd had extensive practice at racing down back hallways due to his penchant for mischief and trouble.

Oh, how confident she'd been that they wouldn't have a subsequent assignation! She was so weak of character!

After meeting the woman who was—or wasn't—his fiancée, she'd steadfastly avoided him. Then, he'd shown up at her door and, with a minimum of sweet-talking, she'd stupidly succumbed to his charm, privately thrilled that he'd fretted enough over her absence to find out where she lived, had expended the energy to check on her.

Still, after he'd gone, she'd vigorously scolded herself. She unequivocally was not going to the manor the following afternoon as he'd requested! Depressed about her decision, but determined, she'd risen and faced the day.

But then the irritating knave had sent a maid out from the mansion, with a huge basket of food draped over her arm, and an elaborate, personally written message from the viscount to Jane as to how he'd selected specific treats for her, and how he hoped they were her favorites.

Once the gift had been delivered, there was no way Emma could refuse it. Jane would have been shattered.

John had informed the servant—an older, reliable type with whom Emma had been acquainted for years—that Emma's presence was required at the main house, that she and John would be making estate visits together.

As they'd previously done just that numerous times, the retainer hadn't thought twice about his ruse.

John had also obligingly said that they would be late, that Emma would join him for supper, so the woman had to remain at the cottage to assist Jane until Emma returned. The servant hadn't doubted that prevarication, either. The viscount was her employer and her master, so she'd done his bidding without question or complaint.

The maid was convinced that Emma had a scheduled appointment with the viscount, so Emma hadn't had the nerve to dispute his claim, for she wasn't about to stir gossip as to why she'd dare spurn Wakefield's demand that she attend him. She'd freshened up and headed out.

As she'd strolled along her usual path through the woods, she'd incessantly reviewed why she'd so easily acquiesced, what she would say when she arrived, what she expected to accomplish before she left. Initially, she'd conjectured that it was another occasion where she would keep John at bay, but somewhere between her leaving her own house and trekking to his, her resolutions had gotten horridly jumbled.

She didn't want to be strong. She didn't want John at arm's length. Her prospects for interaction with him were swiftly dwindling. How long would he tarry at Wakefield before boredom or duty drew him to London?

It was that blasted kiss, she knew. The one he'd bestowed out on the lane in front of her cottage. With the summer sun shining down, and his confessing how much he'd missed her, her heart had cracked into tiny fragments as he'd voiced aloud her deepest, darkest secret: She was in love with him! How marvelous! How terrible!

He was everything she'd ever dreamed about, but

he was also everything her dear, departed father had counseled against. Yet despite how often she'd heard her father's prudent advice, where John was concerned, she couldn't heed it.

Her entire life, she'd pined for a man like John to sweep her away. He had, yet in a few days or weeks, he'd vanish like smoke, disappearing so rapidly that she'd eventually speculate as to whether she'd really known him, at all.

What a forlorn, miserable crossroads that would be!

She'd marched out of the forest and advanced on the manor, when he'd accosted her at the servants' entrance. Without a word, he'd yanked her inside, then ushered her upstairs, and she'd accompanied him with nary a reservation or objection. There'd been such a sense of the inevitable, a destiny she couldn't alter or prevent.

They reached a landing, and he covertly opened the door that led to the corridor, touching a finger to his lips to motion her to silence. As if she'd have made any noise! If they'd stumbled across a servant, she couldn't have formulated a sufficient falsehood as to what she was doing.

He glanced into the hall, which was empty, then he tiptoed out and tugged her after him. In moments, they were scurrying into his bedchamber, and he closed and locked the door behind them.

She did a hasty survey of her surroundings. It was a grand, masculine room, befitting John's importance, with dramatic, heavy pieces of furniture, red drapes and bedding, lush carpets and chairs. His massive bed dominated the center, with carved headboard, crimson drapings, and velvet quilts. It was on a pedestal, two steps above the floor and situated toward the large window, so that the occupants could recline and imperiously gaze across the rolling lawns of the estate.

Though she'd been inside once prior, at the fateful bath she'd given him, the decor hadn't made the same impression. As she'd been preoccupied that day, she'd barely noticed the imposing bed, or the sensual colors and fabrics. Now, in light of what was about to transpire, the room seemed downright hedonistic.

Suddenly, she was in dire need of sensory contact. She yearned to run her hand along the nap of the rich material, to peel off her stockings and curl her toes into the opulent rugs.

Off to the side, there was a table laden with refreshments. Bread, cheeses, pastries, cakes—enough to feed an army for a week. Several bottles of wine, as well as a decanter of brandy, were also available for her delectation.

He'd been so assured of her capitulation!

Certain she'd accede, he'd already untied the bow on her bonnet and tossed it away, had already pulled the pins from her hair so that the lengthy mass swished down her back.

"I missed you," he said, taking both her hands and ducking down to steal a kiss.

"I didn't miss you," she peevishly remarked.

"Liar."

He laughed and wrapped his arms around her, picking her up and twirling her in such fast circles that she was dizzy, and she could recollect no other episode that had been quite so precious. There was nothing so sublime as having John Clayton focus his undivided attention on her.

How would she manage after his departure?

"Maybe I missed you a little," she admitted as he set her down.

"I swear, Em, you drive a man crazy."

"I? How?"

"I didn't think you were coming. Do you have any idea how long I've been lurking by the back door and peeking outside?"

"No. How long?"

"None of your damned business. That's how long." She started to chastise him as to his language, when he halted her. "I know, I know. Don't curse."

"Thank you."

"I'm understanding you awfully well."

How frighteningly true. "Yes, you are. Tell me what you're about, dragging me up here to your bedchamber." As if she had no inkling! "I can't stay."

"Of course you can. There's no one to say where we are. The staff presumes I left an hour ago, and you're not needed at home. We've sneaked off."

"To do what?" She wasn't sure why she was playing dumb. Inside his trousers, she could feel his cockstand, firm and compelling at her belly.

Could she do this? How could she not?

"I want to make love with you, Emma. All afternoon. All evening. All night if I can keep it *up*." He laughed again, scooping her up and carrying her to the bed, and he eased her down so that she was on her knees and toward him.

"Say yes. It will be so wonderful."

It would. How could she resist?

Smiling at her, with those magnificent blue eyes, that dimple in his cheek, he was sin incarnate, a walking, talking magnet of vice and iniquity that lured her basest impulses to the fore.

I'll pretend it's my wedding night, she rationalized.

Now that she'd consorted with John, she had to confront reality: She'd never marry. After falling in love with him, she couldn't pledge her troth to another.

Why not relent? She could learn what it was like to be a woman, a wife, and long after John went to London, she would have her priceless memories. Why not seize this chance?

"I want to make love with you, too," she bravely conceded.

Her surrender was worth it just to see his reaction. He tumbled her onto the bed and followed her down so that his torso pressed her into the mattress from shoulders to toes. Her most sensitive areas were flattened to his, her breasts to his chest, her loins to his phallus, and she was ecstatic that she'd yielded. Like a lazy cat, she stretched, each subtle movement teasing her with the knowledge of what was to come.

"I've been waiting an eternity to do this," he said, and she agreed. It seemed as though the drudgery of their lives had been but stops on the road to this fantastic event. As though they'd both been merely existing until Fate could convey them to this juncture.

"I want to go slowly," she said, "so that later on I'll recall every detail."

"I'll try my best, but I can't make any guarantees. If I don't have your clothes off in the next five seconds, I can't say what I might do."

She grinned like a half-wit. How could she fail to be enchanted by the insolent rogue?

"Why are you smiling?" He was grinning, too.

"Because you make me happy."

"Good."

Tenderly, he stared down at her, and his regard made her wish for so many things that were beyond her ken, and she shoved away the disturbing wave of longing, determined to concentrate on the present and nothing more. When their rendezvous was over, and she was alone at her pitiful cottage in the woods, there would be plenty of opportunity for recrimination and regret.

The encounter became more profound. He was so beautiful that it hurt to look at him, and she had no illusions: If he'd been anyone else, she wouldn't be lying with him. No other man could have enticed her so completely or so effortlessly.

She was doing this for him. Because she loved him. Because she wanted him to be content.

He whispered in her ear, "It will be all right."

"I know," she whispered in reply.

"Don't be afraid."

"I'm not."

Gentle yet urgent, he kissed her, and she hugged him tightly so that she could lose herself in the act. She wanted to be inundated by uncontrollable passion, so overcome by what she was about to do that neither prudence nor discretion could dissuade her.

He intensified the kiss, his tongue engaging hers. Down below, his hands were at her breasts, kneading the soft mounds through her dress, pinching and trifling with her nipples. She spread her thighs, anchoring her feet behind his legs. Her skirt was bunched around her crotch, creating a pillow against which he could push and flex, his hips matching the rhythm of his tongue.

Leisurely, he unfastened her bodice, and as each enclosure was freed, her anticipation mounted.

Finally, he urged the front open and tugged the sleeves down, exposing her thin, worn chemise. He drew that down, too, baring her breasts. Transfixed, he fervidly assessed her bosom.

"Did I ever tell you that I adore your breasts?"

She blushed, unaccustomed to his sexual banter. "Yes."

"They're so fine. You were made for me, Emma."

He tarried at her cleavage, kissing her, making her wild by squeezing her nipples. Just when she was ready to explode from the delay, he suckled at one of the aroused tips. Showing her no mercy, he worked at the extended nub until it was raw and inflamed, then he went to the other, dabbling until she was writhing and making pitiful begging noises.

She was wanton, burning up, but for once, she didn't care. She intended to float on the tide of rising desire. Whatever happened was allowed.

His nimble fingers resumed their task, propelling the remainder of her apparel past her waist, her hips. Through it all, he was kissing and caressing her, murmuring endearments that encouraged her in her licentiousness.

Ultimately, her attire was down her legs, over her feet, and she was clad only in her stockings and shoes. He sat on his haunches so that he could gaze upon her naked torso. She was embarrassed and wanted to hide herself, her instinct to grab for a blanket or to toss an arm over her breasts and private parts, but she forced herself to submit to his scrutiny.

He commenced at her toes, rambling languidly up her legs, her calves, studying her womanly hair, then he slid two fingers inside. His thumb fondled her sex, and she arched up, desperate to come.

"You are so pretty, Emma." He hovered over her, his naughty hand titillating her. "God, I'm going to ride you so hard."

"Finish it!" she barked. Her untended body was at a precipice from which there could be no retreat. "Don't make me wait."

"You have to. You beseeched me to go slowly. Remember?"

He widened her nether lips, revealing her moist, pink core, as he visually evaluated her.

"John!" She couldn't decide whether she wanted him to desist or continue, but she couldn't abide much more torment.

He leaned down, zeroing in on where she frantically needed him to be. "Let's see if we can make you forget you're a vicar's daughter."

With a few deft strokes of his tongue, he prodded her to the edge and flung her over. She came in a torrid rush, her hips bucking against his zealous mouth. She tried to escape the turbulence, but he held her down, pinning her to the mattress as she soared.

Gradually, she descended to earth, and he was chuckling, languorously roaming up, lingering at her navel, her breasts, her nape. He kissed her deliberately, erotically, and she could taste her sex on his tongue. The tang was an invigorating stimulant that left her exhilarated with the need to touch him, to smell him, to absorb his essence into herself.

He was removing his shirt, fumbling with the buttons, and she took over, swiftly unveiling him. She'd changed her mind about the pace. Abruptly, she was in a hurry to have him stripped, to run her hands over that sinewy muscle, to have his virile male flesh melded intimately to her own.

She plucked at the hem, the lapels, yanking the sleeves off, then she snuggled down so that she could find his nipple. She licked and bit at it, and he grew more tense with each lave of her tongue.

While she dallied, she massaged his back, his shoulders, and she reached lower, petting him through his pants, until he couldn't endure the animation. He jumped up so that she could drag his trousers off his hips, down his thighs. In a jumble of fabric, shoes, and stockings, they wrestled and tangled together until they were both sinfully, blissfully naked.

He covered her, but with no clothing as a barrier to sensation, and they molded perfectly. The bristly hair on his chest and legs abraded and tickled her delicate skin. The energy that regularly sparked between them was alive, pulsating, and he was greatly perplexed by the strength of it.

"Do you feel that? Jesus, Emma, it's indescribable."

"Yes."

She was delirious, elated, and he smiled his devil's smile and flexed his hips, letting her savor the glide of his cock across her abdomen. The appendage was adamant, a pounding entity that demanded satiation, and he needed only to move slightly and he would enter her.

With the realization, her fortitude fled, and she *had* to postpone the inevitable, even if it was for a few minutes.

She rolled him onto his back and kissed down his stomach. Without his trousers blocking access, she was able to fully indulge. He was rigid, erect, his cock proudly jutting out, and she ruffled her nose through his manly hair, rooted till she was at the oozing crown, and she took him into her mouth. He rewarded her with a quick inhalation of breath, his abdomen clenching.

Most sane, virtuous women would have considered the deed appalling, but she reveled in the decadence, the abandon. Her level of enjoyment was further indication of her dissolute nature, of how far she'd fallen from the straight and narrow.

He permitted her to wallow, but he was nearing his limit. His body was taut, his respiration labored and rapid.

She braced for the conclusion, when surprisingly, he

twisted away, shifting her so that they were stretched out
with her on the bottom once more.

On witnessing her puzzled expression, he clarified.
"I want the first time to be between your legs."

It should have occurred to her that he'd seek the
normal route, and she could conjure up no excuse to
forestall the culmination, but still, she was nervous.

"Promise me one thing."

"My darling Emma"—he placed a sweet kiss on the
middle of her palm—"I will grant you whatever is
within my power to bestow."

"I need you to swear that you'll pull out at the last.
That you won't spill yourself inside me."

He frowned. "You're afraid we'll make a babe?"

"Of course I am, you big lout." She slapped his bare
backside, and he laughed, then sobered.

"I can't sire a babe, Emma."

"Why would you imagine you couldn't?"

"I haven't. Not in all these years."

If it was true and the promiscuous rascal had no
children, she suspected his lack of procreativity had
more to do with his choice of paramour than any physical defect. Very likely, his lovers didn't want children,
and they were in a position to acquire methods of preventing pregnancy.

Emma had heard gossip of tonics and concoctions
dispensed by barbers, apothecaries, and others who
vowed they were a panacea, but even if they were authentic, they weren't available to women in her world.
In her experience, when a woman had sex, she typically
had a baby nine months later.

"Promise me," she fervently repeated, not sure what
she'd do if he said no. Would she have the mettle to
rebuff him?

Shrugging, he smiled lazily. "As if I could refuse you anything."

Beginning anew, he kissed her, and within minutes, they were once again at the sharp crest of passion.

His competent fingers indolently roved down her torso, each inch bringing him closer, closer. She couldn't impede him, couldn't back down, couldn't alter their direction.

He riffled through her womanly hair, ensuring she was slippery and wet, when there hadn't been any doubt, then he clasped her thighs and spread her, his cock dropping into the correct spot as though it knew the way and needed no guidance.

When he stroked her with the crown, she pointlessly decided that he was too large, that he wouldn't fit, and she fought down a wave of panic.

Instantly, he sensed her trepidation. "Don't be scared, my little beauty." He urged in the tip. "Relax, and let me make you mine."

In an agile, fleet motion, he was inside her. The smooth thrust was graceful, efficient, and hadn't hurt as badly as she'd predicted it might. Yet the laceration burned and stung. Tears welled into her eyes, because of the pain, but also because of the significance of the moment and what it represented.

Though John was aroused, he wasn't stupid, and he recognized what had transpired. He froze, his body turning to stone, an angry scowl creasing his brow, then he jerked away. The evidence of the sin they'd committed— the red of her maiden's blood—was smeared across his phallus.

As if he'd just ascertained that she had the pox, he leapt off the bed and landed on the floor. Hands on hips, he glared down at her.

"Explain yourself."

"What do you wish to know?"

"You're a damned virgin!"

"I was."

She didn't understand why he was so upset. He was such a libertine that he could probably have a virgin on a daily basis. What was one more?

"What the hell are you up to?"

"I *thought* we were making love."

"Bloody right!" He grabbed for his pants and wrenched them on, hastily concealing himself. "What's going on? Do you have some incensed male relative about to dash in and discover us?"

"I don't have anybody," she said quietly, but he wasn't listening. "Not in the entire world."

"Well, it won't do you any good. Do you hear me, Emma?" He ranted on, floundering with his shirt, stuffing his arms into the sleeves. "If this is some kind of . . . of . . . *plot* to compel me to the altar, it won't work. I've had shrewder people than you attempting to coerce my behavior, and they haven't succeeded yet!"

The thick oaf actually surmised that she'd set a marital trap. How could he impugn her motives! The idiotic scapegrace! Didn't he comprehend that she was here because she loved him?

Her virginity had been a gift! How dare he discount it!

"As if I'd have you!" She vaulted off the bed, too, and snatched up her dress, hauling it over her head, then she marched to him till they were toe-to-toe, and she poked an irate finger at his chest. "You think you're some marvelous catch? Hah! I wouldn't marry you if you begged me!"

"Then what are you doing? A virgin gives herself to a man like me for one reason and one reason only:

marriage! Well, I hate to break the news to you, but you've picked the wrong fellow!"

"I certainly did!"

"Are you so foolhardy that you'd assume I'd bed you then wed you?"

"You pompous bastard!" she seethed.

Embarrassed and frantic to escape, she scrambled for her shoes and stockings, prepared to risk fleeing into the hall half-dressed if only she could be away.

She ran toward the door, but before she could exit, he seized her from behind, his arm snaking around her waist. Struggling against the restraint, she kicked with her feet and lashed out with her fists, but his grip was like an iron vise.

"Let me go!"

"No." He battled to hold on in the force of her fury. "I'm sorry. I'm sorry. I didn't mean what I said."

"Yes you did! Unhand me!"

"Emma! Stop it!" he decreed softly, and he snared her flailing arms at her sides. His command sucked the resistance out of her. She went limp and slumped into him.

"I'm sorry," he reiterated.

"It was a gift! A gift for you!" She gave a final, ineffective kick at his shin. "I loathe you!"

"No you don't."

"Yes I do! I absolutely do!"

He started across the room, lugging her along like a sack of coal, and not loosing his grasp for he knew if he did, she'd scurry out of his clutches. He pitched her onto the bed—precisely where she did *not* want to be—and he pinned her down before she could elude him.

"You know, Em, if I didn't already drink, you'd drive me to it."

He chuckled! Which enraged her so much that if

she'd had a pistol, she'd have shot him through the center of his black heart!

"Get off me." He didn't move a muscle, so she added, "Please?"

"Look at me."

"No."

She couldn't maintain her wrath. Any low opinion he harbored was due to her flagrant episodes of lascivious conduct. If he presumed she was a whore, she had no one to blame but herself, and she could scarcely condemn him for inferring the worst. She was tired, distressed, overwhelmed, and saddened, and she wanted to go home and never come back.

He embraced her tightly, which hindered any egress. "I'm sure your friends and neighbors have bandied many despicable rumors about my character—"

"And I believed every one of them," she petulantly interjected.

"I deserved that, I suppose." He swatted her on the rear. "I have my standards, Em. I've never made love to a virgin before."

"Well, let me tell you, you're not very good at it."

"I deserved that, too." He laughed, then balanced his finger on her chin so she had to match his gaze. "Why?" he inquired, bewildered. "I'm not worth it. Why did you do it?"

"Because I wanted you to be the one. Because I love you."

The simple explanation didn't begin to describe her feelings, and he nodded, accepting her profession of affection, but he didn't reply with a comparable attestation. Not that she'd expected a declaration of strong sentiment, but still, now that she'd thoroughly debased herself, it would have been nice to receive one.

"You know I can't marry you, don't you?"

Imbecilic lummox! "Have I suggested you should?"

"No, you haven't, and it makes me crazy. You're the only person I've ever met—besides my brother—who doesn't want something from me." He was probing, intent, and he appeared young, self-conscious, anxious. "Am I forgiven?"

She was astonished that he'd asked for her pardon. Considering his station, he likely never had to apologize to anyone about anything, and the fact that he had was a sign that he entertained some fondness for her.

She was such a ninny! "Yes, you bounder."

Tenderly, he kissed her, sending her defenses plummeting. "I want to try this again," he sweetly cajoled. "Let me show you how it can really be."

Fool! Fool! Fool! she chastised herself, but even as the admonition spiraled past, she was helping him to lift her skirt up her legs, raising her hips so he could ease her dress up and over her shoulders.

With no more discussion than that, he had her naked and willing, ready to acquiesce—once more—to whatever he wanted.

Lord, give her strength! She had no self-control. Not a shred of dignity remaining.

There was no longer a barrier to restrict his penetration, so he easily glided inside. She was sore from his first invasion, so she winced at his second, but her bruised body swiftly acclimated. Reaching for her hands, he spread them on either side of her head, their fingers linked.

He smiled, and she smiled, too, cherishing him, relishing the moment and the man. She was weak, obsessed, daft, haunted by her need for him, and with no further rumination or reflection, she wrapped her legs around him and pulled him close.

CHAPTER FOURTEEN

CAROLINE wandered aimlessly down the dark hall, the polished floor cold on her bare feet. Even though it was midsummer, the rambling residence was drafty, and she tugged on the belt of her robe.

As John had been out all day, touring the estate, she'd wasted the tedious hours, drifting through the lonely mansion, pondering why she'd been so absurd as to believe a visit to Wakefield would rectify their relationship. When he'd finally appeared for an extremely belated supper, he'd seemed different, happy, and content in a fashion she hadn't previously noticed. Depressingly, it had occurred to her that the changes had nothing to do with herself.

After the meal, she'd endured another unpleasant *talk*, and since then, she hadn't had the heart for any diversion. She'd declined to degrade herself by passing the evening in the downstairs parlor, socializing and pretending all was fine, as was her wont when events went awry. Despite how often her mother had counseled against displays of emotion, sometimes a woman simply had to react!

John had said no, and he'd really meant it. Where before, her parents had been a stalwart buffer, convincing her to discount his rejections, she couldn't any longer. Reality was a bitter tonic to swallow, and she hated its harsh taste, but he was sincere and resolved, and his intent had been brutally clear.

There would be no wedding. Ever.

She was despondent, forlorn, angry; she could very well explode from the cauldron of suppressed feelings she was holding inside. Her toleration was gone, her resentment simmering.

As usual, when the conversation had been transpiring, she'd bitten her tongue, had placidly put up with his gentle rebuke over her unbidden appearance, had obediently agreed to his demand that she depart, but afterward, in the privacy of her bedchamber, she'd conjured up dozens of scathing retorts.

How she wished she could have said what she really thought! What she wouldn't give to speak her piece! Just once! If she ever let loose at the inconsiderate scoundrel, she'd likely never stop ranting!

She'd been so sure that her arrival would alter their association, that he'd be proud of her daring, that he'd see her in a new light. But he pictured her as he always had: an immature girl, who was frivolous and irrational, and who needed men to constantly watch over her.

Why . . . if asked about her father—his whereabouts, or how he would regard her behavior, or what he might do if he found out about her trip—once more, she might start screaming.

John's library was on her left, and she walked to the door and went inside. Someone had been there earlier. The last embers of a fire glowed in the grate and warmed the salon to a bearable temperature. Through the dim glimmer of her candle, she strolled about, investigating the paintings, the books on the shelves. The estate ledgers were open on the desk, and she ran her fingers over the lengthy columns of debits and credits, saddened that they represented a position that wouldn't be hers.

How was it that she'd invested so much effort, so

many years, in John Clayton with nothing to show for it?

He'd persistently told her that he wouldn't marry her, but she hadn't wanted to listen, so she hadn't heeded his denials, but the idiocy wasn't all her fault. Others were guilty, too. His father. Her parents and grandparents. Her friends. Everyone had been so certain that he'd come up to snuff.

She couldn't calculate the number of occasions when she'd heard people affirm that he was merely sowing his wild oats. That he'd inevitably buckle down and do his duty. That she had to be patient, accepting. Especially after his father had died, her mother had been ecstatic, assured that she'd soon be overwhelmed by wedding plans.

They'd all been so optimistic; they'd all been so stupid. John would someday carry out his responsibilities. He would marry and sire a son as was required. Only he wouldn't do any of it with her.

She didn't know what he was searching for in a wife, but she obviously possessed none of the traits, and the notion was so discouraging that she couldn't contemplate it. Her entire identity was wrapped up in the assumption that she would one day marry the Clayton heir, so she felt as if the rug had been pulled out from under her.

If she wasn't going to be the Viscountess Wakefield, then who was she?

The concept of going to London, of having to advise her parents, of suffering through people's sarcasm and ridicule, was excruciating! As she had no idea how to withstand such a storm, the vultures would devour her! Unceasingly, she'd been the perfect daughter, then the perfect fiancée, and she'd spent every waking minute demonstrating flawless comportment, not ruffling a feather, making a wave, or causing a brow to raise.

With his repudiation, what horrors would rain down on her? And how would she survive them?

She had no inkling how to persevere through a scandal, how to live with censure and disparagement. Was it possible to die from mortification?

If she somehow managed to brave the catastrophe, she was quite sure her mother wouldn't. The reserved older woman would expire from an apoplexy the first instance that a rumor was bandied about on the lips of another.

Sinking down into the chair behind the massive desk, she buried her head in her hands. How had she traveled to this pitiful juncture? What was she to do next? What would become of her?

Footsteps shuffled down the corridor, approaching the library, and she panicked. For two hours, she'd been roving about. No one else was awake! If she'd deemed otherwise, she wouldn't have come downstairs.

Who could it be? What if it was John? If he waltzed in, she'd absolutely perish!

She couldn't be observed when she was so disheveled! Jerking upright, she took several fortifying breaths, relaxing her facial muscles into an imperturbable, serene smile. Her hair was down, and she couldn't repair it, nor could she reverse the fact that she was attired solely in a thin summer nightdress and robe, so she decided not to focus on what she couldn't correct.

Rising, she forced herself to look as composed as she was able, just as Ian Clayton sauntered in. Her panic turned to dread, then alarm, then fury. How dare he interrupt her anguished reverie! He was a master at ruining everything!

In one hand, he carried a candle, in the other, a plate of food, and it dawned on her that the room hadn't been vacant after all. Apparently, he'd been working on the estate ledgers and had skipped out to the kitchen for a snack.

What ill luck had drawn her in as he'd stridden out? She had to escape!

He was fully dressed, a detail that irked her to no end, though he'd shed his coat and cravat. His shirt was unbuttoned, the sleeves unbound and the cuffs rolled back. She could view part of his chest and forearms, and they were covered with an intriguing blanket of dark hair, as black as the hair on his head. The amplitude of masculine flesh was distracting, and she refused to pay any attention to it, rigidly keeping her eyes affixed to his.

"Excuse me," she disdainfully stated, "but I didn't realize this room was occupied."

"Well, well . . . if it isn't the ice queen," he chided. "What brings you out so late? Are you hoping to scare someone to death with your exemplary manners?"

She was tired of him; she was tired of every male person she'd ever known. Her whole life, she'd endeavored to mollify and placate them, and where had it gotten her? Nowhere, that's where! She was dying to lash out. To say what she felt like saying. To perform whatever impolite, discourteous exploit tickled her fancy.

"Shut up, Ian!" she snapped. "I'm so sick of your mouth! And your attitude!"

"My, my! The lady actually has a temper." Curiously, he assessed her. "And it's showing."

"Go to hell!" There! She'd let him have it! And no one had passed away! How astonishing! How refreshing! How liberating! "You . . . you . . . bastard!"

"Now, now, don't insult my mother."

Wary, he advanced on her, as if he were afraid she might bite. Considering her elevated level of pique, he was wise to fret about what she might do. Suddenly, she felt capable of any coarse conduct.

As she glared at him across the expanse of oak, he deposited plate and candle, and she was furious to note that the blackguard was laughing at her. Didn't anyone take her seriously?

"I'm not about to stay here and be abused by the likes of you."

She stormed toward the door, but he reached out and caught her wrist before she could slip by. His grip wasn't strong or tight, and he wasn't threatening, but the intimate gesture yanked her to a halt. In her world, corporeal contact was so forbidden that she frequently felt as if she were living in a bubble. The heat of his hand, burning through her nightclothes, was shocking and wonderful.

He shifted closer, so that they were shoulder to shoulder, their sides melded all the way down. She'd intended to glower at him, but as their gazes locked, she was mesmerized instead by how acutely blue were his eyes.

The peculiar, inexplicable strength he generated was radiating out, enveloping her. The air around them leapt with invisible activity, as if their proximity were producing sparks.

He frowned and evaluated her, a thousand sentiments playing across his handsome face.

Finally, he inquired, "What's wrong?"

There was such tenderness and concern in his voice, that she was completely undone. Tears surged to the fore, and she tamped them down.

Out of habit, she contended, "Nothing."

"Don't lie, Caro." He used her pet name, but she didn't scold him.

"What makes you think I'm lying?"

"You are an open book to me." His hand slithered down so that he could link his fingers with hers. "Tell me what's happened."

He leaned against the desk, his hips on the edge, and he didn't release her. She didn't sever their connection, either. The attachment was fascinating, enthralling. With bare skin to bare skin, what marvelous sensations were provoked!

A familiarity was burgeoning, the type that spurred the confessing of secrets, the sharing of woes, though she didn't comprehend the reason it would. Perhaps it was because they were alone, or the quiet of the room, or the odd isolation with this man to whom she'd been acquainted for years but didn't know at all.

By giving a tug, he lured her in so that she was cradled between his thighs, and the resulting intimacy was breathtaking.

"Tell me," he repeated. "Is it John? Has he hurt you?"

The vehemence with which he posed the question startled her, and she was left with the distinct impression that if she but asked it of him, Ian would act as her champion. How splendid to have such a virile fellow outraged on her behalf. Too bad there was naught to defend!

"He's not going to marry me, is he?" She'd surmised the answer by herself, but she needed to speak the forbidden aloud.

Studying her, he struggled to be frank without distressing her further. In the end, the truth won out, and there was no easy way to say it.

"No, he isn't."

"Thank you for your honesty." Graciously, she nodded, cherishing his candor as a gift. "I'd allowed others to persuade me that he simply wasn't ready to settle down, but he wouldn't have, would he? No matter how long I waited?"

"No."

The veracity was exhilarating, but oh, how it wounded her! "So you've talked with him about me?"

"A few times," he gently remarked.

"Do you know—" She paused, hating to debase herself by probing but she *had* to understand. She tried again. "Did he mention why he felt I was so unsuitable?"

"Oh, Caro, is that what you suppose? That there was something inappropriate about *you*?"

"What else would I suppose?"

He rested his hands on her waist, his fingers digging into her lower back, and he urged her forward so that her front collided with his torso. Her breasts were flattened to his chest, and strangely, her nipples beaded into taut buds that poked her nightgown—and him!—making her agonizingly aware of herself as a woman. Whenever he moved, she was rubbed across him, creating tingles of agitation that shot through her bosom and downward, making her stomach clench and her loins ache.

Her crotch was merged to his. She was touching him—there!—and her body wept with an impulse to be nearer, inducing myriad anatomical confusions that had her fidgeting and worrying about morals and principles. Though she knew it was indecent to be situated so wickedly, she couldn't fathom why she would want to remove herself.

His mouth was mere inches from her own, and her pulse pounded frantically. She was positive he was going to kiss her, and she was enthusiastically prepared to let him. She'd never been kissed, though she'd incessantly fantasized about what it would be like.

On this horrid night, when her life was crashing

down around her, if Ian Clayton was inclined to kiss her, she wasn't about to dissuade him.

Yet, he vastly disappointed her—being a gentleman just when she didn't want him to be! No kiss was forthcoming!

"Don't blame yourself for John's decision," he kindly asserted. "It didn't have anything to do with you."

"But it must have!"

"Caro, you shouldn't regret this. John couldn't see the fire burning within you. You'd have been so miserable."

He recognized the passion smoldering deep within! How thrilling that he could perceive it! She'd had to douse the flames so often that it was scarcely a flicker. "I'm so ashamed, and I feel so foolish. How will I return to London?"

"You're tough. You don't give yourself enough credit."

"I can imagine the snide comments. It will be so terrible. How shall I abide the humiliation?"

Tears fell, and she didn't try to hide them. He seemed so sympathetic, a true confidant to whom she could acknowledge her worst fears, and she couldn't see any valid purpose for disguising the extent of her wretchedness.

She never bemoaned her fate, having existed in such a sterile, barren environment for so long that she was totally insulated from any event that would effect an upset. Manifestations of emotion were the height of indecorum. Weeping might cause her nose to redden, her cheeks to mottle, so lamentation had to be immediately quashed.

"Have a good cry, darling," he murmured, snuggling her to his broad chest. "You'll feel better when you're done."

His giving her permission to grieve opened a flood-gate, and she let the tears flow. She mourned everything. For losing John's older brother, for losing John. For being twenty-four years old and a spinster. For never being in love or having had the chance to be loved by the man of her dreams.

Through the whole episode, he held her, his large hands running up and down her back, while he whispered endearments in his native Scottish language. She let them permeate her broken heart and troubled soul, and they were a soothing balm.

Gradually, her melancholy ebbed, and as it did, the embrace transformed, becoming something more, something ardent and impetuous. It started slowly, a kiss to her ear, her hair, but he continued on until he reached her mouth, and she did nothing to delay or impede his quest.

Her first kiss was a sweet brush of his lips to her own, and it was so delightful, and so precious, that she could only ponder why she hadn't previously indulged.

Quickly, it escalated as he increased the urgency, gripping her neck and angling them. His tongue toyed with her, dipping in the tiniest amount, and she profusely grasped what he was seeking and welcomed him inside.

Surprisingly, she had an uncanny knack for kissing. She effortlessly deduced what was expected of her, how to participate and garner maximum enjoyment.

She sneaked her arms around his waist, hugging him as fiercely as he was hugging her. Her fingers explored, tracing bone and muscle, learning shape and size. Her breasts and privates were in an even more suggestive situation, and she could feel the ridge between his legs that she'd heard tittered about by married friends.

She'd excited him in a masculine fashion! How

magnificent! How rewarding! At least one man in this despicable house found her beguiling.

He groaned as his mouth took hers again, and he seemed to be in pain. "God, I've been wanting to do this with you forever."

"Forever?" she gulped, flabbergasted.

The embrace intensified. He clasped her backside and cupped her bottom. The move was wanton, amazing, and it aroused her baser instincts. He pulled her to his loins, flexing them together in a novel rhythm that she readily adopted. The bodily conjunction made her strain and stretch, needing more stimulation and never having enough.

He was encouraged by her enhanced involvement, grumbling a moan of pleasure that rumbled through her nerve endings and ignited her feminine instincts. Abruptly, she wanted things from him that she couldn't begin to name. She was ablaze with longing, and bizarrely, she wished he would kiss her all over.

While mentally, she comprehended that she should desist, physically she felt as if she'd arrived exactly where she belonged, that she'd always been equipped for him to handle her in such outrageous, dramatic ways. Whatever depraved deeds he might perpetrate against her person would be precisely what was needed to alleviate the building tension that was driving her to recklessness. If the pressure wasn't assuaged, she might explode!

He caressed her breast! His hand slid inside her nightgown, and he clutched the mound, molding and manipulating it, then his finger and thumb glided to her nipple, pinching and tweaking the nub in an afflicting, seductive manner. Her response was instantaneous and striking; she felt as if he'd jolted her with a bolt of lightning.

How could she survive such commotion? It couldn't be healthy! Such an extraordinary reaction had to be dangerous!

"Ian! Stop it!"

From behind her, in the vicinity of the doorway, John barked the command, but it took several seconds for reality to pervade sufficiently for her to realize that he'd entered the library and was observing all.

"Ian!" he growled again.

His severity penetrated, and with a shriek, she wrenched herself from Ian and leapt away. With the brusque loss of the security of his arms, she was off balance, and she stumbled to find her footing.

"Shit!" Ian griped, then he muttered an epithet she'd not heard before. She wasn't certain of its definition, but the tenor with which he uttered it unequivocally captured her disposition.

She couldn't have been more embarrassed if her father had stomped into the middle of the torrid scene. Her cheeks were flaming crimson, her heart hammering, and she grappled to regain her composure.

Ian rested a supportive, comforting hand on the small of her back, and she lurched away, imposing distance. With the light of discovery shining upon them, she didn't want to be seen as joined with him in disreputable behavior.

What must John think? No wonder he wouldn't have her! Who would? A few hours earlier, he'd clarified his position as to marriage, and her inaugural act as an unattached woman was to trifle with his brother like a common slattern!

Harshly, John queried, "What the hell are you doing?"

At his brutal tone, she jumped, then swiftly discerned that he was scolding Ian and not herself.

"What did it look like?" Ian insolently replied, casually rising from his perch on the desk as if he hadn't a care in the world. "I was kissing Caroline."

The room was charged with a frightening menace. If they'd been holding pistols, the guns would have been drawn and leveled at each other. All because of her!

She'd never witnessed this side of either of them. In fact, she wasn't aware that they ever quarreled. They were never at odds, and to detect that her lewd conduct had instigated discord was an added disgrace.

"Caro, leave us."

John issued the decree, and though she was desperate to flee from his scrutiny, his superior attitude raised her hackles.

For once, she bravely claimed, "You've relinquished your right to order me about."

"That may be"—he didn't take his eyes off Ian—"but you're a guest in my home, and your father's not here. In his stead, I *will* see to your welfare." He glanced at her, and his fury shook her to her core.

"Go!" he declared, and she scurried away like a timid rabbit.

"Caro! Wait!" Ian beseeched, but she didn't hesitate or turn around.

She was mortified, shamed, having heinously perverted herself, and she couldn't bear to ascertain how he might be viewing her. With fondness? With regret? God—with pity?

For one fleeting, joyous moment, she'd lowered her ingrained defenses, had dropped her inhibitions, had let her wild nature take flight, but she'd crashed to the ground rapidly enough—just as her mother had warned would happen should she give free rein to her sordid proclivities.

What had come over her?

Blame it on the night. On the shadows and the isolated room. On the elegant, dashing man.

Temporary insanity, that's all it was. It couldn't have been anything more.

Under control, she rushed out and hastened to the safety of her bedchamber. Too distraught to sleep, she packed her bags so that she'd be ready to depart at dawn.

Ian remained rooted to his spot, listening as Caro's footsteps faded, then he analyzed John as he approached.

He didn't know what explication he could furnish, or why he would feel honor bound to provide one. Especially to John, who hadn't once refrained from engaging in any dubious diversion, but from the deadly gleam in his brother's eye, he could tell that he'd crossed a line that even John—in his jaded state—couldn't tolerate.

There was an overdue confrontation pending, but he was in no mood for it. He had numerous bones he'd like to pick with John that had never been addressed but, as he was still in the throes of arousal, he wasn't in any condition to discuss them. His balls were aching, his pulse racing, his senses overloaded.

As he'd suspected, Caro was a lusty woman, whose prurient attributes had been repressed for so long that she wasn't cognizant that they existed. If John hadn't bumbled in when he had, Ian couldn't predict what he might have done. Would he have proceeded to deflowerment? Would he have ravished her on top of the desk without regard to the consequences?

With her, he'd had to constantly fight a rampant, perilous attraction that couldn't be acted upon. He'd considered her to be like an angel in heaven. Admired, worshipped, but inviolate. To have finally been granted the opportunity to dally with her! How could he have passed it up?

The experience had confirmed his worries about his tainted constitution once and for all. If he could abuse Caro so terribly, then there was no doubt he was the bastard birth status said he was, and thus, completely unworthy of someone so fine. Why did he spend so much time trying to prove otherwise?

Testy, distressed, his body was loudly proclaiming its displeasure as to its lack of alleviation. His thoughts were disordered, and he couldn't be relied upon to respond with his usual astuteness.

John advanced until they were toe-to-toe. "Don't touch her again."

"Or what?"

"You'll have to answer to me."

"God, I'm trembling." Would this be the occasion when they came to blows? Formerly, they'd had their dissensions, but one of them had habitually backed down before tempers raged.

"Fuck you!"

"What are you so upset about? You don't want her," he reproached. "Why do you care who does?"

"I may not want her, but you can't have her." Cruelly, he pointed out, "You're too far below her station."

There was no more demeaning criticism John could have made. They both knew it, and that he had hurled the remark merely indicated how high their passions were running. They were too aggravated for rational conversation, yet Ian was a vain man, and his pride regularly goaded him into all sorts of unsavory trouble. He wasn't about to abide the slight.

"So what are you saying, John? That I'm good enough for your sleazy mistress to sneak into my bed and suck me off in the middle of the night"—he stretched to his full height, meeting his brother's angry glare with one of his own—"but I'm too foul to kiss your pretty little ex-fiancée?"

John hit him so hard that he almost fell down. As he lurched sideways, an ornamental table crashed to the floor and sundry figurines went flying. He clutched the desk, wrestling to stabilize himself.

"Jesus . . . I'm sorry." John was immediately repentant, and he reached out to Ian to steady him, but Ian shook him away.

"Bugger off."

They glowered at one another, John massaging his sore knuckles, Ian swiping blood from a cut on his cheekbone, then John moved behind the desk, wisely putting space between them.

"I'm sorry," he maintained again. "I don't know what came over me."

"You're a prick. You always have been."

A damaging silence ensued, and if either of them broke it, they'd likely express hurtful slurs they didn't mean. Or perhaps the problem was that whatever they might fling would be exactly what was intended, but in the past, the accusations had been judiciously held in.

"I don't think any of those things about you," John said. "I never have."

"Save the confessions for your pedigreed friends."

John sighed and rubbed his bruised hand once more. Disturbed and bewildered at the turn of events, he asserted, "It's folly for you to pursue her, Ian. Her parents wouldn't allow it in a thousand years. You grasp that, don't you?"

"Of course I do," Ian caustically retorted, "but that doesn't stop me from wanting her."

"Why didn't you confide in me?"

"It was none of your damned business."

He couldn't enumerate how often he'd looked the other way, or feigned apathy, while ignoring John's treatment of her, and assuring himself it was none of his concern.

Caroline had been a nagging thorn in his side, and he'd forced himself to discount his fascination. He'd even managed to persuade himself that he was bewitched simply because she was John's, the consummate symbol of every wretched inequity in the world.

Drained, John started to sit and, in the process, peered down at the desktop. In the melee, Ian had forgotten what he'd been doing before Caroline had walked in. The estate ledgers were out and open, when they shouldn't have been. The books had been tucked away since early afternoon, locked in the drawer, with John supposedly having the only key.

Ian's journal, where he'd been copying sums, was next to the accounting records, his distinctive handwriting impossible to disregard. The pages containing his notes were also visible, an incriminating pile of evidence for which there could be no valid justification.

John perused the materials, while he tried to interpret what he was seeing, and Ian braced. This altercation had been looming for an eternity, and he was surprised it hadn't arrived much sooner. Only John's reputed disinterest in fiscal matters, and their father's presence as a wedge to discovery, had kept it from occurring.

"Explain yourself," he said.

Ian shrugged, swallowing down a wave of remorse, unwilling to grovel or apologize. "I've been checking the balances. Calculating my share."

"Your *share* of what?"

"Of what Father promised me for watching over you."

"How long has this been going on?"

"Since I first came to London." Twelve years. Twelve years of deceit and duplicity, of lies and scheming and conniving with his father to John's ultimate detriment.

"Why?"

John was gravely wounded, but Ian steeled himself against feeling any sympathy. His brother had been given so much, but he had scant appreciation for how fortunate he was. "Because Father asked it of me. And it was an enormous financial boon."

"How *enormous*?"

"Ten percent of the profits from each of your individually owned properties that Father was administering for you."

"Ten percent for doing what?"

"For baby-sitting you. For reporting."

John was aghast and stunned. "You were paid to tattle to him about my personal affairs?"

"Every detail I felt warranted his attention."

"That's why we crossed paths in London."

"Aye."

"Our meeting wasn't an accident." The ramifications were gradually sinking in. "You plotted against me. With Father."

"Yes. He sent for me after you moved out on your own. He didn't trust you, and he wanted my assistance."

"Was there an ending date to your agreement with Father? Or did you have license to steal from me in perpetuity?"

Ian hadn't viewed it as *stealing*; he'd worked for every farthing of his blood money. "There was no fixed duration, though I had the authority to terminate our arrangement if I could convince him that you'd changed."

"My, my, what faith he had in your abilities." The

unspoken comment being that their father hadn't had any faith in John.

"I tried my best."

"I'll just bet you did."

Though John valiantly struggled to hide his reaction, his shock was so great that his knees buckled, and he collapsed into the chair, staring blankly at the condemnatory information. "I want you to leave in the morning."

"I'd planned on it."

"When I return to London, I want you gone from the town house."

"As you wish."

Tormented and afflicted, John scrubbed a weary hand over his eyes. "Your thievery is finished. You'll relinquish all your keys, then I don't want to hear from you ever again. I'll have my solicitor contact you to negotiate an appropriate monetary settlement."

"Stuff it," Ian said crudely, spinning around to go. "I don't need any support from the Wakefield coffers. I have plenty in the bank already."

He strolled out, declining to dawdle and rehash the contemptible situation.

At the last second, John said quietly, painfully, "I thought you were my friend."

"I never was." He departed without looking back.

CHAPTER FIFTEEN

IAN strode down the hall toward the foyer. The summer sun had barely colored the horizon when he'd risen for the journey to London. He'd grabbed a bite of cheese and bread in the kitchen, had a horse saddled and ready outside the door.

All he need do was go, but he couldn't make his feet take those decisive steps. So much was left unfinished—with Caroline and with John—and he suffered from the distinct impression that, once he went, he'd never see either of them again.

He stopped by the library and walked over to John's desk, where he deposited a pouch containing the keys their father, Douglas Clayton, had given him. Keys to desks, keys to doors, keys to ledger books. A damning collection.

Briefly, he considered jotting a letter, some message of apology or justification, perhaps a simple farewell, but he couldn't think of any statement that wouldn't seem selfish or greedy. He marched out, refusing to ruminate or ponder the ways he'd betrayed his brother.

He wasn't sure why he'd consented to act as an accomplice with Douglas. In most situations, he hadn't been able to abide the tyrant. When Douglas had first approached him with the idea of spying on John, he'd been annoyed and insulted, yet secretly flattered that the philandering bounder had needed him.

While he'd like to blame youth and naïveté for what

he'd done, they were sorry pretexts. At age twenty, he'd been callow, poor, and easily swayed, but what was his excuse for continuing on when he was twenty-five? When he was thirty?

Could he ever find a valid reason for his conduct? He and John had had their ups and downs, their quarrels and differences. John could be difficult, complex, troublesome, but Ian was no saint, himself. They'd got on famously most of the time, the periods of conflict short and rapidly forgotten.

John was his only brother. What had possessed Ian to suppose that any amount of money was worth losing his friendship and regard?

John had no one whom he trusted. Too often, he'd been duped and deceived. By their father and most everyone else. He didn't absolve others of their sins, and he'd never forgive this. Their relationship was over. Forever.

Ian had uttered some vile remarks that he'd both meant and hadn't, that he regretted yet didn't. Frequently, his pride and envy overcame his better sense. Jealousy goaded him to do things he hadn't intended, to hurt those he loved.

He sighed. What a waste it all was. Their sibling rivalry. His covetousness and resentment. Through his perfidy, he'd grown to be a rich man, yet he reaped no satisfaction from his affluence. What contentment was there in wealth that had been earned by such dubious methods? He couldn't fully enjoy benefits that were obtained at John's expense.

In the foyer, he donned his coat and hat, arranged to exit into the chilly dawn air, when footsteps sounded on the stairs. Anxious, he looked up, anticipating it was John, speculating as to whether his brother had had a change of heart during the interminable night and had decided they shouldn't part on such bitter terms.

To his great surprise, it wasn't John, but Caroline.

For the merest instant, she paused, a hitch in her gait, and he read a thousand emotions on her beautiful face. Joy, embarrassment, bewilderment, animosity. From the blow John had delivered, he'd sustained swelling and bruising to his cheek and brow and, as she noted his injury, her eyes widened with dismay, then she carefully masked any exhibition of sentiment, retreating behind her typical wall of ennui and disdain.

She floated down, her maid trailing after her. They were wearing cloaks, hats, and gloves, and she was obviously prepared to travel without a word of *adieu* to either John or himself, which was understandable. By any stretch of the imagination, the previous evening's debacle hadn't been the Clayton brothers' finest moment, and he wished he could fix what had befallen her, but he hadn't devised a feasible solution.

After incessantly fretting as to her condition, he'd sneaked to her room, not certain what he was hoping to have happen. Luckily, her door had been locked, so he hadn't entered, and he was still trying to figure out why he'd made the effort. The incident in the library had been terrible. Not their lengthy kiss, but how it had ended, with John witnessing their passion, with his admonishment of her as though she were a child, with her humiliation over being caught.

Ian wanted to make it right, but he hadn't a clue as to what his actions should be. He wasn't about to apologize for kissing her, which was what he was positive she'd demand from him. The encounter had been delightful, what had occurred marvelous, and she hadn't done anything wrong.

As she reached the bottom stair, he hesitantly acknowledged, "Lady Caroline."

"Mr. Clayton." She was haughty, contemptuous.

How could she carry on as if they were strangers? A few hours earlier, he'd had his hand on her breast! Anger surged, hot and potent, and he had to quash an impulse to shake her until her teeth rattled.

As if he were invisible, she strutted past him, flaunting her position, her station, and he grabbed her wrist, the subtle maneuver immediately detaining her.

"Couldn't you be bothered to say good-bye?"

"Why would you feel it necessary that I say good-bye to *you*?"

"Pardon me, Your Royal Highness."

She was panicked, afraid that he might allude to their dalliance in front of the maid, and thus her indiscretion would be relayed to her father. "As we're scarcely acquainted, Mr. Clayton, what might I need pardon you for?"

He sighed again. Hating her. Hating himself. "Nothing, Lady C. Nothing at all."

"Well, then—" She shifted away, breaking their physical contact.

"Are you off to London?"

"Yes, although I fail to see how my plans are any of your affair."

"I'm going, too. Would you like me to ride with you?"

"Honestly! As if I require a male escort! I'm twenty-four years old; I can take care of myself."

She strutted to the door, her maid scurrying before her to open it, and he watched her, his venom spiraling as he muttered under his breath, "Impossible bitch."

He hadn't meant for her to discern the crude epithet, but she had. As if she'd been stabbed by his disrespect, she halted. Her back was ramrod straight, her body trembling with ire, and he truly postulated that his boorishness might impel a scathing retort, but he was mistaken.

Fury suppressed, dignity intact, she strolled out without turning around.

For several minutes, he loitered until her coach rattled away, then he went out, mounted his horse, and followed her, eager to catch up with her and gallop on without giving a thought to her welfare.

With a quick tug of the reins, he trotted down the winding drive toward the lane and the village beyond. Before the final curve in the road, he pulled in and gazed at the manor.

The sun was rising behind the house, the orange sky making the masonry glow as though it was afire. He took in the scene, appraising, evaluating, remembering, and as he did, he detected movement in an upstairs window. Narrowing his focus, he endeavored to ascertain who it might be, but he couldn't tell.

Desperately, he yearned for it to be John, and he waved—just in case it was. Then he cantered on, rushing by Caroline's lumbering carriage, hurrying toward London and whatever lay ahead.

Georgina relaxed in her chair, in the center of Wakefield's box at the theater, her eyeglass pressed to her eye as she spied on the opulent, bejeweled crowd.

She held court like a queen, welcoming friend and foe alike during the lengthy intermission, and from her demeanor, no one could have suspected that she was nervous as to her status with John. As her world was filled with vicious, malevolent people—too many of whom she'd maltreated or insulted—she hadn't shared her secret. There was a veritable horde that would relish in her downfall.

For a month now, she'd dawdled at home, with no

information, and she was frustrated and frantic.

Her anonymous note to Caroline Foster had worked like a charm. As Georgina had predicted, the foolish ninny had scampered after John. He would abhor such cleaving behavior, but he'd have hosted her politely, and would have endured many a tedious day entertaining her, which was precisely what Georgina had wanted. Every hour he spent with Lady Caroline would be one he couldn't spend with that slattern who'd captured his fancy.

But still, Georgina was nettled. Since she'd sent Lady Caroline on her wild-goose chase, Georgina hadn't learned a single tidbit as to how the sojourn was progressing. Before quitting the country estate, she'd bribed three servants at the manor, and Rutherford had been on her payroll for an eternity, but she hadn't heard a peep out of any of them.

She'd penned a few flirtatious letters to John, inane, chatty missives to remind him of her, but he hadn't replied. Not that she'd expected he would, but she'd posted them anyway, desirous of prompting him to recall that he had other responsibilities.

What was transpiring at Wakefield? The question—and myriad conceivable, horrid answers—had kept her awake many a night.

The Earl of Derby's box was across from her, and she was disappointed that the pompous ass wasn't in it. If he had been, he'd have been glaring down his pretentious nose at her. Derby protested that it wasn't fitting for John to publicly consort with Georgina, so Georgina liked to be gallingly conspicuous.

Derby had made it clear that his little darling, Caroline, shouldn't have to be dishonored by Georgina's presence in Wakefield's life, but Caroline was such a dolt that she didn't know who Georgina was. If she

peered across the opera house and observed a female
guest in John's box, she was too stupid to wonder who
it might be.

She looked closer. So far, Derby's box had been
empty, but suddenly, the curtain rustled, and an entourage of women sauntered in. Georgina's heart skipped a
beat. Lady Caroline was in the middle of the group,
having slithered back to London without Georgina's
having been apprised!

She fumed. That bastard Rutherford had received his
last farthing! How dare he neglect to warn her of this
monstrous development!

Staring, she assessed the younger woman's elegance, her serene countenance, her unaffected mien.
How could a man bear to marry such a prim, prudish
paragon of virtue? Especially Wakefield. The very notion of their union was laughable.

Her hatred was so strong that Lady Caroline could
probably feel the malice spewing across the theater.
What was the silly twit doing in London? Couldn't she
keep Wakefield occupied for even a few days? What was
the matter with her?

When Georgina had urged the inept noblewoman to
travel to the Wakefield estate, she'd prayed that some
repressed speck of feminine intuition might kick in, that
Caroline would recognize the dangers posed by the
vicar's daughter. Apparently, Caroline was so obtuse
that she couldn't identify a hazard when it was thrown
directly in her path.

Just then, Georgina's friend Portia returned from a
gossip foray in the lobby. She hustled to the chair next
to Georgina and, fairly bursting with glee, she gushed,
"You won't believe what I heard."

"What?"

"Guess which prominent family has spread the news

that their eldest daughter isn't willing to accept a marriage offer from Viscount Wakefield?"

Georgina could barely refrain from leaping to her feet, babbling incoherently, displaying excessive concern over the tidings. She tamped down any reaction, fixed her smile, blandly murmuring, "Really?"

"Yes."

"When was the announcement made?"

"In the past hour. Scuttlebutt has it that she went into seclusion for a couple of weeks to ponder her future." Portia smiled wickedly. "Evidently, after a great deal of soul-searching, she's decided that Wakefield is not the husband for her."

"It certainly took her long enough," Georgina said caustically, showing more interest than she'd meant to reveal. Others in her box, and in the surrounding boxes, were surreptitiously perusing her in order to glean her impression of the reported split.

"Did you know?" Portia queried.

"Of course," she lied. "She actually cried off several weeks ago."

"And you never breathed a word, you naughty girl!"

Georgina raised a brow, pretending a wealth of knowledge she didn't possess. She was treading in perilous territory, aware that John would be furious if he discovered that she'd discussed him, but she couldn't have others inferring that she'd been caught off guard.

Portia was chattering, furnishing some of the more acerbic quips bandied about as to spinsterish Lady Caroline—what a fool she was, what her family would do with her now—but Georgina scarcely listened.

She was in drastic need of fresh air, of peace and quiet, so that she could analyze the debacle in private, and she was seconds away from jumping up and dashing out, which she couldn't do. Impassively, she flicked her fan and used it to cool her heated face, while she mentally calmed herself.

"What did you find out about Lord Belmont's nuptials?" she inquired, deftly switching the subject to another of Portia's favorite topics.

Portia launched into a new tirade, and Georgina feigned attention until she deemed it safe to leave without giving others the perception that she was upset. She tarried until the third act began and, with a whisper to Portia, she sedately walked out, bound for the ladies' retiring room.

Blessedly, it was vacant, and she was alone.

She stood before the mirror, checking her coiffure, dabbing color on her cheeks. In the dim glimmer of the lamp, she appeared twenty, but as she leaned in, the wrinkles she valiantly struggled to conceal were visible.

Spinning sideways, she studied her profile. Her breasts were still taut and rounded, but before long, they'd droop, she'd sag here and there.

With each passing year, her situation became more precarious. She wasn't a youthful beauty, which was what the earls and viscounts of the aristocracy wanted. In other areas of commerce, maturity counted, but not in hers. Age was an enemy to be fought and vanquished.

She wasn't anywhere near to being fiscally stable. She needed time to stabilize her finances. With skillful manipulation of her features, and proficient nurturing of John's tendencies and habits, she'd hoped to hold on to him until forty or after.

If he tossed her over now, what would she do?

Before she'd garnered John as her protector, she hadn't worried about locating another benefactor. When one had moved on, there'd always been another waiting in the wings, but the chances were increasing that no one else would have her after John cast her aside. She was growing old, and the prospect was too grim to contemplate.

She had to lure him home! Had to get him back on familiar ground, so that he'd be removed from temptation. Once she had him in London, he'd recollect how adept she was at keeping him happy, why he'd picked her in the first place. They were a successful partnership, and no one understood him as she did. She'd invested much in their association, and she wasn't about to lose him to some rural harlot's devious machinations.

There were so few available options, but she had to concoct a method by which she could entice him. He was easily bored, was effortlessly distracted, so it was difficult to combine a suitable amount of vice and amusement.

What strategy might excite him sufficiently so that he'd reestablish himself in town?

The solution came in a flash. Her sister! Yes! She'd ask her sister, Gwenda, to visit! Why hadn't she thought of it before?

Gwenda was zealous for any excuse to escape her monotonous routine in the country, as well as the lecherous, elderly swine to whom she was married. Plus, she was enamored of Wakefield and anxious for any proposition that included him.

The three of them had trysted on a singular, decadent occasion, taking sexual licentiousness to a new height. She and Gwenda were a year apart in age and looked enough alike to be twins, and John had engaged in numerous acts with them that had stoked his male fantasies.

After that depraved encounter, he'd been extremely grateful, and she'd been significantly rewarded for bringing the abandoned rendezvous to fruition, yet since then, she hadn't conjured up anything remotely similar.

Feeling more secure than she had in weeks, she returned to the box. She wouldn't depart with Lady Caroline in the house, so she'd have to suffer through the remainder of the performance, but once she managed to flee, she'd race home and draft the indecent invitation.

The moon was up so she'd be able to send a messenger without delay. By dawn, her note would be well on its way to being placed in Wakefield's hand.

Emma stumbled from exhaustion as she sneaked into John's bedchamber. It had been a full seven days since they'd found the time when they could be together, and in the interim, she'd tended to many children who were ill with a pesky influenza that was sweeping the village, had delivered two babies, and had sat with a dying man. After his demise, she'd aided his family in preparations for the funeral and burial. As Harold had no training or aptitude for dealing with bereavement, he'd been no help, and she'd had to lead all of them—minister and mourners—through the painful ordeal.

She was weary, weak from fatigue, her customary store of energy depleted, and when she'd arrived at the cottage, she'd wanted to fall into her bed and sleep for a week. But John's servant had been there, watching over Jane and her mother, and she'd conferred the message that the viscount was expecting Emma at the manor.

The retainer's assistance had been a godsend during the sedulous period, allowing Emma to carry on with her duties, to earn some extra coin. John had also been relaying food, their meager reserve of supplies gradually augmenting. Conditions were improving, her friendship with him resulting in infinite dividends.

When she'd left the cottage, dragging her haggard,

overburdened body through the woods and up the hill, she'd told herself that she'd agreed to attend him merely because she wanted to personally thank him for his generosity, but while she had every intention of expressing her appreciation, she wasn't fooling herself: She was going because she wanted to see him. There were no loftier motives behind her actions.

During the desolate nights, as she'd been awake and toiling away, she'd missed the rogue, and she'd spent the lonely hours thinking of him, wondering where he was, what he was doing, and if he might be missing her, too. She'd dreamed about when she'd be free, once again, to stop by. At the height of her enervation, she'd longed to lie down with him, to doze and rest while he snuggled with her.

Her attachment to him was rash and dangerous, her fondness preposterous and absurd, but she couldn't alter her course. She loved him *and* she liked him, even though there was no explanation for why she would. He was rude, tyrannical, spoiled rotten, a licentious libertine, with a different woman behind every door. Yet, as he'd proven over and over, he could also be kind, considerate, benevolent, and they shared a mutual affection and physical magnetism that couldn't be disregarded.

Why she was attracted to him was an unanswerable puzzle. How she'd let him come to mean so much a complex mystery. She could have sworn she was too astute to embroil herself in any ridiculous indiscretion, but she'd done exactly that, and now she was enmired far beyond any level that was prudent.

She'd set herself up for heartbreak, and her only choice now was to count the days to that terrible moment when he would leave for London.

At his room, she furtively crept in. He was at a table by the window, with various books spread out before

him as though he'd been absorbed with paperwork. At
tired casually in loose-fitting trousers, he was without
coat or cravat, his sleeves rolled up, the buttons of hi
shirt unfastened.

"Well, well," he said, smiling, "if it isn't the Sain
of Wakefield. How honored I am to be graced by you
presence!"

She was flustered by his teasing. "Hello."

He pushed away from the table, and patted his leg
indicating that he wanted her to sit, and she rapidly an
willingly crossed the floor and crawled onto his lap.

"Is there any sacrifice you won't make? Any task
you won't assume?"

"People need me."

"Yes, they do." He kissed her forehead, her lips. "I'
about decided that you were never coming."

"I've been so busy."

"That's what I hear." He kissed her again, lingering
savoring, making her stomach tickle. "I hate it that you
work so hard."

"I don't mind."

Which wasn't precisely true. She felt it her duty to
serve others—it was her nature—but she wouldn't complain if the schedule wasn't so hectic, if she sporadically
had the prerogative to refuse those who came knocking

"You'll be pleased to learn that I've been busy, too
while you were away."

"With what?"

"Reviewing the accounting ledgers. I've designed a
strategy to get the estate back in the black. As you suggested, I've canceled the crofters' rents. For this year
and next."

"My hero."

"I'm not giving you any of the credit, either. I'm
pretending that I conceived of it all on my own."

"I knew there was a gallant heart beating beneath that tough exterior."

"Hmm—" he groused, incapable of a reply, and she pressed her face to his shoulder, hiding her smile. He was uncomfortable with his developing philanthropic constitution, and he wasn't quite sure how to take a compliment. He chafed at her acknowledgment and approval of his charitable deeds.

"And there's one more thing," he said. "I've condemned your cottage."

"You what?" She bolted upright. What would they do? Where would they go?

"Calm yourself," he soothed. "You'll stay in it until a better residence is vacant. Then, you're moving."

"You can't do that!"

"I can, and I shall."

"But I can't afford to pay more than I already do!"

"In exchange for your continued commitment to the community, your rent has been voided."

"Who's been informed of this?"

"The estate agent and myself."

"But what if others find out? What will they say?"

"They'll *say* that you deserve it."

He smirked, and she sagged in defeat. She was too tired to argue. Too tired to fight. Later, with some of her vigor restored, she'd be angry over his high-handedness, would have the stamina to resist his unwarranted largesse, but at the moment, she couldn't muster any outrage.

An unladylike yawn escaped, her eyelids drooped.

"Come." He urged her to her feet and led her toward the bed, and she let out an unrefined snort, and he smiled down at her. "What's so funny?"

He wanted to climb into his marvelous bed to dally. *She* wanted to climb into it and nap for an eternity. They were oil and water, never on the same page, never in accord. How had she deemed them a match?

"You want to make love. I want to sleep."

"I know."

Surprisingly, he guided her past the bed and into his dressing room. A bath had been laid out in his fancy tub, the water steamy and inviting. A fire glowed in the brazier. Soft towels were folded and stacked on a stool. A candle burned, a glass of wine had been poured.

"I thought you might like a bath."

She stared at the tub as though she'd never seen one before. When had she last enjoyed a real bath? Tears welled in her eyes, languor and perpetual travail taking their toll.

"It's still hot," she inanely remarked. "You were so certain of when I'd arrive."

"I've been keeping track of you. When I was advised that you were finally on your way, I had it brought up."

"Oh, John—" she murmured. "You couldn't have done anything nicer."

"If I'd known it was this easy to convince you to call me John, I'd have had a bath drawn for you every day." He chuckled, dipping down to kiss her on the mouth. "After you've finished, I'll give you a back rub, and then you can sleep as long as you like." A few tears dribbled down her cheeks, and he thumbed them away. "Let me help you with your dress."

He started with the buttons, and she stood, her arms at her sides. He stripped her as one might a young child, and the experience was too sweet! Dawdling, he fussed with sleeves, knots, and laces. As each piece was tugged away, he kissed and fondled, cuddled and cooed.

Progressing from top to bottom, he slipped her shoes off her feet, untying her garters and rolling down her stockings. Eventually, she wore only her chemise, and he knelt before her, nuzzling her stomach, burrowing into her cleavage. His divine blond hair grazed her breasts, and she riffled her fingers through it, her entire being aching with gladness.

He yanked her chemise up and over her head, and she was naked, but she wasn't disconcerted. Her nudity seemed perfectly normal, and in an odd fashion, she pictured her body as belonging to him, having been created solely for his delectation and delight.

"In you go." Holding her hand, he stabilized her as she stepped into the tub and sank down into the water, and she emitted a hiss as she immersed herself.

"Would you like me to wash your hair?" he asked as she reclined. "Shall I let it down?"

"No. It would take forever to dry."

"Lean back then." He spurred her to relax. "I'll brush it out."

He pulled up a stool and removed her combs, her hair hanging over the rim, and he dragged through the curly mass in methodical, smooth strokes. The rhythmic motion was tranquilizing, and though she tried to stay awake, to concentrate on every delicious aspect of the extraordinary encounter, she kept nodding off.

"Don't doze in the tub, sleepyhead." He set the brush on the vanity and kissed her cheek. "You'll drown yourself."

She laughed as he took a cloth, soaped it, and massaged her shoulders and arms. He lifted her to her knees, the water lapping at her thighs, and he swabbed her privy parts, her breasts. The rubbing was satisfying, pacifying, but also arousing, the rough nap of the material sending prickles of sensation shooting through her.

He nudged her down to rinse in the water, and she smiled with an abrupt reminiscence.

"What are you grinning about?" he inquired.

"Do you remember when I first came up here? For *your* bath?"

"How could I forget?"

"Would we have made love if your mistress hadn't barged in?"

The mention of his London doxy caused a hitch in the intimacy, but he swiftly recovered. "That was definitely my plan." Mischievously, he said, "I'm wicked that way."

"Yes, you are."

Suddenly, she was intent on pursuing the topic of his paramour. They hadn't ever discussed the woman, but Emma was extremely curious about what John would do when he left Wakefield.

If he could split with her, then travel to London and resume his licentious habits—with nary an intervening respite—what did that say about all of them? About their collective characters? Their morals? The perilous states of their immortal souls?

Lethargy was loosening her tongue, making her utter things she wouldn't have contemplated had her usual circumspection been fully engaged. "Is your mistress eager for your return?"

"Emma—" he scolded.

He couldn't look at her, and she couldn't deduce which emotion was preventing eye contact. Embarrassment over his conduct with the fallen woman? Irritation at Emma's raising the subject? Anger at her presumption? A combination of all three?

"Will you keep on with her after you marry?"

His forearms were balanced on the rim, and he vacillated, cautiously choosing his words. "What I did in my private life wouldn't be any of my wife's business."

"But wouldn't Lady Caroline be upset by the relationship? I can't see you deliberately hurting her."

"Caroline and I are not betrothed!" he snapped. "I made it clear to her that there's no chance for us, and she's gone home."

"But you'll wed someday. Whatever woman ultimately becomes your bride, wouldn't she—"

"Em!" he sharply interrupted. "I won't debate this with you."

He was trailing his fingers through the water, and he appeared baffled, as if she'd poked at disturbing facets of his personality that he didn't care to confront.

She considered him more thoroughly, and it seemed he was distressed, unsettled, as though he were carrying the weight of the world on his shoulders. Being overly weary, she hadn't detected his elevated woe, and she detested that he could be tormented, that he was dejected or despondent.

"If you were my husband, and I found out you had a mistress"—she ruffled her fingers through his hair, wanting only to make him smile once again—"I'd kill her. Then, I'd kill you. Very slowly. Very painfully."

"You probably would." His beautiful blue eyes linked with hers. He was so handsome, so dear. So alone.

"You're worth fighting for, Wakefield."

"Do you think so?" He posed the question as if the notion hadn't occurred to him.

"Absolutely."

He kissed her, a luscious, overwhelming joining of mouth and tongue, then he withdrew. "The water's getting cold. Let's get you out before you catch a chill."

He assisted her as she clambered out, then he took a large towel and dried her. She was still naked when he escorted her to the bedchamber, and he laid her down so that she was stretched out in the middle of the enormous, enticing mattress.

From a dresser, he retrieved a bottle of scented oil, then he scrambled up next to her. "Roll onto your tummy."

She readily complied, pillowing her chin on her forearms, as he straddled himself over her bare behind.

He dribbled some of the oil—it had been warmed!—and smeared it into her skin, then he kneaded her sore muscles. His strong, steady hands dug deep into the tissue, and provided her with a glimpse of what heaven must be like.

Never in her wildest imaginings had she supposed that a man might do such a fantastic thing to a woman. Commencing at the tips of her fingers, then working to the tips of her toes, he touched her everywhere, questing, diligent, frequently plunging into naughty territory. Every pore was ablaze; it was physical debilitation coupled with sexual longing, satiation mingled with a desperate craving to have his lean body slick and slippery and moving against her own.

"Take your clothes off," she commanded, too drained to disrobe him herself.

"Not yet." He shifted to the side. "Turn onto your back."

He rotated her, then meandered down, rubbing the oil into her feet and upward, to her mons, her belly, her breasts. Her hips responded, and he centered himself between her legs, letting her feel his cockstand, letting her flex to relieve some of the building tension.

With his hands on her nipples, he ducked down and rooted through her womanly hair, taking her with his tongue. In a few deft strokes, a powerful orgasm whisked through her, and she was easily swept away after the prior hour of restrained stimulation.

He rode the wave with her, pinning her down as she grappled against his mouth. The stirring agitation abated and he scooted up, kissing her, allowing her to sample the taste of her pleasure on his lips.

Arrogantly, he smiled, preening over the fact that he was so adept at driving her to such a drastic circumstance.

"Bounder," she grumbled happily.

"You are so fine." He spooned her back to his front, covering them both with a blanket. "Rest now," he whispered, his arms cradling her.

"I love you, John," she mumbled, rapidly fading away.

Her eyes fluttered shut, her breathing lagged, and dreams flitted through her head. From somewhere far off, through a jumble of scattered visions, she thought she heard him reply, "I love you, too, Em."

She slept.

CHAPTER SIXTEEN

JOHN lounged in a chair by the window, watching over Emma. Morning had waned to afternoon, and afternoon was on its way to evening, but she continued to slumber.

Previously, he hadn't dawdled with a paramour for any purpose other than fornication, certainly hadn't welcomed one to his bed, or yearned to have her tarry. His experiences with the fairer sex were more rough and tumble, more expedient, the pace and duration driven by the level of his arousal and his impatience for the conclusion.

Emma was different. From the day that a physical relationship had begun to seem inevitable, he'd suffered from a deranged urge to make love to her in his room.

Fool that she was, she trusted him much more than was wise, sleeping soundly in the knowledge that nothing bad could happen to her while he was present. She'd staked out the center of his mattress, her beautiful brown hair fluffed across the pillows, and he was forced to concede that his bed would never be his own again. From now on, whenever he gazed at it, he'd picture her there.

Sighing, he felt forlorn and lonely, pondering what he was doing, clinging to this final rendezvous with her, but he refused to delve too deeply into the answers.

He couldn't explain why he was still at Wakefield, either. His inspection was completed, the books balanced, solutions instituted. The estate agent was a competent individual, who would reliably carry out the procedures John had set in motion.

In a logical world, John would have left when Ian had, would have traveled with his brother to London, would have relaxed and regrouped, then journeyed—with Ian—on their scheduled excursion to audit the Clayton properties in Yorkshire.

How had it all gone awry?

Since that appalling night when he'd stumbled upon Ian kissing Caro, he'd been trying to deduce why he'd gotten so aggravated, why he'd blown up and created such a scene, embarrassing the three of them.

As he had no romantic bond with Caro, he hadn't been cuckolded or betrayed, but he'd been enraged at Ian. His brother knew better, understood his place and Caro's, and he was aware of the reasons she couldn't be his, so what exactly had he been attempting?

Ian had many faults, but he curbed his baser impulses. He wouldn't deliberately compromise a woman of Caro's stature for he couldn't make appropriate reparation. He wouldn't be allowed to marry her, and his imbecilic conduct could only have led to disaster.

How he wished he could go back in time to modify his entrance into the library so that his arrival would have been less humiliating for all concerned, but with Ian, it was so bloody difficult to know how to proceed. Though he pretended indifference to John's position, there had perpetually been an undercurrent to their association, fueled by their joint recognition that all John possessed might have been Ian's. They rarely discussed it, but it was wedged between them, potent and real.

Was it jealousy that had spurred Ian to seduce Caro? Did Ian view her as one more chattel of John's that should have belonged to him? Or was it something more profound? Had there been a smoldering partiality between them of which John hadn't been cognizant?

Well, he'd never find out. His boorish behavior ensured that Caro wouldn't receive him again, wouldn't speak to him, or show up at any event that he might also attend.

As for Ian . . .

John was hurting, despairing over their altercation. He'd had so few genuine friends, and he'd truly assumed that Ian had been one of them. His brother's opportune appearance in London, their chance meeting and burgeoning camaraderie, seemed to have been brought about by affection and esteem.

It hadn't occurred to him that Ian was simply working for their father, that their mutual regard had been built on a lie. With Ian's motives being so suspect, he couldn't determine how they'd gotten along so famously. The man was a marvel. Such an aptitude for pretense could have reaped him a career on the stage!

Had his brother been fond of him in the slightest? Or had it always been about remuneration and naught else? Ian had often seethed with discontentment, but to learn that his antidote for what ailed him was to spy and tattle! Year after year! Especially when they'd frequently and collectively abhorred their father!

John couldn't figure out what it all signified, but he was heartsick and couldn't fathom how they would repair their rift. It wasn't Ian's furtive taking of so much money that had John perturbed. He had no problem with Ian's acquiring some of the family fortune. There were just the two of them, their father's only acknowledged progeny. John had so much, and he was happy to share it. Rather, it was the dishonesty and deception that had him disconcerted.

Ian's sweeping, dispassionate commission of fraud made John realize that he hadn't known Ian at all. The person he'd thought his brother to be didn't exist.

How grievously he felt the loss!

His anguish over their split had kept him at Wakefield much longer than he'd intended. With his maudlin condition at a new low, he'd needed Emma, but while he'd languished, depressed and melancholy and anxiously awaiting her, she'd been gallivanting around the neighborhood, doing her remarkable good deeds, freely seeing to his struggling tenants and numerous villagers solely because she believed it her selfless duty.

At first, when he'd sent the servant to her cottage, he'd expected her to join him forthwith, and he'd been greatly irritated by her reply that she was too busy. No one told him no, and his initial reaction had been to pack his bags and head for London.

The hell with her!

But the notion of going home was distasteful. There'd be scandal over his definitive break with Caro, and he'd have to deal with rumor and conjecture, would have to endure teasing, questions, perhaps even angry repartee with her male relatives. He didn't have the stomach for any of it, and wanted the worst of the uproar to die down.

Plus, Ian would have vacated the town house, and without his irksome presence to liven the space, the residence would seem barren and dreary.

Georgina was the only constant, the lone aspect of his London life that remained the same, but she was no friend by any stretch of the imagination. He'd descended to a sorry state, indeed, when she was the single beacon drawing him back to town.

Reaching out, he riffled through the morning post, retrieving the letter she'd penned, and reading the words once again. Her sister was visiting, and they were eager to entertain him.

Without her being specific, he grasped that it was a lewd invitation, one she hoped would inveigle him to rush to the city, but surprisingly, the lurid enticement held none of the allure it might have a month or two earlier. The concept of engaging in inane lasciviousness had paled in its appeal. With Emma as his lover, he'd enjoyed the emotional intimacy of their encounters, and though the erotic prospects with Georgina and her sister were tempting, he had no inclination to indulge.

Georgina excelled at amusing him, at accommodating his whims and moods, at adapting to his eccentric disposition.

Although she was renowned to be a colossal bitch to those who opposed her, he never had to witness her shrewish side. She comprehended his dearth of patience for conflict or friction, so when they were together, she didn't fuss or whine, didn't complain about her lot. His favor was a valuable boon that had vastly augmented her standard of living, and she went out of her way to please him.

She was the perfect mistress, and any rational fellow—at this very moment—would have been galloping down the road to London, yet he'd loitered at Wakefield, desperate to see Emma one last time. Over the past few days, he'd paid a stable boy to follow her and track her movements as she went about her unpaid missions of mercy, so he'd had full reports of where she'd been and what she'd been doing.

The woman was a ceaseless phenomenon. A font of compassion. A bottomless well of empathy.

And he was furious with her! For giving so much to others who didn't appreciate her, or adequately compensate her for her toil and trouble! No wonder she was exhausted! How could any normal person keep up such a pace? She was insane, laboring so severely, as if she could single-handedly rectify all the ills in the world!

If he didn't care about her quite so much, he might take a strap to her pretty behind. He might anyway! Once she awakened. She needed to have some common sense drilled into her.

Staring at the bed again, he was thrilled to have this opportunity to while away the hours as she rested. He was so glad she was with him, that he wouldn't have to be by himself as he mentally prepared for his departure. He'd made plans to go in the morning, but he could muster no enthusiasm.

When he'd come to Wakefield, he'd deemed the sojourn to be an unavoidable, obligatory chore, but Emma had altered his perspective, had furnished him with a new respect for the estate and the people who depended upon its fiscal prosperity. For the first time since his older brother's death, when burdens he hadn't wanted had been thrust upon him, he saw that he might be able to help others, that despite what his father and others had vociferously claimed, he would be up to the task conferred by his ownership of the extensive properties.

He felt strong, in control, proud of who he was and what he would ultimately accomplish as the lord of the ancient title, and he owed this surge of confidence to Emma. He would miss her so much when he left, and He'd like to take her with him, to establish her in London, though he knew she wouldn't go, just as he wouldn't ask her.

Regrettably, she'd be so far out of her element, would be devoured by his peers. Or more likely, she'd die of boredom. She wasn't the sort to loaf and laze away at some elegant apartment he'd purchased for her. She'd want to heal, to nurse, to minister, while he'd insist that she be available for the exclusive purpose of fawning over him.

They were never in step, never moving in the same direction. No future was conceivable, no permanent connection warranted, but he couldn't make the necessary arrangements to leave her. She was so extraordinary, so different from any other woman he'd known.

When she'd drifted off, she'd mumbled that she loved him, and it was a fine thing to be loved by Emma. Shockingly, he loved her, too, and he'd whispered the same, and it had been grand to profess it.

She'd given him so much, had unlocked his mind to so many possibilities, had transformed his character. Yet, he'd given her naught in return, because he didn't have anything that she valued.

He was so lucky to have crossed paths with her, but how could a man cosset such an unpretentious female?

Suddenly, he was overcome by the desire to be close to her. He wanted to hold her, talk to her, make love to her. His body was unassuaged, loudly protesting his brief foray into supplying her with pleasure but garnering none of his own.

He needed to be inside her, to bury himself in her sweet nature, to luxuriate in her softness, and he stripped off his shirt, trousers, and other garments until he was naked. His cock rose to attention, rude and heavy, fervent for what was coming, and he clutched it with his fist, stroking himself to ease some of the abrupt tension.

Tiptoeing to the bed, he climbed up, and slipped under the blanket with which she was covered. She was warm, fragrant from her bath, and he stretched out, his torso melding with hers all the way down.

She shifted and stirred, slowly rousing. Her eyes fluttered but didn't open, and she raised her arms over her head, flexing her calves and toes. He cupped her breast, taking her nipple between finger and thumb, and the gesture caused her to purr like a contented cat.

"You're spoiling me," she said.

"Someone should. Why not me?"

Rolling on top of her, he squeezed both her nipples, chuckling at how they puckered. His lips slid over one, laving and sucking, and she gripped his neck, cradling him, urging him on.

He was so hard for her, and he'd meant to hastily slake himself in a boisterous, swift copulation, but it was so luscious to suckle at her breast. Tarrying much too long, he reveled in the details that made her so unique.

Her other breast beckoned, and he ambled to it, delaying, savoring, and when he finally kissed a trail up her bosom, when he finally took her mouth, it was a precious, tender embrace. He couldn't get enough of her. Her fondness was a soothing balm, a cherished gift, and he couldn't abide the thought of their parting.

Their lips separated, and apparently, she'd discerned his distress. She searched for answers, trying to distinguish the source of his blatant woe.

"What is it, John?"

"My brother and I had a fight," he affirmed, amazed that he would. He never divulged his private affairs, and he particularly never expounded on Ian—a fact that annoyed London gossipmongers no end.

"What about?"

"Everything."

She chuckled. "That must have been some quarrel."

"Aye, it was."

"What started it?"

"I caught him with Caro, in the middle of the night. They were kissing."

At the mention of his purported fiancée, she tensed and tentatively ventured, "Were you jealous?"

"No, just upset."

"About what?"

"About his behavior. He's not her equal." Even as he offered the idiotic explanation, he was embarrassed. What a horrid opinion to have about his brother! Ian was an admirable man, but John had been imbued with a lifetime of indoctrination about society and rank, and he couldn't set it aside, not even for the sibling whom he'd always treasured.

"We *commoners* are an infuriating lot," she sarcastically asserted, making him feel petty and mean-spirited. "We don't stay in our place when you exalted types demand it."

"I don't know what he was trying to prove."

"You are such a snob." She chuckled again. "Perhaps they merely like one another. Have you considered that?"

"Yes, but it could never be."

"So? Some people can't stop themselves." Quietly, she added, "Even if what they're doing is improper."

She was referring to their own complex relationship, but it wasn't the same as Ian's and Caro's situation. Was it? Was he stupid enough to imply that, because Caro was the daughter of an earl, her virginity held more import than Emma's? The insinuation was ludicrous.

"He was stealing from me, too," he imputed, switching to a topic about which he could muster more conviction as to his outrage.

"Are you positive?"

"He admitted it."

"He didn't seem to be the kind who would."

"No, he didn't." He blushed. "I said some terrible things."

"I'm sure he'll—"

"I hit him," he interrupted, needing to confess. The heinousness of what he'd done was eating him alive.

"Oh, John," she murmured. "How awful."

"I doubt if he'll forgive me."

"Of course he will."

"He loathes me."

"He doesn't. He cares about you too much. I could tell." She laid her hand over his heart, and it had the peculiar effect of making him feel she was rubbing where it ached. "Although if you want to reconcile, it will be up to you. Even if he was in the wrong, you'll have to say you're sorry."

"I hate apologizing. I never do."

"That's because it's so difficult for you to swallow down that enormous pride of yours."

He laughed, relishing that she would be so frank, that she could catalog his faults without making them sound so calamitous. "You are so good for my ego."

"Somebody needs to remind you that you're human." She kissed him gently. "It will be all right. You'll see."

He gazed into her eyes, loving her, revering her, and he grappled to find the fortitude to declare himself, but he'd never previously uttered the sentiment to another, and though he'd fancied himself a courageous man, he couldn't locate the mettle to tell her.

What aspiration would an attestation satisfy anyway?

The word *love*, when expressed to a female—especially one of Emma's background and antecedents—connoted a pledge of devotion, a promise of fealty and constancy, traits he didn't possess and had no idea of how to implement.

He didn't believe in fidelity, hadn't met a woman who could incite thoughts of monogamy or commitment, though Emma definitely made him speculate as to whether such a life might be possible.

When he married, he would wed for the usual reasons: increased wealth, alliances, status. His highborn wife would understand his proclivities, would ignore his bad habits in exchange for the position their union would bring her. Love wouldn't play a part.

Emma would be a bride who would expect and require faithfulness and loyalty, which he knew from past experience he was incapable of guaranteeing. He couldn't follow through.

Best to be silent.

Taking her hand, he kissed it, then linked their fingers. "I'm leaving for London."

"When?"

He swallowed, scarcely able to speak. When he'd journeyed to Wakefield, he hadn't intended to linger. Why, then, was it so painful to discuss his departure?

"At dawn."

She frowned, calculating. "So soon?"

"I need to be away. I should have left days ago."

She smiled tremulously. "I won't ever see you again."

"No, I don't think you will."

There was the strangest rattle in the center of his chest, and he suffered the oddest impression that his heart was breaking. He'd known that he'd fleetingly be at a loss without her quirky company, but until this very moment, when he'd verbalized his plans, he hadn't truly realized how horrible their farewell would be. On himself.

When he'd visualized his going, he'd imagined how arduous it would be for *her,* but *he* was the one hurting. He felt as if he'd been rent into tiny pieces, that he'd be abandoning half of himself if he traveled to London without her.

How bizarre! Women floated by, and he wasn't imprudent enough to grow attached. He was physically attracted to Emma, and the magnetism was significantly elevated, but he declined to read any more into it than that.

Due to the fracturing of his affinity with Ian, he was overly distraught. Once he got back to London, everything would return to normal, he'd be more himself, and Emma would cease to plague him. Her proximity was confounding, but time and distance would cure his fascination.

Still, he'd be a bit more pleased if she'd evince a smidgen of concern over his tidings. He'd braced himself for a display of feminine histrionics, but not so much as a tear had sprung to her eye, and he was extremely put out that she could remain so calm. Or perhaps—a small voice suggested—she wasn't distressed.

Without notice or warning, he'd burst into her life, had disturbed her staid existence. Maybe she'd be elated to have him go.

Wouldn't that be his just deserts? An ironic turn of events! The only occasion he'd actually bonded with a woman, and she'd be relieved when he walked out the door!

"Will you miss me?" he asked. His customary arrogance was markedly absent, and there was a quiver in his tone.

"Yes, you scoundrel. Every second."

"It's been wonderful knowing you," he posed, but dared no more. "I'm so glad we met."

"As am I."

While he wasn't about to proclaim his buried emotions, he'd hoped she'd expound, but she seemed to have been struck dumb, just when he yearned to have her babbling incessantly.

"I want you to spend the night."

"John," she chided. "I can't."

At her rejection, his original response was fury! He was so tired of her spurning his wishes! This was their final assignation. Would it kill her to accommodate him? Couldn't she be amenable? Just once?

But as quickly as the selfish concept entered his head, he shoved it away. This was Emma. Her dedication to her family was an integral component of who she was, and she'd never change. He wouldn't want her to change! When he was, once again, installed at his empty town house, leading his licentious, boring life, he wanted to fondly reminisce, to picture her at Wakefield, busy, fulfilled, stubborn and determined.

"Then stay as long as you're able."

"I will."

"I want to love you over and over." Surprising himself, he disclosed, "I always want to remember what it was like."

"So do I."

He kissed her tenderly, then with expanding vigor, reveling in the joy that emanated from her. In a desperate mood, he was anxious to imprint himself into her very soul.

He would join to her as he never had with another, would penetrate so deeply and so furiously that some of himself would be left behind when the rendezvous was over. At the conclusion, he wanted to be forever transformed.

Nervous, uncertain, he was like a bridegroom on his wedding night. The remarkable episode of bliss had to be a solid foundation that would provide him with memories to last the rest of his days.

"No matter where you end up, Emma," he said fiercely, "you were mine first. Never forget!"

"How could I?"

"Let me show you how much you mean to me."

"I already know."

She smiled and opened her arms, and he felt as if he'd been welcomed home.

Chapter Seventeen

He was leaving! He was really going!

Emma subdued the wave of sadness engulfing her. From the outset, she'd known his visit would be of limited duration, and she'd accepted that their relationship would be temporary, but to have the dreaded moment arrive without any warning!

It was too terrible to be borne, yet she wouldn't succumb to melancholy, would not allow her sorrow to ruin their last tryst.

John had made her feel special and cherished, as though she had a dear husband, but he'd never been hers. She'd shared a tiny segment of his otherwise bounteous and gregarious existence, and she'd latched on to their connection with a rare determination and gusto.

But it was over.

He would return to London, to his vices and iniquities, and she had no illusions. She had been a convenient method by which he'd slaked his boredom and dolor, but she'd been little more than that.

Once he was ensconced in the city, and pursuing his panoply of sordid amusements, he'd forget her straightaway. She'd simply be one of the anonymous women who'd flowed through his life, and who were systematically relegated to his pool of regrettable past history.

The only viable difference between her and the others was that she had been foolish enough to fall in love with the irritating, engaging cad. She couldn't explain why.

Nothing about their association made sense—not their physical attraction, not their odd friendship—but it was potent and irrepressible, and she wanted the assignation to be glorious, to be festive and magnificent, so that when he departed, he'd recall it with an abiding affection.

He too appreciated the gravity of what they were about. The solemnity was manifest in his actions and demeanor. There was an urgency to his kiss, a somberness and tenacity in how he touched her. They were on the same frantic quest to imprint every impression for later dissection.

His hands were at her breasts, kneading the two mounds, tormenting the nipples, and he took one of the extended tips into his mouth. The inflamed bud was overly animated, and with ease, he had her squirming. He nuzzled to her other breast, teasing and laving it, until she was beyond comprehension or restraint, then he continued on, to her stomach, to her navel and down.

Burrowing into her mons, he tickled and licked her belly, his adept fingers fondling her privates. She was wet, eager, and she spread her legs, granting him access and permission. He was wild for her, delving and probing, spurring her to a savage precipice, but when she would have leapt over the brink, he shifted away.

He kissed her inner thigh, then he worked up her torso, thoroughly investigating her body until she was afire in every pore.

When their lips joined again, she seized the advantage, rolling them so that she was on top, so that she would have the opportunity to explore and titillate. She commenced her own journey by caressing his chest, his ribs, dallying with his nipples, until she had him in a frenzied state, his respiration labored, his pulse pounding.

His cock was adamant, demanding, and she obeyed its dictate, taking him in her hand, in her mouth. It was a maneuver she'd come to relish, had practiced with reckless abandon, so she'd discovered numerous techniques by which she could drive him to distraction.

With renewed vigor, she toyed and played, stroking his length, his balls, while her tongue goaded the incited tip. She grazed and trifled until his sexual juices were oozing, his hips flexing. When he could tolerate no more, she permitted him to slip in, to push and toil, in fervent preparation for a stunning finale, but as he'd done with her, she pulled away before the end.

Blazing an ardent trail upward, she was hovered over him.

"Vixen!" He clasped her buttocks and wedged her loins to his. "I'm so hard for you!"

"Good!"

"You kill me with that mouth of yours."

"What a blissful way to quit this earth."

"Aye," he agreed, "what a way, indeed."

In a swift motion, he rotated them so that she was on the bottom once more. He'd ascended to a critical juncture; he was tense, strained, his heavy torso pressing her into the mattress.

"I have to be inside you," he ground out. "Now! I can't wait."

He nudged her thighs apart, centered himself, and she braced for him to raucously plunge in, but instead, he taunted her, sliding in the smallest amount, the blunt crown jabbing and tempting her.

"Tell me how much you want me," he exhorted.

"I do. I want you."

He propelled himself forward, giving her a tad more,

widening her, making her ache and throb. "Tell me that I'm the only one you'll ever have."

She couldn't fathom why such a factor would signify, or why he'd need her to acknowledge how hopelessly attached she was, but she had no difficulty giving him reassurance.

After knowing him and adoring him, she couldn't picture having another man in her bed. John was the great love of her life, and there could be no other after him.

"It's always been you, John. You'll be the only one."

At her avowal, his eyes glittered with a strange incandescence, and he immersed himself in her, taking her in a single, smooth thrust, then he embarked on his race to satiation. Setting a brutal pace, he penetrated her over and over, his hips thumping like the pistons of a gigantic machine. Sweat pooled on his brow, his muscles were taut and rigid.

She wrapped her legs around his waist, locking them behind his back so that he had a spacious cushion, and he reveled in the ecstasy. Raising up, he reached between their bodies, his thumb caressing her, while he persisted with his savage rhythm.

"Say my name," he decreed.

"John—"

"Say it again."

His thumb was unrelenting, compelling, and she arched up. "John!"

"Don't shut your eyes. Look at me the entire time."

Her orgasm promptly overtook her, and she shuddered and cried out. He captured her wail of dismay, swallowing the sound, though he persisted with his flexing.

As she reassembled, he was over her, his palms on

either side of her, and he gazed at her with an intensity that was frightening. It seemed as if he wanted something from her, or that he was about to remark on something profound that would shock and surprise her, but the episode passed as desire flared anew, and he enhanced the tempo.

The power of his movements was thrilling, startling, and he'd progressed far beyond reality or reason, into the realm where only sensation mattered. His exacerbated activity had shoved her across the bed until her head was banging the headboard, and she grappled for purchase, fortifying herself against the onslaught.

Gripping her rear, he lifted her so that their loins were more tightly aligned, and he hurled into her with accelerating strength. He was so near the culmination. The wave emanated—she could feel it—and she steadied herself, anticipating his habitual withdrawal, then the frenetic spew of his seed across her abdomen.

But it never came.

He clutched at her, providing no chance to escape or retreat, and with a groan of passion and despair, he emptied himself inside her, her womb drenched with his essence. It was fantastic, horrifying, unlike anything she'd endured before.

His phallus pulsated with each surge of his release, and though her flesh welcomed his invasion as the normal conclusion, mentally, she was alarmed and aghast.

He'd promised to be circumspect! He'd given her his word! Like an idiot, she'd believed his assurances, had consented to the ultimate sexual behavior. Didn't he understand the consequences? Had he no inkling of the damage he might have wrought?

How could she have trusted him to constrain himself? She knew what he was like, recognized his negligent propensities, as well as his haughty opinion toward those of the lower classes. Yes, he'd guaranteed caution, but when his pleasure was held up against her reputation in the village, he would never deny himself.

Why should he care? He was leaving in the morning. If he left her in dire straits, he wouldn't be around to witness the outcome.

What had possessed her to wander down this dangerous path? She'd thought herself to be smart, discerning, yet she'd acted no better than the stupidest tavern girl who'd let some virile boy slither under her skirt after a hefty dose of sweet talk and false compliments.

What was she to do now?

His body shook, and he dropped down, his weight crushing her as it hadn't previously. Suddenly, he seemed to be smothering her, with his size, his position, his attitude.

"Get off me!" she rabidly commanded, but he didn't budge, and she whacked at his shoulders. "Let me up!"

He leaned back, but he was still partially erect, so he kept his cock implanted, and he searched her face, not able to grasp why she was agitated.

"What is it?" He was genuinely perplexed.

"You spilled yourself inside me!"

"Oh—"

"You swore to me that you wouldn't!"

"I apologize. I was so aroused; I couldn't help myself."

"Are you a child?" She prodded at his shoulders, to no avail. "You're a grown man! Have you no self-control?"

He inhaled, let it out slowly. "You're afraid."

"Of course I'm afraid! I'm absolutely terrified!"

"Of what?"

"Of making a babe, you fool!"

"You can't become pregnant from doing it just once."

"Who told you such half-witted nonsense?"

"Everyone knows it to be true," he claimed.

"Do you have any idea how many babies I've delivered that were conceived after *one* time?"

He smiled hesitantly. "But Em, I can't sire a child."

"And if this is the first?"

"Don't worry. It's not."

"If you're wrong, and I learn in a few weeks that I'm with child, what will you do about it?"

There it was. Out in the open. A dare. A challenge. An affront to his character. By virtue of his illustrious title, he was omnipotent, and could commit any slight or indignity to someone of her station without recompense.

If she wound up in the family way, would honor impel him to marry her? Or, more likely, would he consider that any damage to her was so trivial that it wasn't worth indemnification?

Lamentably, and much too soon, she was brutally informed of his answer.

"What would you expect me to do?"

"Nothing." She tamped down a torrent of desperation. "Nothing at all."

He shifted away from her, his waning cockstand gliding out, and the instant she was free, she scrambled to the edge of the bed and sat up. He rubbed his hand in soothing circles across her back. For a moment, she allowed the contact, treasuring the feel of his warm skin against her own, then she straightened and stood, traipsing to the dressing room where she'd bathed earlier. Her clothes were folded in a neat pile on the vanity.

"Em!" Clearly exasperated, he called after her, and shortly, he marched over to where she was hastily donning her attire. On seeing what she was about, he was offended, and he inquired, "What are you doing?"

"I'm going home."

"But we've got hours ahead of us. There's no need."

For such an intelligent man, he could be so obtuse! "I couldn't possibly stay now."

"Why?" He approached, rested a hand on her waist. "I said I was sorry. Don't be angry."

"Oh, John—" She breathed a ponderous sigh. He hadn't had much experience at making reparation, so he didn't realize that an inept assertion of remorse would never be sufficient.

He snuggled her to his chest and offered as an inadequate justification, "I wanted you so badly, Emma."

"That doesn't make it right."

"But it was wonderful, wasn't it?" He stuck his finger under her chin, urging her to look at him. "You can't be sad."

He was pleading with her, imploring her forgiveness, but for once, she wouldn't bestow it. She stepped away, grabbed her chemise, and slipped it on.

"Can you even begin to imagine what will happen to me if I'm increasing?"

"You're not."

"Desist with your denials!" she shouted. "You're insulting me."

He flopped into a chair and quietly entreated, "What would it be like?"

"Well, I'd have to marry. Quickly." She snatched up her dress and shrugged into it. "I'd either have to surrender to another man's advances, then lie and pretend the child was his, or I'd have to be honest and confess my dilemma and pray that he'd have me."

"Don't ever do that. I couldn't bear to contemplate you with anyone else."

How typically arrogant of him to insist that she

forgo a resolution simply because he wouldn't like it! She bit her tongue against a flood of scathing retorts.

"Fine, then." She perched on a stool and drew on her stockings and shoes, occupying herself in a meager attempt to contain her ire. "Instead, I'd be an unwed mother, which means—at best!—that I'd be a pariah. I'd be cast out of the community, forced to move on with my invalid mother and young sister. With no money and no place to go."

"And at worst?"

"Maybe they'd stone me. Or resort to tar and feather."

"This isn't the Middle Ages," he scoffed. "Don't be melodramatic."

"I'm quite serious."

She rose, anxious to exit without so much as a good-bye, but he wouldn't let her skirt around him. He clasped her hand, cajoling her over and tugging her onto his lap, and she didn't struggle to resist, for she knew that he'd have his way in the end. He always did.

"I'd never let anyone harm you," he ferociously maintained.

"Well, you wouldn't be here to prevent it, would you?"

She stared forward, declining to so much as peek at him, and he nuzzled under her chin, and kissed her nape.

Stunning her to her core, he suggested, "Come to London with me."

"I beg your pardon?"

"You heard me. Come with me."

"As your what?"

Her query confounded him beyond measure, and a lengthy, painful interlude ensued before he could respond.

"As my mistress. What would you suppose?"

"Naturally," she muttered falteringly. "I'd be your mistress."

"I'd set you up in a grand house; you'd never want for anything."

"How about your current mistress? Would you split with her, or would we share you?"

"I'd let her go." But he evinced no enthusiasm for the dissociation, and he was far from being prepared to make it.

"What about my mother and sister?"

"I'd make arrangements for them."

"They couldn't live with me?"

"Well, I had fancied having you all to myself."

Her volleys had him so disconcerted that he couldn't verbalize what he wanted, and his bewilderment underscored how flippant his overture had been.

"And if there is a babe? Then what?"

"I'd . . . I'd . . ."

"I'm sure you mean that you'd support me for the remainder of my life, that you would contribute to the child's upbringing so that he would know and love you, and that you would guide and nurture him as any father would."

"Certainly," he mumbled, sounding as though he were choking on the prospect, and his lack of sincerity hurt and outraged her.

"Stop it! Please!" She jumped up and stomped away from him. "You're embarrassing yourself."

"Emma, calm down. We can work this out."

"No, John, we can't."

She gazed at him then, and her heart broke. He was so handsome and robust, but so despairing and despondent, too. She'd ceaselessly enjoyed looking at him, watching him, studying him. He enchanted her, intrigued and tantalized. He fascinated her as no one ever had, and as he sat there in his expensive chair, the elegant accouterments of the room highlighting all that he was, he appeared so alone, so lost and forlorn, a rich, dissolute man with no friends or family on whom he could rely, or to whom he could turn in a crisis.

When she walked out the door, her mother and sister would be waiting for her. They might be poor, but they had each other. Their small, tumbledown cottage was filled with vivacious chatter, with camaraderie and affection. She passed her days with people who loved her, people she cherished in return.

John had no one. There wasn't a person in the world—save perhaps Ian Clayton—who cared a whit about him.

He'd go back to London, to his gambling and his whores and his decadent habits, and then what? How tragic that his life had so little purpose. That he'd been given so much, but he saw his gifts as burdens. There was so much he could do, so many ways he could benefit others, if he'd open himself up to the possibilities.

Though she yearned to tell him so, to hug and comfort him, to explain myriad methods by which he could find contentment, she kept silent, refusing to be the one who bridged this final gap. He'd created his obstacles, had fostered his image as a cad and a ne'er-do-well, and he thrived on his negative reputation.

He was an adult, with the resources to change his fate whenever he was ready.

She was about to bid him farewell; then she would never see him again, would never hear from him again, but in the coming dreadful months, she didn't intend to worry about how he'd fared. She had her own problems. Problems that were pressing, real, and overwhelming. In comparison, his adversities were petty, and she wouldn't let herself be influenced by his distress.

She couldn't fix everything for everybody.

"I must go." She took another step toward the door and the freedom of the corridor that lay beyond.

"Emma," he repeated, annoyed. He strode over to her, taking both her hands in his. "Not like this. Not when you're so upset."

"It has to be now."

"Come tomorrow. I'll delay my departure, and we'll talk this over."

"I can't think of a single word that still needs to be said."

She wanted only that the hideous scene be concluded, but her determination, and his inability to sway her, infuriated him. "I've tarried here for almost a week just so I could see you one last time," he complained, in a temper, "but all you can do is argue."

"I'm not arguing. I'm leaving."

"You've worked yourself into a lather over some vague, nebulous potentiality, and you're angry with me because I can't give you instant answers to complex questions."

"I don't expect anything from you. I never have."

"So you say!" He waved an irate finger under her nose. "What is it you really want from me?"

"Nothing!"

"Liar," he chided. "You're beseeching me with those pretty brown eyes of yours! To do what? You're intimating that I don't care about you. That I wouldn't provide for you if there was a child. That I have no honor or integrity. I thought you had more faith in me than that!"

"What have you told me, in the past few minutes, that would make me presume you would assist me if I was in trouble?"

"You're asking me to make life-altering decisions in

a thrice, to give promises to you that I'm not certain I could keep. When I can't furnish an immediate solution to a situation that doesn't exist, you're furious that I won't! You're acting the lunatic!"

He threw out his arms in aggravation. "Would you have me prostate before you? Begging you to wed? So be it!" Abruptly falling to his knees, he gripped her hand in his, squeezing it so tightly the bones ached, and he snapped, "Will you marry me?"

Sarcastic, mocking, the proposal was packed with rancor and bitterness, and his wrath inundated her.

Any other woman would likely have discounted his temporary peevishness, would have swooned with giddy delight, so she was convinced that he'd driven her a bit mad, but she could conceive of no worse punishment, no more disastrous eventuality, than to marry John Clayton.

Quietly, she stated, "No. I never would."

Shrinking away from her, he shuddered as though she'd rendered a hard blow, her rejection stabbing him like the sharpest blade, and she was so confused. His offer hadn't been genuine, and he should have been ecstatic to have had it tossed in his face.

He was a man of town, a confirmed bachelor and libertine with exorbitant, exotic tastes, and he would never tie himself to a woman as modest and unpretentious as herself. Why would he be distraught?

Then, as rapidly as she'd noticed his vehement reaction, it was scrupulously masked, his usual mien of bored disdain once again shielding his aristocratic features. He smirked as though he'd anticipated nothing better, and he sauntered out, proceeding to the main bedroom and seating himself in a chair by the window.

Shaken and disturbed by the horrid exchange, she was shattered that these antagonistic remarks would be the last they ever uttered to one another.

Slowly, she adjusted her apparel, dawdling to regain her composure, then she went to the bedchamber. He was engrossed in his paperwork and completely ignoring her. She scrutinized him, aware that she would never have a subsequent opportunity.

Ultimately, he glanced up at her, and he seemed surprised, as though he'd forgotten she was on the premises. Their gazes locked and held, a thousand sentiments flaring between them that couldn't be voiced aloud.

"Thank you," she murmured.

"For what?"

"For giving me this chance to spend time with you. I'll treasure the memories." She paused for an eternity, but he didn't tender a similar observation. Resigned, devastated, she whirled away, when he spoke to her back.

"I'm sorry if I've left you in a predicament. I never meant to. If there's a babe, write to me."

"I wouldn't."

"Why?" he barked tumultuously. "You know I'd help you!"

"Yes, I'm sure you would"—she peered at him over her shoulder—"but then, I'd constantly suffer from the knowledge that my child and I were nothing but a monthly expenditure you were required to pay in order to cover one of your mistakes."

He sighed, the weight of the world heavy on his shoulders, the agony in his eyes excruciating to bear. "It wouldn't be like that."

"It would be exactly like that." Unable to abide further barbs, she sneaked to the door and peeked into the corridor, relieved that it was empty, and she started out.

"Damn you!" he bellowed to her retreating form. "Write to me! Let me know!"

"Yes, yes, I will," she agreed, wanting only to be away, and she ran out without looking back.

CHAPTER EIGHTEEN

JOHN gazed blindly at the passing London streets, but he had no energy to peruse the scenery. The August day was balmy, the lawns in his Mayfair neighborhood immaculately trimmed, the flowers in riotous bloom, but he hardly noticed. He dropped the curtain and leaned against the squab.

In minutes, he'd arrive at the town house, a moment that had plagued him for the entire journey, and he quashed his feelings of dread. There was no reason to lament his being back in London. Neither would he continue chastising himself over what had happened with Emma. It was too late to mitigate or rectify his impetuous conduct.

She was too precious for him to have endangered her welfare, to have hurt or abused her in the slightest fashion, so he couldn't fathom why he'd forged on and spilled his seed inside her.

With a monstrous disregard for her and himself, he'd proceeded, after vowing to her that he wouldn't. The sole rationale he could devise—and how inadequate!—was that he'd been disturbed over his imminent split with her, perceiving that it would be painful and hating that he couldn't satisfactorily alter the outcome. When they'd finally made love, it had been so amazing to be inside her that he'd behaved like an ass.

She was correct in her accusation that he'd comported himself like a callow boy, impulsively progressing, heedless to the consequences, and in an isolated part of him, he was ecstatic that he had. Madly, he hoped she *would* become pregnant. That he'd branded her as his own by planting his child. It was a feral, primal instinct, and from where it had sprung, he couldn't imagine.

While he'd always believed he couldn't sire a child, Emma was prudent to be alarmed. He'd imperiled them both and, when confronted by her outrage, he hadn't extended the merest hint that he'd provide recompense.

His lone suggestion as to reparation had been to make her his mistress! Emma! Whom he deemed to be so unique, so fine. How could he have insulted her so terribly? When he'd raised the possibility, he'd been upset, fatigued, and not thinking clearly, but they were sorry excuses.

He hadn't wanted her for his mistress. And he definitely hadn't wanted to marry her! He'd be a pathetic husband, and he would never saddle such an extraordinary woman with having to perpetually endure his despicable presence.

So what had he intended? What had he anticipated? What result had he planned to effect?

A thousand questions swirled by. What if he had impregnated her? What if—at this very instant—she was increasing with his son? What would she do? What should *he* do? How could he make any of this right? The frantic ruminations had him dizzy with their loud, vehement repetition of the prospects for disaster, and he shoved them away.

He absolutely would not reflect on calamity! Ever since she'd left his bedchamber in a huff, he'd been stewing and fretting. Throughout the trip from Wakefield, remorse and regret had been dragging along behind like a couple of weights wrapped around his neck, until he felt as if they were choking him.

He was glad to be home! He wouldn't pretend otherwise!

Though he'd bungled the attempt, he'd endeavored to mend his gaffe. He'd offered to marry her, which was a boon any single lady in England would have latched on to in a thrice, yet she'd refused him. Yes, he'd been angry and confused when he'd tendered the proposal, but still, he'd made it, and she'd sensibly spurned him.

She understood, as did he, that he was *not* the man for her.

Their relationship was concluded. She'd been naught but a fling, a fleeting, tantalizing amour that had been engaging and amusing, a delicious method for relieving the monotony while he'd been stuck in the country, but she'd been no more than that.

It was done! Over! Finished!

If an inner voice kept prodding him to remember how much he'd liked her, how much he'd cherished her company and had valued her opinion, he didn't have to listen. He could control his despondency! He was away from the ennui and tedium that had driven him into her arms. All of London was, once again, available for his enjoyment and delectation, and he was resolved to indulge in every dissolute, wicked distraction he could find.

Beginning immediately!

Before the week was out, Emma Fitzgerald would be but an unpleasant memory. In a few months, if he immersed himself in his regular array of tawdry pursuits, he wouldn't recall her at all, wouldn't be able to conjure up a recollection of her pretty smile, or her fabulous brown eyes.

She'd be vanquished from his store of reminiscence. And good riddance!

The carriage rattled to a stop in front of the house, and he tarried while the coachmen fussed with the step and readied the door. He alighted, and stood, staring up at his imposing, empty residence. Rutherford had traveled in advance, so the servants would be arranged to accommodate his every whim, but he was in no hurry to enter.

Dawdling, he watched as the luggage was unloaded, then there was nothing to do but march to the threshold. Almost on cue, Rutherford greeted him with an obsequious bow.

He loitered in the foyer, looking around. As he hated to be fawned over, Rutherford had ensured that the staff was conspicuously absent, and it seemed they were the only two in the big mansion.

"Has Master Ian vacated the premises?" he asked impassively.

"Aye, milord. His possessions were gone when I returned."

John sighed. "Did he leave a note? Or information as to where he'll be staying?"

"No, sir." The retainer feigned indifference, when curiosity had to be gnawing at him. Every gossipmonger in the city would be dying to ascertain the particulars, but no one would ever learn any details from John.

Let them speculate to infinity!

He glared at the walls, at the expensive chattels scattered down the lengthy corridor, and he considered going upstairs, maybe ordering a bath and supper, but the hallway to his bedchamber led to Ian's rooms, too, and he couldn't bear to walk past and see for himself that his brother's things had been removed.

Suddenly needing to be away, he spun around and

went outside, calling to the driver who was about to take the carriage to the mews, and notifying him to wait.

"Prepare me for another trip, Rutherford," he said. "In a day or two, I'd like to depart for my tour of the Yorkshire properties. I want to handle my business and be home before autumn wanes."

"As you wish, Lord Wakefield."

"For now, I'm off to Georgina's."

Rutherford's stoic aplomb tottered, and he grimaced, but he quickly recovered, effectively masking his dislike. He snapped to attention, hoping his employer hadn't discerned his lapse.

John approached, studying him, tickled that he'd goaded Rutherford into a response. If the man was bothered enough to betray an attitude, John wanted to know why. "Do you have some problem with my visiting Miss Howard?"

"No, milord." He gulped. "None at all, but what if—"

He couldn't complete the inquiry, so John probed, "*What if . . .* what?"

"What if we were to hear from Miss Fitzgerald? What would we tell her?"

So . . . Rutherford was thinking of Emma, was he? John presumed that they'd been discreet, but not all secrets could be kept. Had Rutherford kept his suspicions to himself, or—more likely—had he blabbed them hither and yon? Well, John wasn't about to fuel any untoward rumors or indecorous conjecturing.

"Are you referring to that vicar's daughter at Wakefield?" He affected no knowledge or connection and—he was convinced—had damned himself to hell in the process. "Why on earth might I be contacted by that irritating piece of baggage?"

Rutherford's disgust and disappointment were obvious. Scathingly, he scrutinized his employer, then murmured, "No reason, I suppose."

"I should say not," John blustered.

Bravely, Rutherford added, "I'd rather come to like her bold style, sir."

Faking apathy, John shrugged and insisted, "I didn't spend enough time with her to distinguish what she was like."

He glanced away, unable to abide Rutherford's blatant condemnation, and he briskly strode out and climbed into the carriage without a word of farewell. His tired driver whisked him away, and soon, he was parked at Georgina's.

Although he was welcome at any hour, he tried to be solicitous and warn her in advance when he'd show up. She didn't know he was in town, so he was being rude, but he didn't care. He was in a reckless mood, and he was desperate to do something negligent, something rash, to bury himself in licentious activity until he was oblivious, until his heart and mind were at rest. He would achieve some peace!

The door was locked, and he didn't knock, using his key and admitting himself. There were no servants about, but he recognized Georgina's sultry laugh wafting down from her sitting room. As she hadn't been expecting him, he could vividly envision what sort of merriment he'd stumble upon.

He ascended the stairs, to the messy salon and the two women who occupied it.

Georgina and her sister, Gwenda, were sprawled on the couches, lounging in brightly colored robes, their hair down, their feet bare. Georgina's robe was tightly cinched, but her sister's was loose, one of her breasts exposed, a thigh enticingly curled on the sofa cushions.

Evidently, they'd been wallowing in their favorite

naughty habits: swilling and smoking. An exotic pipe lay next to a brandy decanter, and the air was hazy and thick with the pungent smell of opium.

It was a depraved, sordid scene, the kind he typically embraced with enthusiasm, but for once, he experienced no charge of excitement. In fact, he was quite revolted, but he tamped down his repugnance, declining to feel any emotion over what he was about to do.

"Hello, Georgina." He leaned against the doorjamb, arms folded over his chest.

"Wakefield!" She leapt up, but the rapid movement pitched her off balance, and she gripped the couch to steady herself.

Her dismay over his unannounced appearance was palpable. Plainly, she wasn't in any condition to entertain him, but she speedily composed herself, pasting a bland smile on her face, and simulating an acceptable pretense of gaiety. "How nice to see you. When did you get home?"

"Just now." He sauntered in as though he owned the bloody place—which he did—and irrationally, he suffered a letdown at her listless, insincere salutation. A likeness of Emma burst into his head. Invariably, she'd been jovial, animated, and genuinely happy to be with him, and he squelched the annoying image.

Georgina was paid, and paid handsomely, to attend him. Affection had never played a role in their association, and he would never have wanted her to exhibit false fondness. He was acting like an unsophisticated dunce!

Gracefully, she gestured to the other couch. "You remember my sister, Gwenda?"

"Of course."

"Lord Wakefield." Gwenda nodded, a hand slithering to her waist and slackening her belt, the lapels of her robe toppling away to reveal more of her nude center.

Lush, voluptuous, alluring, they were a beautiful pair, a daring, adventurous duo who were game for any diversion, but oddly, he felt no tingle of desire. For a brief instant, he was tempted to flee, to abandon them to their deviant routine, and to forgo the pending carnal feast, but as swiftly as the absurd sentiment took shape, he scoffed.

Why abstain? He had ties to no woman, was unshackled by convention or restraint. In forty-eight hours, he was bound for Yorkshire. Before going, he was eager to revel in his preferred pastimes, and he'd not feel any guilt over his decision.

"Would you like a drink?" Georgina queried, smoothing over the awkward silence.

"Yes, I would."

She grabbed a glass, poured whisky to the rim, then delivered it to him. Their fingers grazed, and he inanely observed that there was no flare of sensation at their touching.

He tipped the libation and took his customary protracted swallow, but as he'd scarcely had a drop of spirits since meeting Emma, he'd lost his acclimation, and the stringent liquid burned. His eyes watered, and he almost embarrassed himself by coughing and spitting it up.

Hastily pulling himself together, he advised Georgina, "I had an exhausting journey. I'd like a bath, then a massage and supper. I'm starving."

"Certainly, John." In the intervening period, her poise had reasserted itself, and she pranced about as though she'd like nothing more than to wait on him hand and foot.

She rose on tiptoe, and bestowed an irksome kiss

against his lips, then she exited to summon the appropriate servants.

After she left, Gwenda patted the spot next to her on the couch, flashing a primitive smile that promised numerous episodes of erotic bliss. "It's been a long time, Lord Wakefield."

"Yes, it has."

He crossed the room and sat down.

Georgina idled at her breakfast table, sipping her morning chocolate and contemplating the sealed envelope before her. She was in no rush to open it. Whatever message was contained within would be dangerous, would have the power to transform her life forever.

It held hazardous propensities—she felt it deep in her bones—an instinctive, inherent female premonition of bad news.

The missive was from Wakefield and, without a doubt, would clarify what had befallen John. Before he'd trekked off to Yorkshire, his abbreviated visit had been discouraging. He'd been morose, obviously troubled by a momentous dilemma, and unwilling—or perhaps unable—to rollick due to his preoccupation.

Nothing she'd tried had lured him out of his unusual doldrums, and much of his inclination for vice and corruption had vanished, which was a terrifying discovery for someone in her line of work.

If he persisted with his present direction and totally relinquished his penchant for fast living, what would become of her?

Drastic measures were imperative. She needed to proceed aggressively, but at the same juncture, it couldn't hurt to privately and quietly begin investigating other financial opportunities—just in case she failed in her efforts and her arrangement with John was terminated.

She picked up the envelope and examined it, testing its weight and size in her palm. It had been simple enough to retrieve it from John's daily post. The footman who'd stolen it for her had a gambling addiction and was constantly in need of extra cash, which Georgina was delighted to provide in exchange for the favors he managed.

A woman could never have too many friends in the right places!

She wasn't sure what had compelled her to watch for a letter, but now that the correspondence had arrived, she was elated that her fortuitous acumen had been so acute.

Weary of the suspense, of delaying the inevitable, she stuck her thumbnail under the seal and carefully lifted it. If it wasn't what she'd anticipated, she'd have to resecure it and have it slipped into John's mail with no one being the wiser as to its temporary absence.

Dispassionately, she scanned the text, her lips curving into a small moue of distaste, her heart pounding at the realization of how near she'd come to disaster.

"My dearest John," the tidy, feminine script read, "I regret that I'm forced to write with these horrid tidings, but when we parted, you asked me to contact you should the worst happen . . ."

At the bottom of the page, she shook her head in disgust.

"Foolish, foolish girl!" she chided to the quiet room.

She refolded the paper and tapped the edge against the wood of the table, mulling, speculating, deliberating as to the likely consequences if John received the communication—and if he didn't.

What would he do with the information?

Ultimately, she decided that there was only one viable choice. The prospects of any action he might take to assist the little Jezebel were too grave.

The note had to be destroyed.

If he subsequently learned that the strumpet had written to apprise him of her predicament, it would be far too late for him to intervene, and no one would ever postulate over why her solicitation had been lost.

The post was so unreliable.

A candle was lit on the sideboard. She snatched it up and held the corner of the letter over the flame. Once the document grew too hot, she dropped it on her plate, and it dwindled to a pile of ashes, then she strolled to the hearth and threw the remaining scraps into the fire.

As the last of the evidence disappeared, she used a napkin to brush at her fingers, wiping away any sign that she'd handled the blackened mess, then she went upstairs to dress for her round of afternoon socializing.

Emma meandered down the hall of the vicarage and took in the details of the house where she'd been born and raised. As the domicile was now a bachelor's residence, there were many differences from how it had been when the Fitzgerald family had utilized it, but she was pacified by the familiar surroundings.

I can do this! she murmured to herself. *I can!*

Ten weeks had passed since that dreadful incident in John's bedchamber, when they'd loved so tenderly and fought so viciously. Since that vile encounter, she'd often pondered how two people who'd been so intimate could have come to such a hideous end.

She hated him! She loved him! And she excruciatingly felt every riotous swing of emotion in between.

How could her immense ardor for him have brought her to this despicable low?

Mortified, degraded, frantic, she trudged on to the library, where the housekeeper had said that Harold was finally ready to accommodate her. He'd kept her waiting for nearly an hour, and she'd dawdled in the parlor like a supplicant, checking the clock on the mantel, counting the arduous ticking by of the minutes.

If she'd been in a stronger position, she'd have declined to play his game. He was trying to make a point, or teach her a lesson, when she couldn't fathom what it might be, but she was in a dismal, desolate mood, so she'd lingered.

While she wasn't certain what had transpired between them, it definitely didn't seem as though he still wanted to marry her. The notion that he might have changed his mind set her insides to quivering.

If he was no longer interested, what would she do? What options did she have?

Previously, he'd been a frequent visitor, but now, she rarely saw him. He didn't arrange for picnics or carriage rides, he never stopped by to inquire how she was faring. At church, she and Jane would say their hellos after the service, and he was cool and reserved, his demeanor toward her having reversed dramatically.

She feared that she'd angered him, though she couldn't see how. He could be tedious, fussy, although she'd always tried to be polite, but something had driven him away.

The village social, where the parish celebrated the harvest at the end of September, had been held the prior week, and she'd been so sure that he'd invite her to go with him, but no request had been forthcoming, and it boded ill for how circumstances had evolved.

Her trepidation spiraling, she approached the library.

The door was open, but she knocked anyway, the rift in their relationship making her feel uncomfortable about barging in. Petulantly, she noticed that he was sitting behind what had been her father's desk, involved in paperwork, and he didn't look up when she entered.

She missed her father, missed the invariable rhythm of that era, the ebb and flow where each day had blended into the next, where there'd been no surprises, no catastrophes, no anguish or grief. No John Clayton to wreak havoc.

Her father had been a compassionate man, and he'd spent his life doing for others who were less fortunate. How galling that Harold had been allowed to succeed him! She was inexplicably furious, and she bit down on any comments, lest her wagging tongue spew sentiments she dare not utter aloud.

"Have a seat." He was irritable, as though she were wasting his time.

Busy with adjusting and organizing his documents, he ignored her, incensing her with his discourtesy, but she quashed her spike of temper. Considering the current precarious state of their association, she couldn't display a hint of annoyance.

After lengthy rumination as to her plight, she'd determined that she had to seek Harold's help. She'd written to the exalted Viscount Wakefield, but he couldn't be bothered to answer, and there was no one else to whom she could turn. Not her mother, certainly. Even if her mother had been in full possession of her faculties, she'd never been robust, could never have dealt with such horrible news. Jane was much too young.

Emma had no trusted confidantes and, while she was on amiable terms with many women, she couldn't discuss her condition with any of them. Such a juicy tidbit would race like wildfire through the neighborhood, when Emma needed absolute secrecy.

Though she'd racked her brain, she hadn't devised an alternative. There was no other gentleman of her acquaintance who might aid her. Just Harold. From the first, he'd been infatuated, had seemed almost obsessed with the idea of marrying her. That sort of profound affinity didn't cease overnight. He *had* to still feel some fondness.

She prayed that she could find the words to plead her case—without humiliating herself in the process!

"What is it?" he snapped.

He tossed his papers aside, and shifted in the chair, his fingers steepled over his chest, and there was a particular venom about him that scared her, which was preposterous.

This was Harold! Plain, boring, stodgy, dependable Harold.

Momentarily, she faltered, then regrouped. "I must speak with you."

"In what capacity? As your minister?"

"As my minister but also, I would hope, as my friend."

She smiled hesitantly, but he didn't render any reciprocal sign of affability.

"Shut the door." He nodded toward it.

Rising, she walked over and closed it. His vehement gaze cut into her back, but she returned to her chair, head high, though her hands were quaking, and she tucked them under her skirt.

"I have a confession to make, and I—"

"What?" he barked, interrupting. "I can't hear you."

"Well . . . you've wanted to marry me for many months now"—he was glaring at her so malevolently that she wasn't sure she'd be permitted to spit it all out, so she hurried on—"and I've kept putting you off. It was rude of me, I admit, but recently, I was wondering if . . . that is . . . if you might . . ."

Though she'd mulled over the conversation on dozens of occasions, the reality was nothing like the fantasy. She couldn't verbalize what she required. Her shame was too gigantic, her burden too impossible.

In all actuality, she barely knew Harold, and for her to have imagined that she could beseech him to shield her from scorn, to wipe away her sins before the community, had been a ludicrous plan. She'd simply been so desperate, and her anxiety had her grasping at straws.

She couldn't do it. Not to him. Not to any man.

Ooh, how she'd love to strangle John Clayton! If she could wrap her hands around his neck for ten measly seconds, he would rue the day!

"I'm sorry. I shouldn't have come." She started to stand, but his sharp tone halted her.

"Sit!" he decreed, angrily drumming his fingers on the desktop. "You can tell me whatever it is. We are *betrothed*, after all."

His concern was unmistakably feigned, and *betrothed* was imbued with such rancor and disdain that she shrank away from him, wanting to go, but worried as to how she should depart. Anymore, her musings were so agitated, her panic so enormous, that she couldn't make a valid decision to save her life.

She slid down into her chair, and she was incapable of speech, couldn't explain what she was doing in his library. Tears welled to her eyes. Increasingly, she was overly emotional, and the slightest development set her to weeping. Plus, she was excessively fatigued. From hard work. From lack of sleep. From torment and toil and despair.

"Let me guess," he chided. "You're in a wretched

spot, and you need me to get you out of it."

"I thought I did, but I was wrong. I can't ask you."

"Whyever not, *dearest* Emma? I'm your fiancé! Soon to be your husband! What could have occurred that would be so terrible you couldn't share it with me?"

His insulting manner, his attitude and hostility, were so out of character that she couldn't deduce what had wrought such animosity. Rounding the desk, he placed himself in front of her. He wasn't inordinately tall, but she was sitting down, so he towered over her and seemed extremely intimidating.

"Are you—by any chance—here to divulge that you're with child? And it is by another man?"

She trembled. "How did you know?"

His malice escalated. "So it's true!"

"Yes."

She stared down at her lap, but she could sense his glittering regard drifting to her abdomen, her breasts, and he assessed her in a prurient, contemptuous fashion. The analysis was so meticulous that she felt as if he were viewing her unclothed, and she struggled against the urge to fold her arms over her torso in order to conceal herself from his probing evaluation.

"Did you enjoy your *romp* with your precious viscount, Emma?"

My stars! He knew about John! How could he? "I didn't mean to—"

"Shut up!" He bent down, thrusting his face into hers, compelling her to look at him. "You've disgraced yourself! And me! Do you have any inkling of how sickened I am by what you've done?"

"I can't begin to—"

"I wanted to marry you! To honor and respect you! I'd have cared for you. Provided for you. All I expected in return was that you would come to our marital bed as my virginal bride. Did I demand too much?"

"No."

"Instead, you're soiled, defiled, in the family way! You have the effrontery to beg me to wed you! To rear another man's child as my own!" Before she was aware of his intent, he lashed out, slapping her as ferociously as he could. She lurched away, trying to evade his fury.

"Harlot!" he seethed. He slapped her again, propelling her off the chair and onto the floor.

"Oh, God! Oh, God!" she wailed over and over, clutching her injured cheek.

"So how was it, Emma, fucking your nobleman? Did you take him in your mouth? In your ass?" Each crude remark was like another savage blow. "How far were you willing to debase yourself merely to garner his illustrious attention?"

Scrambling to her knees, she strove to regain her equilibrium so that she could flee, but she was so stunned that she couldn't react. Her muscles wouldn't obey the most elemental command.

No one had ever hit her before, and she was thoroughly unsettled by the barbarism, terrified as to what brutality he might commit next. She endeavored to crawl away, but he grabbed her by the neck, hovering over and shaking her.

"Your story is so pathetic! So obscene! The innocent vicar's daughter, seduced by the great lord!" He squeezed her neck, making her wince and cry out. "What did he use to tempt you? Money? Trinkets? How little did it take to entice you to spread your legs?"

"Nothing," she spat out. "He offered me nothing."

"He must have plighted you something. What was it? Eternal love? Undying devotion?" As though touching her had suddenly become revolting, he let go and stepped away, but not before kicking her in the ribs so fiercely that she couldn't catch her breath. "Well, we see what his bloody promises are worth, don't we? Where is he, Emma? Where is your fancy *lord* now—when he's left you in this dire predicament?"

His rage vented, he moved away, and as the prospect for further violence diminished, her physical alarm waned. She didn't think he'd strike her again, but she couldn't be sure. Confused, disoriented, she huddled on the rug, curled into a tiny ball. Tears flowed down her cheeks.

Harold was correct: How could John have done this to her? How could he—how could any man of conscience—have provoked the calamity then blandly sauntered off into the sunset?

He'd never penned a single note to learn how she fared. Had never sent the estate agent to check on her welfare. The better cottage he'd pledged—that she'd maintained she hadn't wanted—had never come to fruition.

He'd trotted off to London and forgotten her.

His final day at Wakefield, he'd insisted that he be apprised if her worst fears were realized so, once her suspicions had been confirmed, she'd notified him, but he hadn't answered her letter. If he'd harbored any lingering affection for her, wouldn't he have responded? Even if it had been for the sole purpose of passing on a few pounds through the estate agent?

Harold had been her only hope—vague and remote though he had been. What would happen to her? To her mother and sister? She couldn't bear to discern their fate!

Demeaned, ashamed, she couldn't say how long she lay there with Harold watching her from across the room, but his voice yanked her out of her reverie of misery.

"Quit your groveling and get up. I'm weary of you."

Weak and unsteady, she used the arm of the chair to haul herself to her feet. She was a mess, her nose red and mottled from her sobbing, her cheek swollen and throbbing from his beating her. Her hair was in disarray, some of the combs having scattered, and she stooped to pick them up.

"I'll call the banns on Sunday," he abruptly said, "but we can't delay the full four weeks. We'll hedge a bit, and the wedding will be two weeks from today."

She couldn't believe that he'd suppose she'd have him after this. "No, I won't do it."

"You will!" He stomped over to her, looming, frightening her again with his superior size.

"And if I refuse?"

"I will have men from the village drag you to the church, bound and gagged, where I will publicly accuse you of fornication. Then you'll be cast out. With only the clothes on your back."

"My neighbors would never do such a wicked thing to me!" she protested, though she wasn't as confident as she pretended. Who could predict what others might do?

"For someone who claims to have such magnificent insight into the human condition, you really don't understand people very well." He laughed treacherously. "They'll delight in your fall from grace, they'll get a tremendous thrill on discovering that a person as pious and righteous as yourself has sinned so egregiously. Especially with the likes of Wakefield. He's genuinely detested by all."

That wasn't necessarily accurate, not after she'd convinced him to cancel the evictions and defer the rents, but the boons had gone to a handful of the most destitute. What was the general opinion held by others? The Clayton family was often blamed for myriad woes, many of which were the Claytons' fault, and many of which were not. There was a specific element of troublemakers who were filled with resentment and ill will. Would those disgruntled souls follow Harold's edicts just to exact revenge from John?

Harold was exuding hatred of her, and she had to query, "If you loathe me so much, why would you marry me?"

"The benefits will outweigh the detriments." He pulled her close, mashing her side to his front. Against her hip, she could feel his erection! He was cocked as a pole! Repugnant as it sounded, he seemed to have been aroused by the fighting, his enmity spurring his desire.

She battled to get away, to create space between them, but he gripped her too tightly, and he flexed against her thigh, letting her perceive his titillated state. Offensively, he caressed her breast, trifling with the mound, kneading it, painfully pinching the nipple.

"I relish many lewd acts that transpire in the bedroom." He leaned down to nauseatingly lick and bite her earlobe. "Being married to a whore will have its advantages."

"Bastard," she ground out, shuddering with distaste, and he tweaked her nipple harder.

"Of course, my charity does not extend to your demented mother. I'll contact the insane asylums to locate a home for her, but Jane will live with us." He kissed her neck, a sloppy, wet, sickening affair. "Now that I know what a trollop she has for an older sister, my Christian duty dictates that I oversee her upbringing. I must free her from your corrupting influence."

"Never in a thousand years."

He laughed again. "You'll have a roof over your head, and your sterling reputation will remain intact. In exchange for my benevolence, you will do whatever I say. Night after night, my darling Emma. I suggest you prepare yourself."

Summoning her strength, she shoved him off, but she grasped that she'd slipped away from him because he'd released her. He was much larger than she; if he'd meant to further abuse her, he could have with ease.

"You're mad!" she scoffed, distraught and terrorized.

"I will have my way in this," he warned. "Make ready."

She whirled away, rushing out the door and down the hall, and she hastened into the clean, fresh air and sunshine, fleeing his deviance and lunacy, then she ran home without stopping.

CHAPTER NINETEEN

FROM his box in the theater balcony, John stared at his surroundings and heaved a sigh.

In the two months he'd been gone from London, nothing had changed, and he was bored out of his mind. The play was typically mediocre, the same tedious people were present, the same squalid pursuits were available after the show.

Where once he'd have been energized and eager for the lengthy night and myriad amusements it held, he couldn't muster any excitement. He'd lost his patience for the shallow characters who feigned friendship, and for the superficial recreation he'd claimed to prefer, though in all actuality, perhaps he'd hadn't *lost* his interest in frivolous entertainment. He suspected that it had never really been there in the first place.

Amazingly, he was beginning to recognize that much of the decadence he'd embraced was abhorrent to him. He'd been on a reckless, fifteen-year quest to irritate his father, to live down to each and every one of the difficult man's low expectations, affecting many nefarious habits and espousing those most liable to infuriate him.

As a youngster, it had been fascinating and intriguing to test his limits and break all the rules, but the behaviors he'd adopted out of pique and temper had become the norm. He couldn't explain why or how he'd allowed himself to be lured into such a depraved existence, but he couldn't wallow in such a pitiable trough.

Maybe he'd finally grown up. Or maybe his passing much of the summer in the country with an irksome, sassy vicar's daughter had forced him to take a good look at himself—where he'd been, where he was going, what he wanted for the future.

Throughout their abbreviated relationship, she'd chastised and castigated him for his excess and immoderation, had prodded him to shape up and, while he'd believed that he'd ignored her with his routine ability to shut out what he hadn't wanted to hear, some of it had obviously penetrated.

The transformation had commenced after he'd arrived in London from Wakefield. Lonely, out of sorts, irate and disgruntled, he'd visited Georgina and her sister, intending to revel in the indecent pleasures they would have provided before he'd left on his protracted tour of Yorkshire. He'd been prepared to immerse himself in vice, to loll in whatever perversion Georgina might have devised, but in the end, he hadn't been able to go through with it.

He'd tarried briefly, had had a second drink, had engaged in some naughty verbal exchanges with Gwenda, but somewhere between the talking and Georgina's declaring that his bath was ready, his enthusiasm had waned. The allure he'd ordinarily found in such sordid conduct had vanished and, astonishing both the women and himself, he'd finished his whisky and exited without so much as removing a cuff link.

The preceding week, he'd discreetly returned to London, but he hadn't notified her—or anyone else. For the full seven days, he'd been sequestered in the town house, ruminating over his stay at Wakefield, his trip to Yorkshire.

He'd spent the northern journey by himself, with too

much opportunity to reflect and stew, and he'd developed a different view. Of himself. Of the world.

Ultimately, listlessness had driven him to the theater, but as he peered around at the wealthy, lazy aristocrats who shared his social sphere, none of his earlier hobbies, or his cadre of companions, appealed in the least.

Upon his entrance, several of his cronies had joined him, and they would count on him to traipse off with them when the performance concluded. They would gamble and swill, fraternize with prostitutes, but John detested the notion of going out on the town. Their favored diversions seemed so tawdry.

He smiled, recalling Emma Fitzgerald. What would she think if she could see him now?

Since the initial period at Wakefield, when she'd sent his dubious associates running for cover, he hadn't tossed the dice or turned the cards. He'd imbibed of spirits on the sole occasion when he'd been at Georgina's, and he rather liked being sober. The prior decade, he'd languished in a state of constant inebriation, and he'd forgotten how it felt to have a clear head, to jump out of bed in the morning, robust and alert.

And as to his carnal comportment . . .

Well, it appeared that he was about to forsake his notoriety as a promiscuous libertine. Potential paramours crossed his path on a daily basis, but remarkably, he had no desire to partake of their charms. At the Yorkshire estate, there'd been a particularly fetching widow who'd done more than hint that she'd like to initiate an affair, but her seductive suggestions hadn't elevated his pulse, let alone any body parts.

After having Emma as his lover, no one else compared, and he was earnestly pondering whether he was due to remain celibate for the rest of his life.

With her, he'd experienced an incalculable amount of felicity and passion, and he couldn't work up the necessary energy to dabble with another simply for the purpose of physical release. Mere fornication seemed so pointless. If he was going to go to so much trouble, he craved more than corporeal gratification.

He wanted laughter, spontaneity, exhilaration, friendship.

Otherwise, why bother?

Smiling again, he remembered Emma as she'd been when she'd stormed into his library at Wakefield. Outraged, righteous, adamant, she'd definitely been a sight! She'd beguiled and bewitched him as he'd never dreamed possible.

He thought about her often, and it was much more than random retrospection. Perpetually, he contemplated her, speculating as to how she was managing, and if—by chance—she might ever wax nostalgic about him, although presumably, any musings that wandered his way were likely memories of contention, of ire and strife.

His fixation on her was ridiculous and futile, but he couldn't let it go. Continually, he pothered about her, fretting over her fate, so much so that he'd picked up a pen dozens of times, inclined to inquire as to her welfare, but he'd been too much of a coward to commit words to paper. She was probably still so furious that she'd have torn any missive to shreds without reading it.

Of course, she hadn't corresponded, either, when he'd been so positive that she would. The first thing he'd done upon coming home from Yorkshire was to examine the post, searching for her letter, and he'd been stunned to discover that nary a one had been dispatched. If she'd reached out and bridged their gap, the gesture would have supplied him with the courage to respond, but she hadn't, and he couldn't blame her.

Her recollection of their liaison had to be extremely diverse from his own. Had he given her a scrap of happiness? Had there been a single moment when he hadn't been overbearing and domineering? Regularly, she'd chided him that he was conceited, vain, too presumptuous, and he doubted that their separation would have eased her reminiscence.

How he wished he could alter the past!

That last, hideous afternoon had been so terrible, when he'd planned for it to be so wonderful, and it eclipsed everything else that had occurred between them. Their decisive meeting should have been splendid, and it didn't seem fair that the crucial encounter should overshadow all the merriment and joy.

She was still at Wakefield, he knew, because the estate agent had referred to her in a curt sentence, buried in a report. The news had been scant, pertaining exclusively to the fact that he was waiting for a suitable cottage to become available, and he hoped he could get the Fitzgerald family relocated before winter set in.

As it was the only information John had had of her since his departure, he'd reread that tidbit a thousand times, illogically checking for any hidden significance that might be concealed in the obscure comment.

Surely, she would have gotten in touch with him if she'd needed him! If her circumstances had plummeted, she'd have notified him, wouldn't she?

Even as the absurd interrogatory popped into his mind, he shook it away. She'd never seek his help. He had to accept reality! She'd never wanted anything from him, and if he broke down, and stupidly offered her his aid, she'd reject it.

A proud man, he wasn't about to beg her to let him

support her. He had to forget her, to move on, the problem being that he had no direction in which to travel.

Exhaling another heavy sigh, he stood and scooted around his retinue, escaping the box for the corridor. They'd assume he'd stepped out for a smoke or a drink, and that he'd be back shortly. It would be many minutes before they realized he'd sneaked off.

With minimal effort, he retrieved his coat and hat, then he ambled out into the cool autumn evening. It was drizzling, the air refreshing after being inside the stuffy theater, and he stalled under the portico, considering whether to stroll for a bit before hailing his carriage.

Distracted, he spun around to go, not paying attention, and he bumped into a cloaked lady. As he grasped her arm to apologize and steady her, her hood slid down, and he was face to face with Caroline. He was surprised to see her, having understood that—upon the rumors spreading as to her failed engagement—she'd taken an extended holiday to Italy.

"Hello, Caro," he said affectionately. "How are you?"

"How I *am* is none of your business, Wakefield." She jerked her arm away.

He wasn't worth such an expenditure of animosity, and he couldn't fathom why her upset persisted. "Don't be angry." She didn't reply but stared down the street toward her escort who was tagging along behind, and he felt compelled to point out, "We would never have suited. Our split was for the best."

"Absolutely!" she rabidly concurred. "I'm so relieved to be free of your dissipation and carousing. And your wanton strumpets!"

She'd had the audacity to mention his paramours! Her tongue was so loose that he conjectured as to whether she'd had a few too many glasses of sherry.

"I'm sorry if some of my actions embarrassed you."

"No, you're not. You thrived on humiliating me."

"I didn't mean to—"

She interrupted. "So who's your current mistress? Are you still consorting with that horrid Georgina Howard?"

"Caro!"

"Or have you bought an apartment for your little friend from Wakefield?"

"My *friend* from Wakefield?" he repeated, sounding like a moron.

"Don't deny it, John Clayton," she seethed. "One of your dear London chums was kind enough to write me about her last summer."

"You received a letter about me?" He was incredulous, and when she nodded tersely, he asked, "What did it say?"

"Oh, the usual." The *usual*? "How that drab minister's daughter had captured your fancy, and how you were about to make a fool of me all over again. That's why I hastened to the country. I'd imagined I could stop you—ninny that I am." Scathingly, she looked him up and down. "I pity the woman who winds up married to you, Wakefield. I truly, truly do. I'm so glad it won't be me!"

My oh my! She was in a serious temper, and he couldn't soothe her ruffled feminine feathers, yet he yearned for a smidgen of cordiality.

"Have you heard from Ian?" he politely queried, trusting he could whirl the conversation to a less quarrelsome subject than his dearth of integrity.

There'd been no communication with his brother. During the interval John had been in Yorkshire, no message had been delivered to the town house. Rutherford had relayed various inquiries among his colleagues who were in service, but they hadn't unearthed his whereabouts.

"Why would I have been contacted by that vile animal?"

"I thought you two were . . . were . . ." What were they exactly? He couldn't describe what he'd observed that night in his library.

"Your brother is nothing to me," she alleged. "He's a wicked cad, from the lower classes, who forces himself on unsuspecting women, and certainly not the type with whom I'd keep company."

She stuck up her nose, and peered over at her brother, Adam, who had espied John and was speeding toward them.

"Hello, Adam." John struggled for amiability in the middle of the dreadful scene.

"Bugger off, Wakefield!" Adam seized Caro's arm and whisked her inside.

Doleful, disturbed, John lingered long after they'd flounced off.

He'd been acquainted with Caro since she was a wee lass, but he didn't actually know much about her. Clearly, she'd been attracted to Ian, as had Ian been to her. Now that she was ensconced in the bosom of her family, she needed to rationalize her lusty peccadillo by attributing her lapse to Ian's base nature.

How sad that—the one and only instance she'd exercised some abandon—she'd had to justify her conduct by converting it into a painful memory.

He gave up on the idea of walking, and had an usher summon his coach. As he cloistered himself in the conveyance, his head swirled with questions: Who would have advised Caroline about his burgeoning amour with Emma? Who would be so vicious?

People adored Caro; she was too gentle and too passive to have made any enemies. Who didn't like her? Why would anyone want to hurt her? And who had been sufficiently familiar with his activities at Wakefield to be privy to such confidential matters?

Only Ian and Georgina. Ian would never have done such an appalling thing to Caro. Not to any female. Which left Georgina. But why would she? What was her goal?

They arrived at his town house, but instead of getting out, he ordered the driver to Georgina's, and without delay, they rattled to a halt on her quiet street. He peeked out, pleased that a candle glowed in an upper bedroom. On the way over, he'd worried that she might have gone out. As he'd wanted a succinct discussion, he hadn't relished the notion of chasing after her.

He requested that the driver wait, and he hustled through the gate and to the door, knocking. The hour was late so he wouldn't barge in unannounced. He rapped twice more before footsteps were apparent. The butler answered the door, and on seeing who was loitering on the stoop, his brows rose in shock.

"Lord Wakefield! We weren't expecting you!"

"I must speak with Georgina. I take it she's up and will attend me?"

"Well, yes . . . that is she . . . I . . ." Nervously, he glanced up the stairs.

"We'll confer in the parlor." The man didn't move a muscle, so he added, "Immediately."

"Yes, milord. I'll tell her."

He started off, but so slowly that John was irritated. "I'm in a hurry. I'll go up."

"But Lord Wakefield . . . she's . . . why don't you let me . . . could I . . ."

John was already climbing, and the servant bustled along behind, babbling incoherently. When he couldn't deter John, he commenced shouting, "Miss Georgina! Lord Wakefield is *here*! He's coming up. *Now!* I just thought you might like to *know*!"

John disregarded him, suddenly eager for the pending confrontation. In the carriage, he hadn't been precisely sure of what he would say, but his intent had gradually crystallized: He was tired of Georgina. He wasn't the same person he'd been when he'd established his agreement with her, and she no longer fit in his life.

As he ascended, the butler fussed behind him, and he recalled his previous fateful visit when he'd nearly fornicated with her and her sister. Just mulling what he might have done caused an involuntary shudder to ripple through him, another sign of how much he'd changed.

Her door was ajar, and he pushed it open . . . only to find Georgina naked and in the throes of a sexual tryst. She was in a panic, lurching out of bed, and chaotically jamming her arms into a robe. Her Romeo—a man whom he didn't recognize—was scrambling off the other side of the mattress and frantically grabbing for his pants.

He was stocky, balding, with a paunch and a rapidly waning erection.

"John!" Georgina was trembling, distraught, and she raced around the bed to block his view of her paramour. "What are you doing here?"

"I might ask you the same thing."

"I didn't know you were back."

"Obviously."

Fidgeting, she yanked on the lapels of her robe. "This isn't what it looks like."

"Really?" He chuckled. The spectacle was hilariously funny, and he was tickled to have stumbled upon it. "To me, it *looks* like you've been going at it with this hale fellow." He glared at her swain, trying to appear malevolent, when he could have cared less. "What's your name, sir?"

"Lord Wakefield"—the man gulped—"I wasn't cuckolding you. I never would! Don't challenge me to a duel! You'll kill me! I'm awful with pistols, and I—"

John rolled his eyes. As if he'd duel to the death over Georgina!

"Get out!" he commanded. The chap had managed to don his trousers, but not much more, and John scooped his coat and shoes off the floor, stuffing them into his outstretched arms. "Here! Go!"

The man scampered off, and they froze, listening, as the butler escorted him downstairs and shoved him out the door, then Georgina dashed over and coaxingly stroked the center of his chest.

"I can explain."

"There's no need."

"I've been so lonely without you. I've been pining away, day after day, and I—"

"Desist!" He removed her hand.

"Don't be angry, John," she pleaded, mistaking his mood.

"I'm not."

"I've never taken a lover before. Not in all the years we've been together. I swear he's the first!"

"Well, that's if we exclude the occasion you tried to suck off Ian at Wakefield, but since he refused you, I suppose it doesn't count."

She bristled over Ian's tattling—she must have been positive that he wouldn't!—then she nimbly masked her ire. Turning cunning, her mien growing sly, she strove to deduce how to emerge from the fiasco in the best possible light.

"I'll make it up to you," she crooned seductively.

"You've been traveling for an eternity. You're exhausted. Let me relax you."

She took a step forward, and he blanched, choking on the smell of her sweat, her stale perfume, the scent of sex hovering around her.

"I'm not fatigued. I've been in London for a week."

"A week!" she fumed. "But no one—"

She mumbled a curse, realizing that she'd almost admitted a dangerous consequence, and he completed the sentence for her. "No one informed you?"

Affecting calm, she sauntered to a table and poured herself a stiff drink. Though she valiantly endeavored to seem poised and in control, the quaking of her fingers revealed her distress.

"Why would I have people *informing* me as to your comings and goings?"

"That's what I'm wondering."

Cautiously, she scrutinized him, striving to determine the most beneficial reply.

"I hardly need to spy on you," she scoffed. "I'm closer to you than anyone. If I need to know where you'll be, or what you'll be doing, I'll simply ask you."

"So you wouldn't stoop to poking your nose into my private affairs?"

"Definitely not. Who suggested I had? Tell me who it is, and I'll call him a liar to his face!"

"You shouldn't have written to Lady Caroline last summer." He'd leapt directly to the truth; her gasp of affront gave her away. "Your behavior was so out of bounds, and I can't figure out why you did it. What were you trying to accomplish?"

With his query, pretense was abandoned, and she shrugged, erroneously assuming that a dose of veracity would improve her position. "I was hoping she'd scurry to Wakefield and run off that pious hanger-on with whom you were enamored." She swilled her brandy in one swig. "But the silly twit couldn't even do that much."

"You wanted Caro to get rid of Miss Fitzgerald?" The concept of Georgina being jealous of Emma was so ludicrous that it was farcical, and he might have had a jolly laugh over it if he hadn't been so irate.

"Stupid of me, I know, but there it is." She dismissively waved her hand, as though her sins were forgiven because she'd confessed.

The shrew was a marvel. At conniving. At maneuvering. At artifice and intrigue. But scheming against Caro? And Emma?

"I'm glad I came here tonight," he said.

"So am I, darling," she gushed, deeming all was well, that she'd lied her way into absolution. "It's been so long."

"Not long enough," he countered, inducing an unusual scowl to mar her perfect features. "I'm elated that I witnessed your shenanigans, because my decision is so much easier."

"What decision?"

"We're through."

"No!" She rushed to him and clasped his arm. "You can't be serious. Not after what we've meant to each other."

"You've never *meant* anything to me. Nor I to you."

"You're wrong. I did everything for you! Just so you'd be happy! I love you! I . . . I . . ."

The word *love* was so foreign to her character that she could barely pronounce it, and he was disgusted that she'd fliply toss it out. The pathetic machination underscored his resolve to be shed of her.

"My secretary will contact you with a financial settlement to tide you over until you can procure other arrangements. And I'll give you three months to vacate the house, but don't dawdle. I want you gone when the time is up."

Rendered speechless, she glowered at him, then conjured the gall to mutter, "You bastard! After all I've done for you! After all I've endured!"

"You were well paid for your whoring," he crudely remarked, "so don't try to make me feel guilty. It won't work."

Bitterly, idiotically, she blustered, "I'll retaliate for this."

"No you won't."

"I know all your secrets; you'll be ruined."

Enraged that she would dare threaten him, he stalked to her and gripped her by the neck, his thumb and fingers digging in. He supplied adequate pressure to temporarily cut off her air, and she clawed at him, but he was too strong.

"I'm grateful to you for your services, so I will remain silent in my opinions as you search for another protector. However"—he shook her roughly and hurled her onto the bed—"if I ever discover that you've discussed me, my brother, or any of the women in my life with another soul, if you disseminate a single story, I'll personally see to it that there isn't a man in the kingdom who will have you."

"Bastard," she repeated.

"Don't push me, Georgina. You won't like the result. I guarantee it." He stomped away lest, in his fury, he take a belt to her. At the door, he glanced to where she lay. She looked older, her customarily smooth, lustrous skin lined and aged, her countenance worn and weary.

"I don't want to hear from you again," he instructed. "Leave with your dignity intact."

Their gazes locked in an onerous battle, then she rolled onto her back and studied the ceiling. She laughed, an eerie, unsettling chortle, but he was disinclined to dawdle or debate so, on light feet, he spun around and flew down the stairs.

"I've already gotten even," she flung after him. "You'll learn soon enough what I've done. But it will be too late . . . too late . . ."

Her bizarre cackle trailed after him, but he ignored her, unconcerned by her idle gibberish, and he experienced a swell of exhilaration that he'd split with her. The sense of freedom was indescribable.

A creature of habit, he hated discord and strife, so he avoided them like the plague. He continued on in situations much longer than he ought, merely because he loathed the upheaval that change would engender. The fact that he'd sent her packing was another budding trait he could attribute to Emma.

Through her incessant wheedling, she made a new man of him. How depressing that he had no one to note the extensive alterations!

He climbed into his coach, signaled the driver, and they were off.

What a night! When they finally pulled up at the town house, for once he didn't wince at arriving home; he'd treasure the solitude. But as he sprinted up the front steps, Rutherford, himself, opened the door. It had to be after midnight, so his presence was a sinister omen.

"You have a visitor, milord. In the library."

Emma! She'd swallowed her pride! She needed him! How magnificent!

He tamped down his burst of excitement, scarcely able to keep himself from running down the hall like an ecstatic boy.

Feigning apathy, he queried, "At this hour?"

"It's your brother, sir."

"Ian?" he blurted out. After everything that had occurred so far that evening, he couldn't grasp this development.

Ian is here! Does he wish to make amends? Is it bad news?

Since their row at Wakefield, he'd missed Ian terribly, had chafed and fretted over where he was and how he was faring. John regretted their separation, rued every vicious detail of their reprehensible quarrel, and he yearned to restore their relationship to its previous harmony.

"He showed up after you left for the theater," Rutherford was clarifying. "I advised him of where you were, but he didn't want to track you down. He said he'd await your return"—he paused, apprehensive—"and I told him it was all right if he stayed."

"Of course, Rutherford," John said. "Ian is always welcome here. Now, thank you for tarrying, but you may take to your bed."

"If you're sure—"

"I am."

Rutherford nodded and departed, and John was alone in the foyer. He lagged as his retainer disappeared, then he breathed deeply, bracing for whatever was coming, and trying not to be overly optimistic. Considering their prior dissension, any reception was possible. He'd pray for an amicable conclusion, but if the encounter ended direly, he didn't want to be too disappointed.

He walked to the library and went in. Ian was standing by the fire. Impatient and testy, he'd adopted a military posture, his hands behind his back, his fingers linked. Though he was frowning, John's smile spread from cheek to cheek. He was so bloody delighted to see his brother, and he wouldn't pretend otherwise!

Despite their differences, they could mend their rift. He was convinced of it.

"Ian!"

"Wakefield." He displayed no emotion.

"I've been so worried about you. How have you been?"

"This is not a social call."

"Ian, for pity's sake." He was stunned and hurt by Ian's attitude, but he wasn't about to start off fighting. "I'm so glad you're here. I hope you're home for good."

"This is not my *home*." Acridly, he added, "It never was."

John's smile faltered and he sighed. Reconciliation would be much more difficult than he'd imagined. He crossed the floor, desperate to heal their wounds. "Then why have you come?"

"I bring tidings from Wakefield."

From Wakefield? Something has happened to Emma! He stiffened, geared to be battered by a catastrophe. "What is it?"

"Emma Fitzgerald is pregnant." Full of malice and menace, he advanced until they were toe-to-toe. "In order to conceal the disgrace you inflicted upon her, she is about to marry Harold Martin, that slimy, weaselly *vicar*—and I use the term loosely—who was assigned to the parish after her father's death."

"Emma's pregnant?" Weak in the knees, he couldn't absorb the announcement, and he sustained various waves of ecstasy and dread.

He'd sired a child! With Emma! How fantastic! How terrifying!

Why hadn't she written? Didn't she know he'd have helped her? Did she truly have so little faith in him?

"As you could never be bothered to speak with Vicar Martin," Ian was scolding, "you have no idea what a horrendous outcome this is for Miss Fitzgerald, and I can't allow her to suffer it."

"When is the wedding?" was the only question that seemed to signify.

"In four days."

"So soon?"

"Miss Fitzgerald has no male relative to act on her behalf, so I will be her champion."

"She doesn't need a *champion*," John contended. "I love her; I've always loved her. Now that you've apprised me of her predicament, I'll assist her."

Dubiously, Ian assessed him. "Let me make myself more clear: You have two weeks to rectify her circumstances. You will live up to your responsibilities, or you will answer to me."

"What are you demanding? That I marry her?"

"Yes."

"And if I don't?" Facetiously, he inquired, "Will it be pistols at dawn?"

"Precisely."

Ian's hand lashed out. He was clutching a riding glove, and the leather snapped as it cracked across John's cheek. His head whipped to the side, as his heart sank.

Could Ian engage in such a heinous deed? Could he aim a weapon at his only sibling? With intent to maim or kill?

John couldn't. No matter what Ian did.

"Ian, don't be ridiculous. I could never—"

"Place a wedding announcement in the *Times*," Ian interrupted. "I'll watch for it. If I haven't seen it in the next fortnight, you may choose your seconds."

He clicked his heels, a rude gesture of farewell, then he skirted John as though he were repulsive.

"Ian . . . wait!" John implored, but he kept on, showing himself out.

John turned and stared at the flames in the hearth, then he went behind the desk and plopped down in his chair.

Was a dark star following him? Was he laboring under an evil cloud? How had he warranted so much misery and woe on a single evening?

Bone-tired, dazed, shattered, and confused, he leaned against the tall chair and gazed into the fire. Obviously, it was going to take more than a brief conversation or fervent wishing to repair his relationship with Ian. Perhaps he never would, and he had to adjust to the reality that his brother might be forever lost to him.

But what about Emma?

She was about to marry. Could he stop her? Did he want to? Did *she* want him to? If he rushed to Wakefield, would she castigate him for his romantic foolishness? If he decided to block the wedding, was there ample time to intervene? And how should he go about it? Was he prepared to ride into the village, storm the church, and sweep her away in the middle of the ceremony like some crazed knight of old?

The notion made him grin.

God, but he cursed the day he'd met the irritating, aggravating wench.

"Emma Fitzgerald, here I come," he murmured to the empty room. "Are you ready?"

CHAPTER TWENTY

JANE Fitzgerald heard the horse's hooves riding up the lane. There was a carriage or wagon rumbling behind, but she was scared to peek outside to see who was coming.

Emma was gone, and with the news that she would marry Vicar Martin, Jane was terrified that the minister had arrived while Emma was out. What if he planned to move the furniture? What should she do?

She didn't want to be alone with him. Not here at the cottage and definitely not at the rectory. Though she'd never admitted as much to Emma, the man frightened her. She couldn't clarify why. He'd never said or done anything rude, but from how he looked at her and talked to her, she couldn't abide the thought of living with him.

When Emma had first broached the prospect of marriage to Mr. Martin, Jane had listened politely, but she'd been alarmed. She couldn't understand why Emma would take such a drastic step.

They were getting along admirably—considering. Their situation could have been much worse. They weren't starving. Their cottage was cozy and clean, and they didn't need Vicar Martin.

Didn't Emma recognize his strangeness? Didn't she sense the . . . the . . . weirdness that emanated from him?

If only the viscount hadn't forsaken them! Jane had been so positive that he'd been fond of Emma. She'd witnessed their affection, and she was sull smarting from his abandonment.

How could he have left them to the likes of Vicar Martin?

Her visitor dismounted, walked to the stoop, and momentarily, whoever it was knocked on the door. Nervous and afraid, she glanced over at her mother who was rocking peacefully in her chair, undisturbed by the intrusion.

The visitor knocked again. A fire smoldered in the grate, and smoke curled up the chimney, so she couldn't pretend that no one was home, and she hailed, "Just a minute."

She opened the door a crack, and a gust of chilly autumn wind whisked by her. The brilliant afternoon sun streamed in. She blinked and blinked, unable to believe her eyes.

Surely, she was staring at a phantom! A ghost!

"Hello, Miss Jane," Viscount Wakefield said. He was smiling, his golden hair glowing in the bright light. "Do you remember me?"

"Viscount Wakefield?"

"In the flesh." He spun from side to side, as though to convince her he was real. "I would be honored, Miss Jane, if you would call me John."

"I will."

"Where's your sister?"

"Out. Delivering a baby."

"So . . . she won't be here for hours. Or perhaps days."

"Yes."

"Good," he murmured mysteriously.

"Please come in."

Suddenly, she felt better than she had in a very, very long time, and she held the door wide. He entered, silently assessing her mother, then he pulled up a chair at the table as comfortably as if he'd always sat there. She shut the door behind him, but peered out at the yard, where there were several empty wagons, the drivers milling about.

"Would you like some tea?" she queried, as she sat next to him. "We have a bit. I'd be happy to share it with you."

"I don't need any, darling, but thank you for offering." He leaned forward, his arms crossed over one another, and the manner in which he evaluated her made her feel special and important. "Let me ask you a question."

"Certainly."

"What is your opinion of Vicar Martin?"

"I don't like him at all."

"Why?"

"He's mean to Emma."

"How is he mean to her?"

"He's so grumpy, and he harps at her constantly, about how she should be different, when I think she's fine the way she is." She bent forward, too, and whispered, "And he's terrible to Mother."

"How would you like it if Emma married him?"

"I would hate it." Upon confessing her reservations aloud, relief swamped her. "You won't let her, will you?"

"No, but she's exceedingly stubborn. We'll have to work together if we're to stop her."

"I'll help you however I can," she fervently volunteered. "What are we to do?"

John divulged his strategy, and when he'd finished, she grinned, deeming it a grand idea.

"What about Mother?" she inquired. "She's easily

confused, and it's difficult to persuade her to leave the cottage."

"I'll deal with your mother. You won't need to worry over her ever again." He stood. "Will you introduce me to her?"

He held out his hand, and she grabbed for it and squeezed tight, liking how safe she felt with him nearby. "Yes, I will." She led him across the room. "Mother," she softly beckoned, "this is my friend John Clayton."

Her mother frowned, reflecting on the name. "Clayton? Clayton? Are you related to the Viscount Wakefield?"

"Yes, ma'am," he remarked politely. "He's invited you up to the manor for supper."

"How wonderful," she said. "It's been ages since I've gone. Will Edward be joining us?"

John appeared stumped, and Jane confided, "Edward was my father." She blushed, embarrassed to have him observing her mother's befuddlement. "Sometimes, she can't recall that he . . . well . . ."

Sympathetically, John nodded, then he addressed her mother once more.

"Yes, Mrs. Fitzgerald," he kindly fabricated. "Edward sent me to fetch you. He's waiting for you at the house."

"Marvelous."

She rose, and John steadied her as Jane retrieved their coats and bonnets, then he escorted them out into the brisk breeze, and he gripped her mother's arm, guiding her so that she didn't stumble or lose her balance.

At the rear of the line of wagons, a fashionable gig was parked, a driver at the ready, and John lifted her mother in, then started to aid Jane with the high step. At the last second, she whirled and hugged him around the waist, burying her nose in the scratchy wool of his coat.

"I knew you'd come for us!" she blurted out. "I just knew it! I've been praying every night! I'm so glad you're here!"

"So am I." He hugged her in return and kissed the top of her head. "I'm going to take care of everything, Jane. Don't you fret."

"I shan't," she vowed.

He hoisted her up and settled her, tucking a blanket around her legs, then he gave directions to their driver. The man snapped the reins, and they were off at a pace so rapid that her stomach tickled, and she laughed gaily and clutched the strap. Before they rounded the curve in the lane, she shifted on the seat and peeked over her shoulder for a final glimpse of the cottage where she'd lived in dread every single day they'd occupied it.

The group of men were conferring with John. They'd brought axes and hammers, and he gestured toward the dreary, dilapidated shack.

"Let's get on with it," he commanded. "We're in a hurry."

A slow smile spread across her face, and she turned toward the front, refusing to look back.

Emma trudged down the rutted road toward her cottage, forcing herself to keep on. The autumn wind was frigid, and her worn cloak hardly shielded her from the elements. Her toes and fingers tingled from the cold.

She gazed up at the dazzling blue sky, at the angry clouds flitting past. The ground was littered with orange and yellow leaves, the tree branches stripped bare. There was smoke in the air, the smells of the season vividly evident, as the harvest wound to a close and neighbors incinerated their rubbish.

Winter would be upon them soon.

Then what? an inner voice prompted, but she declined to mull the possible, calamitous answers.

The birth she'd attended had been relatively smooth, the laboring quick, and the pain minor. As she'd prepared to depart, the father of the babe had slipped a loaf of bread and some potatoes into her bag, so at least they'd have supper to show for her efforts, but with the dastardly choices she had to make shortly, the notion of a hot meal was scant solace.

How she detested going home! She'd have to endure her mother's vacuous ramblings and faltering health, and Jane's probing interrogations. Jane goaded her incessantly, wanting to know why she would bind herself to Harold. The poor girl was such an optimist! Emma couldn't explain the hideous sins adults were wont to commit, or the depth of her despair.

What was she to do?

The obvious solution was to contact John Clayton again, which she'd never do. She'd debased herself once, but hadn't received a reply to her pitiful letter.

If he'd responded, if he'd had the estate agent drop by the cottage, if he'd indicated the slightest persisting interest, she wouldn't be where she was: fearful, lost, distressed, bewildered.

When she recollected their last conversation, where he begged her to get in touch with him if there was a babe, she saw red. How sincere he'd been! How earnest! What a talented actor!

He'd driven her to desperate measures, had left her without options. She'd vainly tried to solve her dilemma, but all was in ruins. She couldn't marry Harold! Yet, if she spurned him, what would become of them?

Harold had ambushed her by deviously circulating rumors that there was to be a swift wedding. Then the loathsome swine had called the banns during Sunday services! When she traveled through the village, acquaintances slyly palavered as to the need for a hasty ceremony.

No one had been impertinent enough to quiz her as to why they were in such a rush, so she hadn't had the opportunity to deny any gossip, and she wasn't about to raise the topic herself.

Speculation was rampant, and she was trapped, boxed into a corner. If she didn't wed him, the next prattle would be that Harold had gallantly endeavored to rescue her from scandal, but she'd been too pigheaded to accept. Harold would be painted the hero, and she would be transformed into the village Jezebel.

After perceiving his dangerous personality, which he scrupulously hid from the congregation, she had no doubt that he would act on his threats of exposure. While she'd never beheld a public accusation of fornication, she'd heard about the appalling spectacles.

They hadn't journeyed far from the era when women were burned at the stake for lesser offenses, and she couldn't bear to contemplate what fate the male villagers might inflict. Or the female ones. They could be the most vicious.

She literally did not think she could survive the humiliation of being dragged to the church, where her father had done so much good and had been so revered. Harold would hurl malicious, inflammatory comments, describing her liaison with John Clayton. She'd have to kneel, muzzled and fettered, to grovel as Harold repeated her transgressions.

The odds were great that she'd be whipped, maybe stoned, or that she would sustain similar physical abuse. With severe punishment, the precious babe inside her might be injured.

If she was killed, or badly hurt, what would happen

to Jane and her mother? Since they would be relatives of an outcast, no one would be sufficiently brave to see to their welfare.

She plodded on, so wrapped up in tabulating her woes that she wasn't aware of the approaching horse until it was upon her. The animal snorted and pawed at the dirt as the rider reined him in. Too mired in her misery to worry over who was blocking her path, she didn't glance up.

"Hello, Emma," a male said from atop the horse.

Stunned, she halted in her tracks, studying the ground. That seductive baritone could only belong to one man!

She would not peek up at him! She absolutely would not!

As if he were invisible, she skirted him and strode on, glaring down the road, but she could feel his eyes—intent, engrossed, lingering—upon her back. After a dozen steps, he circled the horse and trotted after her.

"Would you like a ride?" he asked.

Warily, she glowered at the large, lumbering creature upon which he was so graciously seated.

Wouldn't she just love a ride? Wouldn't it be fabulous—for a few minutes—to have someone else carrying the load?

Through clenched teeth, she hissed, "Go away!"

She was so furious with him! He'd caused her so much melancholy, so much anguish and tribulation, that she yearned to curl her fingers around his pretty neck and squeeze until he couldn't draw another breath.

If there was a small part of her—a minuscule, tiny, infinitesimal part—that had suffered an absurd, agonizing wave of joy that he'd finally come for her, she paid it no heed. He was too much of a scoundrel to have surfaced when she needed him most. This had to be a chance encounter. An accident. A fluke.

Very probably, he'd been at the manor for a few hours and was already bored. He likely wanted to reduce his tedium by enticing her into a tumble in the grass.

If she'd been holding a pistol, she'd have shot him through the middle of his black heart!

She continued on.

He tagged along, not seeming to mind that she was ignoring him. Eventually, he dismounted, nonchalantly strolling beside her as though he hadn't a care in the world. Which he hadn't.

"You look tired," he asserted.

"Yes, *Viscount* Wakefield. I'm tired. That's generally how one feels when one has been toiling away like a dog."

"Why don't you ride, and I'll walk?" He was disarmingly courteous. "I'll help you up."

"I'm not climbing on that beast."

She stomped off, and he raced to catch up.

"Why don't you like horses?"

"I like horses well enough."

"Did you never learn to ride?"

"Of course I learned!" She was indignant at the insult; every girl of gentle breeding knew how. "We weren't always paupers!"

"Then why won't you get on? You could use the rest."

Incensed, she whirled around, hands on hips, her body tense with pressure. The rat was smiling at her! Smiling! "I fell once, all right? When I was twelve, I broke my arm."

"And you never tried again?"

"No, I didn't, Your Eminent Lordship. Now, if you'll excuse me—"

She hustled off, unable to be so close to him. He was so handsome, so striking. In the intervening period when he'd been away, she'd forgotten, and to see him now—too beautiful, too magnificent, too illustrious, too . . . too . . . everything!—was more than she could tolerate.

As he came up behind her, her pique soared.

"Emma, you seem to be angry with me."

"Angry? With you?" She was so enraged that she could have bit nails in half! She scoffed. "I'd have to care about you to be angry."

He laughed. Laughed at her fury! Suddenly, she fathomed how the most placid of people could occasionally be motivated to murder. At the moment, a messy, heinous homicide seemed like a capital idea.

"I've missed you," he said out of the blue.

She steeled herself, refusing to be moved by the declaration.

"If you're here because you're hoping we'll have a roll in the hay for old time's sake, you can think again!" Abruptly, she stopped, and he did, too. The horse, not expecting the cessation, bumped into him. "I'm to be married on Sunday," she seethed, "so you can hie yourself off to London, to your whores, and your mistresses, and your fiancées who aren't really engaged to you. Do *not* darken my doorstep in the future. Farewell, Lord Wakefield!"

The cottage was round the bend, and she sped toward it, yearning to be sequestered inside where she could cry and lick her wounds in private.

"Emma!" he called after her.

She staggered around, her arms flailing at her sides, and she imagined that she appeared to be a madwoman, dawdling in the forest and railing at the top of her lungs. "What will it take to make you go away?" she yelled.

"Please tell me what it is so that I can effect it immediately! You're not wanted here!"

He shrugged and chuckled. "Sorry, but I'm not leaving."

What did he mean? Not just then? Not for a few days? Not ever?

She was too distraught to decipher riddles!

"I'm needed at home," she falteringly muttered, marching away, frantic for him to desist and depart, to halt the slow, unremitting torture she experienced merely by being in his presence.

"Actually," he gingerly remarked, "I wanted to talk to you about the cottage before you arrived. That's why I rode out to greet you."

His words were an ominous, echoing warning, and she cast about as it occurred to her that the smoke she'd been smelling for some distance had grown much stronger, and the pungent odor of burning wood filled her with dread.

Frenzied, ferocious, she whipped toward him, scrutinizing him, searching for a clue as to this latest machination, but he was an expert at masking his schemes and emotions. She could read nothing in his countenance.

"What have you done now?"

"It was for your own good," he loftily claimed.

Despite her enervation, she ran as fast as she could to the end of the lane. Her heart about to burst from her chest, she stormed into the clearing where her house had once been located, but it had vanished. All that remained were the remnants of the rock chimney and a smoldering pile of charred logs. Most of it had dwindled to ash, but a few flames still flickered. She narrowed her focus, homing in on a sledgehammer someone had left leaning against a tree.

The fire hadn't been random. He'd waited until she was away, then he'd deliberately torched the place.

As though naught were amiss, he neared, his expensive boots crunching through the fallen leaves, his impressive horse prancing behind.

"Where is Jane?" she shouted. "Where is my mother?"

"I have them."

"You *have* them?"

"Yes."

"Where are our belongings? Did you destroy them, too?"

"No. I've confiscated all you own."

The imperious tyrant! "But why? We have hardly anything. What can you want with it?"

"Well, Miss Fitzgerald, you do owe me quite a lot of rent."

The rent? He had the gall to mention the rent? "But you canceled the rent! For everyone!"

"Not for you. You demanded that I not, remember? You didn't want any special treatment."

Was he jesting? Mocking her? She scowled at him, but his gaze was inscrutable. "So you'll auction off our pathetic collection of possessions to make up for it?"

"Unless you can conceive of some other way to remunerate me for my troubles."

"What *troubles* have we created for you?" she huffed. "I wouldn't have permitted a . . . a . . . *dog* to live in that cottage, let alone a family of destitute women. What burden has been levied upon you by our being here?"

"I'm a businessman, Emma," he said irritatingly. "I'd be willing to forego the income if *you* could make it worth my while—so to speak. What could you do that might tickle my fancy?"

They'd had this conversation once before. The day they'd met. How dare he solicit her favors! After all the havoc he'd wrought! After all he'd put her through! From how he was regarding her—as though he were the cat and she the canary—he obviously believed she'd yield in a thrice.

The presumption! The effrontery! She was so irate that she thought she might explode.

"You have the audacity to suppose"—she stalked over to him, ready to kill—"that I would succumb to such a nefarious proposition a second time?"

"Yes." Arrogantly, he clasped his hands behind his back and casually rocked on the balls of his feet. "I have everything you hold dear, everything you cherish. How else will you regain it?"

"Is this how you entertain yourself? Do you travel from property to property, immorally inflicting yourself on your unsuspecting female tenants?"

"I've only done it with you." Annoyingly, he grinned from ear to ear. "You seem to bring out the worst in me."

They were toe-to-toe, and she stared up into his mesmerizing blue eyes, hating him and loving him.

How easy it would be to say yes. To fall into his arms and let him take her up to the manor. She could wallow in luxury, could dine, and bathe, and lounge until she was refreshed and reposed.

Recently, she'd been working more than ever, trying to scrape together extra coins, to garner extra supplies for their larder. The babe, coupled with her excessive schedule, had escalated her exhaustion. She was fatigued, scared out of her wits, her mental state disordered, and she was laboring under a cloud of misfortune.

At the mansion, she'd be pampered and coddled, and the leisurely respite would be expedient. Her diet would stabilize, so she'd add some weight, which would be nourishing for the babe, and Harold couldn't drag her to the church if she was under Wakefield's protection, so she was tempted to acquiesce.

But after . . . Then what?

John would return to London, and she'd be forsaken once more. Left with her broken heart and shattered illusions, her predicament with Harold would aggravate, and she'd be back where she'd started.

Like a fatuous, lovestruck dolt, she pondered him. Her head was tilted up, and the angle made her dizzy. Her pregnancy had been mostly uneventful, with mild morning sickness and sporadic bouts of vertigo. Plus, she couldn't recall when she'd last eaten.

The world spun. She lost her balance, and instantly, he was there, snuggling her to his chest. It felt wonderful to be in his arms, and she inhaled deeply, relishing his scent, his heat. She had every intention of pulling away and standing without his support, but she'd do it in a minute or two. If she moved forthwith, she'd land on her rear in the dirt.

"Are you all right?" he inquired.

Her fate was more bleak than it had ever been, so she'd never be *all right* again, but she lied. "Yes. I'm fine."

Affectionately, he cradled her cheek in his palm. "Is there something you'd like to tell me?"

She perused him as if he'd spouted horns. Was he alluding to her pregnancy? To what else could he possibly refer?

She'd already informed the knave—little good it had done—and she wasn't about to demean herself by rehashing it. She'd die in the streets before she'd beg him for assistance! She'd starve, she'd freeze in a snowbank, she'd sell herself into slavery!

Did she have something to *tell* him? Ooh, yes! A thousand insults were perched on the tip of her tongue, but as they began to spill out, her dizziness increased, her disorientation elevated, her stomach churned and lurched.

She fainted dead away.

Harold lay on his back, an arm thrown over his eyes, sweat pouring down his chest as he struggled to soothe his thundering pulse. The whore who'd rendered the spectacular French kiss had slipped out, giving him a moment to recover before the next round.

Thanks to the pending changes in his life, his climax had been stunning. He was able to generate such delicious fantasies! Frequently, he concentrated on Emma, on how he'd have her under his dominion and control. When he'd been at university, his friend Adrien had taught him numerous methods by which he could exert his supremacy over her.

He liked to have the whores sucking at him while he pretended it was Emma, that he had her tied to the bed, sniffling and pleading.

She was about to find out who stood as her lord and master!

More often, he envisaged that it was sweet Jane who was satisfying him. Jane—with her innocent manner and her child's body. How luscious it would be to have her under his roof and dependent upon him for her very survival! He had many techniques at his disposal that would enlighten her as to gratitude and subservience.

The door opened, and he smiled malevolently. The madam had acquired a new virgin and, since he was such a valued customer, she'd saved the lass just for him.

To be the first to have her, he'd had to pay an ex-

orbitant price, but the cost would be worth it. He would
imagine she was Jane Fitzgerald, and he would practice
with her, bending her to his will as he ultimately would
with Jane.

His randy cock stirred. At Madam's declaring that
he could have the youngster, he'd initially dabbled with
an older whore, slaking his lust so that he could mod-
erate his rampant desire.

Sufficiently sated, he could proceed slowly, could
temper the pace, would make her cry and beseech him
to be lenient. But there was no mercy to be had—as
Emma was about to discover. She would repeat the
vows; he'd situated himself so that she couldn't refuse.
And later . . .

Ah, later . . . Their wedding night would be sublime.

"You there! Girl!" he barked sharply, planning that
she learn to obey from the outset. "Come over here!"

A terse, sarcastic male responded. "I think you've
mistaken me for someone else."

He froze, frowning. Had he dozed off? Was he
dreaming?

No . . . the voice was real and emanating from the
doorway. Alarmed, he rotated to his side, and gulped in
dismay, his cock wilting to a sorry nub, and he crossed
his hands over his genitals, trying to shield his nude
form.

"Lord Wakefield!" he keened weakly. "I can explain."

"I'm sure you can, but do you know what?"

"What?"

"I don't care to hear what your reason might be. In
fact"—he was brimming with disgust—"I don't care
about you at all."

Wakefield left the threshold and sidled nearer. With
Harold prone, the imposing nobleman towered over him.

He felt vulnerable, defenseless, so he leapt to his feet, but being vertical didn't improve his condition. As he was stark naked, it was difficult to exhibit any aplomb.

He was filled with shame, but also quite an amount of rage. Who was Wakefield to barge in and seize the moral high ground? The notorious aristocrat was a profligate libertine, a lascivious roué, for whom no sexual act was too despicable.

"Now, see here, Wakefield," he blustered, extending to his full height, which wasn't adequate to intimidate. "I don't have to listen to—"

"You bloody pervert!" the viscount simmered. "How young do you like them to be? Nine? Ten? Is it just girls? Or boys, too?"

Panicked, he strove to come up with refutations and evasions.

It was one thing to be caught in a brothel; a bachelor couldn't be censured for seeking feminine company! Even a man of the cloth had his corporeal cravings. But he couldn't account for his aberrant predilection for children.

Denial seemed to be the prudent route.

"I've no idea what you're talking about."

"Stuff it," Wakefield growled. "I had a lengthy chat with the madam."

Harold was mortified down to the marrow of his bones. What had the aged harlot dared to confess? What if she'd cited his passion for . . . ?

God, he couldn't even consider it!

She couldn't have told! What could he say as a rejoinder? What could he do?

"Wakefield," he wheedled, "can't we discuss this?"

"No."

"But you understand how a man has . . . *needs*."

"Trust me, Vicar Martin, no *man* of my acquaintance has your sort of *needs*."

A sudden thought occurred to him: Why was Wakefield in the whorehouse? It couldn't be a fortuitous appearance! He must have come for the same purpose as Harold! The hypocritical ass!

"Why are *you* here, sir?" He used the reproachful tone he exuded from the pulpit. "You malign me when we are about to engage in identical behavior! I suggest you clean your own house, before you condemn the grime in another's."

Wakefield chuckled, a menacing, vicious sound that sent chills down Harold's spine. "You assume that I would stoop so low as to partake of the trollops in this place?"

"Why else would any fellow visit this foul den of iniquity?"

"Why, indeed?" Wakefield stepped closer. He seemed immense. Tall. Broad shouldered. Muscular. Trembling with indignation.

Fully dressed!

Harold recoiled, but the bed frame blocked retreat. Longingly, he gazed at his clothes that were neatly stacked on a chair. He'd give his right arm to grab for them, but Wakefield was an impenetrable wall, preventing movement or escape.

"It's not sporting," he tried to assert, "to berate a chap for reveling in the same base tendencies that you enjoy."

"Unlike yourself, I'm not here to fornicate."

"Then why?"

"Merely to advise you that you're finished at Wakefield parish."

"No!"

"You need not return to the vicarage. Even as we

speak, your belongings are being packed and removed."

"You can't do that!"

"I already have."

He couldn't lose his job! He'd waited years to secure the lucrative assignment! If he was discharged, how would he earn a living? His fashionable wardrobe and jaunty carriage would be forfeit. He'd have to relinquish Emma, and then, being poor once more, he'd never persuade another bride to have him.

The ignominy! Gad! No one was ever fired from a vicar's post! It simply wasn't done! He'd be disgraced, humiliated, a laughingstock.

How would he rationalize a dismissal to his father? What would he tell his mother?

"I'll write to the bishop! To the archbishop! I'll protest! I'll appeal! I'll . . . I'll . . ." Only a fool would believe that he could alter what had transpired. Wakefield was too powerful and influential. He would get his way.

Fury swept over him, and with hostility spurring him on, he unwisely admonished, "Who are you to chastise me? With your reputation, you're in no position to judge!"

"Point well taken." Wakefield nodded agreeably. "But as my lovers are adults, I don't have to sneak around in the dark."

"As with Emma Fitzgerald? Your *affair* with her was certainly aboveboard, wasn't it?" Upon his referring to Emma, he received a staggering reaction from the pompous ass, and he preened inwardly. So . . . the viscount had a soft spot, did he? Best to exploit it.

"I fucked her, you know," Harold prevaricated. "Several times. She wasn't much of a catch after spreading her legs for you, but I—"

Wakefield punched him so hard that he flew across the room. Arms buffeting, he crashed into the vanity, the bottles on top clattering to the floor as he grappled for purchase. Blood poured out of his nose and down his chest, and he clutched his face.

"My nothe! My nothe!" he moaned. "You broke my nothe!"

"Stand on your feet, you slimy bastard!"

Panting, wailing, he rose to his knees, and Wakefield hit him again, then again, repeatedly knocking him to the floor. He kicked Harold in the groin, the blunt toe of his boot making direct contact, and doubling Harold into a howling, whimpering ball of agony.

As the worst of the pain ebbed, Wakefield loomed over him, clasping him by the neck, and shaking him like a recalcitrant dog. "If you ever utter her name aloud, if you so much as reflect upon her, I'll kill you. Now, I'm sick of the sight of you. Get out!"

Wakefield lifted him by an arm and a leg, and tossed him into the hall and, with a noisy thump, he crumpled into a heap against the opposite wall.

Patrons and whores from the surrounding rooms were peeking out from every door lining the corridor, anxious to ascertain the cause of the commotion. The stairs were at the end of the gauntlet, and he was naked, covered with blood, his nose and cheeks swollen and throbbing.

"Go!" Wakefield bellowed, lunging after him. "Get out of here, Vicar Martin!"

At Wakefield's specifying of his title, there was a collective, shocked gasp, then titters, then boisterous guffaws and belly-quivering mirth that enraged and scandalized him. They shrieked with jolly humor, gesturing at his withered genitals, his ruined face.

Wakefield picked him up and flung him, gradually propelling him toward the stairwell.

"My clotheth!" he begged. "Pleathe!"

He held out a hand in supplication. The insane aristocrat couldn't mean to cast him out unclad? Could he?

Wakefield slapped at his outstretched limb, and terrified, Harold scrambled, lurching to the stairs, where he tumbled down.

A whirlwind of violent umbrage, Wakefield rushed after him, jabbing and shoving to speed his progress. He landed in an ungracious pile, sliding into the main parlor where guests were drinking and prattling with the whores.

As he rolled into the room, there was a profound, astounded silence, then they began to merrily chortle just as the onlookers had in the upper passageway.

He stumbled toward the front door, which a huge, hulking giant of a fellow had obligingly opened, and he hastened out into the frigid night, the cacophony and malicious sniggering trailing along behind.

Wakefield stalked after him, a dangerous, deadly bully, following him out onto the porch and into the yard. Harold ran for safety, pebbles and twigs cutting into his bare feet, but he scarcely noticed. At the edge of the woods, he paused and glanced over his shoulder, but Wakefield was still there, limned in the moonlight.

"Go, you revolting weasel!" he taunted. "Don't cross my path again!"

Wakefield threw an object—Harold saw it launched. It was a large rock, and surprisingly, the viscount had excellent aim. The stone hit Harold in the center of the chest, pitching him backward. Wakefield hurled another, then another, each striking with penetrating accuracy.

Cold, exposed, and alone, Harold screamed and fled into the trees.

CHAPTER TWENTY-ONE

EMMA stirred on the bed, and John peeked over to see if she was finally awakening. She had to regain consciousness sometime. A person couldn't sleep into infinity.

When she'd fainted at the cottage, she'd given him a fright, and he'd dashed to the manor with her cradled in his arms, certain she was at death's door. She'd been pale as a ghost and thin as a rail, and she hadn't roused the entire journey, not when he'd lugged her onto the horse, not when they'd loped through the woods, not when he'd carried her up the stairs, or had had the housekeeper undress her and tuck her in.

He'd definitely raised a ruckus as he'd sauntered inside. The grumbling had commenced when his retainers had recognized Emma, and it had elevated to an impossible clamor as he'd taken her directly to his bedchamber. His servants were a conservative lot, and they weren't too keen on the concept of his putting their Miss Fitzgerald in a compromising position.

To save his sorry hide, he'd had to do some fast talking. Only his adamant, stentorian insistence, to all present, that he planned to marry her as soon as the vicar from the neighboring parish could visit Wakefield, had staved off a full-fledged revolt. He'd had to show them the wedding bands he'd purchased in London before they'd believe him.

The brilliant gold rings had settled nerves and provided sufficient guarantees as to his intentions, so that they'd let him proceed, though they'd hovered in the corridor, equipped to barge in should Emma need their assistance.

At first, he'd been terrified that a dreaded illness had seized her, or that she was about to waste away from a hidden infirmity. Despairing and concerned, he'd whispered as much to the housekeeper, but she'd laughed and patted his hand, assuring him that Emma was merely worn out from the hectic pace she'd been keeping since his departure.

Then, he'd confided that Emma was increasing, but the older female hadn't been shocked. Apparently, rumors had been flying as to Emma's plight and the prospect of her nuptials with the generally loathed Vicar Martin, but John's name hadn't been linked to the scandal. With the truth revealed, the group was in a hurry to rush out and disseminate the news, so he'd dismissed them, but not before he'd suffered through a lecture as to Emma's delicate condition.

He hadn't understood that pregnancy could excessively fatigue a woman, or that a heavy workload was bad for mother and babe. Actually, he didn't know very much about the state at all, having made it a point to avoid those who were in the family way, but now that he'd been apprised of the details, he could wring Emma's bloody neck.

What was she thinking, being so heedless of her health?

The housekeeper had scolded him, contending that Emma would need extensive rest, ample diet, and pampering for the remaining months of her ordeal. She'd glared at him as though she were challenging him, or leveling a massive burden that he'd fail to assume.

As if it would be a cumbersome hardship to spoil Emma! He couldn't wait to begin!

Tiptoeing to the bed, he watched her, as he'd been doing for many hours. He enjoyed studying her, assessing her smooth skin, drifting with the rise and fall of the quilt as she inhaled and exhaled. Sporadically, she mumbled, her reverie cluttered and distressing, her forehead wrinkling with worry. Once, she'd murmured his name—at least it had sounded like his name—and he liked it that even after so much time had passed, he could disturb her slumber.

When she was alert and in possession of her faculties, she might pretend she didn't care, she might rant and rave and try to discourage him, but when she was asleep and vulnerable, she called for him.

He tried to take some comfort in the fact.

While he'd made mistakes, had behaved badly and irrationally, his blunders had occurred because he was crazy about her. His monumental affection made him say things he didn't mean, and effect results he'd never contemplated.

He wasn't very adept at apologizing or fixing his errors, so he was wandering into unfamiliar territory. She had little patience for equivocation or folderol, so he needed to tread cautiously. He'd botched things so royally that he couldn't suppose he'd have many more chances to make amends.

Shifting about, she rolled onto her back and flung an arm over her head. Her curly mass of hair was spread seductively across the pillows. She was so beautiful, so remarkable, and if he played his cards right, she'd be his forevermore—the trick being to get her to agree without too much fuss or aggravation.

It had been an eternity since he'd held her, since he'd lain with her. From the day he'd left for London, he'd been able to dwell on nothing but how much he missed her. Without his being aware that it was happening, she'd become the better part of himself.

She'd thoroughly ingratiated herself, but he hadn't a clue as to how she'd accomplished it. He was utterly bewitched, his feelings for her powerful and potent, spurring him to odd and erratic conduct. Over the years, he'd stoically grasped that he'd have to eventually marry, but he'd eschewed the notion, declining to progress toward what he'd postulated would be an arduous nightmare.

How wonderful, how refreshing, to find that—in the end—it wasn't difficult in the slightest.

The center of his chest began to ache, and he felt as if his heart were inflating with an incredible amount of joy. He rubbed at the spot, smiling, reflecting on how fortunate he was.

Suddenly anxious to be unclad and snuggled with her, he stripped off his clothes.

He'd done this once before, had bathed her and put her to bed, then he'd climbed in with her. On that fateful afternoon, he'd made one horrid gaffe after another.

By spilling his seed inside her, he'd broken his vow. Then, to his great shame, he'd let insolence and arrogance rule his haughty tongue. She'd been panicked, trapped and alarmed, and he'd been too overbearing to offer her the promises she'd needed to hear.

Pride had goaded him into leaving her to fend for herself, to endeavor and toil beyond her limits. In her forlorn search for aid, he'd driven her into the arms of Harold Martin. If Ian hadn't communicated the pending disaster, John couldn't have achieved a providential arrival to stave off catastrophe.

He shuddered to imagine what Martin might have ultimately done to her—and her mother and sister.

Though a fire crackled in the grate, the flames had died, the temperature had cooled, and he shivered, the floor icy under his feet. He lifted the blankets and crawled in, easing himself down so that he wouldn't startle her.

The bed was a warm cocoon, and he stretched out, an arm under her shoulder, the other on her waist, a thigh over her hip. She was nestled close, and he shut his eyes, letting his starved sensations fill themselves with the feel and smell of her. Contentment resonated through his veins.

Without hesitation, she cuddled herself to him, and though he'd envisioned that the encounter would be chaste and restrained, his untended cock swelled to attention.

He'd not had sex in months, not since the decisive occasion he'd made love with Emma, and his anatomy emphatically and bluntly reminded him of the lack. His unruly physique should have embarrassed him, but he couldn't muster any chagrin. Emma had perpetually aroused him to novel heights, and he wasn't surprised to ascertain that naught had changed.

With an insane voracity, he lusted after her, and he couldn't conceive of his desire waning in the next fifty or sixty years. An hilarious, unbidden vision flashed—of himself as an old man. He'd be chasing her around their bedchamber, still randy, still unassuaged, still craving the satiation he obtained only in her company.

Flexing his hips, he relished how his cock surged against the silky softness of her abdomen. He flexed once more, just because it felt so exceptional, and she arched her hips and met him in mid-stroke, her body as ready and eager as his own.

Fleetingly, she accepted his presence, smiling and purring, welcoming the subtle connection as though she were in the middle of an erotic dream and he was correctly performing his role. Then abruptly, she froze, her muscles contracting, a frown marring her brow.

Time seemed to pause, her breathing arrested, then her eyes flew open. There was an interlude of clear disorientation, where she didn't comprehend where she was or who she was with, then reality crashed down.

"You!" she snarled as if he were a dog that wasn't allowed in the house.

"Hello, my darling Emma."

He kissed her on the mouth, but she lurched away and rose onto her elbow. Gaping about, she was frantic to identify her surroundings, and several seconds ticked by before she distinguished that she was in his bedchamber.

"How long have I been asleep?" she asked between clenched teeth.

"Sixteen hours, give or take a few minutes." He reached out and twined a strand of her hair around his finger.

"How did I end up in your bed?"

"You fainted, and I brought you home."

"Why, thank you very much," she fumed, "but this is *not* my home! How dare you presume so much!"

"Did I ever tell you how cute you are when you're angry?"

"Ooh . . . I must get out of here!" She pitched the blankets back, and the chilly air hit them both, causing her to look down and note that she was bare. So was he. "Aah!" she screeched, scooting away. "I'm naked!"

"Just how I fancy you."

Wildly, she clutched at the bedding, trying to shield herself from his prurient, roving regard, but to no avail. He adored her being in the nude, and he wasn't about to glance away, or act the gentleman to her unanticipated outbreak of maidenly modesty.

If it was up to him, he'd never let her get dressed again.

"How did I come to be disrobed?"

"At your service, Miss Fitzgerald." He lied effortlessly, letting her infer that he'd removed her garments, piece by delicious piece, and that he'd reveled in every mischievous, decadent, inappropriate moment.

"You . . . you . . ." Her puritanical tongue couldn't wrap itself around a word that was insulting enough to describe him. "Where are my clothes?"

"I burned them."

The destruction of the pitiful apparel had been an inspiration, and he was abundantly delighted that he'd had the foresight to dispose of everything. The elimination had garnered him a threefold benefit: She couldn't run off without being accoutered. In the interim, he'd have her sequestered and nude. When the finery he'd ordered for her was delivered, he'd have the pleasure of observing her fashionably turned out.

If he lived to be a hundred, he would never permit her to wear black, gray, or brown again.

"You *burned* my clothes?"

"Every last item."

Indignant, she dissected him as though he were a species of foul insect she'd like to step on and grind under her heel.

"What am I to do? Lounge in your bedchamber like a harem concubine, catering to your personal whims, and ministering to your carnal needs?"

"Precisely."

"You're commanding me to do this?"

"No. I'm rather hoping you might wish to of your own accord."

"And if I refuse?"

"You can't."

"I'm a prisoner, then?"

"Not a *prisoner* exactly." Her temper ignited and flared with each exchange, and he chuckled inwardly, pondering how far he could push her before she snapped. "Don't forget: You have debts to work off."

"Debts!"

"You *do* recall your unpaid rent?"

"Of all the outrageous, dictatorial, underhanded—"

"I love you." There! He'd said it aloud, the first time ever, and he was especially proud of himself.

"Well, I hate you!" she hissed in response.

He laughed. After the myriad ways he'd scorned and discarded paramours over the prior decade, how hilarious, how fitting, that his sole declaration of strong sentiment should be completely discounted!

"No you don't," he gently chided.

"Yes I do!" she insisted. "I really do!"

In a quick motion, he gripped her by the waist and yanked her across the mattress, situating them so that he was on top of her. His torso weighed her down, his thighs cradled hers, and his cock slipped between her legs, throbbing with a reckless urgency at being so near its lush destination.

At the end of her rope, she didn't struggle or try to escape, seeming defeated after having battled too long and too strenuously. The fight went out of her. Her body was limp, her arms slack, and he was devastated to detect tears in her eyes.

"Don't do this," she beseeched. "Please! I can't bear to go through it all again!"

"And what is it, my dearest Emma, that you deem you'll be forced to *go through*?"

"You'll sweet-talk me into lying with you. For a

day. Or a week. I always relent!" She gulped down a flood of misery. "Then, after I do, you'll return to London."

She assumed he was toying with her! That this was a temporary visit! How marvelous it would be to prove her wrong!

"I'm not going anywhere."

"I don't believe you."

What a hard nut to crack! Desperate measures were called for, and lest he lose his nerve, he blurted out, "Will you marry me?"

"Stop it! It wounds me when you act like this! When you flatter me with compliments you don't mean! When you—"

He kissed her, cutting off her tirade. For a brief instant, she resisted, then she sighed and mellowed.

"Marry me," he repeated as their lips parted.

"No!"

He rested his palm on her stomach, and he massaged in slow circles, picturing the tiny child sheltered within. "Isn't there something you need to tell me?"

As it dawned on her that he'd discovered her secret, fury clouded her gaze. "I did tell you!"

"When?"

"As soon as I suspected. I wrote you a letter."

He tensed, his focus narrowing. Since his contentious, hideous meeting with Georgina, he'd conjectured as to what her warning had referred, and if it might have concerned Emma. Was she alluding to a letter? Had she somehow stolen it?

If she had, there were many methods by which he could find out, as well as many ways to extract revenge.

His ex-mistress would permanently rue the day she'd crossed him.

"You wrote to me?"

"Yes, but you never answered." Tears dribbled down her cheeks, and he swiped them away. "You never came for me."

"So you thought I didn't care?"

"Yes. I've been alone. All this time."

She started to cry in earnest, and he clasped her to his chest, hugging and caressing her, rubbing his hands up and down her back. It aggrieved him that she'd felt she couldn't depend on him, but then he'd spent his life perfecting indifference to a fine art. What else could she have concluded?

"Ssh," he soothed, "it's over. Everything will be all right. I'm here now."

"I've been so scared."

From his tough, tenacious Emma, it was a huge admission, and he smiled, kissing her hair, her cheek. "I didn't receive your letter, Em. I swear it."

"Then how did you know?"

"Ian learned of your situation somehow. He notified me, and I came at once."

"I was afraid that I would have to marry someone else, and I couldn't have borne it. I was so confused, and I was so . . . so frightened about—"

"Don't fret over Harold Martin," he interrupted, astounding her with his total insight into her predicament. "He won't ever bother you again."

"But he knows all about us, and he threatened to—"

He tamped down on his rage, unwilling to have her perceive how provoked he'd been by the vicar, even as he speculated as to what coercion the perverted swine had used to terrorize her, but he truly didn't want to be apprised. If he ever unearthed all the facts, he'd be compelled to hunt down and murder the offensive weasel.

"Mr. Martin and I had a heart-to-heart chat," he said as placidly as he was able, "and he's decided that this isn't the job or the town for him. He's moved on."

"You're certain?"

"Aye."

She trembled fiercely, her relief enormous, and she seemed to recognize that he and Martin had had more than a polite discussion, yet she didn't press, and he was glad. He wouldn't dream of alarming her further by relating where he'd found the despicable reprobate, or what he'd been up to.

"Thank you."

"You're welcome."

He studied her, staring into her heavenly brown eyes, so content and happy merely to be with her. Brimming over, with felicity, with his affection for her, he said in amazement, "I'm about to become a father."

"Yes, you are," she acknowledged.

"So I ought to become a husband, too." He pinned her to the bed. "Miss Fitzgerald, there's a proposal on the table, and your reply was unsuitable. I won't settle for anything but yes."

"You're serious . . ."

"Bloody right, I'm serious!" he irritably stated. The woman was lethal to his pride! "Do you think I've nothing better to do than to flit around the countryside, offering marriage to ungrateful females?"

"What benefit could there possibly be for me in marrying you?"

"Emma!" he barked in exasperation. "How about a roof over your head? Food in your larder? Clothes and stability and security?"

"That's all well and good," she began maddeningly, "but what about—"

He was a vain man, and she'd needled him to petulance. He couldn't tolerate a subsequent slur to his intentions or his integrity. Annoyed, he queried, "Do you have any idea how many women in this world wish they were in your position?"

"That's what I'm worried about. How many women will I have to—"

"None. They're gone. Forever."

"Your mistress, too?"

"I split with her before I left London."

"What of the drinking? The gambling?"

"Done."

She assessed him, dubious, incredulous. "Really?"

"You've had an extremely detrimental effect on my base character. Spirits and wagering bore me to death. As to other women"—he scoffed—"nary a one can tickle my fancy."

"Why?"

"Because they're not you!"

"You expect me to believe such nonsense?"

He sobered. This might be his only chance to make her understand how much he treasured her. He kissed her again, a simple melding of lips and tongues, and he was exhilarated as she joined in the euphoric embrace. "As husbands go, I'm not much of a catch."

"No, you're not."

"But I will always cherish you, I'll always look after you, and I promise I'll love you all my days. Till I draw my last breath."

"Oh, John . . ."

"Say yes, Em. Marry me."

"I am such a fool," she muttered. For an eternity, she was silent, pensive and introspective, and he panicked because—for once—he couldn't decipher her musings. The quiet went on and on as she struggled toward a resolution.

In the end, she inquired, "We'd live here at Wakefield?"

He could barely keep from shaking his fist in triumph. "Most of the year."

"You'd watch over my mother and my sister?"

"As if they were my own."

"You'll be a devoted father to my children?"

"I hope we have a dozen."

"If you ever stray, you'll meekly acquiesce to castration?"

"You drive a hard bargain, Miss Fitzgerald, but for you"—he chuckled—"I'd consent even to that."

"I mean it, John. If you speak vows, I'll demand that you honor them. I'd be crushed if you took another after me."

"I know that. I never could."

Searching his face, she probed for equivocation or vacillation, but encountered none, and ultimately, she accepted that his pledge was genuine.

She sighed, giving in, giving up. "Yes. I'll marry you."

There'd never been any other choice. No other conclusion would have been adequate or satisfactory. He couldn't explain why he'd dawdled and procrastinated. Usually, he wasn't so oblivious, and he blamed his paucity of astuteness on being dictatorial, on narcissism and pomposity and presumption, and he was so relieved that he'd come to his senses before it was too late.

If he'd lost her, due to his stupidity or conceit, he couldn't guess what would have become of him. How would he have carried on without her?

"When? Tomorrow?"

"Well, I'd like a bit of time to plan. I don't even have any clothes to wear for the occasion." She caustically appraised him. "Someone seems to have burned all mine."

"A week, then. I can't wait any longer."

"A month."

"Two weeks," he haughtily intoned, "and that's final."

"Yes, Viscount Wakefield," she obligingly conceded.

"It's so pleasant when you do as you're bid."

"Don't get used to it."

He laughed, once more, full and loud. There'd never be a dull moment, being wed to her!

He was tired of the wooing, tired of the verbal moil he'd had to endure in order to win her over. Their separation had been wretched, and he was ready to experience some of the rewards of being an almost-married man.

"Now . . . about those debts you need to discharge—"

"My debts! Of all the nerve!"

She attempted to leap off the bed, but he held her down. When she couldn't flee, she pummeled him with her fists, but as they were prone, she couldn't land any effective blows.

He reached down to fondle and caress her, and the instant he touched her intimately, her opposition ceased. She gazed up at him, her ardor and regard shining through, and she nodded, a gesture of permission and capitulation. He kissed her tenderly, then he moved to center himself between her luxuriant thighs.

"Where were we?" he asked, grinning.

"We were arguing over how I should repay the money I owe you."

"Ah, yes. We'd determined that sexual favors would mitigate your arrearage, but we hadn't debated the terms any further."

"We agreed on no such thing," she said, sounding prim and proper. "I won't be bullied."

"Fine, then. I shall establish the conditions with no input from you." He pretended to consider, then imperiously commanded, "You will accommodate me, in any fashion I request, as often as I require your services, from now until the wedding."

"I can't abide it when your aristocratic tendencies are showing."

"I know. That's what I love about you."

"Despotic lout," she grumbled.

"Think of how much fun you'll have reforming me."

"I have my life's work cut out."

"Yes, you do." But that's when Emma was at her best, fixing, providing succor, arranging, helping. What a lucky, lucky man he was!

A sly feminine smile creased her cheeks. "So, my *lord*, Wakefield, how would you have me begin? What is it you desire?"

The answer was so basic. So elemental. So essential.

"Just you. Only you."